HUNT AT OWL CREEK

Bitter lies. Sweet revenge.

HUNT
AT OWL CREEK

CAREN HAHN

Hunt at Owl Creek by Caren Hahn

Published by Seventy-Second Press

www.carenhahn.com

Copyright © 2022 Caren Hahn

ISBN-13: 978-1-7352272-7-6

Cover design by Andrew Hahn.

Edited by Rachel Pickett.

Printed in the USA

Bitter lies. Sweet revenge.

HUNT

AT OWL CREEK

CAREN HAHN

Hunt at Owl Creek by Caren Hahn

Published by Seventy-Second Press

www.carenhahn.com

Copyright © 2022 Caren Hahn

ISBN-13: 978-1-7352272-7-6

This is a work of fiction. Any references to historical events, real people, or real places are used fictitiously. Names, characters, places, and incidents either are the products of the author's imagination or are used fictitiously.

Cover design by Andrew Hahn.

Edited by Rachel Pickett.

Printed in the USA

For Chris. Growing up with you was an adventure worthy of fiction.

BOOKS BY CAREN HAHN

CONTEMPORARY MYSTERY:

THE OWL CREEK MYSTERIES

Smoke over Owl Creek

Hunt at Owl Creek

AVAILABLE ON KINDLE VELLA

This Side of Dark

What Comes After

ROMANTIC FANTASY:

THE WALLKEEPER TRILOGY

Burden of Power

Pain of Betrayal

Gleam of Crown

HATCHED

Hatched: Dragon Farmer

Hatched: Dragon Defender

Visit carenhahn.com to receive a free copy of *Charmed: Tales from Quarantine and Other Short Fiction.*

Renee,
A new threat is stirring in
Owl Creek. Are you ready?

HUNT AT OWL CREEK

OWL CREEK MYSTERIES BOOK 2

CAREN HAHN

SEVENTY-SECOND

PRESS

1

VAL'S STOMACH dropped in a sickening jolt as the ladder swayed backward. She gripped its sides with one hand and one forearm, trying not to drop the heavy drill. Her teeth clenched around the head of a screw, biting back a curse as she wished for her dad's missing tool belt. She shifted her weight and the ladder settled again, her stomach settling with it.

Beneath her was the porch roof, its slope forcing her to lean the stepladder against the farmhouse at an angle, making the whole set-up precarious. If she fell, the porch roof would catch her fall, and she probably wouldn't roll off onto the ground fifteen feet below.

Probably.

She really didn't want to fall.

Val lifted the new decorative shutter and braced it in place with her shoulder while she readied the drill. This would have been so much easier with another pair of hands, and she wondered if she should have postponed the project until Joel could help. But it shouldn't be this hard to replace a stupid shutter, and she didn't want to be the needy girlfriend who always had one more favor to ask.

Girlfriend.

Is that what she was? She and Joel had talked to each other almost every day in the three weeks since the shooting in the pump house, but it seemed too soon to call him her boyfriend. She didn't want to rush anything, especially since she'd just barely learned her husband was still alive.

The thought stoked a low-level rage that flared whenever she thought of Jordan. Faking his own death to escape prosecution hadn't just turned her life inside out, it had given her false permission to move on. When she'd come back to Owl Creek, she'd been working to put Jordan behind her, thinking he was dead. But now he'd returned and upended her life again.

The sun was setting over the western hills, the temperature dropping with it. While she worked, the squeak of trampoline springs kept rhythmic time and served as a beacon to tell Val where Abby was. For all the acres of property surrounding them, she still didn't feel comfortable letting Abby leave the yard after everything that had happened that summer.

Val slipped the screw from her mouth and rested the tip on the predrilled hole.

Almost there…

She pushed against the drill and pulled the trigger slowly. It whined as the screw turned, but there wasn't enough force for the screw to bite the wood. Val pushed harder.

With a lurching sensation, the ladder slipped under her and she slid with it, sending the screw flipping into the air. Her arm scraped against the window trim as she scrabbled for a handhold, fumbling to a stop against the porch roof with her knees—and ego—bruised.

Val swore and picked herself up. The asphalt shingles were hot from the late August sun, chafing like sandpaper against her bare knees. She heaved the ladder against the side of the house again and shook it, making doubly sure that it was stable.

It had seemed like such an important thing to replace the broken shutter. But that meant replacing all four so they matched, and she'd stripped out three of the rusted screws holding the shutters in place. Now she had no idea how she was going to remove them to make room for the new ones. Crowbar? Pliers? This small project was turning into a big headache, making her wonder if a potential buyer would have even noticed the broken shutter in the first place.

All at once, Val realized the squeak of the trampoline had ceased. She stepped back to the edge of the porch to see around the corner of the house.

Abby was standing on the trampoline, her little body barely making it sag in the center. She wasn't jumping. Instead, she was standing still, watching toward the horizon.

"Abby? What's up?" Val called.

Abby pointed. "There's somebody out there. Do you see?"

Val shielded her eyes against the golden light glittering over the fallow field.

"Where?"

"They're by the trees. Look."

Val frowned and reached for her phone as she climbed over the window ledge. The rough wood scraped the tender skin inside her thigh, but she barely noticed. Her attention was focused on dialing Joel's number.

He didn't answer, but he sent a text a few seconds later.

Sorry, can't talk. Working.

Val sighed. She sent a thumbs up.

She couldn't expect Joel to run out to her place every time she had a couple of trespassers. Ever since Eliza Bellingham's remains had been recovered from the abandoned well, kids from town had occasionally tried to break into the pump house. Joel had even caught a couple with unlit fireworks, a completely insane idea considering the forest fires that had ravaged the area during the peak of summer. Apparently the social life in Owl Creek hadn't improved in the decade since Val had been a teen.

Abby was standing on the porch when Val exited the house, looking toward the dirt road that led to the pump house.

"Go inside and get in your pajamas," Val said, keeping her tone light. "I'll be back in a few minutes."

"What if it's that man?" Abby's voice was tinged with fear. "What if he came back?"

Her face was round with the softness of childhood, and her green eyes almost glowed in the warm light. Her question broke Val's heart.

"He won't ever come back. That man is long gone. It's probably just a couple of kids. We're safe, I promise."

Val didn't mention that the intruder Abby had seen was now dead, and their friend Carter had killed him. She'd managed to keep those details from her, as well as what had really happened to Carter. It had been hard enough to explain to Abby that their friend had died not far from their house. Telling her that Joel had shot Carter to save Val's life would have been too much.

It was amazing how much you could dismiss by calling something a very sad accident.

But Val hadn't been able to return to the pump house since. Now, with phone in hand and heart beating faster than it should at a brisk walking pace, she made her way to the dirt road.

She tried not to think of that day, but it was hard not to. It's where her mind went whenever she was awake at night listening to the sounds of the old farmhouse settling. It was all she could see if she had to go outside in the dark alone.

With the nights getting longer, she didn't know how she was going to make it through winter.

The sun slipped behind the hills as she approached the pump house. Joel had boarded up the broken window and installed a new padlock on the door, and so far none of the trespassers had succeeded in breaking in. A clanging sound accompanied a loud thump as Val rounded the corner of the pump house, skirting a bicycle discarded in the grass.

Two kids, looking to be in their early teens, were standing at the door. One was striking the new padlock with a big rock and cried out as he smashed his fingers.

If Val hadn't been so annoyed, she would have laughed. Instead, she planted her feet and folded her arms.

"It's harder than it looks in the movies, isn't it?"

They whirled, eyes wide and flooded with guilt.

"So, boys, am I calling the cops to report you for trespassing? Or are you going to run home and tell your friends never to come back here?"

In answer, the one without a rock grabbed the bike and took off down the dirt road. The other—a freckled kid with a mullet—watched him go helplessly, cradling the heavy rock like he wasn't sure what to do with it.

"Looks like your friend chose for you. Better go before I change my mind and call the cops anyway."

"Yes, ma'am. Sorry." His face was red with shame, and Val hoped he was the kind of kid who would learn from his embarrassment.

She watched as he followed his friend across the ombre fields, shouting for him to wait. Shadows were growing long, and the whole valley was nearly consumed by twilight as daylight leached out of the sky like a drained sponge wrung out to dry.

A cool breeze sent a chill up her neck, and Val

suddenly realized she was alone in this place of shadows and nightmares.

Hugging herself, she set off up the road at a trot, leaving the pump house behind.

Barry Krenshaw vomited on the asphalt next to the Wallace County Sheriff Yukon, splattering brown chunks on the white paint. Joel jumped back just in time.

Larry swore. "Come on, Barry! Couldn't you have done it in the bushes?"

Barry groaned, and Joel was distinctly grateful he'd parked his Charger on the street.

"All right. Anyone else here capable of telling us what happened?" Larry asked the small group gathered at the edge of the parking lot.

They were at the Moon Apartments, a small single-story complex that sat behind the Owl Creek library. The two buildings sat in an L shape and had nine side-by-side units between them. Curious neighbors gathered on stoops and lined the edge of the gravel lot.

Travis Krenshaw, Barry's brother, sat on the front step of apartment number three.

"I'll tell you what happened," Travis bellowed. "She ran over my foot! They all saw it!"

He gestured toward his girlfriend, Suzie, who stood nearby, smoking angrily.

"It was an accident," Suzie argued back. "Ya'll

know it weren't on purpose. I was just trying to back out. I can't help it if his foot got in the way."

Larry looked at Joel and raised his eyebrows in a question. *Which one do you want?*

"Suzie, let's come talk over here," Joel said, leading her away from the onlookers.

Suzie stalked after him to stand under a large cedar on the other side of the dirt parking lot.

"Barry says you were angry with Travis," Joel began. "Can you tell me why?"

"Barry is a lying drunk. Look at 'im. Why would you listen to anything he says?" She gestured with her cigarette toward Barry, who was now sitting on the ground with his head between his knees.

She had a point.

"He also said Travis was pounding on your car window. Why would you ignore him?"

She shrugged. "No reason."

"Suzie, do we really have to do this? Neighbors said you two had been going at it for an hour. What were you arguing about?"

"It wasn't an argument. They're blowing smoke out their butts." She exhaled smoke as she said it. Her skin was tanned and wrinkled like leather, her collarbones and shoulders bony. Everything about her was tough, and she hardened more each time Joel questioned her.

This was the third time this week.

"So you're telling me that Travis starts pounding on your car window while you're backing out, and you don't think to stop and find out what's going on?"

"Look, I don't know what to tell you. I was in a

hurry; he got in my way. But I didn't mean to run over him."

"You weren't angry at him?"

"Nope."

"Because we're going to have to bring both of you in. It's standard procedure when someone's injured in a domestic violence incident. And I—"

"Domestic violence!" Spittle flew from her lips. "This ain't domestic violence! It was an accident, and if you can't tell the difference, I'm wondering if your badge is plastic, Detective."

Joel ignored her outburst. "If there was anything else going on between you, now would be a good time to tell me. You're sure this doesn't have anything to do with where Travis was on Monday night?"

"I'm done talking about that," she snapped. "He didn't have nothin' to do with that girl. He was with me."

A siren and flashing lights announced an approaching ambulance. As it slowed to turn into the parking lot, Suzie swore.

"Who called the ambulance? We don't got that kind of money." She walked away from Joel, her bony shoulders rounded as if she were headed into battle.

So far she'd stuck to her story that Travis had been with her the night a teenage girl had been assaulted in the nearby park. Travis's record and the girl's description of her assailant made him the prime suspect, but Suzie had sworn they were together that night.

Now neighbors reported an angry fight which

ended in Suzie running over Travis's foot. It sounded like vengeance to Joel.

In the aftermath of Eliza Bellingham's body being discovered seven years after the teen disappeared, the whole community was on edge. No one was feeling it more than the deputies assigned to Owl Creek. Peter Moyer had filed a lawsuit against the sheriff's office, claiming they'd contributed to his son's death by mishandling the investigation into Eliza's disappearance. And with the most recent attack—even though the girl had escaped without any injuries—the pressure was on to find the perpetrator. But without direct evidence, and with Suzie providing Travis an alibi, their hands were tied.

Joel's personal phone buzzed with a text, but he ignored it. He would much rather be at Val's on a Friday night than at the Moon Apartments smelling vomit and sweat and cigarette smoke in the late summer evening. Paramedics were inspecting Travis's foot while Larry stood nearby, handcuffs in hand. Suzie stood over Barry, gesturing angrily. Barry moaned, drawing the attention of another paramedic.

What a mess.

Joel went to his car to get his own cuffs. When Suzie saw him approaching, she dropped her cigarette and ground it into the dirt.

"Oh I see how it is. You can't get Travis, so you're going to arrest me on some trumped up charge hoping I'll turn on him."

"Come on, Suzie, let's go."

"Feed my dog, will ya, Barry?" Suzie said, placing her hands out, palms up.

Residents from the other building were coming out now. The warmth of the day had faded quickly with the setting sun, bringing a promise of fall and cooler temperatures. One teenager even wore a sweatshirt.

As Joel escorted Suzie to his car, a loud barking laugh drew Joel's attention to the far end of the building. He knew that laugh.

Mason Pearson was a couple of years younger than Joel, but Joel remembered him well. He'd never liked him much in high school. Mason had been small and wiry then but had made up for it with a chip on his shoulder to rival a bully twice his size. Quick to anger, he didn't seem to have mellowed out much over the years, judging by the scuffle he'd started at the alumni softball game over the Fourth of July.

Joel and a few others had intervened, and Mason had taken a swing at him, spitting out a stream of racial slurs at the same time.

Now he stood near a woman Joel didn't recognize, and Joel's gaze lingered as he took her in.

She was watching from her porch, the elevated view making her stand out from the rest. But it was more than that. Her appearance showed an attention to personal hygiene he wasn't used to seeing from the typical Moon Apartment residents. Nor did she share the same aura of desperation.

Interesting.

Nothing caught his attention like something that didn't fit.

Joel walked over to Barry and crouched down, trying to gauge if he would get anything useful out of him. His shirt stank of puke.

"What do you think?" Joel asked the paramedic who was checking Barry's pulse against his watch.

"I think he's not going to remember much tomorrow. If you've got any questions for him, better ask him now. But he's all right." Dropping Barry's wrist, he said, "Get some rest, and make sure you stay hydrated. And stay off the bottle, all right?"

Barry waved a hand. "Sure, sure. Thanks, brother."

"Barry, can you tell me what Suzie and Travis were arguing about?" Joel asked. "You were there, right?"

"I dunno. I try not to get involved when they get going."

"Do they fight a lot?"

Barry made a slurping noise as if he'd forgotten how to swallow. "Sure. I been tellin' Travis it ain't worth it, but he don't listen."

"What's not worth it?"

"Suzie. Livin' with her and all that. But he says he can't leave her."

Joel glanced up to where Travis was being loaded in the ambulance on a gurney. "He can't leave her? Or he won't?"

"Both, I guess."

"Why not?"

"She won't let him."

"What does that mean? Has she threatened him?"

Barry threw back his head and cackled. "She's a

spitfire but I doubt she weighs a buck-oh-five soaking wet. Could you see Travis being scared of her?"

"Then what do you mean she won't let him leave? How is she making him stay with her?"

"D'you think he'll be able to use that foot again? I hope he won't be a cripple. Travis should sue her for damages." His words slurred together. "I'm gonna go home now."

Barry gathered his feet under him and pushed himself up to stand. Joel straightened, stretching his cramped muscles, and Larry joined him. Together they watched Barry stagger to the second apartment unit. People moved out of the way to let him pass.

"Do you want me to call Brian to go to the hospital?" Larry asked.

"I'll go after I take Suzie in. Travis won't be going anywhere for a while."

"Especially on that foot. I swear the thing's already doubled in size. It'll be a good long night in the ER. Lucky you," Larry added with a grin. He was older than Joel by about fifteen years, and Joel appreciated his easy-going attitude that took everything in stride.

Joel's phone buzzed again as he walked to his car. He checked it quickly, feeling a little thrill at seeing Val's name.

I just chased off a couple of kids trying to break into the pump house without calling 911. You're welcome. I expect my badge when I see you tomorrow.

He thumbed a quick answer.

First you have to stop calling it a badge.

Right! Shield. Not sure why you cops can't do the decent thing and use the same terms as the rest of us.

Because you're wrong.

Harsh! Does the arrogance come with the shield?

She included a wink emoji and Joel smiled to himself before slipping the phone back in his pocket.

Suzie glared at him from the back seat, her mouth moving in a silent tirade.

Larry was right. It was going to be a long night.

2

"WHAT WILL we do if a train comes?" Abby asked, standing at one end of the giant trestle bridge and eyeing the railroad track warily.

Val stepped onto the metal grating that ran along the shoulder, allowing pedestrians to walk safely over the ties. Fifty feet below, the north fork of Owl Creek collected into a deep green pool perfect for swimming. A rope hung from the lower bridge supports—and had for as long as Val could remember—issuing an invitation to daring teenagers.

She gestured to Abby encouragingly. "Trains don't run on these tracks anymore. Come on, don't you want to see the ghost town?"

Abby looked at the tunnel entrance yawning at the opposite end of the bridge. Cut into the mountain, the tunnel curved out of sight so no light was visible from the other end.

"Are you sure we have to go in there?"

"It's not as dark as it looks, I promise," Joel said, slipping a backpack onto his shoulders. It held their picnic dinner while Val's backpack held sunscreen and water bottles.

Val reached for Abby's hand. "I've got you. I promise you won't fall."

Abby stepped onto the grate, and Val positioned her own body nearest the safety rail, a flimsy-looking thing with three narrow cables providing the only protection between her and the steep drop below. Joel followed behind, and their footsteps vibrated the walkway.

The sound of a car made Val turn. A red Honda crossover had come to a stop on the dirt pull-out next to Joel's truck. That was unfortunate. They were on a little-used road that led the back way over the hills from Owl Creek to Salmon Ridge, and she'd hoped to have the place to themselves. A man and woman got out of the car and moved to the sign describing the history of the abandoned silver mining town and the original railroad that had supplied it.

She turned back to watch her feet. "I'm so glad Goldendale is still standing, especially after the wildfire season we've had. I haven't been here in years."

"I used to come here all the time with my family," Joel said. "Estella stepped on a nail once and it went right through her sandal and an inch into her foot."

"Ow." Abby winced. "I hope there aren't any nails there now."

Val squeezed her hand. "You're wearing tennis shoes, so that'll help. But pay attention to where you're going. It's over a hundred years old, so stuff will be falling apart."

"Whoa. That's older than Grandpa Fisher."

Val snorted. "Yes. Way older."

Jordan's parents were in their mid-sixties.

The trestle bridge ended, and Abby veered off to the side of the path where a pile of rusted spikes sat.

"Look, Mom!" She picked one up and brandished it like a sword. "This is the biggest nail I've ever seen! Can I keep it?"

"Better not. They must be there for a reason."

Abby's shoulders sank as she dropped it, and Val bit her tongue watching her wipe the rust from her hands onto her pink cotton shorts.

They followed the railroad tracks into the massive tunnel. Val slipped her sunglasses up to rest on top of her head, allowing her eyes to adjust to the dark. The ribbed interior of the tunnel sported graffiti, but the ground was free of litter. A pleasant breeze funneled toward them from the other end, providing cool relief from the late afternoon sun outside.

Abby tried walking on the steel rail like a gymnast on a balance beam, but she slipped off after a few steps and settled for leaping from tie to tie, confident now that the ground was solid beneath their feet and not open to the river below.

Val slipped her hand into Joel's, keeping to the gravel shoulder where the footing was level. Their steps echoed in the cavernous space, the grinding of rock beneath their feet.

"I wasn't sure you'd make it," she said. "I haven't seen you very much this week."

"Sorry. This lawsuit is making everyone so tense right now. Our reports have to be triple-checked and watertight."

"I still don't understand why Peter Moyer is suing the sheriff's office. It wasn't deputies who killed his son."

"No, but finding Eliza's body stirred up a lot of pain, and he's looking for someone to blame. With everyone responsible either dead or in prison, all he can do is blame the cops who didn't get it right the first time."

He kept his voice low. The couple from the Honda had entered behind them, their chatter drifting to Val and Joel.

Abby whooped. "Listen, Mom! It's an echo!" she cried, sending the noise reverberating through the tunnel. They rounded the corner, and bright daylight from the exit filled their view.

"Well, I'm glad you could be free today. Things have been so busy with school starting that I don't know where August went."

"I know. We still haven't had our *Stranger Things* marathon, but October might be best for that anyway."

Val smiled to hide her discomfort. Everyone was raving about the new show on Netflix, and Joel had invited her to watch it at his house since she didn't have high speed internet. But she hadn't figured out what to do with Abby.

When she and Jordan had wanted to watch a show

by themselves, they simply stayed up late after sending Abby to bed. But this was different.

Very different.

"Maybe I can ask Eileen if she's free to watch Abby next weekend."

"Cool." He looked at her with a gleam in his eye, and she knew he was thinking the same thing when his eyes flickered to her lips.

Val ducked her head, fighting a smile. In front of Abby, she wouldn't allow more affection than holding hands. It had been hard enough telling Abby about her father. She didn't want to complicate things by rushing things too soon with Joel.

They emerged from the tunnel into brilliant sunlight. The mountainside had been cut away to accommodate the rail line, forming a steep cliff rising on one side and falling away to the river on the other. There was no shade or relief from the unrelenting sun, and the gravel slowed their progress.

"This is taking forever," Abby complained. "Can we have our picnic right here?"

"On the rocks and the train tracks?" Val asked incredulously. "I promise it's not far. Do you see that bend ahead? Right around that corner it opens up into a little meadow, and we'll be there!"

"Then we'll see the ghost town?"

"Yep. All four buildings."

"Three," Joel corrected. "The house is gone. Finally collapsed."

"Okay, three."

"I'm glad we're coming in the day so we don't see

any ghosts," Abby said. "Do you think we might see Bigfoot?"

"Better keep an eye out just in case."

Joel said, "My dad always used to say the first one to see Bigfoot got an ice cream cone."

"Did you ever see him?" Abby asked, her eyebrows raised so high they disappeared under her bangs.

"Nope. Which is good because he likes to take little girls and carry them away to the woods!" At this, Joel lunged for Abby and swooped her up into his arms. She squealed in delight, showing gaps in her teeth where she'd lost her canines. Joel swung her up onto his shoulders.

"Is that better?" he asked.

"Yes!"

Val caught Joel's eye and grinned. He didn't have children, but he was adapting to Abby like a natural. When they rounded the bend, the meadow spread before them awash in the brown and golden tones of late summer—dried grass speckled with sticker weeds, dandelions, and wildflowers. Madrone trees edged the forested hillside, and rhododendrons, ferns, and vine maple filled in the understory. The green foliage was muted with a coating of dust from weeks without rain, a pop of color emerging in the shadows where the vine maple were already changing colors.

In the center of the clearing, shaded from the afternoon sun by the mountain, sat three buildings that looked like they could have come out of an old western movie set. The church was most recognizable, with a wooden steeple standing proudly in spite of missing planks in the siding and a gaping belfry. Behind it stood the building that had once served as the general store and post office in one, with its covered porch still intact. Where the old house had once stood was now an empty plot, and in the distance the accompanying barn sagged.

A picnic table had recently been installed near the church, the concrete pad still smooth. The table surface was thickly painted and untouched by vandalism.

Val dropped her pack on the picnic table as Abby looked up at the church steeple, shading her eyes against the bright sky.

"Is that it?" she asked, her face scrunched up in disappointment. "I thought it was a ghost town, not a couple of old buildings."

"This is it," Joel answered, swinging Abby back down to the ground. "Goldendale, a bona fide ghost town built in the late 1800's and abandoned for some reason I don't remember now. It probably says on the sign."

"Let's go check out the church," Val said, taking Abby's hand.

She remembered the spot as a gathering place for teenagers and vagrants, but someone must have been caring for it now because there was no litter or vandalism anywhere. There weren't any historical arti-facts left inside the church, and the interior was just a long, empty room with identical squares cut for windows on either side. An information sign showed a diagram of how it might have looked when used as a church on Sundays and a schoolhouse during the week.

Abby leaned out the nearest window, her stomach pressed against the ledge.

"I see a dragonfly!" She pointed.

"Can you imagine having your whole entire school fit in this one room?" Val asked.

Abby turned and looked over the room. "When are we gonna eat?"

Val caught Joel's eye, and he slipped off his backpack.

"Here. You can get a head start."

Abby ran out the door with the pack, and Val moved to follow, but Joel grabbed her hand and pulled her back. Just inside the doorway, with one hand on her waist, he pulled her in for a quick kiss.

The tenderness of his lips made her stomach flutter. It was so brief that when he released her, she felt a little breathless. Wanting more.

Val looked into his dark eyes and grinned. "Why, Mr. Ramirez," she said in a mock western drawl. "I do believe you've intentionally distracted our chaperone."

"That I have, indeed, Ms. Rockwell." He pantomimed tugging on a hat brim. "I'd be a poor lawman if I didn't know how to take advantage of... opportune diversions."

He leaned in, and Val giggled. Then she caught sight of a man in the distance pointing a camera in their direction.

"Someone's trying to take a picture of the church," she said. But Joel's nearness made her heady, and she didn't want to move.

"Now isn't that a shame," he continued in his mock accent and brushed her lips gently with his own.

"Come on, Abby's waiting."

She stepped out of the doorway, vaguely realizing it wasn't the late summer afternoon that made her feel so warm.

With the other visitors exploring the buildings—one of whom had a professional camera and seemed intent on capturing every angle of the historic settlement—Joel was happy to draw out the meal. Abby was an expert. She'd eat a bite or two, then launch into a rambling dissertation about whatever subject popped into her head, and upon which she was an authoritative expert.

Dragonflies came first, with lengthy explanations about why they had four wings because two were for going up and down and the other two were for going sideways. Then there was Bigfoot, including a theory on why she and Val hadn't seen him yet in spite of living in Owl Creek for three months.

Joel and Val did their best to carry their own conversation under the running current of Abby's monologue, but she always seemed to catch when their attention was lagging and would ask a probing question to draw them back in. It was cute for the first few minutes, but after a while, Joel found it exhausting. He wondered how Val could stand it day after day without a rest, but she seemed content and unruffled. She seemed to have perfected the art of tuning out all but a few necessary bits so she could respond appropriately when put on the spot. Was it a cultivated skill or something that came instinctively with motherhood?

By the time the food was packed away, the shadows from the mountain had grown long, stretching over the ravine. The opposite hillside was aglow with late evening light.

"Should we take a picture?" Val suggested. "What do you think, the church or the store?"

"Let's do the store," Abby said. "I want to stand on the porch."

She took off at a run and Joel and Val followed at a leisurely pace.

"Let me do it," Joel offered as Val pulled out her phone.

She handed it over and joined Abby on the porch, crouching down so she was closer to Abby's height. Abby posed with a jaunty hand on her hip, her round belly sticking out with childish exuberance.

Joel took a couple of shots and then a woman's voice behind him offered, "Do you want me to take it so you can be in it too?"

Joel looked up. The woman wore a sleeveless denim top that was so long Joel couldn't tell if it was supposed to be a shirt or a dress. Her straight bangs brushed against her sunglasses, and her smile was warm, but Joel hesitated. Not only because it was Val's phone he'd be handing over, but because he didn't want to insert himself in the mother-daughter photo.

But Val called from the porch, "Yes, thank you. Come join us, Joel."

Joel handed over the phone and climbed the rough wooden steps. Val leaned against him, and as he reached his hand around her waist, an unfamiliar feeling washed over him. He couldn't remember the last time he'd posed for a picture like this. Not just with a couple of guys after the annual Turkey Bowl at the high school football field each Thanksgiving, but with someone who made him feel like he belonged to a family.

Suddenly he felt nervous, like he might be doing it wrong. The fear of screwing this up hit him so hard he almost couldn't breathe. Every sense seemed amplified, from the smell of Val's skin, to the feel of her soft cotton t-shirt under his hand where it rested against her waist, and the thump of Abby's foot against his shin as she wobbled on one leg.

The woman held up Val's phone.

"Say cheese!" she said brightly.

"Cheese!" they replied as one, Abby loudest of all. Joel desperately hoped his smile didn't look as terrified as he felt.

And then it was over. They broke apart, and Abby ducked inside the doorway, scanning the interior.

"I need to go to the bathroom," she whispered to Val.

Val pursed her lips. "All right. Let me grab my pack, and we'll go find a spot. You can do it like a real cowgirl."

Abby curled her lip in uncertainty.

The woman with the blunt haircut watched them go and held Val's phone out to Joel.

"What a cutie," she said, watching them disappear into the forest. "Is she yours?"

Joel considered Abby's fair skin and blond hair and wondered how she could ask.

"No, she's not." Then, when the woman seemed to expect more, he added, "I'm friends with her mother."

"Are you from around here, then?"

"Owl Creek."

"Ah. Can I ask what you do for work? I'm from New York myself and always curious about how people live in small towns."

"Our main industry is timber, but I'm in law enforcement."

"Interesting. My name's Rebecca, by the way." She offered her hand, and Joel shook it. Her hand was small in his, but her grip was firm.

"I'm Joel. What brings you all the way out here?" He thought he detected a faint midwestern accent, not New York at all.

"I'm an investigative journalist for *LensFlare* magazine. I'm doing a piece on the Fisher family and hoping to get an interview with Valerie Fisher."

Joel's stomach plummeted.

"You're a reporter." It sounded accusing.

Rebecca's smile widened. "Not that kind of a reporter. Ours is a serious publication that's well-respected for our thoughtful treatment of the people behind the issues."

"I don't think I should be talking to you. Val came back to Oregon to get away from people like you."

"Not like me. I promise I'm just trying to understand her experience and give her fair treatment in the press."

"She doesn't want any sort of treatment in the press. She wants her privacy."

Rebecca shook her head. "That's impossible. Jordan Fisher's crimes have brought all the family into the spotlight. His wife and daughter won't be ignored. You have to understand, if she gives me an exclusive interview it'll be everywhere for about ten minutes and then they'll move on. But if she avoids them, she won't have any control over what comes out."

Joel looked back toward the hillside where Val and Abby were emerging from behind a madrone tree.

Not now. Please don't come back now.

"I have to go. Please leave her alone. She doesn't want any part of it."

But Rebecca wasn't finished. She laid a hand on his arm to hold him back while she dug in her bag for a business card. "Just give her my card. Please. She's welcome to reach me anytime, day or night. I'm giving her an opportunity to be proactive and control the narrative. Otherwise, there's no telling what might happen."

Joel took the card and slipped it into his pocket. He'd leave it up to Val to decide. But as he joined Val and Abby, he couldn't help but think of Rebecca's final words. Did she mean them as a friendly warning? Or a threat?

"We needed this," Val said as they drove back down the mountain, passing an area blackened from recent wildfire. "Everything's been so…"

She trailed off, trying to find words to describe the past few weeks. The flurry of media attention surrounding Carter's death and the discovery of Eliza's remains. The excitement of getting a job at the bank and the stress of figuring out how to be a working single mom. The new, uncertain relationship with Joel.

"This was really nice," she finished.

Joel reached for her hand.

"It was." But he didn't say any more.

He'd been subdued while they explored Goldendale and hadn't shown much interest in lingering. Val had secretly been hoping for a romantic moment watching the moon rise, though she hadn't figured out how to manage it with Abby. Instead, at Joel's insistence, they'd packed up and left before the sun had fully set.

By the time darkness swallowed the winding forest road, Abby's soft snores drifted from the back seat. The truck's headlights illuminated a deer crossing sign riddled with bullet holes.

Val seized the opportunity for rare privacy.

"All right, Joel. What's bothering you?"

He glanced at her, and the corner of his mouth twitched. "Who says something's bothering me?"

"How long have we known each other? You might have gotten better at hiding it, but I can tell. Something's up."

She swiveled in her seat so she could give him her full attention. He had such a nice profile. His cheekbones were pronounced and his long black lashes had inspired a fierce jealousy when she was a teenager. When she looked at his lips she had a hard time not thinking about kissing him in the church. Maybe when they got home tonight if Abby stayed asleep...

"You remember that woman who took our picture?"

"Yeah." Val returned abruptly to the present.

"She's a reporter from New York looking for an interview." He pulled a business card out of his shirt pocket and handed it over.

Val had never heard of the *LensFlare* magazine and wondered why a reporter from New York would be interested in Eliza Bellingham.

And then it hit her.

"About Jordan?"

Joel nodded.

Val swore and leaned back in her seat. Blood drained out of her face, and her hands tingled. This couldn't be happening.

"What did you tell her?"

"I said you weren't interested. She gave me her card in case you change your mind, though. She said she's doing a whole write-up about the Fishers. Including you."

Val dragged a hand through her hair, thinking of the photographer. "They were together. Joel, that photographer was with her. He got pictures of us today. Pictures of you and me together."

Joel raised an eyebrow. "Does that bother you?"

"Well, yes!"

"Why? I don't care."

Panicked thoughts swirled in Val's mind. If Joel was dragged into this, what would the media do to him? What would it mean for them both? She'd seen first hand how brutal they could be. And what about Abby? She was starting school on Monday. What if people in Owl Creek found out who her dad was? What if kids in her class heard things and repeated them to her?

"Hey." Joel's hand was on her shoulder, a comforting pressure. He slid his fingers to the back of her neck and massaged gently. "It's going to be okay. They're going to be way more interested in Jordan and his parents than you. Especially once the divorce goes through."

Val snorted without humor. "However long that'll take." But she leaned into his touch, wanting him to be right.

After the past six months, she had very little room for optimism when it came to Jordan. The man she'd married, in spite of all the advantages of influential parents, education, and wealth, had turned out to be a crook who preyed on senior citizens and defrauded them of millions of dollars. Val had only learned about his double life the day federal investigators had shown up on her doorstep with a search warrant. The same day they'd found Jordan's suicide note.

For six months, Val had struggled with a strange mixture of both grief and anger, thinking Jordan was dead. Once she'd learned he was alive and had faked his death to avoid prosecution, there was only room for anger.

The most important thing now was protecting Abby. Whatever it cost her personally.

It was late when they arrived at the farmhouse, the night air pleasantly cool and filled with a cacophony of crickets and frogs. Inside was stuffy from the heat of the day, and Val set about placing box fans in windows while Joel carried Abby upstairs. In her sleep, Abby cuddled against him, a study of contrasts with her fair skin against his dark. It made Val's heart ache seeing her so small and vulnerable. Jordan's betrayal would shape Abby's life in a way Val couldn't fully understand yet.

Val followed them upstairs, and when Joel laid Abby on her bed, she stirred.

"Hey baby, let's get you in your pajamas," Val said.

Joel left the room, closing the door behind him, and Val gently eased Abby out of her clothes. She tenderly guided arms into sleeves and slipped her nightgown over her head. At that signal, Abby, who had stood motionless in her half-sleep state, collapsed toward the bed.

"Nope, not yet." Val caught her and half carried her toward the bathroom at the end of the hallway.

"Do you need help?" Joel asked.

"Nah, we're almost done."

It was another few minutes of tending to the zombie child before she was curled up in bed and Val was able to straighten her cramping back. She closed Abby's door and moved out to the hall. Joel was waiting for her, standing near the doorway to her bedroom. The box fan in the bedroom's open window hummed. A gentle breeze brushed Val's skin.

Joel's eyes were dark in the shadows and Val felt drawn to him with an almost physical pull. The hallway was narrow, and it was only a small step before she was close enough to touch him.

She ran a hand up his arm and to the back of his neck, pulling him to her and pressing her lips against his. She kissed him insistently, hoping to drive away thoughts of the reporter and Jordan. He responded in kind, his hands moving up her sides, pressure against her ribs. The darkness of her bedroom was inviting, a whisper of wind cooling her skin.

She tried to give in to the feeling of being wanted, of discovering new love together, but it wasn't enough. Even with his touch, she thought of Jordan. Her mind raced with thoughts of Abby across the hall. Abby who still wouldn't talk about Jordan's betrayal. She thought of seeing Joel with that reporter and how the woman had laid a hand on his arm as if confiding in a friend.

Instantly Val gasped and pulled away.

"I'm sorry, I can't." She staggered back a step, her body warm and her breathing fast. "This isn't going to work."

"What's wrong?" Joel's voice was husky with desire. Moonlight traced his features, and Val folded her arms to stop from reaching out to him.

"I have to think about Abby. If it were just the two of us, then it would be different, but it's not. She's still so confused about Jordan, and I don't want to do anything to make things harder for her."

"I could leave before she wakes up."

"It's more than that. Seeing that reporter today…I don't know what's coming, but I need to be very careful. For all our sakes."

The only response was the fan blowing night air in from the window. Val could smell Joel's aftershave on her skin, and it filled her with longing.

He rubbed the back of his neck and released an almost imperceptible breath. "All right. I get it. Maybe things aren't ever going to be simple between us."

"I'm sorry, Joel. I don't know what else to do."

"It's okay. I told you before that I don't want to screw this up. If you need to slow things down, I can respect that."

"Thank you." But it felt like an apology as she showed him to the door.

3

JOEL SLOWED his car to a stop before turning into the gravel parking lot for Donovan Lumber Company, the mill that employed the majority of Owl Creek's residents. The employee parking lot was further down the hill and accessed through another entrance closer to the plant. This lot was smaller, serving the administrative offices as the public face of the mill.

The one-story building was covered in weathered gray cedar and looked like it was decades overdue for a remodel. Larry's Yukon was parked out front, and before Joel had closed the door to his car, Larry came out the front door shaking his head.

"Hope you brought some valium. He's gonna need it."

"Is he freaking out?"

Larry stopped, his boots scuffing rock. "I get why he's upset. But he's seen too many cop shows. He thinks we should be calling in the FBI."

Joel climbed the three steps and before he could reach the glass door, it was flung open from inside.

"Joel! You're here. Thanks for coming."

Kevin Donovan was in his early thirties, but his receding hairline made him look older. He'd graduated high school a few years before Joel and had returned to Owl Creek as soon as he finished his degree at Oregon State so he could prepare to take over the business from his dad. Randy Donovan had retired last year, and Joel knew from rumors around town that many employees weren't thrilled about the change in command.

Joel understood how it felt to be dismissed because of youth and inexperience. When he'd been promoted to detective, some inside the sheriff's office had assumed it was only because of the publicity surrounding the Stan's Market incident. What they didn't understand was that with the publicity came increased scrutiny, and more days than not he'd wished it was someone else who had been given hero status that day.

He wondered if Kevin felt his own career was an uphill battle trying to please people who would never think of him as anything but a usurper.

"Sorry to call you in on a Sunday," Kevin said as he locked the door behind them. "I guess they meant to leave it overnight so it was extra ripe when I found it tomorrow."

Standing at the front desk was a middle-aged white man with a pronounced paunch and a younger woman whose heart-shaped face was framed by two black braids, one draped over each shoulder. With a start, Joel recognized the woman he'd seen at the Moon

Apartments on Friday night. She wore the grim expression of someone trying to be strong in the face of a shock.

Kevin gestured to them both. "This is Hannah, our new front desk gal, and Alex is our accountant. Hannah is the one who found it."

"Where is it?"

Joel pulled on gloves as Kevin led him down the hallway to his office. The dark-paneled room was dimly lit by sunlight leaking through the closed mini blinds. In the corner nearest the window hung a cat skinned from head to foot. Stretching long and lean from bound rear legs, its pink muscles were shiny and taut.

The carcass was already beginning to turn in the heat, filling the room with the scent of decay.

Joel approached carefully. "Was there a note or any sort of message?"

"Not that I've found, but I haven't really looked. Once Hannah called me I told her to leave the room and call the police. I figured you'd want to see it just how they found it."

Joel nodded as he examined the paracord that suspended the creature from a hook in the ceiling.

"How long has that hook been there?"

"Ages. It's for plants, but I'm not really good with them."

Joel turned the rod to crack open the blind slats. Wide windows on either wall met in the corner of the room, forming a nook where the cat hung like a grotesque piece of art on display. One window was latched, but on the other the latch was open.

"This window isn't locked. Did you open it recently?"

Kevin stepped up next to him, peering at the latch. "No. I almost never open these windows."

Joel pulled the slats down to better see the unlocked window. Outside, a narrow evergreen shrub stood like a placid sentinel next to an azalea spreading tiny leaves dotted with shriveled blooms. Judging by the height of the azalea, the ground was close enough that someone could have pulled themselves up from the outside.

"Do you remember if the blinds were open—"

Joel turned just as a bullet struck the window. He jumped back so fast he hit the cat and sent it swinging as the rifle's delayed report cracked through the air.

"Get down!" he ordered Kevin, dropping to the floor.

"What the—"

Joel dragged him down and pushed him toward the large oak desk, adrenalin tasting metallic in his throat.

"Get to the desk. Move!" He unholstered his duty weapon, counting two more shots. Sheltering on the other side of the desk, he reached for his radio.

"12-99 at Donovan Lumber Company. Requesting all units respond for shots fired."

Larry's voice came over the radio. "You all right in there?"

"A single shot hit the window on the south side. You see anyone out there?"

"No one. I'm sitting tight until backup comes. If they're on the hill, they've got the advantage."

Joel grabbed the telephone cord hanging off the

edge of the desk and pulled the whole unit down. He thrust it at Kevin, who fumbled with it, pale and trembling.

"Call the front desk. Tell your folks to take shelter in a closet or bathroom, anywhere without windows. Tell them to lock the door and don't come out until a deputy tells them it's safe."

Kevin nodded shakily but hit the wrong button twice, swore, and tried again.

Hannah's voice was clear coming through the receiver. "Everything okay in there?"

"Yeah," Kevin answered. "Uh, no, but we're okay. Someone's shooting out there, so, uh, you need to take cover."

There was a pause. "You're serious? Alex, Kevin says someone's got a gun, and we need to hide."

"Somewhere without windows," Kevin added. "Police are on their way." He hung up and looked at Joel. "Now what?"

"We wait," Joel said. "We don't want to expose ourselves."

"What if he comes for us?"

Let's hope he comes for us and not your office staff, Joel thought grimly. "Backup will be here soon. What's the best way to get word to your employees at the plant? We need them to seek shelter. Lock it down. No one in or out until given the all clear."

Kevin made another phone call to a plant foreman and relayed instructions.

In the silence that followed, Joel strained to hear any sound over the rushing of blood in his head. Any sign that an intruder was coming for them. It was like Stan's Market all over again, only this time he was the one trapped. Had it felt like this for the two armed thieves? Had they known how it would end?

One of them had. Austin Wilson—barely old enough to vote—had been trying to talk his older companion into surrendering. But when the other man had fired a warning shot, Joel had feared the worst: that their delay waiting for the team from Medford was costing lives. He'd made a rash decision, counting on his knowledge of the grocery store's crowded layout to give him the advantage. It had worked, and eight lives were saved. But when he thought about Austin lying dead on the floor with two holes in his chest, and the expression of fear that had made him look even younger, Joel wished it could have been nine.

Smelling his own sweat, he wondered how well the shooter knew Kevin's office. Would he suspect where they'd gone for protection?

In the distance, the comforting sound of a siren wailed.

"I wasn't even supposed to be here today," Kevin muttered. "How did he know I'd be here?"

"The cat."

"What?"

"The cat was to lure you to the window. The question is, how did he know someone would be here to find the cat? Who knew Hannah and Alex would be working today? Is it typical for them to work Sundays?"

"No. It's the end of the month, and Alex is training Hannah to help with payroll. They came in over the weekend instead of trying to fit it in during the work day."

"Your receptionist does payroll?"

Kevin's voice held an edge of defensiveness. "It's a hybrid position. Alex needs a dedicated assistant, and some of the duties overlap, so it makes sense."

Hybrid position sounded suspiciously like trying to pay one employee for the work of two, but Joel didn't say so.

More sirens sounded in the distance, drawing closer. Joel eased forward into a crouch.

"Stay here. Don't come out from behind that desk."

He edged over to the window, staying just out of sight in the shadows below the sill. A large hole made a webbed constellation in the glass, distorting the view outside. If Joel could get the shooter to reveal himself, that would give the units outside a better chance of locating him.

An American flag hung on the wall, and Joel eased it out of its bracket. He reached out with the pole and snagged the paracord, swinging the cat toward the window. It crashed against the metallic blinds.

Kevin swore. "What was that?"

"Just the cat."

No more shots were fired. The shooter was gone or knew better than to expose himself.

Larry's voice came over the radio. "We're securing the exterior of the building. Everything still okay in there?"

"Kevin and I are inside his office. Two employees— a man and a woman—are sheltering in the lobby."

"Door's locked. Is the interior secured?"

"Give me a minute."

Kevin stood, watching the cat swinging ominously back and forth.

Gun in hand, Joel stepped to the door and pulled it open, noting a bullet hole in the lower part of the wall near the door. The shooter must have been positioned high on the hill for it to hit at that angle.

Systematically, he opened each office door as he went down the hall, checking to make sure the room was empty. When he got to the third door, he pulled it open to reveal a supply closet. Alex and Hannah were inside, Alex sitting on a five-gallon bucket and Hannah typing away on her phone.

She looked up, startled, when he opened the door.

"You both okay?" Joel asked.

"Yeah."

Joel nodded and finished his search, then went to the front door.

Three more deputy SUVs had joined Larry's, as well as a truck from a neighboring county and a car from Pineview's city police department.

Larry waited on the other side of the glass door, now wearing a vest. Perspiration glistened on his forehead.

"Kim and Brian are searching the hill. More units are on their way. You wanna show me what happened?"

Joel led him down the hallway just as the reception phone rang. Hannah answered it, her voice professional in spite of the charged undercurrent. She seemed made of stronger stuff than either of the older men.

"Donovan Lumber, this is Hannah speaking."

Joel and Larry were almost at Kevin's office door when Hannah called them back.

"Detective! I think you should hear this."

Her face was drained of color, and her hand shook as she held out the receiver.

Joel walked back and took the phone. "Ramirez."

"That was a warning, Puss," a man's voice said on the other end. "Next time I'm blowing his brains out. Yours too, if you get in my way."

The line went dead.

Hannah was a more confident witness than Alex. Where Alex responded with a lot of uncertainty and contradictions, Hannah was very clear about what she'd experienced.

"I noticed it right away, as soon as I went into the office. The way it was silhouetted against the window at first made me think it was a person standing there, and it startled me." She leaned forward slightly in her chair, eager and attentive.

"What time was this?"

"A quarter to noon, because I was hoping to go shopping with my friend and thought we could wrap things up by one, so I'd looked at the clock before I went in."

"Do you have a key to Kevin's office?"

"I don't need one. He never locks it."

"And have you ever noticed him opening the

windows for any reason? Or has he ever asked you to open them?"

Hannah paused. "There was a day a few weeks ago when we had a big thunderstorm. We opened all the windows in the building to take advantage of the fresh air."

Joel remembered that afternoon well. That was the storm that had started the fire that nearly burned down the Rockwell house. The day he'd killed Carter.

He pushed the memory away.

"Do you remember who opened the window that day? Was it you or Kevin?"

Hannah's confidence faltered, and she looked apologetic. "It might have been me. I'm not sure, sorry. It hasn't been open since, though, I can promise you that. The way the sun cooks his office in the afternoon, he would have noticed for sure."

They were sitting in another office far from the activity going on at the opposite end of the building where Larry and Brian were collecting fingerprints and photographing the scene.

"Have there been any threats before this? Even mild ones?"

"No. I mean, people are upset, of course. This contract negotiation has been a mess. And sometimes things can get pretty heated in the meetings with the union reps, but I don't think anyone's ever made a direct threat."

"Can you get me the names of everyone involved in the negotiations?"

"Of course. I'm on all the email threads."

Hannah's dark eyes sparkled when she smiled. Joel wondered if Kevin was smart enough to hire her for her intelligence or if he'd hired her for that smile.

"Can you tell me again about the phone call?"

Hannah's smile faded. "I answered the phone and a man asked to talk to you. That's it."

"He asked for me specifically?"

"No, he just said, 'Put the police on the phone.'"

"No name?"

"I'm pretty sure he just said 'police.'"

"Thank you. I'll let you know if I have any more questions."

Hannah moved toward the door and then paused. "I'm glad you were both okay. What a miracle that the shooter missed you."

Joel smiled, but as she left the room he thought about the shooter's warning. Shooting through a glass window was trickier than it looked, and the shooter's vision would have been impeded by the closed blinds. Had he intentionally missed, or had Joel gotten lucky? And with the perpetrator still on the loose, how long would Kevin's luck hold out?

Whoever the shooter was, he knew Joel. Hearing that nickname, Puss, had made him feel like he was seventeen again. Angry and trapped, helpless to do anything except laugh it off. A reference to the Puss in Boots character voiced by Spaniard Antonio Banderas, the nickname had spread like wildfire for a few weeks during his junior year. It hadn't taken long before it adopted sexual connotations, and although he'd tried over the years to forget it, occasionally it still reared its ugly head.

Joel was seized with a desire to text Val, just to let her know he was okay. But then he remembered his commitment to give her space. Vowing not to be the first one to reach out, he put his phone away.

In the distance, the steady thrum of a helicopter grew louder until it seemed to vibrate the whole room.

Larry appeared in the doorway. "News is here. You wanna make a statement?"

Joel looked out the window to see a news van pulling into the parking lot. Would Val learn about the shooting from the news? Would she be angry that he hadn't told her first? But what was there to tell? No one had gotten hurt, and Kevin was the one at risk.

"I thought Larson was on his way." It was an election year, and the sheriff was quick to get in front of the camera.

"Not here yet. I can stall if you're still camera shy."

"I'm fine." Joel shot him a look to see if he was teasing, but Larry looked serious. Worried, even. It's true that Joel had been avoiding the press since Carter's death. To prove he was over it, he collected his thoughts and prepared to face the reporter.

Carter's replacement covering the southern end of Wallace County was a man with long black hair pulled back into a bun and a narrow beard that barely defined his jawline. He was talking to Hannah, and the way she kept touching her hair reminded Joel of a self-conscious woman on a first date wishing she had a mirror.

They waited until the county chopper disappeared

over the hill before beginning the recorded interview. When Hannah was finished, she turned and offered Joel an encouraging thumbs up as she walked away.

"Detective Ramirez," the man greeted, reaching out a hand. "I'm Wesley Peters. Would you mind if I ask you a few questions about what happened here today?"

They ran through the basics, and Joel gave as little information as possible without making it obvious he was stonewalling.

When the camera turned away, Wesley stepped forward with a strained smile on his face.

"Keeping things pretty close to the vest on this one, eh?"

"Just trying to do my job. If you'll excuse me…" Joel turned away but Wesley's voice stopped him.

"Carter always spoke so highly of you, Ramirez. I hope we'll be able to work together as well as the two of you did."

Joel stared at him. "You know it didn't end well, right?"

"You mean with your bullet in his chest and him at the bottom of a well?" Wesley shrugged. "I'll take my chances." He gave a little salute and turned his back.

Joel watched him go, wondering whether to be annoyed or impressed at his bravado.

Figures moved through the trees on the slope, rifles at the ready. The hillside was wooded, and Joel knew it would be a beast to search. Search and Rescue dogs were on their way, but it was a volunteer team, and Joel wasn't sure they'd ever worked a scene quite like this.

Kim was taking pictures of the flower bed beneath

Kevin's office window. The layer of red volcanic rock was a popular landscaping choice for businesses who didn't want much upkeep. She straightened as Joel approached.

"If they came in through this window, they picked a good entry point. They could have done a whole line dance with their drinking buddies on these cinder rocks and it wouldn't have left a trace."

"We'll need to set up checkpoints in all the parking lots to make sure he doesn't leave with the employees."

Kim nodded. "You doing okay?"

"Sure." He didn't mention the way his skin crawled when he turned his back to the slope. "It's the phone call that's getting to me. He knew it was me on the other end, so he must have seen me enter the building. Why wait for an audience?"

"Maybe he wanted this kind of response. Maybe he's got a flair for the dramatic."

"He knew me. He called me Puss." Even after all these years his jaw clenched to say it.

Kim's eyes narrowed. "Hold on, where have I heard that before?"

"It's a stupid insult carried over from high school. Cropped up again at the softball game on the Fourth of July."

"Right. When you broke up that fight. Wasn't Kevin Donovan part of that?"

But Joel had already turned and was headed back toward the office. He found Kevin inside, talking to Hannah near the reception desk.

Kevin's skin was sallow, and his lips seemed too red. He ran a hand through his hair as Joel joined them.

"Have you caught him yet?" he asked.

"We're setting up a perimeter and calling in air support and search dogs. What can you tell me about Mason Pearson?"

Kevin looked at him blankly. "My brother-in-law?"

"He's your brother-in-law?" This isn't what Joel had expected.

"My wife—Bonnie—he's her brother. Do you need to talk to him or something?"

"Are you on good terms? You guys got in a scuffle a couple months ago during the softball game."

Kevin's shoulders stiffened. "Look, that was stupid, but it was nothing. Mason's a bit of a hothead and he was celebrating a little too much, you know? But it wasn't anything. We get along great."

"You know Mason, too, don't you?" Joel asked Hannah.

She blinked in surprise. "I do, yes. How do you—"

"Did he know you would be working here today?"

"No, I don't think so. We aren't that...I don't know him that well. He's just a guy in the same complex. Oh that's right, you were there Friday night when poor Travis...yeah, Mason lives there. You get to know everyone in a small place like that."

"Did you recognize the shooter's voice? Is there any chance it could have been Mason?"

"This is ridiculous," Kevin objected. "There's no way Mason would have done something like that."

Hannah shot a look at Kevin. "No. I don't think so. I didn't recognize the voice at all."

Joel silently agreed. Mason's voice was higher than the caller. High and strident. The voice on the phone had been considerably deeper.

"Why are you asking questions about Mason?" Kevin demanded. "What does he have to do with this?"

Joel didn't want to explain about the nickname. "We're going to have to talk to all your friends and family, see if they have ideas about who might have wanted to hurt you. Do you have a number for Mason?"

"Sure." Kevin reached for his phone. It buzzed twice in quick succession, and he scanned the screen. "Uh, do you know how long this is gonna take? Bonnie's really worried."

"It's best if you don't leave until the area is secure."

"I have that list of names you asked for." Hannah handed Joel a computer printout with email addresses and phone numbers of half a dozen men and two women. "This is everyone who's participating in the contract negotiations."

Some Joel recognized, and one in particular, Harry Frandsen, made him pause. Frandsen was the family name of a couple of kids who had terrorized the neighborhood when Joel was young. They'd been called Icky and Sticky then, but Joel knew them now as Isaac and Steven Frandsen, petty criminals who cycled in and out of the county jail on a regular basis.

"Do you guys have CCTV on this place?"

"There are a few cameras down in the plant,"

49

Kevin answered. "Nothing up here. We've never needed them."

Voices sounded from down the hallway.

"What do we do with it now?"

"Does Colleen Radford still have pigs? Her farm is just up the road."

"Good idea. I'll give her a call."

"Either that or call sanitation."

Brian stuck his head into the room, holding the skinned cat by the paracord.

Hannah made a noise of disgust and turned away.

"We're done with the cat unless there's anything else you need from it."

"Thanks, I'm good."

"Have you got a trash bag or something we can put it in?" Brian asked Kevin.

Kevin shuddered and looked to Hannah. She hesitated for a moment, then—when Kevin didn't move—she let out a soft sigh of resignation.

"Yeah, let me get you one."

She followed Brian out the door, and Kevin watched her go.

"You know, it's none of my business," Joel said. "But whatever you're paying her, it isn't enough."

4

THE FRONT DOOR of the farmhouse stood wide open, welcoming a breeze through the screen door. The afternoon had warmed, but Val hadn't yet closed the doors and windows to trap in the cool morning air. So when the knock came on the screen door, it was too late to pretend not to be home.

Val had been looking over her budget and trying to figure out how to make things stretch until she got her first paycheck at the end of the week. There would be no new school clothes for Abby, but it was hot enough that she could wear her summer clothes for a few more weeks. Owl Creek was full of families who could barely make ends meet, so Val didn't expect to have a long list of school supplies like at Abby's last school. But the zipper on Abby's backpack was broken, and her lunchbox had disappeared in the move.

Startled by the knock, Val closed her laptop and

glanced at the clock. It was early afternoon on a lazy Sunday, and she wasn't expecting company. Her first thought was that it was Joel, and she felt both nervous and excited to see him after the awkward way the previous night had ended.

Instead, when she rounded the hallway, she saw a woman standing on the porch. She was dressed in a black sleeveless top and pencil skirt, and Val immediately recognized the blunt cut hair. It was the reporter who had followed them to Goldendale the day before.

Grateful that Abby was upstairs, Val approached the door.

"I know who you are, and I don't have anything to say to you except get off my porch." She reached for the door to close it.

"You don't remember me, do you? You went by Val Rockwell then."

Val paused. The woman removed her sunglasses so Val could better see her eyes. Annoyed with herself for taking the bait, Val tried to think what was familiar about her.

"I was at Fargher Lake, too. My name's Becca Sheffield. We played volleyball together sometimes? Such as it was." Her chuckle held embarrassment.

At the sound of her laugh, Val caught a memory of a blonde with her wispy hair tied up in a bandana. Could it have been this woman standing before her now? If she looked past the filled-in features, trying to imagine the skeletal structure underneath, it might have been her. Over the years, Val had only stayed in touch with a few of the girls she'd met at the eating disorder residential treatment program. Even those she'd lost contact with after Jordan's betrayal.

She stepped onto the porch, careful not to slam the screen and alert Abby that she'd gone outside.

"You told Joel you were a reporter."

"I am. I'm in New York now." Becca had a gleam in her eye, as if she couldn't believe it herself.

Val knew that feeling. After believing she would never have anything positive in her life again, even simple victories felt like a miracle, let alone major ones.

Becca continued, "I asked for this assignment because I remembered you. People don't understand what it's like. The battles we face. I wanted to be the one to tell your story, to make sure it was done right."

Val snorted. "Sorry to waste your plane ticket, but I'm not talking to anyone. I just want to be left alone."

"I can understand that, I really can." Becca's voice was gentle, but persistent. "I can only imagine how hard this has been for you. And battling Ed on top of it. He's a real tyrant, isn't he?"

"My recovery is going fine," Val said. She didn't want to get personal with a reporter, no matter their shared history.

"Good. I'm so glad. I don't want to do anything that would make things worse for you and your daughter. My goal is simply to tell your side fairly and help people see that you're the victim here."

Val cringed at the word *victim*. "I don't care what people think. I just want them to forget about me."

"Sure, I get it." Becca looked around at the fields and forested hills that surrounded the property. "You've got a nice little slice of paradise here. This is the place that time forgot, isn't it? But in the rest of the country, your husband's crimes are big news. You ever get on social media?"

"No."

"It's probably for the best. I'm going to be honest with you, the tide of popular opinion can change like that." She snapped her fingers for emphasis. "I'm offering you a chance to get ahead of it. Put your story out there before the rumors can get too entrenched to contradict. Because we both know that in today's social media climate, truth is mostly about perception and whose voice is loudest. If you speak first, no one else's voice will matter."

For a moment, Val considered it. Could she share her story in such a way that she looked innocent but not helpless, sympathetic but not naive? She shook her head. There was no possible version of her story that wouldn't make things worse for Abby. The same tactic that her lawyer had drilled in to her six months ago was still the safest line: No comment.

"I have to think about my daughter. I'm sorry you came all the way out here for nothing, but the answer is no."

Becca nodded as if she'd expected this. "Just think about it. If things get bad enough and you change your mind, I promise I'll do everything I can to help. We Fargher Lake girls have to stick together," she added with a smile.

Val watched from the porch as Becca went to her car and drove away. Then she picked up the phone to make a call she'd been putting off for weeks.

Val hadn't talked to her mother-in-law in over a month. They'd never been close, exactly. Jeanette's disappointment had been clear when Jordan had decided to marry a college drop-out from Nowheresville, Oregon. Val's upbringing hadn't prepared her to live with the upper class, and every social interaction in those early years had marked her as an outsider. But Val had always appreciated that her senator mother-in-law had made an effort to guide her through the strange public life that came with marrying a Fisher. Ironically, Jordan's death had brought them together, bonding the two women in a way nine years of marriage hadn't. She'd even been supportive when Val had moved Abby across the country, though Val knew it had broken Jeanette's heart.

When Val learned that Jordan was alive and had returned to the States, there had been so much to say she couldn't think of how to start. Jeanette and Charles had been equally silent. She hoped she could still count on their support, but everything had changed for them too. Would they side with Jordan?

The screen door slammed as Abby came outside wearing knit shorts that were twisted off-kilter on her hips.

"Creampuff! Here kitty kitty," Abby called to the stray calico cat who'd adopted them over the summer.

Val intercepted her, tugging at her shorts to straighten them, her phone tucked against her ear.

Just when Val thought her call would go to voice-mail, Jeanette answered.

"Valerie?"

"Hi, Jeanette."

She released Abby who darted down the steps, calling for the cat.

"How are you? How's Abby?" Jeanette asked.

"We're...okay. We're keeping busy."

Val didn't know how much Jeanette had heard about the events over the summer, but it was safe to assume she'd heard enough. Val walked out of Abby's earshot to the line of apple trees against the fence. The apples were beginning to drop and lay neglected on the ground, soft and brown where they were beginning to rot. Wasps hovered over the sweet fruit.

"It's so good to hear from you," Jeanette said. "I've been wanting to call, but I know it's probably so difficult for you and Abby right now. I didn't want to intrude." Her tone was controlled and formal, her professional demeanor worn like a mask.

Val immediately felt guarded. "How have things been for you and Charles?"

"Oh, we're doing all right. We're getting through it."

Val couldn't help but contrast the trite dismissal with her memory of Jordan's mother at the memorial service. She'd been composed and gracious, but Val had seen how bone white her knuckles had looked as she'd clutched her handbag, and she remembered the brittle way Jeanette had hugged Val as if she would shatter if she leaned too far into the embrace.

"Have you...seen him?" Val's throat closed on all the words she wanted to say. *Is he sorry? Is he sorry for hurting me?*

"We have. It's..." Jeanette paused as if collecting herself. "I'm glad he came home. But the question is, what can we do for you?"

"Honestly, Jeanette? I need your help. I want to file for a divorce, but Jordan left me with nothing. My mom can't afford to help, and I was hoping you might consider helping me navigate the process."

There was a long pause on the other end of the line.

"That makes sense. This is a difficult time for us all. I understand completely."

"Thank you." Val breathed out a sigh of relief.

"Remember, though, these things take time, and it would be best not to rush into anything. You never know how this will all play out. Jordan's legal team tells us that he's probably not looking at more than a few years in prison. Of course, it would have been better if he hadn't fled the country." Her voice took on the hard edge of an exasperated mother, but it was gone in a flash. "These cases don't generally include long sentences, so let's give it some time and see where it goes. I'm sure you can see how it would be good for Abby to let things settle before making any permanent decisions."

Anger pulsed in Val's head like static. "What would

have been good for Abby would have been to have a father she could trust. A father who didn't steal and betray his family and then pretend to be dead while he ran off and left them to clean up the mess!"

"Now, Val, I understand how you feel. But not all their evidence is quite as clear cut as all that. The lawyer says that he has a good chance—"

"This isn't up for debate," Val snapped. She tried to keep her voice low, but it was hard with the fury in her veins. "I get it; you're his mother. But I can never forgive him, Jeanette. Not after what he did. If you think I could ever love him and be his wife…" The thought almost made her choke.

"I'm sorry, I don't mean to upset you. I just want you to consider that how you feel now might not be the way you feel a year from now. Give it time."

"It's over. Surely you have to see that. For Abby's sake, we need a fresh start. But I can't afford a divorce lawyer right now. I was hoping you'd be willing to help like you did with the move."

Another long pause. "Maybe we should have this conversation in person. Would you and Abby be willing to come to Chicago so we can talk about it? We'd love to see you both. I'll get Henry working on finding flights right away."

"No. That's not going to work for us. I'm in a new job, and Abby starts school tomorrow. If you're not willing to help us—"

"Of course we'll help. You're our family, Valerie. And if you really think a divorce is the best thing for you and Abby both, then we'll support you. But let's figure out the details together before we get a lawyer involved. The process will be so much easier if we're all on the same page."

Just who did Jeanette think Val was trying to divorce? Jordan or her? But of course, in a way it would be like divorcing the whole family. Suddenly, Val realized this phone call was a mistake.

"Just to be clear, I'm not trying to keep Abby from you. You're still her grandparents and always will be. But I can't be Jordan's wife anymore."

Jeanette's voice was softer when she replied. "You married a complicated man, Val. But just because he wasn't as good as you thought he was, doesn't mean he's as bad as you think he is either."

Val couldn't respond because she knew it was true. It was easier to think of Jordan as nothing more than a villain who'd lied and coerced and cheated for his own selfish gains. But the truth was that he'd also been unfailingly kind to her and absolutely loved being a dad. When they'd gotten married he'd been filled with a desire to change the world for the better. How he'd lost his way, she didn't know. She'd never had a chance to ask him.

Jeanette was offering her that chance now.

When she didn't answer, Jeanette seemed to take this as a good sign. "Think about what I've said. Let's not do anything right away. I'll put out some feelers and see what I can come up with, but promise me that you'll give this a chance to settle? With enough time, you might feel differently."

"Thanks for taking my call, Jeanette. Give my best

to Charles."

Val hung up before her mother-in-law could realize she hadn't promised her anything.

5

VAL WASN'T sure who was more nervous, Abby or herself. It was the first day of school, and Val had made arrangements to go in late to work so she could take Abby. She'd worked out a babysitting arrangement with a retired woman who had once worked with Val's mom at the Owl Creek library, but on the first day of school Val wanted to hold Abby's hand as she walked to class.

The grounds of the Owl Creek Elementary School didn't swarm with children the way Val remembered from her own childhood. A lot of families had moved away over the years, and Val hadn't fully appreciated the toll it had taken on the school community until seeing the children line up by grade.

Abby gripped Val's hand. Her backpack sat lightly on her shoulders with a stiffness that said the year was new and fresh and it hadn't yet succumbed to the weight of countless papers and library books and home-packed lunches.

"Look! There's Ms. Newman."

Abby's second grade teacher looked young enough to be a recent college graduate, but at Back-to-School night she had assured Val that this was her fifth year of teaching. Not much taller than the sixth graders, she nonetheless commanded attention in a way that suggested she would lead with firmness and affection. As they'd left the school that night, Val and Abby had both felt optimistic.

But now, surrounded by unfamiliar faces, Abby clung to Val's hand.

"You're going to do so great," Val said reassuringly, as much for herself as for Abby.

They stood in line, waiting as Ms. Newman greeted each student with a high five and a quick question about their day.

"And how are you this morning, Abigail?"

Abby shrugged and dutifully slapped her teacher's palm, but it lacked enthusiasm.

"Fine, I guess."

"What did you have for breakfast this morning?"

"Cereal."

"Yum! I like cereal too."

"It wasn't waffles though."

Val winced. Jordan had made waffles for the first day of school last year. She hadn't remembered, but Abby had.

"Waffles are great too. Maybe you can have them soon," Ms. Newman said.

Abby shrugged again.

How could Val not have realized Abby was

expecting something special for the first day of school? Wondering how she could make it up to her, she smiled as Ms. Newman talked about the fun things they were going to do that day—"design our own nameplates and pick our cubbies when we get into the classroom"—until she moved on to the next student.

Val crouched down to look Abby in the eyes. "I wish I'd known you wanted waffles today. Maybe we can make them on Saturday, what do you think?"

"Okay."

"Next time, if there's something extra special you're hoping for, do you think you could tell me? Then I can try and make it happen."

Abby squinted against the morning sunlight as she looked up at Val. "Really?"

"Of course. I'll always try."

Abby relaxed a little after that, and when it was time to file in with her class, she even managed a smile and a wave.

When Abby disappeared inside the doors, Val paused and let out a sigh. She knew she would wonder all day how Abby was doing, but for now she was in someone else's capable hands.

To be honest, it was kind of liberating.

As Val walked to her car, she overheard two moms gathering their preschoolers to start the walk home.

"That's so scary. Ben said they were on lockdown for two hours while they searched for the shooter."

"Did they find him?" the other woman asked as she bent to buckle a flailing toddler into a stroller.

"No. Ben didn't want to go to work today. It's bad

enough they're all stressed about whether or not they're going to strike, but now? The guy fired at police. Clearly he doesn't care who else gets hurt."

Val slowed. She hadn't been in touch with Joel since Saturday, but surely he would have told her about a shooting, wouldn't he? She pulled out her phone and did a quick search, landing on a story about a shooting at the mill. She scanned the article quickly until the name Ramirez jumped out at her.

"No one was injured, and we believe this was a targeted incident, not a threat to the public at large."

Had Joel been on the scene when the shots were fired? The article didn't say, and Val read and reread the quote until it meant nothing, just a collection of words.

She scrolled down to see if there was anything else, and then she saw it. A headline for a national news article under a picture of Jordan with his hand raised toward the camera. He was dressed in a tuxedo, and in the background—just visible over his shoulder—was Val.

She was half turned away, so only part of her profile could be seen, and even that was a little fuzzy. But it still hit Val like a gut punch. Winded, with blood rushing to her head, she opened her car door and hurried inside as if the Prius could protect her from what she was seeing.

"Wolf in sheep's clothing—Jordan Fisher's victims speak out," the headline read. Underneath, the subheading stated, "How Chicago's Golden Boy scammed millions from middle-class retirees."

Val switched off her phone and threw it on the passenger seat as if it had stung her. How many people looking up the shooting would see that same article? Who in Owl Creek knew her husband's name? Would they recognize Val?

She grabbed the steering wheel and breathed deeply. She'd been informally using her maiden name since coming back to Oregon, but Abby had never been anything but Abigail Fisher. The people of Owl Creek might live in a bubble, but they weren't stupid. Someone was bound to figure it out.

Mason Pearson drove a light blue Chevy Silverado with a rusted tailgate and a large Trump Pence 2016 sticker on the bumper. Joel timed his visit to the mill so he was waiting for Mason when the shift let out. At 3:30 p.m. on the nose, a stream of employees spilled onto the parking lot with hard hats in hand and tired smiles as they discussed plans for the evening.

Mason's beard made him blend into the crowd, and it wasn't until he veered off toward his truck that Joel could be sure it was him. He stepped forward to intercept him.

"Hey, Mason."

Mason looked him over and paused. "What's up?"

"Do you have a few minutes? I have a couple of questions for you."

Mason dropped his hard hat and lunchbox in the bed of the truck. He had never gained much height, but his build was sturdy and exuded strength. He smelled like fresh cut wood and tobacco.

"I've got a couple minutes. What can I help you with?"

"I understand Kevin Donovan is your brother-in-law."

"Yep."

"I'm interviewing family and friends to get a better understanding of who might be responsible for the shooting yesterday. It's just standard procedure. How long have you known Kevin?"

"Uh, he and Bonnie have been married for seven or eight years. So a little longer than that, I guess."

"What can you tell me about their relationship?"

"As far as I know they're doing great. Why are you asking me, though? Shouldn't you be asking him?'

"These are just routine questions. How would you say they're doing financially?"

Mason looked up the hill toward the mill office. "I guess they're fine. He owns the mill, right?"

"Can you think of anyone who would want to hurt him?"

"I don't know. Not that I can think of."

"I know that you and he don't always see eye-to-eye, and I thought—"

"Who told you that?"

"Uh, the softball game on the Fourth? You took a swing at me when I tried to break it up, remember?"

Mason looked down at his boots. "You never should've got involved. It was no big deal."

"So, if it was no big deal, tell me what it was about."

"Just...nothing. Sometimes he thinks he's better than the rest of us, and I was tired of taking his crap."

"He said you'd been drinking."

"Maybe. It was the Fourth of July. I had a day off. Why are you asking me about this now? What does it have to do with the shooting?"

"Maybe someone else was tired of taking his crap. Do you know of him getting into fights with anyone else besides you recently?"

Mason's eyes darkened. "I didn't shoot at him if that's what you're implying."

"Do you own any rifles?"

"That's my business, not yours."

Joel nodded as if it were no big deal. "Like I said, this is all routine. But just to cover our bases, where were you yesterday between eleven and one?"

"Well, I...let's see. I went to Pineview to look at microwaves. Mine burnt out last week."

"Did you get one?"

"A microwave? No."

"Do any other shopping? Anything you can produce a receipt for?"

Mason rubbed his eye and blinked. "Yeah, I did. You got a warrant or anything?"

"Nope. We're just chatting."

"Whatever. I've gotta go."

"One more thing." Joel paused and flipped to the next page of his note pad.

Mason reached in his back pocket for a can of

chewing tobacco, Skoal brand with a green label. He opened it and dipped his fingers for a pinch, then slipped it into his lip with practiced ease.

"Do you remember what you called me at that soft-ball game?" Joel asked. "Do you remember calling me 'Puss'?"

Mason worked the wad in his lip and spit into the dirt. "Is that what this is about? Did you get your feelings hurt because I called you Puss? Jeez, let it go, man."

Everything inside felt tightly knotted, but Joel kept his voice calm. "Do you know anyone else who still calls me that name?"

"Why, you lookin' for an apology?"

"Believe it or not, it's relevant to the investigation. It could help us find who tried to kill your brother-in-law yesterday."

"I dunno, man. I think I've heard some of the other guys use it."

"Do you have names?"

"Fine. Me and Ben Christensen were at The Trader talking about how you...you know...shot Carter and everything. Jason Garfield joined us, and I'm pretty sure he used it."

Joel wrote the names on his notepad.

"Anyone else you can think of?"

"No. Are you done? Can I go now?"

Joel stepped away from the truck. Mason climbed inside, and the engine roared to life with a deep growl. He backed out, wheels crunching gravel, then floored the accelerator as he climbed the incline to the road, leaving a black cloud of exhaust in his wake.

As Joel walked to his car, he checked his phone. It had been two days since he'd last heard from Val. How long should he wait before reaching out? He wanted to show her he could give her whatever space she needed. On the flip side, he didn't want her to think he was sulking about her not sleeping with him Saturday night.

Ah, the awkward nuances of a new relationship.

He looked up at the hill that rose behind the office building. Whoever the shooter was, he'd picked his location well. That time of day the hill was lost in shadow, so even if someone down at the mill had happened to look up, they probably wouldn't have seen any movement on the hill. Either this guy had really lucked out, or he'd known exactly what he was doing.

Val tucked Abby into bed and kissed her goodnight, grateful that it was still early enough in the evening that she could enjoy some quiet time to herself. Sure, she would spend it on the mundane tasks of folding laundry and packing lunches for the next day, but it was still time to explore her own thoughts with her guard down.

When she'd picked up Abby after school, she'd been relieved to find her daughter bright-eyed and enthusiastic about the day. She'd already made two friends, she announced, and Ms. Newman had let her do the calendar.

Val had listened to her stories until they ran dry,

trying to stay as engaged and optimistic as possible. But constantly lurking in her thoughts was the online article she'd seen that morning. The never-ending question of *Will we be safe here?* nagging at the back of her mind.

A dozen times she'd thought about texting Joel. Half a dozen times she went so far as to write out a text, but then discarded it. She couldn't seem to find the words.

Just heard about the shooting. Hope everything's okay.
Trite and impersonal.
OMG, Joel! What happened at the mill?
Too reactive.
You all right? Call me when you get a minute.
Felt too much like he owed her something.

She picked up her phone now and tried again. She stared at the screen, trying to come up with the right words. The more time passed, the more awkward it would be that she hadn't acknowledged it at all.

I heard some crazy stuff happened at the mill yesterday. Everything okay?

Before she could talk herself out of it, she sent the message.

It was a long half hour before he replied.

Never a dull moment. How was Abby's first day of school?

His refusal to answer her question annoyed her. It felt almost…guarded.

Great. She's excited to go back.

That's good.

Now what? There was so much Val wanted to tell him. So many questions she wanted to ask. But it didn't feel right over text.

Would you have time to go to lunch this week? I'd have to keep it short, but with Abby in school it might be nice just the two of us.

She paused before sending it. Maybe the second line was too much. Should she erase it?

Her phone vibrated in her hand with an incoming call. Startled, she meant to dismiss it but swiped the wrong way and answered instead.

"Is this Valerie Fisher?" a woman's voice said.

"Yes."

"Mrs. Fisher, I'm with the Chicago Sun-Times, and I'd like to ask you a few questions about your husband—"

Val hung up so fast she fumbled her phone and nearly dropped it. She'd changed numbers after she'd moved. How had the reporter gotten her new phone number?

She looked again at the unsent text. What was she doing trying to pursue a new relationship with so much hanging over her from the last one? But Joel was her closest friend here and the only one who knew all she'd been through.

She erased the last part about being just the two of them.

Would you have time to go to lunch this week? I'd have to keep it short.

Joel's reply was quick.

Not sure I'll have time this week. Lots going on at work. Maybe next week?

Val cringed. It was so hard to tell tone over text. Was he really that busy, or was he trying to distance himself from her?

Sounds good.

But she didn't push to set a date. Dissatisfied, but not knowing what else to do, she turned off her phone.

6

A FIGURE PULLED Joel's attention to the lawn in front of City Hall as he drove down Main Street. The morning had dawned cloudy and cool. A light mist blurred the edges of the brick building and the man standing alone in the fog. Joel didn't recognize Peter Moyer at first. He'd only met the older man once over the summer, when he'd questioned him about the details surrounding his son Ryan's brutal murder.

Now Peter was dressed in black slacks and a white button shirt, looking more like a waiter than a protester. Except for the posterboard sign he held with the words MY SON DESERVED BETTER on the front. His dog, an aging boxer whose name Joel didn't remember, sat at his feet.

Joel slowed as he prepared to turn into the alley that led to the sheriff substation behind City Hall. The boxer raised its head, but Moyer didn't move a muscle.

He stood as still as a statue, his silent protest an indict-ment not only on the sheriff's office but the whole community.

Joel's heart went out to the grieving father. As far as Joel knew, he was alone in the world; Ryan was an only child and his death had taken everything Peter cared about. It wouldn't have happened if the public hadn't turned on him, convinced he was responsible for Eliza Bellingham's disappearance. Now that Eliza's body had been found and Ryan exonerated, it seemed Peter's pain had reached a breaking point.

Joel pulled up in front of the station, a manufac-tured building that sat behind City Hall like an afterthought. There was no lawn here, only a small strip of river rock that divided the station from the City Hall parking lot.

Kim was standing at Kathy's desk as Joel walked in, scribbling on a notepad.

"Kathy's out today, so we've got to man the phones."

"Good to know. Is she okay?"

Kim shrugged. "The doctors don't have a clue what they're doing. I keep telling her she should ask for a referral to the research hospital in Portland."

"Her specialist in Eugene isn't working out?" Joel couldn't remember the last time he'd talked to Kathy about her health, and he suddenly felt guilty. She always carried on with a smile, so it was easy to forget she spent most days in pain.

"I don't know. She only sees him a couple times a

year, so how much good can he do?" Kim's expression brightened. "But I've got some good news for you. Suzie Fryer says she's ready to talk about where Travis really was a week ago. Seems she's had a change of heart and is remembering things a little differently than she did the last time you talked to her." Kim's dark eyes sparkled with humor.

"Well, that's something."

The door opened and Larry entered, bringing a gust of cool morning air.

"Whew!" he said as the door shut behind him. "Did you see Peter Moyer out front? Creepy sonofagun."

"I think it's sad," Kim said.

"Sure, it's really sad. But with the fog and the light it was like something out of a scary movie. Not how I wanted to start my Tuesday morning."

Kathy's phone rang and Kim looked to Joel.

"Your turn."

"All right, I'll grab it in my office."

He left Kim and Larry talking about Peter Moyer and hurried to his office, shifting his coffee thermos to grab the phone and pick up the call from the main desk.

"Sheriff's office, Ramirez speaking."

As he fielded a call about a deer that had been hit by a car but was still alive, he looked over his notebook. He'd made a list of those who had been most tenacious in calling him Puss. There were a handful of others besides Mason, including Isaac and Steven Frandsen.

The tricky part was, it could have been anyone. The school was small enough that even those who didn't use the name would have heard it. He hadn't recognized the voice on the phone, though, so he didn't think it was anyone he'd stayed friends with into adulthood.

"A deputy will be right out. Thanks for letting us know," Joel said, hanging up the phone. He called out his office door. "Who wants to go put a deer out of its misery?"

"You took the call," Kim called back. "Sounds like it's got your name on it."

Joel went to the doorway. In a tone of mock disappointment, he said, "As much as I want to, I've got the union president coming any minute now. Besides, you love animals."

Kim wrinkled her nose. "Deer aren't animals. They're long-legged rodents. Did I tell you how they've chewed my big beautiful blueberry plants to twigs? Left them alone for almost ten years and suddenly this is the year they've mowed them down like they're an offense to nature."

"Sounds like this is right up your alley, then."

The outer door opened, and a small white man with a receding chin and bulging eyes walked into the building.

"My name's Derrick Proctor, and I'm looking for Deputy Ramirez," he said.

Kim shot Joel a dark look. He fought a smile as she reached for her keys. To Derrick, he extended his hand.

"I'm Joel. Let's step into this room where we can chat. Thanks for coming in, Mr. Proctor." The union president's hand was sticky with perspiration.

"Of course. Anything I can do to help. Violence like

this doesn't help our cause, believe it or not. It only turns public opinion against us."

"So you don't think anyone in the union was responsible?" Joel asked as he gestured to a chair. He placed his phone on the table, the voice recorder active.

"I would have a hard time believing it. How do you know for sure the shooting was even related to the contract dispute?"

"We're exploring all leads. Do you have any theories of your own?"

Derrick smoothed his hair. "I wouldn't want to waste your time speculating."

"Hey, your speculating might save someone's life. You never know. Tell me what you think is going on."

Derrick narrowed his eyes. "Here's a thought. Kevin Donovan set it up himself. Insurance covers the cost of the window, no one is hurt, and public opinion turns against the union and in favor of Donovan. He wins."

Joel nodded. "Anything else?"

"Well, there's always the personal angle. Maybe an upset girlfriend. Maybe his wife is cheating on him and wants him out of the way."

"Do you have any reason to think that?"

"No more than you suspecting members of the union."

"Let's talk about who you work with. Any of them ever talk about wanting to hurt Kevin?"

Derrick pulled back. "Even if they did, I wouldn't take it seriously. They've gotta blow off steam, you know? It doesn't mean anything."

"I'm just interested in who you think might be capable of something like this."

"Desperate men will do desperate things. You never know what someone's capable of if pushed far enough. But in answer to your question, no, I don't have any idea."

"How are the negotiations going?"

"They're not. Donovan refuses to meet with us. The deadline is this Friday, and it's looking more and more like we'll be striking on Monday." Derrick's eyes almost glowed as he said the words, making Joel suspect this was exactly what he wanted.

"Labor Day."

"It seems fitting, don't you think?"

"Where were you on Sunday morning?"

Derrick's bulbous eyes narrowed. "I was at church with my family. We got home at noon, and then I took my boys to the park to swim in the river. There were lots of people there. Do I need an alibi?"

"If you can write down a few of the people who saw you there, I'd appreciate it."

"I didn't try to shoot Kevin Donovan."

"I'm not saying you did. We have to cover all our bases, starting with the easiest ones. Sounds like we shouldn't have any trouble verifying your whereabouts." He pushed a sheet of paper toward Derrick.

Derrick scratched down a few names. "There were a lot of people there. But I starred the ones I actually talked to, so hopefully they'll remember."

Joel traded his paper for the list he'd made earlier. "Do you know any of these men?"

Derrick looked over the list. "I know Mason Pearson. And Frandsen...any relation to Harry? But the rest, no, I don't know them."

"How well do you know Mason?"

"A little. Everyone knows Mason. Why?"

"Is he part of the union?"

"I don't have to divulge that information. About half of the employees at DLC aren't. I wish we could get them to see how much more power they'd have if we could all be united."

"Harry Frandsen has been part of the negotiation team, right?"

"Right."

"How has he responded to negotiations stalling this week?"

"Same as anyone. We're all annoyed, but not surprised. Donovan doesn't have half the integrity his dad did."

"It sounds like people aren't too happy with him being in charge."

"I'm stating the facts, not opinions."

"Do you own any rifles, Mr. Proctor?"

"Sure. I've got a little twenty-two for plinking and a 12-gauge shotgun."

Joel noted these down. The preliminary ballistics report had indicated the rifle the shooter had used was a .30-06.

"Well, thanks for coming in. If you think of anything else that could help, give me a call. And good luck with the negotiations. I hope things can get resolved peacefully before anyone gets hurt."

Derrick bristled at that. "We don't like violence,
Deputy. Our first priority is to take care of the workers.
We don't want to see anyone get hurt. But we're also
not going to back down while men like Donovan flex
their muscles and rob their employees. He's not as
untouchable as he thinks."

Mist rose off the river as Val drove over the bridge into
town. The temperatures had cooled overnight into the
fifties, and Val was wearing a light sweater over her
Wallace Community Bank polo shirt. Abby had opted
for a sweatshirt, even though the forecast said it would
be hot later in the day.

Val had been excited to wake up to clouds. Summer
didn't go down without a fight in southern Oregon,
especially a summer as blazing hot as this one. But these
cool mornings were a welcome reminder that fall was
on its way and eventually the heat would break.

As she passed City Hall, Val did a double take. A
small crowd had gathered on the lawn, black figures
looking otherworldly in the morning fog, like specters
rising from a cemetery.

"What are all those people doing there?" Abby
asked from the back seat.

"I'm not sure."

Val had seen the older man with the sign the past
two days. It had taken a while before she'd realized it
was Ryan Moyer's father. The sight broke her heart. But

this was more than just one man. If she had to guess, at least a dozen or more people were there.

They weren't just holding JUSTICE FOR RYAN signs either. Val recognized a handful of SHIELDS FOR SHERIFF campaign signs, with red stripes and a large white star against a blue background. Sheriff Larson was up for reelection in November, and it looked like some of his opponent's supporters were jumping on the chance to use the Moyer protest to get their own candidate's name out there.

The presidential election was already divisive enough. Owl Creek really didn't need to create their own election drama.

Val handed Abby off into Eileen's care and drove into the parking lot at Wallace Community Bank a few minutes later. She pulled down the visor in her car and checked her reflection in the mirror before going into work.

"You're a warrior," she whispered to herself. "You are enough. You are loved."

Popping in a breath mint, she grabbed her bag and hurried across the parking lot to the bank. She pulled open the heavy glass door and stood aside as an older, white-haired woman wearing a light sweater approached the step.

"Good morning, Mrs. Page."

"Thank you, Valerie. It's a little chilly this morning, isn't it?"

"It is, but I think it feels great," Val said.

Mrs. Page was a regular at the bank, preferring to

do everything in person instead of relying on the internet. Val wasn't sure she even owned a computer.

"It looks like Brandi is open," Val said as they stepped inside.

Brandi waved from across the lobby. "Hi, Mrs. Page. I can get you sorted if you'd like."

While Mrs. Page shuffled across the tile floor, Val slipped behind the counter and dropped her purse and lunch into the drawer. She hated being late and felt waves of shame as she opened her window next to Brandi. She unlocked the till and quickly counted out her cash, and by the time Mrs. Page left, she was finished.

"I saw Gina's post on Facebook," Brandi said. "I can't believe she went skydiving! It made me feel woozy just looking at the pictures. She's insane!"

"I know. Isn't that crazy? I don't know what she was thinking." Val didn't mention that she wasn't on Facebook. Gina had texted a few pictures to Val, knowing that was the only way Val would see them.

"You couldn't pay me enough money to jump out of a plane. Unless—"

"Val, would you come here for a minute?" Maddie's voice carried across the lobby. She stood in the doorway to her office, and Val felt a fresh wave of shame over being late.

She smiled nervously at Maddie as she entered the office, then her smile fell as she caught sight of the framed illustration of Amy Geddon from the webcomic *Robert Apocalypse*. Abby loved the comic and asked almost daily if she could read more. But just the sight of it reminded Val of Carter and made her palms sweat.

"How are you feeling, Val?" Maddie asked, gesturing for Val to take a seat.

"Fine. Thanks." Maddie seemed to be waiting for more, so she added, "Things have been a little busy this week with Abby starting school, but we're settling into a groove."

"That's good. And how about with Jordan? How are you managing things there?"

She said it so casually that it took Val a heartbeat to realize what she was asking. When she did, she felt sick.

"What do you mean?"

In answer, Maddie turned her computer monitor so that Val could see it. Her browser was opened to a news article with the headline, "Senator Fisher's son makes first appearance in court." The picture showed Jordan in a three-piece suit, his hair cut short and a beard lining his chin. It was so startling to see a recent picture that Val bit back a gasp.

"You told me he was dead," Maddie said flatly.

"I thought he was. I didn't know he wasn't until just a few weeks ago." The room was suddenly warm and sticky, even as Val felt cold.

"So...that puts us in a strange situation. Nothing I've read seems to implicate you in his crimes, but if word gets out that you're working here, it could look bad for our institution."

Val fought the urge to look away. She made herself look Maddie in the eye.

"Look, I know I didn't tell you everything that

happened. I was trying to put it behind me. I thought he was dead and we could start fresh. I'd hoped Abby and I could keep our distance from it."

"I understand. But Val, can you tell me truthfully you weren't involved in his illegal activities?"

Val's spine went rigid. "Of course I wasn't! I didn't know anything about what he was doing until the day federal investigators showed up on my doorstep. By then, Jordan was long gone."

Maddie frowned. In sympathy or suspicion, Val couldn't say. "How is Abby holding up?"

Val's gaze strayed to the photo of Amy Geddon. "It's rough. She already lost her dad once, and now she has to lose him all over again. She doesn't understand what's going on, and I'm trying to keep as many details from her as possible."

Maddie sighed and twisted a bracelet circling her wrist.

"Look, you and Abby have had a hard time, and I don't want to make things worse. I just want you to be aware that if anyone at the corporate office gets wind of this, they might think it's best if you find somewhere else to work."

Her words stung.

"Does anyone have complaints about my work?"

"No, of course not. But institutions like ours can't be too careful. I'm not saying that will happen, but it might be worth having some back-up options just in case."

Maddie stood and crossed the room, her ugly words

hanging in the air between them. She paused before opening the door.

"I will say, Val, if they do hear about it, it won't be from me. Maybe that makes me a disloyal employee, but I'll take that chance."

Val knew she meant it to be comforting, and she tried to muster a grateful smile as she left Maddie's office, but she couldn't feel anything but dread.

7

WHEN VAL PICKED up Abby from the babysitter's house after work, Abby gathered her things quietly and greeted Val without her typical enthusiasm.

"Abigail's been a bit glum today," Eileen said, shading her eyes against the western sun. In spite of the cool start to the day, the afternoon had warmed to summer heat. "I tried to distract her by making play dough, but she never really snapped out of it."

"Did something happen at school? She seemed fine this morning when I dropped her off." Guilt gnawed at Val. She was grateful to have Eileen's help, but there was still a part of her that worried she was a bad mom for not taking Abby to school and picking her up each day.

"She didn't say. Her teacher didn't mention anything either. I can ask tomorrow, if you'd like."

"No, that's okay. I'll talk to her, and if I can't get to

the bottom of it, I'll email Ms. Newman. Thanks, Eileen."

"Take care, my dear," Eileen said as she closed the door.

Abby was waiting for Val in the back seat of the Prius, buckled and looking out the window at a hawk circling overhead.

"That's a big bird, isn't it?" Val observed as she got in the driver's seat.

"Mmhmm."

"Is it a hawk or an eagle? I can never tell."

"I don't know."

Abby was typically eager to share random trivia about the animal kingdom, courtesy of a summer spent watching PBS children's programming. So for her to miss the opportunity Val had set up for her was even more disconcerting.

Val kept an eye on Abby in the rearview mirror as she took the rural highway out of town, passing the property that looked like a department store graveyard. It was part hoarder, part horror, with a collection of mannequins perched on discarded furniture, cars, and appliances.

Val had never seen the owner—she could barely make out a blue house behind the heaps of junk—but the scenes nearest the road were changed frequently, so she suspected he made his changes under cover of darkness.

Abby called it the Creepy House, and Val had to agree. Sometimes the mannequin scenes were whimsical and festive, but other times they were disturbing and adult-themed, with sexual or violent overtones. Because of the way the road curved in front of the yard, it was impossible not to see them while she braked to navigate the turn.

Today, three mannequins stood shoulder-to-shoulder wearing backpacks as if in line for the school bus. One of the figures held a large Nerf gun that had been painted black to look like a semi-automatic rifle.

Val watched Abby as she slowed to take the corner, wondering what she was thinking. But she watched the mannequins pass without comment.

"Hey Gabby-girl," Val said, using a nickname Jordan had started when Abby learned to talk. "Is everything all right?"

Abby shrugged.

"Is there something bothering you? You worried about anything? Just tired?"

Another shrug, her narrow shoulders rising and falling almost imperceptibly.

"We'll have to make sure you get to bed early so you get enough sleep tonight."

Abby didn't respond. She watched the dry yellow fields and forested hills pass outside her window as they followed the county road to their turnoff.

Taking the dirt road slowly so to avoid kicking up too much dust, Val let her mind wander to Joel. It had been days since she'd heard from him. He hadn't exactly warmed up to her invitation to go to lunch, but maybe he really was slammed at work.

Of course, then there was that constant voice in her head that said he was probably trying to avoid her because he was losing interest. It was usually followed up with a suggestion that she binge anything she could get her hands on, or stop eating altogether. When she'd been with Jordan, somehow it had been easier not to listen to that voice, but it had gotten a lot louder since he'd been gone.

At Fargher Lake they'd taught her to think of her eating disorder as an abusive ex named Ed. Jordan had intuitively known when to treat Ed like a serious threat and when to laugh him off. His support had carried her through pregnancy and childbirth and helped her establish Abby as her North Star when Ed threatened to make her relapse.

Now she heard Ed's voice louder than ever, telling her that she wasn't good enough for Joel. That she was unlovable and undeserving. That it was a good thing she hadn't let him stay the other night because he would have been disgusted by her. That no one would ever love her again.

Val took a deep, shuddering breath. Becca Sheffield was right. Ed really was a tyrant.

The house came into view, its mismatched shutters drawing her attention. She really needed to find time to finish replacing them. But not tonight. Tonight she was going to focus on Abby and eating a nutritious dinner. Hopefully she could turn her daughter's day around to end it on a positive note.

"What was your favorite part of school today?" Val asked Abby as they climbed out of the car and headed to the porch.

"Um, I made a new friend at recess. Her name is

Kara."

"That's awesome! What's her last name? Maybe I know her parents."

"I don't know, but she has an older brother and a dog named Riddle."

"That's so great! I love making new friends."

Val unlocked the door and held it open for Abby, who dropped her backpack just inside the door.

"Hook, please, young lady."

Abby paused and bent over her backpack. She unzipped the pocket and retrieved a long piece of construction paper that had been folded in half to fit inside.

"I have to do this All About Me poster," she said, handing it to Val as if she were delivering bad news.

"Oh, great! Do you want to work on it together?"

Val unfolded the poster and things clicked into place. Right in the center was a large space meant to feature Abby's family. Something that would have been simple enough for her classmates was painfully complicated for Abby. No wonder she was depressed.

"I think we could have a lot of fun with this," Val said cheerily. She pointed to the columns in the margins. "Why don't you get the markers and while I work on dinner you can start filling out your favorite food, favorite color, and when your birthday is."

That would give her a little more time to think of what to do about that big gaping question at the center of the poster. *Who is your family?*

Abby walked away, and Val picked up her backpack and hung it on the hook near the door.

Working on the poster lightened Abby's mood a little, and by the time dinner was finished, Val had an idea.

"What do you want to use for a family picture? Do you want to use a photo or draw it yourself?"

Abby's fingers were tinged red and blue with marker.

"Beau brought his poster back today, and he had a photo of his family."

"Is that what you want to do?"

"Well, yeah, but…what about Daddy? We can't take a picture with him. He doesn't live with us now." Her gaze flitted up just briefly, as if nervous of what she would see if she looked at Val.

"That's true. But you know what we can do? We could use one of our old pictures with Daddy. What about the one from when you were a baby?"

Abby recoiled. "No one else is going to use baby pictures."

"Maybe not, but I'll bet your class will love it. Or you can use the last one we took together before…" *Just say the words. If you don't say them, how will she ever learn to talk about it?* "The last one we took before your dad went away."

Hope glimmered in Abby's eyes. "Are you sure it's okay?"

"Absolutely." Val made a mental note to email Ms. Newman and prep her to direct Abby's presentation down safe paths.

"Can I put Creampuff on the poster too?"

Val laughed. "Of course!"

While Abby worked, Val went out to the porch to watch the sunset. The western trees were black silhouettes against a peach sky layered in wispy clouds. The outline of those trees was as familiar as the farmhouse. There was a douglas fir that stood taller than the rest, and next to it the drooping branches of an ash tree formed a heart from this angle.

She pulled out her phone, wondering if she should text Joel. Struggling to think of anything to say. It was strange to feel uncertain with him again. Nothing beat the excitement of a new relationship, but she wished she could skip to the part where they were comfortably reading each other's minds and finishing each other's sentences.

She tried to think of something light to text him, something to reestablish a connection. Abby was usually a safe topic, but not today.

Abby's school project triggered an identity crisis because she doesn't know how to portray her family, was definitely not it.

The screen door opened, and Abby came out with her poster.

"I've got everything except the picture."

"Let me see." Val took it and held it up dramatically, making a show of reading through her childish scrawl. "Wonderful job. You even wrote 'astronaut' all by yourself?"

She'd spelled it 'astrnot.'

"I think we have some glue in the spare room, so let's—"

A shrill squeak pierced the air.

Abby's eyebrows arched. "What is *that?*"

"I have no clue. Maybe a bat?"

But this didn't sound right. It was urgent and insistent. Something was in distress.

Val looked to the border of the yard where an old rhododendron dropped paper-dry blossoms to the ground. The grass grew long beneath its spreading arms where the mower couldn't reach.

Creampuff leaped nimbly out of the grass, something dangling from her mouth. But it didn't look like a mouse. It was too bulky and didn't have a visible tail.

"Look! Creampuff caught something!"

At Abby's shout, Creampuff dropped the critter, and Val realized what it was as it hopped in a frenzied rush across the yard.

"It's a bunny!"

Without thinking, she ran down the porch steps and chased after it, suddenly feeling protective. Creampuff got there first, but when Val yelled, she zipped away.

Val scooped the little rabbit into her hands. It writhed and squeaked like a child's toy, so small she held it still with one hand wrapping over the top like a blanket.

"Oh, let me see! It's so little!" Abby cried.

"It's just a baby."

Val examined it for injuries. She couldn't see any gaping wounds in the fading light. Creampuff watched from the edge of the yard, seemingly unconcerned that her dinner had been stolen beneath her nose.

"Can I hold it?"

"Sure. It's calmer now." The squeaking had stopped, but the bunny's heart still thumped rapidly against her palm. It was breathing hard and fast. "Hold out your hands."

Carefully, Val transferred the bunny to Abby's little hands. But as soon as Val let go, the bunny twisted and lurched from Abby's grip, jumping to the ground. Creampuff streaked across the yard and pounced, pinning it to the ground.

"Creampuff!" Val and Abby shrieked together.

The cat batted at the bunny, then let it go, chasing it to a clump of purple asters. Toying with it. The bunny's shrill cries filled the air.

Val grabbed Creampuff by the scruff of the neck, pulling her off her prey. The cat darted away, and Abby hovered near Val.

The baby bunny seemed to have expended all its strength and lay still in defeat. Val gathered the ball of fur into her hands and looked it over. The bunny's ears were flat against its head, its eyes black and glassy. Behind its ear, the fur was wet and matted. Val's fingers came away dark in the failing light.

With a sinking feeling, she turned to keep the wound out of Abby's line of sight.

"Is she okay?" Abby asked. "Poor little baby."

"It's not doing so well. Creampuff got it pretty good."

"She just needs her mommy. Her mom will take good care of her."

Val pressed her lips together. *Some things moms just can't fix.*

"Why don't you go in the house and I'll try and find its mom."

Abby was hesitant to leave. "Please let me hold it," she whined.

"You can pet it but I'm going to hold it to make sure it doesn't try to escape again."

Val knew it didn't have any chance of escaping, and she suspected the bunny knew it too. Was she imagining that she could see a glint of despair in its glassy black eyes? Its squeaking was softer now, but somehow that seemed worse. Val's hand was sticky. There would be no second chance for this bunny.

Abby stroked its small head and ran a finger along its back. "Can I give it a kiss?"

Val suppressed a shudder. "Better not. Hurry inside and get ready for bed. I'm going to look for the bunny's mom."

After one last pat, Abby obeyed, dragging her feet and turning to blow kisses to the bunny as she went.

The baby bunny's heartbeat fluttered against Val's hand. What could she do? Creampuff was nowhere to be seen, but she knew better than to think the cat had forgotten about the bunny. The thought of listening to the desperate shrieking for as long as Creampuff delayed the inevitable death was more than she could bear.

She'd promised Abby she would find its mother, but there was no sign of the mama rabbit. If she'd heard her baby, why hadn't she come running?

Val reached under the rhododendron and gently placed the bunny on the ground. Feebly it tried to shuffle away, then stopped and collapsed to the ground.

Val glanced around the deepening shadows of the

yard. She knew this was the way of things in the wild; the strong preyed on the weak. Creampuff probably killed baby bunnies nightly. But Val had felt the bunny's warmth and heard its anguished cries. She couldn't just abandon it to a long and torturous death.

But to put it out of its misery…could she do it? The ball of fur lay there, squeaking plaintively.

Val cupped the bunny's body with one hand and cradled its head with the other. Beneath the fur she could feel the bones of the skull and neck, so tiny and frail under the skin. It would be so easy to end its suffering now. But something so easy had never felt so hard.

She whispered a countdown. "Three…two…one."

With a quick pull and twist, she snapped the bunny's neck and the squeaking ceased. Val shuddered and threw the dead bunny into the field on the other side of the fence, where Creampuff or a coyote would be welcome to it later.

Some things moms just can't fix.

Wiping her trembling hands on her pants, she headed toward the house.

Joel hadn't been to McGowan's since Carter's death. Now he straddled a four-legged stool and waited for Gary to finish chatting up another customer before ambling over to Joel's end of the bar.

"Just a club soda and lime tonight."

"You sure? You look like you could use something

stronger." Gary looked him over critically as he reached for a glass. "Any luck finding that shooter?"

"I should ask you the same thing. You probably get all kinds of chatter passing through here every night."

Gary placed his drink on the bar and added a wedge of lime. "Wish I could help you on that one. Doesn't matter what side of the contract debate you're on, that's going too far."

A hand clapped Joel on the back, and he turned to see a familiar bearded face leaning over his shoulder.

"What's that you've got there, Joel? Gary, get him some vodka to add to that, will ya?"

"Not tonight, thanks, Luke."

"Well at least come join us over at our table. Brad's onion rings won't eat themselves."

Joel followed gratefully. McGowan's felt a little darker without Carter, and Joel hadn't been sure he was up for it. But Luke and Brad didn't even mention Carter as they pushed the basket of onion rings toward him.

"How's the hunt for the shooter going?" Brad asked. His curly hair sprang out under a ball cap with the Donovan Lumber Company's logo on the front.

"Giving me heartburn. Things have been quiet at the mill since, though, right?"

"Define 'quiet,'" Luke said. "Everybody's so tight right now, they're gonna need a laxative to crap straight. That shooting didn't help things at all. If anything, Kevin's digging his heels in, and it looks more and more likely we're going to strike."

"I think he set it up himself," Brad said. "Trying to

make us all look bad and give him an excuse for not compromising."

Joel had wondered the same thing, but if Kevin had orchestrated it, he was a better actor than Joel would have guessed.

"If he's stubborn enough to stage a shooting, do you think a strike will work?"

"It's got to," Luke said. "He doesn't care whether or not we can live off our wages. He only cares about padding his own pockets. Have you seen that big house he's building out up Skyline Road? Near the trestle bridge?"

Brad nodded. "That's in the Salmon Ridge school district. He won't even be living in this town, or sending his kids to our schools. He thinks he's too good for us and doesn't care how impossible it is for us to live on lower wages."

"What about his argument that he's trying to avoid layoffs?"

Brad and Luke exchanged a dark look.

"It's a dirty tactic, threatening us so that we feel grateful even to have a job." Brad said. "It's the kind of thing that makes me wish the shooter hadn't missed."

Luke chuckled sourly.

Joel took a drink, debating about whether to say it. "If the shooter hadn't missed, you'd be going to my funeral, not Kevin's. I was the one standing at the window when the shots were fired."

They both looked at him, eyes wide with surprise.

Brad swore. "Sorry, man. We didn't know."

Luke nodded. "Glad you're okay."

"Me too. I've got a question for you both. Do you guys remember in high school that stupid nickname that went around for a while?" He gritted his teeth to say it. "Calling me Puss?"

Luke laughed. "Oh yeah! I forgot about that."

Brad grinned, shaking his head. "Puss in Boots."

"Do you remember who started it?"

"No, why?"

"Just curious."

"That was a long time ago. Didn't last very long though, did it?"

"Kids are dumb," Luke said, shrugging it off. "You don't even have an accent."

Joel didn't point out that he wasn't even Spanish.

Brad watched him closely. "Is someone giving you a hard time?" He sounded a little defensive, protective even.

"It's come up again recently."

"I'm just glad we didn't have Facebook or Snapchat back then. Or whatever the kids are on these days," Luke said. "MySpace was bad enough."

Brad snickered. "How long has it been since you've thought of MySpace?"

Their eyes wandered to the television screen above the bar that was showing a baseball game. The Dodgers were leading against the Cincinnati Reds, but Joel couldn't muster the energy to care.

When his phone buzzed, he reached for it. His heart tripped to see a text from Val.

I'm officially the worst person in the world. I just murdered a baby bunny with my bare hands.

Joel stared at his phone, dumbfounded. That was not what he'd expected.

You did what?? he replied.

It was awful. Poor thing was attacked by the cat. Had to put it out of its misery.

It was followed by an emoji of a person feeling sick.

Val was tough, and Joel knew she had hunted with her dad as a kid, but to kill a baby bunny? This was a whole new level.

What did Abby think?

I sent her inside. She thinks I helped it find its mother. I'm a Bunny Killer and a Liar Mom. Where did I go wrong?

Your secret's safe with me.

Good, because you're officially a co-conspirator now.

A warmth of familiarity washed over him. How could a few texts affect him so much?

Three dots indicated she was still typing.

"Dude, what's that smile for?" Brad was watching him with a smirk. "Is she someone we know?"

Luke reached for his phone, but Joel snatched it away and slipped it in his pocket.

"Ha! I think that's a yes," Luke said with a wide grin. "Tell us! Who are you hooking up with?"

"And that's my cue." Joel finished the last of his drink and stood to leave.

"You can't go yet. You didn't eat your share."

Joel grabbed one of the crispy onion rings and pushed the basket back across the table. "See you guys later."

Luke cat-called him all the way to the door, but with eyes on his phone, Joel barely even noticed.

8

JOEL PARKED in the shade of a fragrant mimosa tree spreading its fern-like canopy over Harry Frandsen's yard. Some of the feathery pink blossoms had shriveled to brown and were starting to drop, littering the ground and threatening to leave a sticky residue if he left the Charger there too long. Joel's mother had always cursed the one that grew in the yard of his childhood home for that very reason. But to Joel, the heady scent went hand-in-hand with late summer, and as a kid he hadn't minded the mess.

An oscillating sprinkler waved lethargically across the brown lawn that looked to be more weeds than grass. Plastic squirt guns in bright green and blue lay discarded on the dried lawn, and a tricycle sat in the driveway, its front wheel bumped against the tire of a white minivan.

Joel stepped over the tricycle and avoided another

squirt gun laying on the front stoop as he reached for the doorbell.

A young boy opened the door and brushed his hair out of his eyes to look up at Joel. He wore swim trunks and held a lime green Otter Pop in one hand.

"Is your dad home?" Joel asked, pulling off his sunglasses.

"Yeah, he is." The boy didn't move. He sucked noisily from his popsicle. The interior of the house was dark and cool, and the smell of sautéing onions made Joel realize how long it had been since he'd eaten.

"I'm Joel Ramirez from the Wallace County Sheriff's Office. I need to ask your dad a few questions."

"Cool."

This kid just didn't get it.

"Can you tell him I'm here?"

"Banner, who's at the door?"

A woman came around the corner and stopped when she saw Joel.

"I'm looking for Harold Frandsen, ma'am. Joel Ramirez from the Wallace County Sheriff's Office."

She scowled at the boy. "Why are you just standing there? Go get Daddy. Sorry about that, Officer." She offered an apologetic smile, but her eyes looked wary and she didn't invite Joel inside. Instead she hovered, using herself as a barrier between Joel and her home.

When Harry appeared behind her shoulder, Joel looked for some family resemblance to the kids Icky and Sticky who had called him racial slurs and tried to run him down on their bikes. He couldn't see it. Harry's beard was neatly trimmed, and his denim shirt strained a little over his belly. He reminded Joel of a high school science teacher.

Harry stepped onto the front stoop and closed the door. There was no sign of recognition in his eyes as he reached to shake Joel's hand.

"How can I help you?"

"Mr. Frandsen, I need to ask you a few questions about the union's contract dispute with the DLC mill. I understand you've been involved in negotiations."

"Sure, happy to help. Is this about that shooting?"

"Do you think the two are connected?"

"They have to be, right? Why else would someone be taking a shot at Donovan?"

"Do you know of any specific threats against Kevin Donovan? Anyone in the union who's been especially upset?"

Harry shifted and folded his arms. "Nah, not in the union. The folks who aren't part of the union have been screwed the most. They don't have any way of fighting back, you know? But that's the way it goes when you don't join up. We've gotta take care of our own."

"That seems like things could get contentious. Have you had any bad blood between members of the union and those who aren't?"

"No more than usual."

"Describe the usual for me."

"Look, things are pretty stressful right now. No one wants to lose their job, and those who don't have the protection of the union are more likely to get the ax. Donovan thinks he can keep everyone happy by cutting pay instead of laying people off, but that hurts everyone. Better to cut some loose so they can move on and the rest of us can still feed our families. I don't mean to be callous. That's just life."

"Do you own any firearms, Mr. Frandsen?"

Harry's calm demeanor didn't falter. "Nope."

Joel paused. Guns were as common in Wallace County as wolf t-shirts and flannel.

"No firearms at all?"

"I'm not that into them, but if I were, I wouldn't have to report them to you anyway."

"Are you any relation to Steven and Isaac Frandsen?"

Harry frowned. "They're my cousins. Why?"

"Do they work at the mill?"

"There's no way either one of them could pass the drug test. They could be locked up in the state pen for all I know."

"So you aren't in touch?"

"No. They're family in name only."

They weren't currently incarcerated. Joel had checked. Though Isaac had an outstanding bench warrant for missing a court date.

"Thanks for your time, Mr. Frandsen. I'll let you get back to your dinner."

His phone rang as he walked back to his car.

"I'm headed over to the mill," Larry said when Joel answered. "Kevin Donovan got a threatening letter, and I thought you might want to join me."

"Sure, I'll meet you there."

Joel checked the time. He'd worked late every night this week and couldn't remember the last time he'd eaten something that hadn't come out of a package. The grab-and-go diet and lack of exercise were getting to him, but tonight was shaping up to be more of the same.

The mill was located on the edge of town across the street from the elementary school. Larry waited in his Yukon, the engine running to keep the air conditioning on. He shut it off when Joel pulled up next to him.

"Any luck with Frandsen?" Larry asked.

"He thinks the non-union employees have more reason to take a shot at Kevin than anyone in the union. They'll be the ones hurting the most when the dust settles. Have we got current addresses for the Frandsen twins yet?"

"Still working on it," Larry answered as they headed to the office.

Inside, Hannah greeted them with a smile. "He's waiting for you, Detective. Go on back."

Kevin Donovan was wearing a kevlar vest when he welcomed Joel into his office. He'd moved his desk away from the corner, and two metal filing cabinets now sat directly in front of the window. The blinds were drawn tight.

The overhead light fixture was made of amber glass, and without the natural light from the windows, it made the air in the room feel murky.

"Hey, Joel, thanks for coming in. I'm trying to avoid

being seen out in public too much. I'm sure you understand."

"Let's see these letters."

Kevin reached for a large Ziplock bag. "They've been coming in all week. Most of them have come here, but a few were sent to the house."

Joel pulled on a pair of gloves and took the bag from Kevin. He laid the letters out on the desk. Most of them were typed, with a few handwritten ones mixed in.

"Any envelopes?"

"No return addresses."

At first glance, they looked to be written by different individuals. Maybe as many as eight. One caught his eye. It was typed and printed on a basic laser printer. It was the words that struck him.

You've been warned. Next time I'm going
to blow your brains out.

"This is what the man on the phone said after the shooting."

"Do you think it's him?" Kevin's forehead was beaded with sweat.

Joel didn't answer. He put the letter back into the pouch and looked around the room. "Anything else give you concern? Any sign that you've had an intruder or someone's been on the property who shouldn't be?"

"I don't even know what I'm looking for. Everything makes me jumpy these days."

"I'd like to take a look at the mill's financial records, if that's okay. Just a matter of routine."

Kevin flushed. "Oh. Those are confidential, and with the contract negotiations going on...I'd hate for them to get into the wrong hands."

"Which is exactly why they may be pertinent to finding out who has a motive to kill you. I can get a court order, if you'd prefer."

"No, that's fine. I'll have Alex get you whatever you need. Just, don't share anything with the union."

Clearly Joel had struck a nerve. "How are the negotiations going?"

"I'm not about to give in to the demands of terrorists. When they're ready to own up to what they did, then we'll talk."

"We don't know that anyone in the union is responsible. You might consider trying to reach a compromise before the weekend is over. A strike isn't in anyone's best interest."

Kevin's phone rang. He lifted the receiver from the cradle and covered it with his hand. In a low voice he dismissed Joel with a firm, "I know what's in my best interest. Just do your job and find the guy who's trying to kill me."

Joel tucked the pouch of letters under one arm and headed back out to reception where Larry was chatting with Hannah. She held out a bottle of water that was so chilled droplets of condensation formed before it passed from her hand to his.

"How's it going?" she asked. "Are you any closer to catching the shooter?"

Joel forced a smile. "We're giving every lead the attention it deserves."

She grinned. "That sounds like police-speak for 'stop asking questions.'"

Now his smile was genuine. "It takes time. Half the people in this county own a rifle like the one the shooter used. I don't suppose you've remembered anything more since we last spoke? Anyone else who knew you were working on Sunday?"

When Hannah shook her head, a tendril of black hair fell into her eyes and she swept it away. "Just the names I gave you already."

Joel lowered his voice. "How are things in Kevin's personal life? Do you know if there's any stress other than the contract dispute?"

Hannah glanced over his shoulder down the hallway. "No, but I haven't been working here long."

"No marriage or financial problems?" Larry asked.

She shrugged. "Sorry, I'm useless. Secretaries are supposed to know all the juicy stuff, right? As far as I know he's happily married, and I assume he's doing fine financially. He had me make a dinner reservation once at that casino in Salmon Ridge…what's it called, The Wheelhouse? That's pretty expensive, right? But usually he keeps his personal stuff separate from work."

"If you think of anything," Joel said, "you have my number, right?"

"Of course!" Her eyes shone a little too brightly.

He wondered if Larry saw it too, because he felt the weight of his hand on his shoulder.

"Thanks, Miss Quinton. We'll get out of your hair now," Larry said genially.

When they got out to the parking lot, Larry paused before he got in his SUV. "I've been thinking about that word they used. Puss?"

"Yeah?"

"Could it have meant something else? You're assuming it was someone you went to school with. But maybe it was just a coincidence. Maybe he was referring to something else."

"Maybe." Joel had been under stress, and emotions were high. Maybe he wasn't as objective as he thought. But the way Joel felt when he'd heard it, it was like the shooter had been specifically taunting him.

9

WHEN FRIDAY FINALLY CAME, Val greeted the weekend with relief. Maddie hadn't said any more to her about Jordan, but Val's nerves were shot from waiting for the other shoe to drop. During her lunch breaks, she'd researched local divorce attorneys, trying to find one she could afford who seemed competent enough to take on Jordan's lawyers. Jeanette hadn't come right out and said it, but Val suspected she and Charles would be throwing their weight behind their son.

Abby was lighthearted when Val picked her up from Eileen's after work. She swung her backpack by the strap and threw it into the air, catching it before it hit the sidewalk.

"Are we doing anything fun tonight?"

"What sounds fun to you?" Val asked.

"I don't know. Make cookies?"

"That's a great idea." Nice and low expectations. Val could handle that.

While Abby climbed into the car, Eileen followed Val down the sidewalk to the curb.

"She's such a delight. It's such a shame you're going through so much right now with her father."

Val looked at her sharply. "What did she tell you?"

"She said that everyone thought he'd died, but it was a mistake. She also said he can't live with you anymore because he did some bad things. It's really hard on her, I can tell. Hard on you both, I imagine."

"It is."

"Is there anything I can do?"

"No, but thanks. You're already doing so much. Taking care of Abby is so helpful."

"Is it okay if we talk about her dad, or should I leave it alone?" Eileen's eyes were lined with concern.

"Honestly, I don't know. I'd like to find a counselor for her, but I haven't been able to find any in the county that specifically work with children. So I'm just making things up as I go."

"Oh, I'm so sorry." Eileen squeezed her in a one-armed hug that smelled of lavender. "You're doing a fine job, though. She's a lovely child."

Val was surprised at how much she appreciated the affirmation. "Thanks, Eileen. Have a good weekend."

Her mood tempered, Val tried to put a smile on her face before she got in the car.

"Is Joel coming over tonight?" Abby asked.

"Not that I know of, why?"

"He always comes over on Friday nights."

Always was a stretch. Val could only remember two

Friday nights Joel had visited. But when you were seven, two was enough for a pattern.

"Do you want him to come over?"

"I didn't get to show him my new backpack yet."

"Sounds like we'd better invite him then."

Val called Joel directly.

"Hey, are you free tonight?" she asked when he picked up.

"Define 'free.'"

"As in, would you be open to coming over for chocolate chip cookies and a possible backpack review?"

"A what?"

"Abby wants to show you her new backpack. I'll warn you, she's expecting high ratings."

"Tell her I take my backpacks very seriously." Joel's voice was warm with a smile. "Let me wrap up some things here, and I'll head over."

Val hung up with a new lightness in her chest.

As they drove out of town, Val realized the mannequins had been changed again. Today's scene seemed harmless enough, featuring a family seated around a dinner table with an assortment of mismatched dinnerware. Val caught a glimpse of a tarnished silver urn in the center with a featureless mannequin head balanced on top.

Odd, but she could handle odd.

Val allowed herself to relax and enjoy the view of golden fields glowing in the evening heat. Autumn was just around the corner, the first of the maples starting to turn in the distant hills. Soon the grass would be greening up with rain, and she'd be wearing sweaters and boots. The anticipation of changing seasons always thrilled her, and tonight it was enhanced with the expectation of seeing Joel.

But when she reached the farmhouse, her eagerness withered. A white news van was parked in the driveway, and a camera crew was already set up and filming the house.

Val slammed on her brakes.

"What are those people doing here?" Abby asked, indignant.

There wasn't any room to turn around unless she went all the way up the drive. Could she reverse and make her way safely down the hill? There was little to no shoulder, and she didn't want to end up in a ditch. She had to think fast.

A man holding a microphone spotted her and pointed. As one, the crew turned and saw her approaching. The man with the microphone and another shouldering a camera ran for the car.

Val thought about Jeanette's poise in front of the camera and tried to channel her mother-in-law's dignified calm.

Easing the car forward, she parked next to the house, her mind racing.

"I hate reporters!" Abby complained. "Are these ones going to stay here all night like the ones at our other house?"

"I don't know. I sure hope not. Here's what I want you to do. Take my keys. This one opens the front door. You know how to unlock it right?"

Abby nodded as she reached for it.

"I'm going to talk to them while you run into the house. After I get out of the car, count to three and then run as fast as you can. Once you get inside, go upstairs to your room but stay away from the windows so they can't see you. Got it?"

"Okay."

Val gripped her purse and reached for the door handle.

"Don't forget, count to three."

As soon as she stepped out of the car, the man with the microphone stepped forward.

"Good evening, ma'am. I'm Wesley Peters with the Channel Six news. I'd like to ask you some questions about your husband's arrest."

Val was hyperaware of the camera pointed at her and tried not to look at it. Channel Six was Carter's station. Did Wesley know about their relationship? Did he know that Carter had tried to kill her not far from that very spot?

Thinking again of Jeanette, she took a deep breath and straightened her shoulders.

Abby's door slammed, and Val resisted the urge to look at her. Hoping she wouldn't have any trouble unlocking the door, Val listened for her footsteps running up the porch steps.

"I'm afraid you've wasted your time, Mr. Peters. I don't know anything about the case against my husband."

"Did you know he faked his death to flee the country?"

"I can't comment on what he did or didn't do.

Thanks to marital privilege, the case will proceed without me. You probably know more about what's going on than I do."

The screen door slammed, and Val edged away from the car.

"Mrs. Fisher, how much did you know about your husband's crimes? Do you know what he did with all the money?"

The cameraman had planted himself in Val's path. She felt the tell-tale restriction of panic closing in. She hoped her expression didn't betray her.

"I have nothing more to say. Please leave me and my daughter alone."

"How much did you know about your husband's illegal activities? Did you know he faked his own death?"

She tried to move the other direction around the car, but a woman was there, demanding,

"Mrs. Fisher, why won't you answer the question about whether you knew about your husband's crimes? What are you trying to hide?"

A familiar sound caught Val's attention: tires on the road. Joel's gray pickup was rounding the final bend to the house. The news crew turned to greet the newcomer. Dust swirled around the truck as Joel braked to a stop behind Val's Prius.

He opened the door, and Wesley Peters snapped back to Val.

"Mrs. Fisher, what is your relationship with Detective Ramirez?"

Val's throat seemed to close. She couldn't think of anything to say.

Joel slammed the door and stalked past the reporter. "Peters, get your crew out of here. There's no story here."

"That's for me to decide, Ramirez."

"Go find some real news and leave Mrs. Fisher alone." Something about Joel's demeanor made the cameraman step back so Val could get past. She tried not to run to the porch, remembering Jeanette, but it took every bit of her self-control. Joel's hand was at her back, protective.

She walked into the house to be met with the stuffy heat of an enclosed space. But she didn't dare open the windows, not with the news crew on her front lawn.

"You okay?" Joel asked once they were inside.

"I was trying to distract them so Abby could get inside. Maybe that was the wrong thing to do." Val dropped her purse on the kitchen table and ran up the stairs to find Abby. She was sitting on the floor next to her bed, hugging her stuffed cat pillow.

"You did great! Nice job," Val said. She was aiming for enthusiasm, but the tremor in her voice sounded more like fear.

Abby's eyes were wide. "I hate it here. Why can't they leave us alone? Why can't we go back home? I want to see Daddy."

Val sat on the floor and put an arm around her. "I know, it's so hard. But you were so brave. Do you still want to make cookies tonight? Oh, and guess what! Joel's here and wants to see your backpack."

Abby's face paled. "I left it in the car!" She jumped to her feet and ran to the window.

"It's okay. We can do that later."

"What if the reporters take it?"

"They won't. It'll be fine. Come away from the window."

Val pulled her gently away and tried to envelop her in a reassuring hug, but Abby squirmed away.

"Okay, then. When you're ready, Joel and I will be downstairs making cookies."

As Val reached the door, Abby shot out one last complaint. "He's not my dad. I only want Daddy, not Joel."

Val's ears rang with her words, and she hoped Joel hadn't heard.

He was waiting downstairs near the living room window, standing just out of sight, watching the reporters. He hung up his cell phone as Val entered the room.

"I've made a couple of calls. They should clear out pretty soon."

"I didn't know they were here. I would have warned you if I'd known."

Joel slipped his phone into his pocket and reached out a hand for her own, but she didn't take it. Her heart raced with the words she knew she needed to say, but she didn't know how to say them.

"Joel. This was a mistake. I'm sorry, it's not your fault. I shouldn't have tried...I was stupid."

Joel dropped his hand and looked at her for a long

moment. "Do you mean inviting me here tonight? Or do you mean...everything?"

Val felt something crack deep inside her. She could take it back. It wasn't too late.

"I mean...us. Trying to do...whatever this is. My life is such a mess right now, and it's not fair of me to drag you into it."

"You didn't drag me into anything. I'm here because I want to be. These past few weeks haven't been perfect, but they've been the best I've had in a long time."

"Me too. And in a simpler life it could have been great. It's not your fault; you've been amazing. But the way things are now, I just don't see a way for us to be together."

Joel stepped close enough that she could feel his warmth. His eyes were intent, searching.

"I don't mind waiting. We can slow things down. I can wait however long you want. Just please, don't give up. I know we can make this work."

She wanted to lean into him, to relax and let the stress of the week ease away. But if she didn't end things now, it would only get harder. She never should have let things go this far as it was.

"I can't, Joel. I'm sorry."

A veil dropped behind Joel's eyes, a dark impenetrable mask of pain.

"Breaking up isn't going to stop people from telling stories about us."

"It's not that. I mean, that's part of it. I have to think about Abby. I need to have everything watertight when I file for a divorce. I can't have anything screwing that up. Not even you."

Joel turned back to the window. "They're clearing out. Do you want me to leave?"

No, she didn't want him to leave. She wanted him to stay. She wanted to forget the reporters and spend the evening together like nothing had happened. But it wasn't about what she wanted.

"I think it's for the best. I'm sorry."

Joel's nod was almost imperceptible. He walked to the front door and paused before opening it.

"Tell Abby her backpack gets five out of five stars from me."

Then he walked out without a backward glance.

10

JOEL PULLED into the alley next to McGowan's looking for an open parking spot. There was just enough room for one row of angled parking, leaving a narrow space for one-way traffic to get around as long as everyone pulled all the way forward. Every so often some punk would let the back end of their king cab truck hang out and cut off the traffic flow, but most of McGowan's regulars knew better.

Joel's headlights illuminated the light gray building, and he pulled forward until the front of his grille nearly touched the cinder block wall. He didn't feel particularly social, but a dark ache had settled into his chest as he drove off the mountain, and he knew that being alone tonight would only make things worse.

He was used to being alone. It shouldn't be that hard to go back to it. But in the two months since Val had come back into his life, he felt like something had healed that he didn't even know was wounded. Now, it felt like the scab had been clawed open.

For tonight, all he wanted to do was make the pain go away.

He didn't blame Val. He'd known he was taking a risk by getting involved with her so soon after Jordan's betrayal. He knew better, and he only had himself to blame.

He replayed the past week in his mind and wondered if he should have done something different. Things had seemed so good when they went to the Goldendale ghost town. What had he done wrong?

Before the divorce, Lacey had complained that he never opened up to her. Did Val feel that way too? She'd said it wasn't his fault, but Joel had a hard time believing it. If he'd done things right she wouldn't have felt the need to break up.

He pulled the door open and stepped inside, pausing to let the cheer of alcohol-fueled camaraderie wash over him. It was Friday night, the start of a three-day weekend, and the bar was buzzing. It smelled like fried food and cheap beer, and he ordered both before joining Larry and Brian at a booth on the wall furthest the TV set. He saw Brad and Luke on the way, meeting Luke's fist bump in greeting as he passed.

"Didn't expect to see you here tonight," Larry said when he sat. "Thought you'd be out with Val."

"Is that where you've been lately?" Brian asked. "I didn't know you were a couple."

"Not a couple. Just friends." Joel took a drink to

avoid looking at them, letting the rich malty flavor slide down his throat.

Larry exchanged a look with Brian. "Joel forgets what we do for a living. He thinks he can lie to our faces and we'll believe him."

"Shocking," Brian murmured, giving him the side-eye.

Joel grunted. "All right, so it's complicated. She's still married, you know? We're taking a break to figure things out."

"Right," Larry said. "I forgot about that. Sorry."

"That sucks," Brian grumbled.

"How about you, Brian? Things going all right with Trish?"

"No complaints. She's got the boys this weekend, so we're thinking of taking them up to Diamond Lake. They love going out on the boat."

"Sounds great." Joel felt a twinge of jealousy.

"We were just talking about if the strike's going down," Larry said, smoothly changing the subject. "I wouldn't be surprised if Donovan asks for police protection after what happened this week."

"Would Sheriff Larson do that? We're short on deputies as it is, and with the holiday weekend…"

Larry shrugged. "Depends on how important it is to keep Donovan happy. I think Larson is pretty worried about image right now. With the election right around the corner, that Moyer lawsuit couldn't have come at a worse time."

Brian frowned and lowered his voice. "Trish said someone's started a Facebook group called 'Justice for

Ryan' or something, all about drumming up public support for Moyer. She says it's turned into a roasting session. People coming out of the woodwork with complaints against the agency, some of them decades old."

Joel grimaced. "Nothing like social media to feed a mob."

His order was called, and as he made his way up the counter, a woman called his name.

"Detective Ramirez?"

Hannah stood at the bar dressed in slim-fitting jeans and a tank top. Her black hair hung like a curtain over her bare shoulders, and her eyes sparkled as she smiled.

"Hey there, Hannah." He nodded to her as he reached for his order.

"Food to share?" Her dark eyes flickered to the basket of wings and potato wedges.

"Yeah, I'm here with a couple of guys from work."

"I thought you might be here with Mrs. Ramirez." She glanced at his left hand and took a sip of her drink.

"No, I'm not married." He checked her left hand before thinking.

She noticed and smiled. "I'm neither. Not married, but not single either. My boyfriend's finding a parking spot. Is it always this busy on Friday nights?"

It must have been a new boyfriend judging by the effort she'd put into her appearance. Flawless makeup, a little too much perfume. She looked stunning, but Joel observed the fact in a detached sort of way. He preferred Val's natural and effortless beauty, the way she could look just as attractive in a baseball cap and pony-tail as she did dressed to the nines.

"It can be," he said, turning to leave. "Have a good night."

"Detective?"

He turned back, and as he did, he glanced at the TV above the bar. An ad for the evening news was running, and he recognized the new reporter, Wesley Peters. Joel froze. A picture of Val with Jordan Fisher flashed over Wesley's shoulder. Jordan's arm was around her waist in an intimate gesture as they smiled at someone off-camera. The volume was down, but the headline read "Local woman tied to fraud scandal."

In seconds, the spot was over and an ad for an upcoming action film took its place.

Joel blinked and realized Hannah was waiting for a response from him.

"Sorry, what did you say?"

She glanced away shyly, not meeting his eyes.

"Oh, it's just that I feel weird that you know my first name, but I don't know yours."

"Joel."

"Nice to officially meet you, Joel."

Some part of his brain recognized that smiling was the right thing to do in this instance, but he couldn't seem to make his face obey. Blood was rushing in his ears, and he hurried back to his table, scanning the room to see if anyone had recognized the woman on the screen.

No one else seemed to have noticed.

Larry was laughing as Joel sat down. "How do you

even get a nickname like that? Icky and Sticky…it's like a bad SNL sketch."

"I don't want to know," Brian said. His smile fell as he caught Joel's expression. "Everything okay?"

"Yeah, sure." Joel picked at the spicy wings and glanced at the clock. The late news didn't air until eleven, giving ample time for the teaser ad to run. How long before someone noticed?

Making a decision, he said, "I think I'm going to head out."

"Already? You just got here. What's up?"

"Nothing."

Larry snorted and shook his head. "You're so full of crap."

"All right, look." He lowered his voice and leaned in. "There was a reporter at Val's this evening—the new guy, the same one who covered the mill shooting. It looks like he's airing a story about her tonight."

Brian murmured in sympathy. "That's too bad."

"I can't stand that new reporter," Larry said. "Every time I see his man bun I want to punch him in the face."

"Guys. I was there too."

Brian and Larry looked at him.

"You've gotta be kidding."

"Seriously, Joel? You're smarter than that."

"I didn't know. They were waiting for her when she got home, and I drove up right after. It's not even like we were together."

"Like that matters," Brian said. "You're gonna have a lot of explaining to do when Larson finds out."

Heat flushed up Joel's neck.

Larry looked at him steadily. "Go home. There's nothing you can do about it now. But don't make it worse by hanging around here. Probably for the best you two are taking a break."

Joel's stomach felt sour. "Here, keep the wings. I couldn't eat them now anyway."

He couldn't leave the bar fast enough. He stepped out into a chilly breeze, the late summer night cool in spite of the warm asphalt radiating under his feet. The evening that had seemed so promising had gone from bad to worse.

He rounded the corner to the dark alley, reaching in his pocket for his keys. A black truck waited at the entrance to the alley, and he picked up the pace, knowing they probably had an eye on his spot.

Before he reached his truck, a deep throaty growl erupted behind him, and he turned. Headlights barreled toward him, closing fast.

He was exposed, caught in the middle of the alley.

He lunged out of the way, stumbling between two parked cars as the truck thundered past, the roar of its engine vibrating in his chest, leaving behind a cloud of diesel exhaust and the smell of burned rubber.

Joel stood, his heart hammering in his chest.

"Whoa, dude! Are you okay?"

A man and woman jogged toward him from the alley entrance.

Adrenaline rushed through him fast and furious.

"Are you okay?" the woman repeated, breathing heavily from the short run.

"What did you see?" Joel asked. "Make or model?" It was too much to hope for a license plate.

"I'm not sure." She looked at the man. "A truck. I think it was a GMC?"

"No, it was a Nissan," he said. "It had some of those hitch nuts on the back. You know, the fake balls?"

Joel looked around for other witnesses, but the street and sidewalk were empty.

Still jittery with how close he'd come to being crushed, he climbed into his own truck and took a couple of deep breaths.

Sometimes he really hated this town.

11

THICK BATTER HISSED as Val poured it over the waffle iron, then clamped it down and flipped it over in one fluid motion.

"Can I have that one?" Abby asked. She sat on the counter nearby, her legs dangling out from underneath her nightgown.

"Better get dressed first. Hurry! See if you can get back down before it's ready."

Val swatted Abby's bottom affectionately with the spatula as she climbed down and ran toward the stairs.

While the waffle iron cooked with a steady click, she looked at the list she'd started making the night before when she couldn't sleep.

Sole custody
Sole responsibility for medical decisions
Child support?
No alimony

Visits no more than twice a year (1x
summer, 1x Christmas), with Jeanette
or Charles present

The list went on. Since it was Labor Day weekend, she wouldn't be able to make phone calls until Tuesday, but she wanted to get her thoughts together before she talked to a lawyer.

Abby bounded down the stairs just as Val slid the golden waffle onto a plate and set it on the table.

"Perfect timing!"

"Do we have any strawberries?"

"Just maple syrup."

There was a rapping sound on the screen door and Val untied her apron.

"That must be the realtor. You eat your breakfast and then brush your teeth, okay?"

"Got it," Abby said with a mouthful of waffle and syrup dripping on her chin.

Val had been relieved when the realtor said she could fit her in on Saturday morning to take a look at the property. Val's mom would help pay for small repairs and improvements on the house, but most of her pension went to pay for her condo in Phoenix and there wasn't much left to go around.

Val slipped the list into the back pocket of her jean shorts and opened the door.

Then stared.

It took one heartbeat—two—before her brain made sense of what she was seeing.

The man standing there took off his sunglasses and

in his eyes she read an apology before he even opened his mouth.

"Mrs. Fisher, I don't know if you remember me or not—"

"Of course I remember you, Special Agent Giles. What are you doing on my porch?" Val gripped the door, grateful for the screen between them.

Giles was dressed in a suit and tie. Pink spots appeared in his cheeks, whether because of the heat or Val's rude welcome, she wasn't sure. The surrounding trees hummed with the steady drone of insects as she waited for his answer.

"This is unexpected, I know. But I was wondering if I could have a minute of your time."

"Why not just call me?"

He shifted his weight. "Frankly, Mrs. Fisher, I didn't think you would talk to me."

He was probably right about that.

"So you flew all the way out to Oregon to have a chat? I wouldn't think you'd have that kind of time. Shouldn't you be working to put my husband behind bars?"

She winced inwardly, but he didn't seem to notice the slip. She'd been trying so hard to stop thinking of Jordan as her husband. She was trying to move on and put him squarely in her past. All it took was one of the federal agents showing up at her door and she was back in those dark days over the winter when she'd been so desperate to get her old life back.

Giles held his hands out in a placating gesture. "I understand that I don't have a right to ask for your help, and I promise what I have to say won't take long."

Val wished she had it in her to tell him no, but the truth was, she wasn't angry at Giles. He represented the loss of everything she'd known, but it wasn't his fault. That was all on Jordan. Giles had been respectful and considerate in the way he'd behaved toward Val and Abby, treating them with as much compassion as if they too were victims of Jordan's fraud.

"I'd rather you didn't come inside but we can talk on the porch," she capitulated. And then, because the morning breeze felt so good against her skin and she felt ten degrees hotter looking at his suit coat, she offered, "Would you like some water?"

"Yes, please," he said gratefully.

Val returned to the kitchen and grabbed a chilled water bottle from the refrigerator. It was left over from their trip with Joel to the ghost town, and she felt a pang of remorse as she grabbed it. Had that just been last week? How naive she'd been, thinking she could pursue a new relationship with impunity. That the world would mind its own business and let her live in peace.

Abby was sitting at the table, licking the excess syrup from her plate.

"It wasn't the realtor after all," Val said as she closed the refrigerator. "It's a man who has some questions about Daddy. I'm going to talk to him on the porch for a few minutes, so I want you to stay inside."

"You're always talking to boring people."

"Don't I know it. Rinse your plate when you're finished, and wash your face. It's covered in syrup."

She returned to the porch and found Giles sitting on one of the plastic chairs, his suit jacket draped on the porch railing. She chose another chair, this one covered in dried paint splotches from a long-forgotten crafting project, and handed him the water bottle.

"So, what brings you all the way out to Owl Creek?" Val asked.

Giles looked around at the wooded hills and fields rippling with dry summer grass. "It's a nice place you have here. Too bad about that fire on the mountain. It looks fresh."

Val's stomach clenched the way it always did when she thought of that day.

"We were lucky." *In more ways than one.*

"Mrs. Fisher, I know things haven't been easy for you, and I admire your determination to make a good life for your daughter. How much do you want to know about the case against your husband?"

Val leaned back, considering. "To be honest, the biggest question I have is how can I use it to fast-track our divorce and get him out of our lives for good."

"I can understand that. If I were in your shoes, I would want the same thing." Giles's smile looked strained. He had the beginnings of a five o'clock shadow, suggesting he'd flown through the night. "But of course, it's not that simple."

"You're not here to give me divorce advice, are you?"

"No. Mrs. Fisher—"

"Please don't call me that."

He blinked. "What do you want me to call you?"

"Ms. Rockwell works."

"All right. Ms. Rockwell, I pride myself in never yet having had a case go to trial. Usually the evidence is so tight that the defense doesn't want to risk it. It's not a question of whether he's guilty or not, it's a matter of how willing he is to cooperate and how lenient a judge will be in sentencing."

"Is Jordan cooperating?"

"Jordan Fisher fled the country for six months, which is the opposite of cooperating," he said drily. "But we've run into a bit of a snag. Jordan claims to have information about another case that I can't disclose here but that's of particular interest to the Department of Justice."

"Please tell me you aren't planning on cutting a deal with him."

"Not exactly. He's only asking for one thing, but it's not ours to give him." His voice was neutral, but his eyes betrayed him.

Abby.

"No. No way." Val stood, the blood rushing from her face. "He abandoned us. He abandoned her! He has no right." Bile rose in her throat, choking off the words. She strode to the door and then back. "You came all this way for her?"

Giles rose. "Just a visit. Nothing permanent. You can still pursue whatever terms you want in the divorce."

"Do you have any idea what it does to a little girl to bury her dad and then find out six months later that he ran away and lied to her? She thinks it's her fault!" Val hissed in a near whisper, anxious not to be overheard from inside. "She's not a toy to be played with! I'm not going to give him what he wants and make her suffer for it. It's going to take years to fix the mess he made as it is!"

Giles was shaking his head before she'd finished. "I get it. Truly, I do. I wouldn't even be here if I didn't think there wasn't some value for you too."

"What value?"

"This could actually help your daughter—"

Val snorted her disbelief.

"Hear me out. If she could see Jordan for herself it could help her come to terms with what's happened. Seeing him for herself, knowing that he still loves her, that's gotta mean a lot to a seven-year-old."

The truth of his words was like a hot needle in Val's heart. Her pulse raced and it was hard to draw breath.

"Get off my property."

"Ms. Rockwell—"

"Go. The answer is no. I have nothing else to say to you."

She turned and went in the house, feeling a perverse satisfaction in the slam of the screen door behind her.

Abby stood in the hallway with a Lego construction in her hands. As she took in Val's expression, her hands drooped to her sides.

"Hey," Val said, her voice shuddering with the effort of masking her anger. "What have you got?"

"I made the Fero City bridge from *Robert Apocalypse*." Abby pronounced the comic carefully to make sure her consonants were correct. "Look, it's got the same towers, and here's the spot where Doctor Menace put the bombs."

Val leaned against the door and sank to the floor, gathering Abby close. Over Abby's chatter, she heard the start of an engine and felt suddenly drained. How long would she have to fight for a future for herself and her daughter?

How long would the past keep dragging her back?

12

WHEN JOEL GOT the call on Monday morning that the union workers were striking at the mill, it was almost a relief. He'd spent the weekend home alone and had gotten so miserable that he'd broken one of his own rules.

He'd Googled Val and Jordan.

What had started as a desire to understand her better and ease the pain of their breakup had spiraled into a miserable cesspool of self-pity. Val's life with Jordan had been nothing short of a fairy tale. Was there any wonder that he hadn't been able to hold her interest?

He'd never been so happy to have an excuse to go to work on a holiday.

Joel drove out to the DLC mill and found Brian and Kim already directing traffic on the main road. The parking lot was full of picketers, men and women holding handmade signs like I'D RATHER BE WORKING,

HONK 4 FAIR WAGES, and I JUST WANT TO FEED MY KIDS. Joel even saw a few children in the crowd.

Derrick Proctor was handing out water bottles and soda in the shade at the edge of the parking lot. A bull horn sat at his feet.

Joel parked his car across the street at the elementary school and walked over to join Brian.

"Is Kevin here?" he asked, looking at the office. The blinds were drawn and all looked dark.

"No. Spending the holiday with his family. Office is closed."

Cars slowed as they passed, honking and waving, boosting the energy of the crowd. A forklift truck moved in the distance, a reminder that the plant was still functioning at some level with the nonunion employees.

A white news van pulled up, and the driver rolled down the window to call out to Kim.

"Hey, Deputy! Can we park here on the shoulder to get some footage?"

"You can park across the street at the school," Kim said, then stopped the oncoming traffic to give them a chance to turn.

Seeing the news van spiked the energy of the crowd further. The chanting increased in volume, and signs stood straighter, bouncing with vigor. Joel took a few photos with his work phone, wondering if any of the picketers was the shooter from last week. It was probably for the best that Kevin wasn't here.

"Joel! Joel, come here!"

Hannah waved to him from under the shade tree.

Joel stepped over the dry ditch separating the road from the parking lot and joined her.

"You don't think this is a conflict of interest?" he asked.

She grinned. "I'm not waving a sign, am I? Besides, I'm on my own time."

"What's Kevin going to say if he finds out?"

She shrugged. But a few seconds later he felt her lean in and heard her voice low in his ear. "He thought it was a good idea. Get a feel for what's going on, you know?"

"Be careful," Joel warned. "If someone's out to hurt Kevin, you don't want to get caught in the middle."

Her smile faltered, and her gaze flickered to the chanting crowd.

Clouds chased across the sky, offering periodic relief from the overhead sun. Most of the picketers were dressed in hard hats and boots as if they'd just stepped away from the plant. Joel recognized Brad and Luke standing near the new DLC sign and gave them a nod. The sign looked expensive and Joel wondered how long it would be before a disgruntled employee vandalized it.

"She looks so much shorter in real life, doesn't she?" Hannah asked, drawing his attention to the reporter talking energetically to the camera, her short hair dancing in the breeze. "Is that a requirement for being a reporter? The guy that was here last week was pretty short too."

Joel thought of Carter and didn't respond.

"He actually gave me his number; can you believe it? So unprofessional."

Joel didn't point out that Hannah hadn't seemed to mind at the time, remembering how she'd preened while talking to Wesley Peters.

"How about you, Joel? You didn't say the other night. Are you single?"

The question made him wince inwardly, but he kept his tone neutral. "For all intents and purposes, yeah."

Hannah laughed. "What's that supposed to mean?"

"Hannah!"

Joel turned with Hannah to see Mason Pearson approaching. He wore a flannel shirt over a tank top and carried a sign that said HONEST WAGES 4 HONEST WORK. When he saw Joel, his smile faded.

"Hey Mason." Hannah's tone was playful. "Do you know Joel?"

"Yeah, of course." Mason didn't reach for Joel's hand.

"Are you a member of the union?" Joel asked.

"That surprises you?"

"Your brother-in-law doesn't seem to think very highly of it."

"Yeah, well, he doesn't run my life. I just want to bring home my check at the end of the week." He turned from Joel and focused on Hannah. "You want to get off your feet? I've got some camp chairs if you want to take a break."

"Well…" Hannah looked at Joel and back at Mason, as if conflicted.

Joel took a half step away. He didn't want to be on any scale that was measuring him against Mason Pearson.

That seemed to make up Hannah's mind.

"Sure. Just for a bit." She followed Mason and disappeared into the crowd.

Joel watched them go, wondering how a smart, attractive woman like that could tolerate Mason's company for more than five minutes.

And then he saw it. A backpack rested under a thorny bush near the steps to the office. Gray and nondescript, it was nearly invisible in the shadows.

Suddenly alert, Joel pulled Derrick aside. "Do you know who that backpack belongs to?"

Derrick frowned. "Can't say." He turned to a couple helping with the cooler. "Anyone leave a backpack over there?" They looked around and shook their heads.

Joel flagged Kim over. "There's a backpack hidden in the bushes near the office entrance. No one seems to want to claim it. I think we'd better clear the crowd."

Kim's mouth hardened and she reached for her radio, switching it off. "I'll tell Brian. We've gotta get this group to turn off their cell phones. Do you think someone's at the school? Maybe we can use one of their phones to call it in."

Joel returned to Derrick as he shut off his own phone. "Mr. Proctor, I'm sorry to tell you this, but we're going to need to evacuate the area for everyone's safety."

Derrick's mouth dropped open. "You're yanking my chain."

"I'm afraid not. We need everyone to vacate the premises. Help me get these people to the far end of the baseball field." Joel gestured across the street.

Derrick looked as if he wanted to argue, but instead he wiped the sweat from his forehead and picked up the bull horn. "Hey y'all!" he called out. "We're gonna need to move this across the street for now. It seems there's some kind of security issue, and we need to move the demonstration. Let's go nice and orderly."

Murmurs in the crowd grew, overwhelming the chanting.

"What kind of issue?"

"Is there another shooter?"

"Tell them to turn off their cell phones as a precaution." Joel shifted to keep the backpack in view.

"Folks, go ahead and turn off your phones. No need to run, please, just walk."

Brian stopped traffic from both directions while the wave of picketers started to move. At first it was a trickle and then they flooded the street, their pace picking up as word spread of a gunman.

Brad fought the crowd to come near Joel. "What's going on? Is it the shooter?" He looked nervously up the hill.

"Suspicious package. Might be nothing, but we need to check it out. Get across the road with everyone else."

"You mean there's a bomb? Dude, if there's a bomb I'm not sticking around." He turned to the man next to him. "Let's go."

Hannah appeared next to Joel, her expression grim. "How can I help?"

"Get across the street to the baseball field like everyone else."

But Hannah moved a few paces away and started helping direct the flow of people.

"You're just fine. No need to run," she said to a woman who tried to break into a trot and then stumbled into a man who'd stopped to pick up a fallen sign. "Watch out there."

"You two," Joel called to the reporter. The cameraman was filming the mass exodus. "Get past the baseball fence. That'll get you safely out of the way."

The crowd buzzed with excitement and anxiety, rumors flying faster than their feet.

"Someone called in a bomb threat."

"No, it was the shooter."

"I've got my shotgun in my truck. Should I grab it?"

Picket signs were dropped and water bottles left abandoned.

Kim returned from the school just as the last civilians cleared the parking lot. She and Brian moved their Yukons to close the road to traffic then joined Joel across the road.

"Where did you see it?" Brian asked, raising a pair of field glasses.

Joel pointed to the office entrance. "It was right next to the stairs, just under a bush."

"I don't see it."

"Look for something gray in the shadows."

Brian handed over the binoculars. "You try."

Joel adjusted the lenses and focused on the shrubbery in front of the office. It was hard to see with the sun's overhead glare.

"It's there; I promise."

"The state police bomb squad will be here in the hour," Kim said. "They'll find it."

The blonde reporter stood near the crowd gathered in the outfield, interviewing anyone willing to go on camera about what they'd seen. As the minutes stretched long and enthusiasm waned, she turned her attention to Joel.

"Detective, can you tell me exactly what you saw?"

"I can't comment on that."

"But you saw something suspicious, is that correct?"

"We'll know more when the OSP unit gets here."

"That's the bomb squad you're referring to?"

"Yes."

"Do you think this has anything to do with the DLC union strike that started just this morning?"

"I can't answer that."

Eventually the reporter lost her verve and told the cameraman to pack up. "We've gotta get back to the station," she said to Derrick. "Sorry, folks, can't wait all day."

Watching the news van drive away, some of the picketers gave up and sat on the crunchy brown grass in the outfield. Others drifted away. When the bomb squad van arrived, Derrick tried to get them to pick up their signs and start chanting again, but the energy was gone.

He left the fence and stalked to Joel, looking murderous. He pointed his finger at the mill across the street.

"I sure hope that wasn't just a diversion tactic, Ramirez. Look at us; the picket line has fallen apart!

Half the picketers are gone. Half! Morale is vital, and it's been effectively crushed on day one!"

"We're just trying to keep your people safe. Excuse me," Joel replied. He jogged across the baseball diamond to join Kim.

"Here he is," Kim said to a trooper in protective gear as Joel joined her.

"Where did you see the package?"

"In the bushes next to the office steps."

"We've searched all the plantings, and there's nothing there."

Joel looked at Kim. Her confusion matched his own.

"Nothing?"

"You said it was a backpack, right?"

"Yeah. A gray backpack. It was mostly in shadow."

"You saw it too?" he asked Kim.

"I did. But I left to use the phone at the school. Not sure what happened after that."

"Who was supposed to be keeping eyes on it?" he asked, looking at Joel.

"It got a bit chaotic there, and I couldn't see it the whole time," Joel admitted. His throat felt dry. He looked at Kim for reassurance, but she avoided meeting his eye.

"Well, I don't know what you saw, but there's nothing there now. We'll do another sweep to make sure before bringing all those people back."

Across the baseball diamond the disgruntled strikers were leaning against the outfield fence.

Derrick was the first to come forward.

"Well?"

"Good news is, they haven't found anything. You all can resume your demonstration."

"Resume? Just like that?"

"Yep, all clear."

"Then what was that all about? We just lost more than two hours and over half our crowd."

"I'm sure you can understand why we needed to be cautious."

Derrick swore and stomped away. The nearest picketers shot Joel dark looks.

As they passed, he overheard a bitter, "You know he's friends with Donovan, right?"

"Donovan's got the police in his pocket now," came the reply.

Even Luke shook his head as he passed. "Not cool, man."

A few of the strikers were more brazen, yelling profanities and flipping Joel off as they passed.

Hannah followed in their wake, her expression regretful. "You were just doing your job. Why can't they see that?"

Joel didn't reply. There was nothing he could say that would assuage the crowd.

He was more concerned about what had happened to the backpack.

13

VAL KISSED Abby goodbye and handed her school backpack to Eileen.

"If it's hot this afternoon, don't leave your jacket out on the playground. Make sure you put it in your backpack so you can bring it home."

"I will," Abby promised as she stepped into Eileen's house.

"I packed her an extra after-school snack today in case she decides not to eat the sandwich crackers again."

Eileen stepped aside as Abby entered the house and pulled her sweater tighter against the morning breeze. "You didn't need to do that. I told you, I have lots of snacks."

"I know, I just…I'd like to."

Eileen gave her an expression that Val recognized. The *You're one of those helicopter parents* look. Maybe she was, a little. But she couldn't explain to Eileen why it was so important that she be able to take care of Abby in these little ways. How the fear of all that she couldn't fix sometimes kept her up late at night making lists until she ran out of paper.

"You might want to avoid Main Street if you can. My son said the protest at City Hall has exploded, and traffic on Main Street is a mess."

Val suppressed a smile. In this town, where traffic problems were unheard of, "a mess" might be as simple as a two-minute delay waiting on utility workers.

"Better there than so close to the school. I think that was all too upsetting to the kids."

Eileen shook her head. "No, they're still demonstrating there too. I'm talking about the Moyer group. The anti-police protests? But you probably know all about that."

Val shook her head. "I'm not on social media, so I'm kind of out of the loop."

"I just figured with your boyfriend being a cop you'd know all about it."

Val's smile dissolved. "I don't know what you're talking about."

Eileen flushed. "I'm sorry, was that supposed to be a secret? It's all over the news, dear. Pictures of the two of you together. I figured you knew."

"We're not…we're just friends."

"Oh, I've made you upset. I'm sorry, I shouldn't have assumed. The media never gets it straight, do they? Like all that stuff they're saying about the police. You know how social media is. No one even bothers to check their facts before sharing it with all their friends."

Val felt slightly winded. "I'm sorry, I'm going to be late for work. Thanks for warning me about the traffic."

But instead of going the longer route, she purposefully drove down Main to see the protestors for herself. She'd seen the small group in front of City Hall for the past week, but this was different. Dozens of people dressed in black aggressively waved signs that said NO JUSTICE FOR RYAN and DOWN WITH POLICE CORRUPTION. There were more SHIELDS FOR SHERIFF campaign signs, too, as well as homemade signs like TIME FOR A NEW SHERIFF IN TOWN.

Some of the protestors had brought lawn chairs and were setting up like it was a picnic. She slowed down while a few people jogged across the street waving handcuffs like a theater prop.

What had happened to this town? Owl Creek was about as conservative as it got, and Val had never seen anything but pride in their local law enforcement. As she passed the alley that led to the small manufactured building that served as the sheriff's office substation, she thought she saw Joel's Charger. Was he doing okay? How was he getting through all this?

Should she call him? Would he want to hear from her?

Then she remembered what Eileen had said about their relationship. Now was not the time. But she couldn't stop thinking about him as she parked behind the Wallace Community Bank.

She smoothed her skirt and checked her reflection as she passed the car window. She knew better than to look at herself in distorted glass—especially when she was wearing the unflattering work-issued polo shirt—but lately she'd been slipping into some of those old habits.

"You are a warrior. You are enough. You are loved." She murmured the mantra as she crossed the parking lot.

"Hey Val!"

Brandi caught up with her just before she reached the door, her heels clicking against the asphalt.

"Brandi!" Val paused for a brief hug. Brandi had been gone the day before, having extended her Labor Day weekend for a trip to the coast. "How were the dunes?"

"So great." Brandi's tongue piercing gave her a slight lisp when she spoke. "I didn't want to come back. How was your weekend?"

"It was—" Val searched for words to describe the ambush by the news crew, an unexpected visit from Agent Giles, and breaking up with Joel before they'd fully been a couple.

She gave up on adjectives.

"I had a realtor come out to take a look at the house."

"Oh yeah? How did that go?"

Val shrugged. "About how I expected. But we've got a solid plan forward, I think. The nice thing is, my mom can afford to price it low. We're just hoping we can find a buyer who will think it's charming, not fifty years outdated."

"I love old historical homes." Brandi adjusted her purse strap on her shoulder and reached for the door.

"Wouldn't it be great to take on a restoration project like that? It would take a lot more money than I make, though."

"Exactly my problem."

Brandi laughed.

They walked into the bank, and Val stopped, pulled up short by the sight of Maddie and the two loan officers standing in a huddle. They stopped as if in mid-conversation, guilty expressions on their faces. None of them would meet Val's eyes.

"Morning," Brandi said. "Everything okay? What's going on?"

Maddie recovered first. "Nothing. Just catching up. How are you both?"

"Great," Brandi said, but Val couldn't speak.

"Good," Maddie said breezily and turned to go to her office.

Val put her purse away at her desk, conscious of several pairs of eyes on her, then fled with as much dignity as she could muster to the restroom.

Locking the door, she pulled out her phone. She couldn't avoid it any longer. She had to know.

She typed her name into the internet browser, then hit Search.

The first result almost made her drop her phone. She covered her mouth in disbelief.

There was a picture of her and Joel at Goldendale, kissing in the doorway of the abandoned church.

"Valerie Fisher's secret boyfriend," the headline read.

Another article featured a picture of Joel with Abby

on his shoulders. Abby's face was cropped out of the photo, but Val was there at his side, smiling.

"While husband Jordan Fisher sits in jail, wife moves on."

"Valerie Fisher dumps criminal husband for law enforcement hero," was accompanied by a picture of Joel in full uniform.

Another article with Jeanette and Charles was head-lined, "Senator Fisher refuses to comment on daughter-in-law's affair."

"No, no, no, no, no." Val covered her face with her hands. Jordan's divorce lawyer would have a field day. She was an idiot. After everything she'd been through, she hadn't learned.

There was no hiding.

Heart racing, she leaned over the sink and ran cold water. Wetting some paper towels, she patted her neck and chest, trying to ground herself in the cool, coarse texture. How could she go back out there and face the other women?

She breathed deeply, counting with each exhalation.

She could do this. She'd faced investigation by federal agents, her husband's suicide, and a killer she'd once trusted as a friend.

She could face a bit of office gossip.

The crowd at City Hall had swollen in size to spill over onto Main Street. Joel recognized a few faces he'd seen at the strike. As he turned into the alley that led to the station, something hit the car. He jerked in his seat as a water bottle skidded across the road, but whoever the culprit was had blended back into the crowd.

Just what he needed.

Kathy was on the phone when he walked in.

"He's just come in now. Give me a minute, and I'll send you right back." She placed the call on hold and dropped the receiver to her shoulder. "Kevin Donovan is on the phone for you. I'll give you a minute to get back to your desk. Oh, and Sheriff Larson is on his way down," she added over her shoulder as he walked past. "He's coming to address the protestors."

Joel's desk phone rang before he sat down.

"Good morning, Kevin," he answered.

"What's going on there, Joel? It's been over a week, and you still haven't made any arrests. I drove through town yesterday and saw the crowd at City Hall. Honestly, I'm beginning to see their point."

"I know it's frustrating. These things take time. Have you had any additional threats since the strike started?"

"Not me, but Hannah's car was broken into."

"There at the mill?"

"No, at her house. But I have a hard time thinking it wasn't connected."

Joel wasn't so sure. Hannah lived at the Moon Apartments where deputies got so many regular calls they knew most of the residents by name.

"If she files a report, I'm sure it will come to my attention."

"I'm sick of feeling like a sitting duck. I won't let my

son go to school, and my wife is afraid to even go to the store."

"I understand. But I assure you we're doing everything we can to find the shooter. One thing that would be helpful is if you would turn over your laptop and let our team at the county take a look at it."

"I need my laptop for work," Kevin said briskly. "You had dogs on that hill, couldn't they find anything?"

"I can't discuss specifics, but I can assure you this case is top priority." The dogs had led their handlers to tire tracks on the back side of the hill, but the tracks had disappeared once they hit asphalt.

"Thanks for checking in, Kevin. If you change your mind about the laptop, you can bring it in at any time. Otherwise, I'll let you know if anything changes."

Joel hung up and looked over the white board where he was keeping notes about the timeline the day of the shooting. He'd interviewed the members of the bargaining team, but they could all account for their whereabouts. Maybe it was time to look further into Kevin's personal life.

He went out to the front office and found Larry leaning against the counter with a coffee mug in his hands and a grim expression on his face.

"Anyone take a report from Hannah Quinton about a break-in to her vehicle?"

Larry shook his head. "Not that I know of. You seen some of those signs out there?"

"Yep."

"There's stuff about Austin Wilson too."

154

"You're kidding."

Kathy removed her glasses and pulled out a cleaning cloth from her desk drawer. "It's that Facebook page. All kinds of stuff getting dredged up on there."

Joel pictured the kid standing next to the chip carousel at Stan's Market—his wide eyes and open mouth as he crumpled to the floor.

"It's not just the Facebook page," Larry said, but he couldn't quite meet Joel's eyes as he said it.

"No, I guess not." Kathy focused more intently on her glasses.

The room suddenly felt a few degrees warmer.

"You know they're exaggerating, right? Whatever those reporters are saying about me and Val?"

Larry's gaze flickered to Joel and away. "Sure."

Before Joel could reply, the outer door opened, and Sheriff Larson entered the building followed by Joel's supervisor, Lieutenant Greg Cooper. The walls trembled as the door shut, the whole manufactured building seeming to flex to make room for them.

"Well, that's quite a mess you've got out there," Larson said in greeting. He was a tall man with what was left of his hair graying aggressively. Out of uniform he looked like a kindly grandpa, but Joel knew better. He'd recently seen him go toe-to-toe with a US Marshal without giving ground and knew he fought like a bulldog when the time called for it.

Joel just hoped he'd fight on his side.

Cooper's face was closed.

"Ramirez, let's have a chat."

"Yes, sir."

Joel led Cooper to his office and closed the door behind him, the only sound the hum of the air conditioning unit in the window. He was suddenly conscious of the radio sitting on his desk instead of in the charger where it belonged and the take-out box with his half-eaten lunch sitting forgotten in the corner.

"Have a seat." Cooper gestured to the two plastic chairs in front of his desk, turning one so it faced the other. "How are you holding up? It's been a rough month, hasn't it?"

The fatherly concern was almost worse than if he'd yelled.

"I've had worse."

"True." Cooper frowned. "You and I both know you can't be blamed for the Wilson boy. You made a tough call when innocent lives were at stake. If you'd hesitated, the outcome could have been much worse."

My bullet, my fault, Joel thought, but he said nothing.

"Unfortunately, with that Moyer lawsuit hanging over our heads, the court of public opinion isn't very favorable right now. This isn't the time for sloppy mistakes."

"I understand."

Cooper leaned forward and rested his forearms on his knees, steepling his fingers together. "Can you explain to me what happened at the mill? Before you answer, I want to remind you that good people make mistakes under stress. You wouldn't be the first cop who thought they saw something they didn't. Something like seeing a cell phone and thinking it was a gun, for example."

The reference to Austin Wilson was like a barb under Joel's skin.

"So tell me, did you actually see a suspicious package at the mill, or did Kevin Donovan ask you to disrupt the demonstration in some way?"

Joel held his gaze, his pulse quickening. "I saw a backpack sitting next to the steps, hidden under the bushes. Kim saw it too. We followed protocol and cleared the area, but in the chaos I lost sight of it."

Cooper nodded as if he'd expected this. "Unfortunately, the union is crying foul. The news coverage Monday night was all about the bomb threat, not the issues they were hoping to raise. It works in Donovan's favor and makes their members nervous about coming to the picket line."

"I followed procedure. I don't know what else to say."

"Look, I have to ask the hard questions because the public is asking them of the sheriff. Horace Shields is pouncing on anything to use against Larson. I have to make sure the shooting last week isn't affecting your judgment."

"It's not, sir."

Cooper leaned back. His voice took on a harder edge. "Then can you tell me why half my office thinks you're having an affair with Jordan Fisher's wife?

Joel's heart skipped a beat.

"Where did you hear that?"

"Is it true?"

"No, sir."

"Ramirez—"

"We're friends," he insisted. His face burned, and his mouth felt like cotton. "We've been out a few times, it's true, but there's nothing going on between us."

"Really? Because every time her name comes up lately it seems to be attached to yours."

"We've known each other a long time. She's going through a hard time, and I'm one of the only people she trusts."

"I've seen the pictures, Joel."

"What pictures?"

"You and her together. Kissing."

Joel groaned and collapsed into his chair, head in his hands. "Jeez, I can't believe we're having this conversation. Yes, we kissed. No, we're not…together. I haven't even seen her in almost a week. There's nothing going on."

Cooper sighed, and the plastic chair creaked as he shifted. "What did I tell you when you were fresh out of the academy, Joel? What two things have ruined more cop careers than all the other factors combined?"

"Booze." Joel's jaw tightened. "And broads."

"Exactly. I've seen a lot of smart men get really stupid when a woman is involved. Normally, I'd say it's none of my business as long as it doesn't affect your job. But I don't need to remind you that this is an election year. Jordan Fisher's name is synonymous with corruption. His mom is a senator for crying out loud. You can't date his wife and think it's not going to be everyone's business. Unless you don't want to work in law enforcement anymore."

Joel's gaze snapped to his boss. "Excuse me, sir?" His hands tingled with a rush of adrenaline.

"No, that's not a threat." Cooper shook his head. "Sorry, that was out of line. Don't go running to HR on me now. My point is just to remind you that you're under a microscope in this job, and everything you do reflects on this agency. With the election coming up and this lawsuit bringing out every low-life who's ever had a complaint against us, it's a rotten time to draw attention to yourself."

"I understand."

"Now, having said that, I'm pulling you off the DLC shooting."

Joel should have seen this coming, but it still felt like a slap in the face. He tried to keep his face impassive.

"Marion Sanders will be taking over from here on out. Send her your files, and bring her up to speed."

"Yes, sir."

Cooper sighed and leaned forward, resting a hand on Joel's shoulder. "Lay low a while and keep your head down. You're a good cop. Give it enough time, and this thing will blow over. Just stay smart."

He stood, and Joel moved to open the door. But before Cooper passed through, he looked Joel in the eye and added, "And if you know what's good for you, stay away from Mrs. Fisher."

14

"Mom, your phone is ringing."

Abby ran into the living room wearing velour leggings and a Christmas sweatshirt featuring a snowman with black pom-poms for coal.

Val was holding a warrior yoga pose and had left her phone in the kitchen to avoid being distracted by the buzzing. She kept it silenced all the time now to avoid almost daily calls from news stations and online magazines.

"It's okay. Just put it on the table."

"It's Grandma."

"Oh." Val blew out a deep breath and stood. Maybe her mom had changed her mind about painting the house. But when she took her phone from Abby, it was a photo of Jeanette that smiled at her from the screen.

She swiped the screen to answer and made her way outside to the porch for privacy. The sun was setting earlier each evening, and she was momentarily surprised at the chill on the breeze. It would be late in Chicago.

"Hi Jeanette."

"Val, how are you? I've been so worried about you and Abby. Is everything okay?"

"We're fine. Why do you ask?"

"I saw a picture of reporters parked outside your house. Are they harassing you?"

"It was just the once. What do you need, Jeanette?" Val was surprised at the calm in her own voice. She braced her foot against the west balustrade and leaned into the stretch, watching the last of the light drain from steel-gray clouds, making way for tiny pinpricks of stars.

"I just want to make sure you're okay. Because if you and Abby ever need a safe place to go, I hope you know you're always welcome to come back to Chicago."

Val grimaced. She'd fought too hard to get where she was. She wasn't about to surrender control by going back into her mother-in-law's orbit.

"Thank you, I appreciate the offer. Abby's making friends at school, and my job is going well, so things are working out for us."

"That's good," Jeanette said again, but she sounded disappointed. "I talked to Henry today, and he said there hasn't been any word about divorce papers being filed. Thank you for taking some time to think about it before rushing into things."

"It's not that; I just need to save up some money first. Plus I want to find someone who will be a good fit, and that's taking a while."

"I see. Well, I understand. I was wondering,

though, how you might feel about letting Abby come out here for a visit. We miss you both so much, and I think it would really mean a lot to her to get to see her dad."

Alarm flared in Val's chest. "That's out of the question. Abby isn't going anywhere."

"You'd be welcome to come too, if it makes you feel more comfortable. It wouldn't have to be a long visit, just something over a weekend."

"Has Agent Giles been talking to you?"

Jeanette's voice was flat. "This isn't about the case, Val, or trying to earn points with a judge. This is about what's best for Abby. You can't tell me she doesn't miss her dad."

"Of course she does. But that doesn't mean—"

"And he misses her too. He misses you both. I know you don't want to hear this, but he still loves you, Val. He knows he doesn't deserve your forgiveness, but that doesn't change how he feels about you."

Nausea churned in Val's stomach. But somewhere deep inside, a small piece of her warmed, like a shattered bit of her heart had broken through its iron casing.

Desperately, she tried to shove it back.

"I'm sorry, I don't mean to upset you," Jeanette said when she didn't respond. "I know you think you're doing what's best for Abby by keeping her away. But just because it's best for you doesn't mean it's best for her."

When Val found her voice it came out tight. "You don't know what's best for her either. You don't know what it's like to have to build a new life for your daughter all alone."

"Really?" The word held a sharp edge. "You're going to take that line? I've seen those pictures of you and that detective."

Shame burned Val's chest, creeping up her neck.

"I thought he was dead, Jeanette. Jordan made me think he was dead! If you're looking for a cheater, look at your son. And for the record, Joel and I aren't seeing each other. The media has blown things out of proportion."

Jeanette sighed. "Forgive me, Val. It's really not my business. I do want you to be happy. I suppose I'm afraid of losing you and Abby, and seeing those pictures made me worry you'll move on and cut us out of your life."

Val tugged the elastic out of her hair and shook her ponytail free. "We won't cut you out. You and Charles will always be a part of our lives. I just don't know what that looks like yet. Give me some time. Things are shifting every day, and I need a chance for things to settle."

"Very well. Thank you for taking my call, Val. My offer still stands. If you change your mind, you and Abby are always welcome here."

"Goodnight Jeanette."

Val ended the call and saw a text had come in while she was on the phone. It was from Joel.

She had to read it twice because the feeling of longing that welled up at the sight of his name made it hard to take in the words.

Hey. Do you have time to chat?

It was followed by another one ten minutes later.

Never mind, I know it's a bad idea.

She opened a reply and then paused. What could she say?

What she was feeling was, "I'm so lonely and I miss you and all I want is to hear your voice."

But she couldn't say that.

She typed, *Sorry, I was on the phone.* Then paused. Added, *I've been thinking about you.*

The front door opened, and Val sent the text before she could reconsider.

"Mom, you've been out here forever. Are you still on the phone with Grandma? Can I talk to her?"

"I just hung up. Sorry, you would have liked that, wouldn't you?"

"I miss Grandma. And Heidi." Heidi was Jeanette's Cavalier King Charles spaniel who tended to be festooned in ribbons and bows whenever Abby was around.

"I know. She was asking if you wanted to come visit."

"Really?" Abby's eyes widened hopefully. "Can I? Oh please, can I?"

Her enthusiasm felt like poison in Val's heart. She tried to hide it by keeping her voice light. "Maybe. Not right now while you have school. But I'm sure we can figure out a time."

"Yes! I'm gonna go pack!"

"Wait! I didn't mean—"

But Abby was already gone, the screen door slamming in her wake.

Val checked her phone again.

Joel had responded with two words.

Me too.

She felt ripped apart with hope and despair. Elation that he was thinking about her. Frustration that she couldn't tell him how she felt. Uncertain what it meant. For all she knew, he might be thinking about her the same way he thought about his ex-wife Lacey.

It was enough to make her crazy.

She dialed her sister. Arizona didn't follow Daylight Savings Time, so for those months out of the year their clocks were in sync and it wouldn't be too late to call.

Gina picked up on the second ring. The sound of the TV was in the background.

"Hey Val, give me just a minute." Her breathing changed as she moved, the sound of the TV fading. "Okay, what's up?"

The alertness in her tone was constant these days any time Val talked to her.

"I can't do this any more, Gina. Would you and Mark be willing to loan me the money to hire a lawyer? You don't have to decide now. Just think about it and talk to—"

"I don't need to think about it. We've already talked about it, and the answer is yes. Yes, of course! The sooner you can divorce that tool the better."

"Oh Gina." Val sagged with relief, unexpected tears burning her eyes. "Are you sure? I won't be able to pay you back for a long time, and I know Jeanette will hire the best for Jordan. It's going to be expensive."

"Don't even worry about it. This is your future we're talking about."

An hour later, Val sat at the kitchen table with a list and a plan. She felt a little stunned at how generous her sister and brother-in-law were being. For the first time in weeks, she glimpsed a future without Jordan, without feeling trapped by him and his crimes.

She picked up her phone again and looked at Joel's text. She wanted to tell him what she was doing but suddenly felt shy. What if he didn't want to give things another try when this was all over? Val had assumed they would have another chance, but maybe she was the only one who wanted one. Joel's life had been fine before she came along and screwed it up.

Her enthusiasm dampened.

Stop it. You're catastrophizing, she told herself.

One thing at a time.

She shut off her phone and put it away.

Joel finished loading dishes in the dishwasher and checked his phone again. Val hadn't texted back, but he kept checking. He should just be glad she'd responded at all.

He turned on Netflix but couldn't find anything that looked good. He'd already finished *Stranger Things* and had hoped to show it to Val since she didn't have high speed internet at her house. Seeing it on his feed just gave him a bitter taste in his mouth.

After a few minutes of scrolling, he turned off the TV. This was stupid. He could sit there alone feeling sorry for himself or get off his couch and do something worthwhile.

In ten minutes he'd changed into running clothes and grabbed his lights before heading out the door. The streetlamps were on, casting pools of orange light at each intersection. Goose bumps formed on his arms, but the cool air would feel good after he warmed up.

Joel lived on one of the few roads in Owl Creek that had sidewalks, but he preferred asphalt over concrete anyway, so he stuck to the smaller streets as he wound his way through the dark neighborhoods. He wasn't out to prove anything to himself. He only wanted to clear his head and ease the stress of the past week. Cooper's visit. The protestors. Breaking up with Val.

He settled into a comfortable rhythm, just his feet pounding the blacktop and his breathing in his ears. The steady pumping of his heart. The feel of his muscles stretching as he lengthened his stride.

He already felt better.

An empty lot on Main Street had recently been converted into a small park—little more than a green space with brick paths and benches. But there was a restroom, which meant a water fountain, and Joel's route took him there twenty minutes in. He switched off his lights and waited for his breathing to calm before getting a drink, swallowing quickly between breaths.

Satisfied, he wiped his mouth and stepped away, then noticed someone sitting on a bench nearby. In the low light, he thought he recognized her profile but had to step closer to be sure.

Hannah was sitting alone, looking out at Main Street. Down the road, lights and a low murmur of noise indicated that some of the protestors were putting in a night shift. But here, it was empty. The bank sat on the corner, cracks in its plaster facade unnoticeable in the dim light. Directly across the street was Stan's Market, the little grocery store where high school students or mill workers could grab a sandwich or rotisserie hot dog on their lunch break.

Hannah's hair was pulled back into a bun, emphasizing her dramatic widow's peak. Her eyebrows were drawn together in focused contemplation. Without her ready smile, her features looked harsh in the light from the streetlamp. Joel suddenly felt like he was intruding and decided to keep walking.

She stirred and saw him, and her gaze was so intense she looked angry. Then recognition flashed in her eyes, and her expression softened.

"Joel."

"Hi Hannah. Are you waiting for someone?"

She shook her head. "I was just out for a walk, It gets a little noisy at the apartments sometimes, so I like to walk here when I need to clear my head."

"That area can be a little rough. Keep your doors locked."

Hannah smiled. "It's temporary. I just needed a place to land when I moved here. It won't be long-term."

"Where did you move from?" Now that his body was cooling, Joel felt chilled. He needed to get moving again, but something about Hannah's pensive mood made him want to stay. Maybe she was homesick. Maybe it was something worse. But his gut told him not to go.

"Most recently Southern California. But my mom moved to Pineview about five years ago."

"So you came here to be closer to her?"

Hannah looked away. "Something like that." She looked across the street at Stan's, its old gingerbread detail side-by-side with freon. "This is a cute town. Feels safe, you know?"

Joel felt a sudden rush of heat thinking about three years earlier when he'd been crouched not far from this spot, responding to a call of an armed robbery gone bad. The more recent memory of shooting Carter followed, as it always did. He could almost smell the ozone from the storm.

He shivered. "You never know about a town like this. One day it's the kind of place where no one has to lock their doors. The next, it's a scene of senseless violence."

"I guess you would know that more than most. I heard about that reporter. Is it true he wasn't armed?"

169

CAREN HAHN

Her voice held an undercurrent of something Joel couldn't name.

"Someone doesn't have to be armed to be dangerous. He was trying to kill an innocent woman."

"Your girlfriend?"

Joel hesitated, the well-worn protest on his tongue. But Hannah was looking at him with such intensity he replied, "Yeah, you could say that."

Hannah looked away. "She's lucky you were there." But it sounded cold, like she knew those were the right words but didn't believe it herself.

If Joel had to guess, he would say there was anger simmering beneath the surface. But his teeth would start chattering soon if he didn't get a move on.

"Hannah, I already told Kevin, but you should know too. The DLC shooting has been reassigned to a detective out of Pineview. I spent some time today bringing her up to speed, so you might be hearing from her."

Hannah looked at him, eyebrows raised. "Why?"

"It's…" *complicated* is what he wanted to say. "Sometimes this happens in an investigation. She's great, though. Kevin mentioned that your car was broken into recently. He seems to think it could be connected, so I wanted to give you a heads up that Marion Sanders will be your best contact if you have to make a report."

Hannah looked troubled. "Good to know. Thanks, Joel."

"Be safe, Hannah."

He set off at a faster pace than before, trying to raise his body temperature. Instead of finishing his circuit, he headed straight home with thoughts of Hannah on his mind. Funny how you could get one impression of a person when you only saw them in a certain setting. She was professional and upbeat and intelligent, but tonight he'd seen a sign of something deeper beneath the surface. An unnamed suffering, perhaps.

It got under his skin, and he replayed their conversation all the way home, trying to figure it out. The final blocks were uphill, and he pushed to maintain his pace, his lungs burning and the taste of exertion in the back of his throat. When he reached the last intersection, he stopped, his breath coming in heaving gasps. With his arms behind his head he walked the rest of the way home, letting his pounding heart settle.

He smelled it before he got there.

The acrid scent of dead skunk intensified the closer he got to his house. He scanned the road, looking for the roadkill, but the street was clear. It wasn't just fresh spray. There was an added scent of decay.

It was definitely centered around his house. He searched his trash can, under the Charger, and in the shadows of his yard where his porch light didn't reach. Finally, he opened his mailbox and gagged. His running lights confirmed the culprit, a mangled skunk with crushed skull and fresh entrails. A plastic, star-shaped badge—the kind of cheap toy a kid might wear with a cop costume—rested on its fur.

Joel looked around but knew the perpetrators would be long gone. The street was empty. Had they been waiting for him to leave or just gotten lucky with their timing?

He took a couple pictures with his phone, then closed the mailbox. The skunk wasn't going anywhere, and he needed a shower.

15

Saturday dawned gray and overcast, the perfect weather to finish replacing the shutters on the house. Val needed a project to keep her from stewing in her own self-loathing.

She needed a win. A big win.

Getting the tools and ladder out of the shop, climbing through the window of Abby's bedroom, and setting everything up on the porch roof took a good hour. By the time she was ready to turn her attention to the shutter, a fine drizzle had started. At first it was little more than a nuisance, but over time it soaked through her flannel shirt, chilling her.

The crowbar she used to pry off the stripped screws was slippery, and she scraped her knuckles against the house until they bled. Tears of frustration and pain stung her eyes until she finally pried the last bit of broken shutter off and let it fall to the roof.

Val looked in satisfaction at her work. Splintered

wood and twisted screws lay at her feet, but she'd done it. Now it was just a matter of attaching the new shutters.

Except that the drill bit snapped off with her first pilot hole.

Val sighed. That was the only bit she'd been able to find in the shop. And she'd learned from replacing the first shutter that trying to screw three more in place without pilot holes would be a huge waste of her time.

She dragged her wet self back in the house, gathered up Abby, and drove into town to the hardware store. Clouds hung low over the surrounding hills, looking like their undersides had been smeared by an artist's thumb. The drizzle was just light enough to need windshield wipers, but the blades streaked across the glass leaving an unwiped band directly in her field of vision.

One more expense she would have to squeeze into her budget before the steady rains settled in for the fall.

Boone Road was more colloquially called "the river road" because it followed the river out of town in a twisting stretch of tight curves with no shoulder. At the edge of town, near the city limits, the hardware store sat across the street from the library and Moon Apartments.

As they passed the city park adjacent to the library, Abby asked, "Can we go to the park today? We haven't been in forever."

Val glanced at the playground equipment shrouded in mist. "It looks pretty wet today. Let's come back another time when it's sunny. But we could stop by the library for a few minutes after the hardware store, if you want."

"Yes! I love the library!"

It probably helped that the librarians handed out suckers to kids who returned their books on time.

Val had avoided the park for weeks ever since Joel had mentioned the attack on a teenage girl after dark. As she pulled into the hardware store parking lot, she wondered if anyone had been arrested. But that made her think of Joel and triggered a surge of regret.

She really needed to make more friends, but that was hard when she stirred up scandal everywhere she went. Besides Joel, Brandi at the bank was probably the closest thing she had to a friend, but their relationship was still in the superficial stages without any real emotional depth.

The hardware store smelled like fresh popcorn from the machine located near the door. Abby made a beeline for it, snagging a complimentary bag and shoving popcorn in her mouth as she followed Val to the aisle with the drill bits. It was a busy day at the store, and Val was so worried about seeing someone she knew that she grabbed the cheapest set of bits she could find and hurried to the cash register, Abby leaving a trail of popcorn kernels in their wake.

A young woman with large gauged earlobes was working the till, and she did a double take when she looked at Val.

"Are you on TV? How do I know you?"

"No, sorry."

The girl tapped a long nail on the counter. "You look so familiar. I swear I know you from somewhere."

Val shrugged and pretended to be absorbed looking for her wallet.

"I've got it!" the cashier announced as she placed the set of drill bits in a bag and printed Val's receipt. "I saw you on that Facebook page. What was the deal with all that?"

"I'm not on Facebook. Thanks."

Val grabbed the bag and ushered Abby toward the door so fast that Abby fumbled the popcorn in her hands and dropped it on the floor.

"Mom! You made me spill!"

"Sorry. I'm sorry," she repeated over her shoulder as she pulled Abby away, stepping over the mess.

"But Mom, my popcorn!" Abby squealed as they passed through the doors and out to the parking lot. "I want a new bag."

"Not this time. We've got to go."

"But that's not fair! It's your fault I dropped it!"

"I'm sure we'll be back another time."

Abby yanked her hand out of Val's.

"This isn't fair. You won't let me go to the park, and now you won't let me get more popcorn. Why did we even come to this stupid store?"

"The world isn't going to run out of popcorn, I promise. You ate almost the whole thing anyway. Let's go home and make lunch if you're so hungry."

Val opened the car door and tossed her purse on the passenger seat. Over the roof of the car, she saw Abby standing still, her arms folded mutinously.

"Abby!" Val snapped. "Get in the car. Now."

Abby glared at her, but she obeyed. She climbed into her booster seat and slammed the door shut.

"This is stupid. I hate this day."

"Join the club. It's not my favorite day either."

Val started the engine and turned on the wipers to clear the mist from the windshield. She felt waves of resentment coming from the back seat as she pulled out of the parking lot, but she was still jittery and couldn't think of anything except the look on the clerk's face.

There was a Facebook page? Did everyone in town know her personal business?

"You promised we would go to the library," Abby said, her voice heavy with indictment.

Val glanced at Abby's reflection in the rearview mirror. "You're right; I'm sorry. Do you think you can forgive me?"

Abby grunted.

Val pulled over near the auto repair shop across from City Hall. Two men crossed the road in front of her, one of them holding a sign that said, THE BODY COUNT IS RISING with a list of names. Ryan Moyer was at the top, and Val felt a jolt to recognize Carter's name near the bottom. Apparently the protestors weren't taking the weekend off.

She turned around to look at Abby and took a deep breath. "I'm sorry about your popcorn. And I'm sorry I forgot about the library. I'm doing the best I can. Things are really hard right now, but they'll get better. I promise."

Abby stared out the window, refusing to make eye contact.

With a sigh, Val pulled back onto the road. She'd needed a win, and instead she felt like she'd crashed and burned.

The car was silent as Val took the county road out of town. She really needed to do some more research into therapists. How there couldn't be any child psychologists in all of Wallace County, she didn't know. She added it to her mental list for after she finished the shutters.

As they rounded a sharp bend and the yard with the mannequins came into view, Val gasped. An old piece of plywood had been propped against a water heater, and the words "Owl Creek's Famous Whore" had been painted by hand.

The scene featured a female mannequin in a negligee kneeling before a male mannequin in a police uniform. Another mannequin in a business suit stuffed with Monopoly money looked on. The suggestive posture made Val's blood rush hot to her face. She braked hard and pulled onto the shoulder.

"Where are we going?" Abby asked from the back seat.

"I need to check something."

"What does w-h-o-r-e spell?"

Before Val could think twice, she pulled into the driveway and put the Prius in park.

"Oh no, not the creepy house! Why are we here?"

"I'll be just a minute."

Heart racing with anger, Val picked her way through the mounds of electronics, bookshelves, old lamps, dismembered mannequins and overgrown shrubbery to reach the house. The old rambler sagged on its foundation and smelled of rot before she even reached it. Treads were missing on the steps, and she had to step carefully to avoid a nail protruding from the porch. The front door was cracked with peeling paint, its old brass handle tarnished almost black.

She turned and looked back at the car. She could barely see it through the junkyard and couldn't see Abby in the back seat at all. Hoping this wasn't the worst idea she'd ever had, she knocked on the door.

As the minutes stretched on, a prickling sensation raised the hairs on her neck. Like she was being watched. She wiped the rain from her face and knocked again.

Just when she was about to give up, the door opened with a squeal of age and exhaustion.

The man who stood there was middle-aged and clean-shaven. His jowls drooped like twin pouches, and his skin was lined and marked with sun damage. The scent of old cigarette smoke poured out of the house.

"Yep?" he said by way of greeting.

Suddenly Val wasn't sure what to say. She tried to rekindle the anger that had driven her to the door. Why was she the one worrying about being rude after what he'd done?

"Excuse me, Mr…" She paused, waiting for him to offer his name.

He didn't. His eyes held no light. They were dead. Shark eyes.

"My name is Valerie Fisher," she explained. "So I'm sure you can understand why I might take objection to the display you put in your front yard."

"It's none of your business what I do on my own property."

"It is if you're committing libel against me."

"Who says that's libel? What makes you think I was talking about you? I don't even know you."

Val folded her arms. She was sticky with sweat in spite of the cold.

"I'm not stupid. Who else would you be talking about in this town? You know under the circumstances a judge would rule in my favor. But I'm not interested in taking you to court. I'm just asking you to take down the scene. For my daughter's sake, if not for mine."

At this, his eyes flickered to the car with interest. Val shifted protectively in a vain attempt to block his view.

"Go ahead and sue if you wanna waste your money. I haven't done nothing wrong. It's my right to do what I want on my property. And you're trespassing, Mrs. Fisher. Better get your little girl home while you still can."

The menace in his tone gave Val a chill, and she stepped back, hurrying off the porch. Suddenly anxious to get back to Abby.

A sharp heat in her ankle made her gasp. She'd rubbed against the barbed threads of a frayed cable emerging from the tall grass, and a bright beaded line of blood formed on her ankle. Cursing her thoughtlessness, she picked her way more carefully to the car.

"Can we go now?" Abby asked as Val climbed inside. "I really don't like it here. These mannequins are gross."

"Yeah, we're leaving."

Val reached reflexively for the hand sanitizer she kept in the car. The door to the house was closed, but she couldn't help feeling like the man was watching her from the darkened windows. She couldn't leave the driveway fast enough.

16

JOEL FINISHED MOUNTING his new mailbox in the dark. After working all weekend he'd had to make a special trip to Pineview to find a new one. The high cost was like adding insult to injury, but there was no way to save the old mailbox after he'd extracted the skunk with a pair of barbecue tongs. The tongs went in the trash with it.

Tired and hungry, Joel went inside and laid his drill on the counter next to his off-duty weapon. The contents of his refrigerator were uninspiring, a witness to how much he'd been working since the shooting. He found an open package of bratwurst that still had good color and threw one in a skillet and a potato in the microwave.

While he waited for them to cook, he scrolled through the Justice for Ryan Facebook group. He'd avoided it until now, not wanting to read the anti-police sentiment and twisted half-truths. But with the protests growing each day, it was increasingly necessary to know what they were dealing with. As far as he knew, he was the only one who had been targeted at home, but that didn't mean the other deputies were safe.

When he saw his face superimposed on a Puss in Boots meme, anger washed over him. It had been posted by Mason Pearson, and Joel couldn't properly read the comments for the blood pounding in his head. They numbered in the hundreds, some in support, some coming to his defense. He scrolled past, knowing he would have to look at them more closely again when he calmed down.

Several people mentioned old cases from before Joel's time. At times like this he missed Carter's uncanny ability to know everything that was going on with everyone in this community. Sometimes his helpful insights opened up a line of investigation that Joel would have missed otherwise. In exchange, Joel had given Carter exclusive access to stories which had earned Channel Six news the reputation of being the leading source for news in Wallace County.

Thinking of Carter now brought another rush of anger. Instead of pushing it aside as he usually did, Joel closed his eyes and let himself feel it like his therapist had taught him, trying to sort out what was fueling it. Carter who had lied, who had tried to kill Val to cover his crimes, who had given Joel no other choice than to fire. It wasn't Joel's fault. All of it was Carter's choice.

It wasn't his fault.

But why were his eyes wet, and it was suddenly hard to breathe?

Then the *if onlys* started. If only he'd made the connection to Eliza Bellingham sooner so Carter could be apprehended before he threatened Val. If only Carter hadn't gone looking for Sam Howser, an altercation that ended with Sam dead and Carter responsible —pushing Carter over the edge. If only Carter hadn't gotten involved in drugs in college and then shared them with Eliza, leading to her death. If only he'd called law enforcement instead of hiding her body on Val's property and keeping it a secret for seven years. If only Carter had surrendered and let Val go so that Joel hadn't been forced to shoot him to save her life.

If only Joel had been smart enough to figure it out sooner.

He was angry at Carter, yes, but he was also angry at himself. It didn't make sense—he'd done the right thing—but emotions didn't have to make sense to be real. The truth was that he'd cared for Carter. Carter may have been a murderer, but he was still his friend, and Joel would have to live with that guilt for the rest of his life.

The microwave beeped, reminding him that he hadn't yet eaten. Joel rubbed his eyes and took a deep breath. It hadn't hit him so hard since the early days after Carter's death. Now the rush of emotion was fading and leaving him feeling…cleansed. Like he could live in his own skin for another day.

Maybe he should make an appointment to see his therapist.

Marnie called just as he speared his brat out of the sizzling pan. He cleared away the emotion in his throat before answering.

"Cooper got a call from the sheriff's office in Harney County," she said. "They've been watching a new sovereign citizens' organization out there and think some of their people have come out here to give your protest a little juice."

"Are you talking about Ammon Bundy's group?"

They'd watched closely the armed standoff between feds and the far right terrorist group that had occurred in Eastern Oregon earlier that year.

"This is a splinter group made up of disaffected followers of Bundy. Popped up after the Malheur occupation and call themselves Patriot Pride."

"That sounds ominous."

"So far they haven't done anything more than make the sheriff's office nervous. They claim to be more peaceful than Bundy, but their core members aren't exactly stand-up characters. Lucky for us, they've apparently taken a big interest in the Moyer lawsuit."

"Why? What would a wrongful death suit have to do with them?"

"That's the weird part; we don't know. Nothing about this case seems to fit their agenda. It could be that they're trying to establish themselves somewhere else, and they're scoping out the area for sympathizers."

Joel sighed. "Just what we need."

There were plenty of right-wing citizens in Wallace County who gave deputies more than their fair share of trouble when they felt their personal freedoms were

threatened by the rule of law. Joel had once had a rural
resident fire a warning shot at him while chasing a
suspect through the woods on his property. Even when
he'd identified himself, the man hadn't cared and had
warned him that law enforcement or not, a trespasser
was a trespasser and he had a right to defend his property. He'd held Joel at gunpoint for forty-five minutes
until backup could verify Joel was who he said he was.

But these were separate individuals well known to
law enforcement, not an organized group with an anti-
government agenda. Just the thought of an organization
like Bundy's getting a foothold in Owl Creek made
Joel's blood pressure rise.

"I managed to finally track down Steven Frandsen
today," Joel said. "He's working at a garage in Salmon
Ridge, and his employer verified that he was working
the day of the shooting."

"Who does that leave from your nickname list?"

"Mason Pearson's still on there, but it could be
anyone with the way he's spreading it. Thanks to that
Facebook page, it wouldn't even have to be someone
who knew me in high school. Do we know when the
page was started? Was it before or after the shooting?"

"That's a good question. I'll look into it. Have you
talked to Mason's sister? Kevin's wife?"

"Not yet. I'm planning to go out there tomorrow. I
still don't know what's going on between Mason and
Kevin, but the fact that they're both trying downplay
any conflict makes me wonder what they're hiding."

Marnie's voice became muffled as she talked to

someone on her end. Joel realized suddenly how late it was and wondered if she'd called him from home.

"Let me know if you learn anything from the sister. I've gotta go, but I wanted to give you a heads up about that Patriot Pride group. I know Larson is worried about how things will look if the sheriff presence is too strong, but don't hesitate to ask for help. "

Joel hung up, and his phone screen switched back to the Justice For Ryan group. Seeing the Puss in Boots meme sickened him. He needed some fresh air.

He threw on a hoodie and jogged down to the Moon Apartments. Dry leaves skittered across the road as he approached the park near the library. The empty soccer field was obscured in shadow as he followed the sidewalk to the back side of the apartment parking lot. A single streetlight at the corner cast a murky orange glow over the parked cars. He stood under the giant cedar where its spreading limbs would keep him hidden in shadow.

The window to Mason's apartment was lit from inside, but the blinds were closed. His Chevy sat out front of his apartment, and Suzie's red coupe sat a few spaces down. In front of the other building, Joel thought he recognized Hannah's gold sedan from his visits to the mill.

He systematically took pictures of the license plates of all the cars in the lot. If Mason were involved in the shooting, he hadn't acted alone. It hadn't been Mason's voice he'd heard on the phone the day of the shooting; he was sure of it. They were still waiting on the phone company to provide records of the DLC business phone lines, so there weren't any leads yet from that direction.

The tall cedar creaked overhead, its branches rustling in the wind. Just as Joel was contemplating returning home, the door to the apartment where Hannah's car was parked opened. The man who stepped out didn't look familiar. He was tall and had a dark goatee, but as his back was to the light, it was hard to see his features clearly.

He was carrying a white trash bag, suggesting a level of familiarity, and Joel realized this must be Hannah's boyfriend. He waited for him to return inside before moving out from under the tree. But when the man returned from the dumpster, Hannah met him in the doorway, her arms folded across her chest.

The man stopped, and the light from the open apartment door fell on his face. Indistinguishable tattoos crawled up the back of his neck. He wore a ball cap with a logo Joel didn't recognize, so it was hard to say, but if Joel had to guess, he would say he was in his early thirties. He had the powerful build of a man used to physical labor.

Joel couldn't make out their conversation, but the man's voice sounded urgent. Hannah turned and shut the door with finality. If this was a boyfriend, Joel suspected the relationship was on the way out, which would explain Hannah's simmering anger when he'd run into her last night.

Hannah's boyfriend stuffed his hands in his jacket pockets and turned toward the library. Joel pressed his back against the rough bark of the cedar until the man disappeared around the corner.

Joel made himself wait two minutes before moving from his spot and heading home. As he did, he caught himself wondering how a man like that had attracted a woman like Hannah. But people were strange, and he was the last person to comment on someone else's choice to fall in love.

17

"You still haven't seen it?" Brandi's eyes were wide with incredulity. She tapped a glossy fake nail against the counter, the end tipped in royal blue with a metallic sheen.

"We can't stream anything out there. The internet is too slow."

"Wow. That's like the Dark Ages."

Brandi said it with pity, and Val laughed.

"I'm sure Netflix will still be there when we move to a house that's more 21st century." She didn't mention how many times Joel had invited her to watch *Stranger Things* at his house. Now she cringed inwardly anytime Brandi brought it up.

"But you have to watch it so I can talk to you about it. It's so cool. They get the Eighties vibe so perfect, and Barb has become an internet sensation. I love it!"

Before Val could point out that even she didn't

remember the Eighties and Brandi was younger than she was, the desk phone rang.

"Wallace Community Bank, this is Valerie," she answered brightly. "How may I help you today?"

"Where's the money?"

"I'm sorry?"

"Jordan Fisher is going to prison, and you're off screwing your old boyfriend. So where's the money? Did you take it? Because if my sister—"

Val pressed the disconnect button so fast the receiver was still at her ear. She replaced it on the cradle, her hand trembling.

Brandi eyed her curiously. "What was that all about?"

"Wrong number," Val muttered.

Someone had found out where she worked.

The phone rang again, and Val looked at it, unable to move. Unwilling to answer.

Brandi picked it up. "Wallace Community Bank, this is Brandi."

Val watched Brandi's face, waiting for her expression to change, but she stayed politely disinterested.

"Sure, let me get her for you." Brandi pulled the phone away from her ear and covered the receiver with her hand. "It's for you."

Val nodded and took the call on her own desk phone.

"This is Valerie." She kept her voice professional and turned away from Brandi so she wouldn't see her face. An angry tirade spewed out of the other end of the phone. A woman's voice, hard and bitter, accusing her of being just as crooked as Jordan.

"Mmhmm," she said, trying to keep her voice from betraying the sick feeling creeping through her middle.

When the woman on the other end started in on Abby, Val decided she'd let it go on enough.

"Thanks for the call. Have a good afternoon." She hung up.

Blessedly, Brandi was busy with a customer, so Val had a couple of minutes to compose herself. Her heart raced, and her limbs tingled. She wanted to tell someone but at the same time felt deeply ashamed. What would Maddie do if she found out? What if the bank manager decided she was too much of a liability and let her go?

Brandi finished with her customer and turned back to Val.

"You all right?" she asked.

Val forced her face to relax into what she hoped was an untroubled expression.

"Oh. Yeah," she said. "That was my realtor. I'm not sure why she didn't just call my cell. If she calls again, will you tell her I'm not available? I don't want her to get the idea that it's okay to call me at work."

"Yeah, no problem."

"Thanks. Now, tell me who Barb is and why she's your favorite."

The distraction worked. Brandi's eyes lit up, and Val relaxed a little listening to her settle into an enthusiastic monologue about a television show Val cared absolutely nothing about. But the phone call nagged at her the rest of the afternoon, like a predator stalking her just out of sight.

Whoever had the gall to make harassing phone calls at Val's place of employment probably wouldn't be easily deterred. How long would she be able to keep it to herself?

Gray clouds hung heavy in the sky as Joel took the county road out of town. The nights were getting colder, and the turning leaves in the hills speckled in bands of red and gold against the deeper evergreen forests. Every year, the change in seasons reminded him of his mom who had grown up in Southern California and never tired of the wonders of having a real autumn.

As he slowed down for the sharp bend near the Rogers house, he was grateful that his mom and sister didn't live in Owl Creek anymore. They would have blown a gasket to see the lewd display Brett Rogers had made to mock him and Val. It gave him a rush of anger every time he saw it, and he could only imagine how it sickened Val to drive past it every day.

Not that he could keep the news about what was happening in Owl Creek from his family forever. Estella had texted him that morning from Portland with a link to an article about the protests.

WTF, Joel? was all she'd said.

Business as usual here in OC, he'd responded.

Are you okay?

Fine. You and Garrett finish that deck yet?

Your powers of evasion are on point, as usual. Do I need to call Mom?

Only if you want to get her worked up for nothing.

Maybe it's time you left that town once and for all. They need cops up here too.

Portland PD? No thanks.

She hadn't said anything more, and Joel could almost feel her fuming in her silence. He knew it came from a place of love, but her worrying didn't do anyone any good. Least of all his mom, who still thought she'd abandoned her adult children by moving to Florida. The unspoken rule between Joel and Estella was not to share anything stressful with their mother so she didn't rush back to Oregon out of guilt. She was happier than Joel had ever seen her, and he wasn't about to be the reason she gave up her new life.

He turned onto Skyline Road that wound the back way through the mountains to Salmon Ridge. If Joel followed Skyline far enough, he would reach the historical trestle bridge and the Goldendale ghost town. He tried not to think about that carefree day with Val and Abby. Had it only been two weeks ago? Already it felt like another life.

How had he spent the past three years alone and yet now couldn't remember how to get along without another person? It was like being with Val had cracked open a part of him that was left gaping and raw in her absence, aching to be filled.

The forest foliage was thick, obscuring the road, and Joel almost missed the private drive that led to Kevin Donovan's house. The dirt road had the unmistakable look of being newly cut out of the mountain and he was grateful the recent rain had settled the dust in the air.

The road climbed steeply up the mountain and ended at a clearing that looked out over the river below and wide swaths of charred forest from the summer's fires. The trees were black toothpicks against a gray backdrop, like something out of an apocalyptic film set. The Donovans were lucky it hadn't come any closer to their secluded hideaway.

In the middle of the clearing a concrete foundation had been poured, and the framing for a home had started, hinting at the shape of an attached garage and a wide bank of windows that would someday look out over the valley. A single-wide trailer sat off to the side in a grove of douglas firs. Joel's first thought was that it was a construction trailer until he saw the minivan and heard a child's shout.

The wooden steps were slick with condensation.

When Joel knocked, a woman's muffled voice issued a sharp command and everything in the trailer grew still.

Footsteps creaked on the other side of the door, and it opened a crack, a brass chain spanning the gap.

"Who is it?" The woman's voice was thin and spiked with anxiety.

"Joel Ramirez with the sheriff's office, ma'am." He held his shield to the gap for good measure.

The door closed as she slid the chain across, then opened again.

"What can I do for you, Mr. Ramirez?"

Joel hadn't known Bonnie Pearson in school—she was a year or two older—but he immediately spotted the resemblance to her brother. They shared the same wide-set eyes and narrow jaw, but Bonnie's face was softer and fuller.

"I'm sorry to bother you at home, Mrs. Donovan," Joel said, "but I wanted to chat with you about what's been going on at the mill. Get your perspective as Kevin's spouse."

"I thought you weren't working on this case anymore. Kevin said with all the protests it had been assigned to a detective out of Pineview."

"Marnie Sanders, yes. But I'm still assisting and had a few questions for you if you wouldn't mind. It shouldn't take long."

Strident sounds of a complaining toddler started up in the back. Bonnie paused and looked over her shoulder.

"Patrick, I told you to leave your brother alone. Go

turn on a movie in your room, why don't you? Sorry," she said, turning back to Joel. "He's supposed to be in school. It would really be great if you would catch the guy who tried to shoot Kevin so our family could leave the house again."

"We're doing everything we can. What do you know about this contract dispute with the union?"

Bonnie leaned against the doorframe. "I don't know all the legal stuff behind it. I just know that my father-in-law handed over a mess when he retired. We're all hoping things will turn around if Trump wins the election. He's promised to revitalize the timber industry, you know?"

"Are you aware of any threats against your husband prior to the shooting? Any conflicts going on outside of work?"

"No. Everyone likes Kevin. Or they did, before all this stuff started happening at the mill."

"Can you tell me a little about your husband's relationship with your brother?"

Bonnie folded her arms. "Mason and Kevin? They get along good. Why?"

"They've never had any conflict?"

"No, not that I know of."

"Because I remember they got into it pretty good over the Fourth of July."

"That was nothing. Just guy stuff."

"Can you tell me what it was about?"

"I don't remember. Nothing important. They'd forgotten about it by the fireworks that night."

"So that was unusual?"

"Yeah."

"Interesting. Because if throwing a few punches at your brother-in-law is that rare, it seems you'd remember why you got so mad at him."

Bonnie's eyes darted over Joel's shoulder to the long drive. "Look, things have been pretty stressful lately. There's a lot of pressure on Kevin and Mason doesn't always know when to keep his mouth shut."

"Do you know where Mason was on Sunday, August twenty-eighth? The day of the shooting?"

"He doesn't report to me, why? Does he need an alibi? Do you think he tried to shoot Kevin?"

"I'm just pursuing all possible leads. And that includes accounting for the whereabouts of the man who just two months ago was seen publicly fighting with your husband."

Bonnie's eyes darkened. "Mason wouldn't do something like that. Kevin is my husband and the father of my boys. Mason wouldn't do anything to hurt him."

Joel changed the topic. "It looks like you're going to have a beautiful home. When is it supposed to be finished?"

"I'm not sure. Next spring, I think."

"Who's your contractor?"

"Why does it matter?"

"Mrs. Donovan, I'm trying to find the man who tried to kill your husband. That includes looking at anyone who's recently done business with him and figuring out if there are any hard feelings there."

Bonnie sighed. "Jason Halstead was our contractor. But he quit so Kevin's looking for a new one."

Joel looked up from his notepad. Jason Halstead was one of the names Mason had given him when he asked who else used the Puss nickname.

"Why did he quit?"

"You'll have to ask Kevin about that." The way she said it tugged at Joel's mind. Like there was resentment buried beneath her words.

"So they ended on bad terms?"

"I didn't say that. Kevin didn't want to make a big deal about it, but he said Jason was price-gouging us. They had a chat and Jason decided he didn't want the job after all. And now we're stuck because everyone else is booked out so nothing's getting done."

A chill breeze gusted at Joel's back and Bonnie shrank further into her bulky sweatshirt. Joel wondered how well the heating in the trailer worked.

"I'll let you get back to your day, but can you tell me the firearms you and your husband own?"

"Let's see, he's got a rifle and a shotgun. Not sure what kind."

"It would be helpful if our ballistics team could take a look at them. Just to rule them out. I could take them with me now and return them as soon as we're finished."

Bonnie was shaking her head before he'd finished. "I don't think Kevin would like that. You'll have to talk to him about it."

"Well, thanks for your time. Here's my card in case you think of anything else."

Joel headed back to his car, passing the skeletal dream of a grand house. Why had Bonnie been reluctant to tell him about their contractor? Maybe it was time to get a warrant for Kevin Donovan's financial records and find out why the owner of the largest mill in this part of Wallace County couldn't manage to find someone to finish building his house.

18

Val saw the flat tire from across the parking lot. Of course. A perfect end to a miserable day.

The morning had started rough, with heavy rainfall and clogged gutters causing a sheet of rainwater to fall from the porch roof, soaking her and Abby as they ran to the car. By the time she'd dropped Abby off at Eileen's and made it to work, her hair was limp and dripped on her shirt. Her khaki pants were speckled with rain. Then Brandi had been out sick, so the day had dragged out as grim as the weather—dreary and lifeless.

Finding a flat tire at the end of the day was like rubbing salt in a wound. There was a mechanic's shop down the road on the site of an old gas station. With the nearest car dealership an hour away in Pineview, Mike not only fixed up most of the cars in town, he also served as a broker of sorts for Owl Creek residents looking to buy and sell their cars. Val had bought her first car from him, a 1972 Lincoln Continental that had been stolen off the streets of West Lafayette during her first semester at Purdue.

Val sheltered under her umbrella as she walked the four blocks to the shop, hoping Mike would still be there. The demonstration at City Hall looked to be taking on permanence. Unlike the picketers at the mill, who seemed unchanged from day to day, the crowd of protestors on Main Street grew almost daily. It made Val uneasy seeing the tents and canopies that had been set up on the lawn. What did they want? How far would they go to make their point?

The noise of the driving rain drowned out all other sound. The street had been closed to vehicular traffic in front of City Hall, and Val worked her way through the crowd, drawing glances. Her bright blue Wallace Community Bank polo shirt stood out among dark flannels and black raincoats and ponchos. Wet signs sagged and were hard to make out in the gray rain, but she recognized the name Ramirez on a few of them.

A picture of Puss in Boots made her stop and stare, anger rushing hot up her neck. That was too far. Resorting to personal attacks was bad enough, but seeing the old racist taunt from high school triggered the same feelings of indignation she'd felt then.

When she finally reached the garage, her anxiety spiked as she realized the open sign was turned off. But there were cars parked under the covered shelter where a gas pump had once stood, and when she tried the door, it opened.

An older man with a thick mustache and long gray ponytail was sitting in an orange overstuffed chair behind the tall counter. He looked up at her over a pair of bifocals.

"Hi, Mike," she said apologetically. "I know you're closed, but this is a bit of an emergency."

"Let's see, you're either Gina or Valerie. But I'm not sure which."

Val smiled. "I'm Valerie. And I'm really sorry to interrupt like this. I've got a flat tire, and I can't make it home without fixing it."

Mike leaned over to look out the office window. "Where's it at?"

"At the bank. I just got off work and noticed it was flat."

"Didn't your daddy teach you girls how to change a tire?"

"Yeah, he did. But I've never actually had to do it. I've only owned this car for about six months. I don't even think it has a jack."

"I'm only teasing, darlin'. I'll get you fixed up right." Mike grinned, revealing a gap where two of his front teeth were missing. "What kind of car is it?"

"It's a blue Toyota Prius."

"You've turned into one a' them granola-crunchers, eh?" He wheezed a laugh as he heaved himself out of the chair.

Val's smile felt strained, but he didn't seem to notice.

"Why don't you take a seat, and I'll be right back. No sense in us both going out and getting wet," he said as he shuffled to the door.

Val thanked him but couldn't sit. The upholstered chair was worn in a vaguely Mike-shaped impression and gave off an air of exclusivity. Instead, she stood at the window and watched him drive away in the red truck. Her pants were wet below the knee, and her ankle boots had leaked, leaving her feet wet and cold.

From her vantage point she could see both the sheriff substation and the lawn in front of City Hall where the protesters were gathered. How must Joel be feeling having to go to work every day and face that? She knew how much Austin Wilson's death haunted him, how uncomfortable he'd been being painted a hero for something that filled him with deep regret. To see him being painted as a villain now made her want to rush to his defense.

Val reached for her phone almost without thinking. When she pulled up their text thread, she stopped, looking at his last text.

Me too.

Was it fair to keep pulling him back into the craziness that was her life?

Maybe things aren't ever going to be simple between us, he'd said.

At the time, she'd seen it as accepting a challenge. But now, she realized, it could have shown a change of heart. A desire for space.

She wished she'd never changed their relationship by telling him how she felt. She needed a friend more than she needed a lover, and if she'd thought things through, she would have realized how pursuing one would cost her the other. It was too late now to go back to just being friends.

Through the rain, Val recognized Mike's truck returning, and she held the door open for him as he brought in her tire.

"Here we go. I'll get you fixed up in a jiffy. Can you get that other door for me?"

Val obeyed, opening the side door that led into the garage. "Can I get you anything? Coffee? A cinnamon roll from the bakery?"

Mike grinned. "Now you're talking. I think she's open 'til six."

Grateful for something to do, Val walked down the block to Lori's bakery. It was a tiny shop featuring baked goods and specialty sandwiches, and the cinnamon rolls were legendary in Wallace County. Each one was the size of a dinner plate and could feed a family of four.

Val bought two, thinking she'd give one to Eileen as a thank you for keeping Abby so late. When she returned to the shop, she found Mike in the garage frowning over the tire.

"How's it going?"

"Not so good, Miss Rockwell. This tire's done been vandalized. You're gonna need a replacement."

"What do you mean?" Val stepped forward and laid the bakery box on the counter.

"See right here?" He pointed to an area of the side-wall. When he pushed on it with a screwdriver she could clearly see the inch long gash.

Val swore under her breath.

"I agree. You're lucky they didn't get any of your other tires. If you want, I can order a new one. Won't take more'n a couple days. Is your spare any good?"

Val stared at him. "I have no idea."

Pity softened the lines around his eyes. "Let's go back there together. I'll take a look at your spare and make sure it's sound and then get you on the road again."

As they rode back to the bank, Mike hummed along with the radio tuned to Pineview's country music station, and Val sat in wooden silence. Someone had slashed her tire. Someone who knew where she worked and what kind of car she drove.

"I'll bet the bank has cameras," Mike said as they pulled into the parking lot. Her little car looked bereft without its back wheel. "You tell police, and they'll probably be able to find out right away who did it."

Right. Police.

Val gripped her phone. Two weeks ago she would have texted Joel, and he would have taken care of it for her. Now...well...

"I'll call them tomorrow," she lied. "Thanks for your help, Mike. You're a lifesaver. I know you're working past your time."

"It's nothing."

But as Val sat in the dry cab of the truck and watched him install her spare in the rain, she felt an overwhelming burden of debt.

This is why you came back to Owl Creek, a voice inside reminded her. *To get support and a soft place to land.*

It was a good reminder that there were still kind people in this town. Lately, she'd begun to wonder.

19

Joel was almost relieved when Kathy interrupted to tell him Hannah Quinton had come to see him. He'd spent the past hour on YouTube watching videos posted by Patriot Pride and suspected his scowl would harden into something permanent if he didn't have a distraction.

Hannah was chatting with Kathy when he came to the front desk.

"Don't they have jobs?" she was saying. "How can they spend all their time here day after day?"

Kathy shook her head. "It's disgusting. One of our deputies had bottles thrown at her house last night. Broken glass everywhere, and she's got kids!"

"But what's the point? What do they want?"

"They want to drum up enough public support to put pressure on the sheriff to accept responsibility for Ryan Moyer's death," Joel said. "And if that won't work, pressure the court to rule in his family's favor."

"I thought the sheriff's office was working toward a settlement."

"That's beside the point," Kathy said. "However it started, it's turned into a way for the lowlifes in this town to get power over law enforcement. That's what they care about. Getting back at the deputies who arrested their brother for drug possession or busted them when they were beating their kids."

"That's awful." Hannah arched a dark eyebrow thoughtfully. "But it's not so bad to have more accountability for police, right? Better training and resources to prevent burnout and bad judgment?"

"Sure," Joel said with a smile. "We all want that. But that costs money, and no one wants to pay for it. It's easier to put a catchy slogan on a sign and march in front of City Hall. What can I help you with, Hannah?"

"Can we..." she glanced at Kathy, "speak privately?"

"Of course. Come on back."

Hannah followed him to his office and sat before his desk, clutching her purse on her lap.

"I feel kind of weird doing this, but you asked me if anything was off in Kevin's personal life. Well, I've been paying attention and...I don't know; it might be stupid. But I figured it was better to tell you just in case it's important."

Joel reached for a pen. "I understand you want to be discreet, but you're doing the right thing. The shooter is still out there."

"I know. That's what I keep telling myself. But I've never been much of a gossip and it just feels...icky."

"Sure, I get it. What's bothering you?"

Hannah fingered a tassel on her purse's zipper. "He's been on the phone a lot lately, and it doesn't always sound like work stuff. And he's really stressed. I mean, of course he's stressed. Someone tried to kill him. But I heard him yesterday afternoon talking to his wife, and I've never heard him get that mad. I wasn't trying to eavesdrop, but I couldn't help it. It sounded like they were arguing about owing someone money. I don't know, but he sounded really defensive."

"What did he say? Did he mention any names?"

Hannah shook her head. "Not exactly. I heard him say something about promising to pay somebody, and then he said something like, 'if your brother doesn't keep his mouth shut…' and then I couldn't understand the rest." She blushed and looked at her hands. "I feel so guilty telling you any of this. I don't know what he was talking about, and it's not any of my business. But if it helps find the person responsible…" Her dark eyes met Joel's with a plea for understanding.

"Have you ever seen anyone come to the office you don't recognize? Or has he left for appointments that he didn't put on his calendar?"

She tilted her head in thought. "Now that you mention it, there have been a couple of times he's left work early without telling me why."

"And there's nothing on his calendar to explain his absences?"

"No. Which is odd because he's usually good about putting everything on his calendar."

"Do you remember any specific dates?"

She smiled apologetically. "I'd have to check on my computer. Sorry. But I can let you know when I get back to the office."

"That would be great. And thanks for coming in. I know it's not easy to share things that make other people look bad, but you're doing the right thing."

"Thanks."

She stood to leave, and Joel reached for his keyboard. He was already mentally drafting an affidavit for a search warrant of Kevin Donovan's personal financial records and didn't realize Hannah had paused at the door until she spoke.

"Have you eaten lunch yet? I was going to grab something before I go back to work, but if you haven't eaten yet, maybe we could go together. I'd feel a little safer than going alone, to be honest, with all those protestors out there."

"I'm not sure being seen with me is going to make you safer," Joel said with a wry smile, but he checked the clock. "I can take a few minutes, if you don't mind just grabbing sandwiches at the bakery."

Hannah flashed a glowing smile. "Perfect. I'll drive."

Val had seven missed calls when she checked her phone during her lunch break. One was a call from Mike saying he had the new tire and to come over anytime to get it installed. Hoping he could squeeze her in during her break, she grabbed her lunch and headed to her car.

She still hadn't filed a police report about the vandalism to her tire. She told herself it was because she'd been busy, but she knew it wasn't that.

The sky overhead was bright blue with clouds as white as cotton, great big shapes drifting overhead. A car horn honked out of sight down Main, coming from the direction of the protest. Val nibbled on a cheese round and ran through the rest of her voicemail as she crossed the parking lot.

Two messages were from divorce lawyers she'd reached out to after her call with Gina. She was narrowing her options, trying to find someone who seemed not only competent, but aggressive enough to take on Jordan's lawyers.

The rest of the calls were from reporters looking for interviews.

Becca Sheffield—the reporter who had followed them to Goldendale—had left a message, another in a long line of invitations to set the record straight by giving an exclusive interview. The other three were from news agencies wanting the same thing.

Val deleted them all.

Nearing her car, she slowed down. Something was on her windshield, the shadow of it visible as she approached from the rear. She glanced at the other cars in the parking lot, expecting to see a flier for a local business, but the other windshields were clear.

She rounded the front of her Prius to get a better look. It was a small yellow mailing envelope, tucked under her driver's side windshield wiper, with an adhesive label affixed to the front. She slipped it out from under the wiper blade and glanced around, half expecting to see who had left it, but the parking lot was empty.

VALERIE FISHER was typed out in all caps.

Val's appetite vanished, replaced with a feeling of dread. What now?

She slipped her finger under the flap and tore it open, then slid out the contents.

They were photos, just simple 4x6's that could have been printed at the Walmart or Walgreens in Pineview. The first showed a picture of the Owl Creek Elementary School, with kids and parents milling around in the organized chaos of after-school pick-up.

The second was zoomed in on one particular child. Val immediately recognized Abby's teal backpack and blond ponytail.

Her stomach dropped.

The next was of Abby walking up the sidewalk to Eileen's house.

Abby was wearing different clothes, so it had been taken on a different day.

There was even one of Abby playing on the play-ground during recess.

Val's mind raced, trying to make sense of it. She searched the envelope, looking for some note of expla-nation. The skin on the back of her neck prickled with the sensation of being watched. She spun around and scanned the surrounding trees and buildings, but she was alone.

With shaking hands, she shoved the pictures back in the envelope and unlocked her car. All thoughts of keeping her distance from Joel evaporated. She felt desperate to get to the station. Joel would know what to do.

She'd forgotten about the protestors.

Main Street was closed the solid block in front of City Hall, each end barricaded with a sheriff's deputy directing traffic down the side streets.

Val swore under her breath. She turned down the side street, and two teenagers spotted her. They yelled something unintelligible, and one brandished his middle finger.

Not wanting to park near the protestors, she drove a block further down the street to the fire station and walked back. With relief, she saw Joel's black Charger in his typical parking spot.

Feeling jittery and sweaty, she hurried up the steps to the building and pulled open the door.

Kathy's face lightened as she entered. "Well hello, Val. It's so good to see you! What can I do for you?"

"I need to talk to Joel." Val was a little breathless from her walk. Her heart pounded in her chest. How long had the packet of pictures been sitting there? Was Abby safe?

"I'm sorry, he just stepped out to go to lunch. Is there something I can help you with? Or do you want to leave a note?"

"No. I'll wait if that's okay."

She couldn't sit, so she went back outside and paced in the shade of the building. She dialed the school while she waited.

"Hi, this is Valerie Rockwell."

"Oh hi, Valerie! How can I help you?" The secretary had worked at the school when Val was a little girl and knew each child and most of the parents by name.

"I'm just checking to make sure Abby—Abigail—made it to school this morning."

"Sure thing, let me check. Yep, it looks like her attendance was marked."

Val wanted to ask her to go check the classroom personally to see for herself, but she held back.

"Thanks. I appreciate it."

She hung up and held her phone against her chin, thinking. There was someone else she could call. She didn't know if he'd be able to help, but it would be better than stewing helplessly in her own anxiety.

Just when she thought she'd have to leave a message, he answered.

"Giles here."

"Hi. This is Valerie Rock—Fisher. Valerie Fisher."

"Hello, Mrs. Fisher." Giles sounded surprised. "What can I do for you?"

"I just found a package of photos of my daughter left on my windshield. Pictures of her at school and the babysitter's. No note, nothing. And…I'm kind of freaking out."

"You said you just found them?"

"Yes."

"I assume you've reported it to your local law enforcement?"

"Not yet. I'm…soon. I just…you show up on my doorstep asking for me to let Abby visit Jordan, and a week later this happens. What's going on, Giles?"

"I'm sorry, I don't have any answers for you, Mrs. Fisher. But when I get—" He paused as a wave of shouting swelled from the protestors. "What is that noise in the background?"

"Oh. Sorry, I'm outside. There's a protest around the corner."

"Are you safe?"

"Yeah, I think so." Val looked over her shoulder toward City Hall.

"Sounds like your local law enforcement have their hands full. When I get off the phone with you I'm going to call the FBI office in Eugene. Is it okay if I give them your number?"

A gold sedan with California plates pulled up to the curb next to the station. Val's heart leaped as she recognized Joel in the passenger seat. But who was the woman driving? She looked a little familiar, but Val couldn't place her. She was young and attractive, though, and Val's mind went blank watching Joel get out of the car.

"Mrs. Fisher?"

"Uh, yeah, that's fine. Please do give them my number." She turned away, angling her body so she didn't have to see Joel with the other woman. She didn't want to know.

Except she *did* want to know. Was he already seeing someone else?

No, that wasn't important. All that mattered was keeping Abby safe.

That's all that ever mattered.

She walked a few steps out of sight around the

corner of the building. Giles was still talking about what she could expect if the FBI decided to open an investigation, but she'd only picked up half of what he'd said.

"I'll touch base after I talk to them, all right?" he finished.

"Thank you, I appreciate it."

"But don't wait. Go to your local police."

"I'm doing that right now. As soon as I hang up."

"Good. I'll talk to you soon."

"Thank you, Giles."

Val hung up the phone and turned around.

Joel stood at the corner of the building, watching her. His eyes were unreadable behind his dark sunglasses.

Val's heart squeezed painfully at the sight of him so close but so impossibly distant. Seeing him with another woman made her acutely aware that he wasn't hers.

"I'd like to think this is good news," Joel said, "but judging by the week I've had I'm betting it's not."

"No." She strode forward and handed him the envelope. "I found this on my windshield."

"What is it?" he asked without taking it.

"Pictures of Abby."

He frowned. "Come inside. I need some gloves. I assume you've touched them?"

"Yes." Val cringed. "I didn't know what it was. I wasn't thinking."

"It's okay. Is your car here too?"

"It's down the street. Across from the fire station."

He nodded and moved aside so she could walk ahead of him to the station. When they reached the door, he opened it and ushered her inside, his hand gently brushing the small of her back. Just briefly, but the gesture was so familiar and comforting that when it was gone, the absence of his touch left almost a physical ache in its place.

Hold it together, Val.

She couldn't let her feelings get in the way now. Not when there was so much at stake.

20

JOEL STOOD shoulder-to-shoulder with Larry and Kim in the conference room, examining the photos Val had found in the small mailer. He could imagine how upsetting it must have been to Val. She was at Kathy's desk now, calling work to tell them she'd be late coming back from lunch. Joel found himself checking and rechecking that she was still there.

"Can Val place the other dates?" Larry asked, pointing to the picture of Abby in front of the school. "She says Abby wore these clothes yesterday, right?"

"Yes." Joel picked it up with his gloved hands, gingerly holding it by the edges.

"We need to talk to the babysitter," Kim said. "See if she's noticed anything. Find out who has access to Abby while she's in her care."

"The post office is right there by the bank. Both of them should have CCTV. There are a couple of residences near there too, right? We need to talk to them all and see if anyone saw anything."

"Could this be related to the dad?" Larry asked, looking at Joel.

That had been his first thought too.

"Let's bring Val in and ask her." He hated that he didn't already know, that he was going to have to be brought up to speed like everyone else in the office.

"Aren't you supposed to be relieving Brian?" Kim asked Larry.

Larry glanced at the clock. "Right. Lousy protestors. Fill me in when I get back. Anyone messes with this kid and I'm gonna mess with them."

Joel went to the door and invited Val to join them. He pulled out a chair for her, and the questions started before she sat.

"Should I take her out of school? How can we know what they're planning? How do we stop them?" Her voice was firm, even angry.

"It's too soon to say. We don't know anything at this point. But once we've dusted these for fingerprints and checked the bank's CCTV, that should give us something to go off of."

"The code on the back. Can it tell you anything? Where they were printed or when?"

"Not likely. A fingerprint match would be our best lead. That and video footage from the bank."

"They upload it to an off-site server. I can ask Maddie to get it to you. And..." Here she blushed and looked away. "You might want to get footage from Monday too. Someone slashed the tire on my car."

Joel exchanged a look with Kim. "You didn't report it?"

"No. Sorry, I was going to."

Her cheeks went darker, and Joel understood what she wasn't saying. She hadn't wanted to report it because that meant she would risk seeing him.

Pain rose in his chest, and he quickly buried it. His voice sounded flat to his own ears.

"Have you gotten any other threats? Anything else suspicious?"

She shook her head.

"I'd like to look over your car. Would you be able to leave it overnight?"

"I...it's my only car. I have work, and Abby has to get to..." She stopped herself, and her shoulders sank. "What am I saying? Yes. Keep it. However long you need."

"I know you've had some unwanted visitors on your property lately. The kids with the fireworks and the news crew." He looked away, reminded uncomfortably of the night she'd broken up with him. "Have there been any others?"

"Um...a special agent with the IRS, but I know he didn't have anything to do with this. In fact, I called him and he wants to help."

"What's his name?"

"Giles...I think his first name is William? Willard? Something like that. He said he'd call the FBI and see if there's anything they can do to help."

"Ah." That explained the phone call he'd overheard. "They usually investigate missing children cases, and

Abby isn't missing. But under the circumstances, with your…husband who he is," he hoped she didn't notice his slight stumble on the word, "they might get involved sooner."

"What do these pictures even mean?"

"How did you feel when you saw them?" Kim asked.

Her eyes were luminous. "Terrified."

"That's exactly what they mean," Joel said. "They're an act of personal terrorism."

"But…why?"

"How much do you know about your husband's victims? Could this be an act of revenge?"

Val leaned back. "I don't even know. Giles could tell you. He's the lead investigator on Jordan's case. Let me get his number." She grabbed her phone and handed it to Joel to write down the number. "There were some really angry people, though. A man cornered me at a grocery store once last March. He said horrible things about how his dad had killed himself over the shame of losing all of their retirement savings. I tried to sympathize with him—at the time, I thought Jordan had killed himself too—and he just got more and more angry. He grabbed me and shook me, and I could…" Her voice trembled, and she paused for a breath. "I could feel his spit on my face. Another customer finally pulled us apart and I was able to get away. Never went back to that store. So yeah, I guess with Jordan back alive and all that coming out, people might be angry enough for revenge."

Kim caught Joel's eye and frowned. Joel's jaw tightened. He felt a wave of protectiveness and tried to push it away. By Val's choice she wasn't his to protect, no matter how much he wanted to.

"I'll talk to this Special Agent Giles," Joel said. "Under the circumstances, it's very possible that we're looking at a connection to Jordan's arrest. Anyone else bothering you lately?"

"Let's see, I've gotten a lot of calls, but no other visits. Then there's the…" Again her face flamed red, and she looked uncomfortably at Kim. She bit her lip and pushed the words out as if she couldn't get them out fast enough, "There's the man who owns the mannequins."

The room suddenly felt ten degrees warmer.

"Has he ever threatened you?"

"Well, I…" She cleared her throat. "I did try to talk to him about…what he's been doing. I was pretty upset, and he…he didn't threaten Abby directly, but it was implied."

"How did you talk to him? Phone?"

"No, I went to his house." She winced at Joel's expression. "I know, it was stupid."

"Yeah, it was. Guess that means someone needs to talk to Brett Rogers too," he said to Kim.

Kim grimaced. "Larry can take that one."

"When was it you had this conversation with Mr. Rogers?"

"That's the mannequin man? Um, that would have been last Saturday."

"You mentioned you've been getting calls. What sort of calls?"

CAREN HAHN

"News stations. Local and from home. Chicago, I mean. But I've deleted their messages. Sorry."

"It's okay," Joel said, hiding his frustration. Val's aggressive desire for privacy was eliminating their leads.

"I've also gotten a few harassing phone calls about Jordan at work. Mostly from the same woman, I think."

The front door opened, and Marnie Sanders entered the building. Not great timing. Joel needed to talk to her about his conversation with Hannah but didn't want to divert his attention from Val.

Val noticed him watching Marnie and stood.

"I'd better go. I'm going to pick up Abby from school and take her home, just to make me feel better. Although…if I'm leaving my car, I'll need a ride."

She looked to Kim, but Kim smoothly turned away.

"I've gotta run too. Good to see you again, Ms. Rockwell."

"I can take you home," Joel offered. "Just give me a minute."

"It's okay, I know you're busy—"

"It's fine," he said before she could talk herself out of it. "Hold on a second."

He left her in the interview room and closed the door behind him.

Marnie watched Val through the window. "Is that Valerie Fisher in there?"

"Yeah."

"I thought I recognized her from the news."

"Someone left pictures of her daughter on her car today while she was at work."

"How old is the daughter?"

224

"Seven."

Marnie frowned. "I don't understand what's happened to this town. It's like you've crammed a year's worth of incidents into the past two weeks."

"What can I say? We're over-achievers in Owl Creek."

"I was just talking to the office staff at the school to see if anyone was there the day of the shooting and thought I'd stop at the mill to see the secretary. Hannah? But they told me I'd find her here."

"You just missed her. She was heading back to work. Let's compare notes when you're done, see what you think about her story."

"Sure." Her eyes flickered over his shoulder to the interview room. "I'll give you a call later."

Val was standing when Joel returned, fidgeting with her phone. "It might not look good to leave together. Let me go first and walk down toward the fire station. You can pick me up there."

"I'm not sure that'll make much of a difference."

"I know, but I'd rather not be seen together when you've got protestors just outside."

"Fine."

Kathy watched her walk out. "Glad to see you two working things out."

Joel grunted noncommittally, relieved when Kathy's phone rang so he wouldn't have to say more.

He gave Val a few minutes before driving down the block to the fire station. She was sitting on the edge of a brick planter on the street corner and slid into the passenger seat without looking at him.

It was only a two-minute drive to the school to pick up Abby, and they made it in silence. With so much left unsaid, it was impossible to find the words.

———————

Val stepped into the school and was greeted with the smell of childhood nostalgia. Sue welcomed her as soon as she opened the office door.

"Good afternoon, Val! Are you picking up Abigail?" She reached for the phone.

"Yeah. Thanks. Do I need to sign her out?"

"Sure, right on that clipboard there."

Val found the clipboard on the counter and quickly wrote the date and time while Sue called Abby's classroom teacher. She paused at the last field on the form: Reason. What reason should she give for withdrawing Abby?

Someone's stalking my daughter

Worried about her safety

Mom freak-out moment

She scanned the other entries above hers for ideas and finally wrote down, "Family event."

"This is a closed campus, right?" she asked Sue as she waited for Abby to arrive. "You don't just let people in and out."

"Of course. No one comes into the building without coming through the office first, and all parent volunteers are required to have a background check. We take safety very seriously."

"What about the playground? There are those entry

points in the fence near the neighborhoods behind the school. Does anyone monitor those?"

"We've closed off the gaps that used to be there when you were a student. Now no one can access the playground without going through one of the gates, and those are locked during school hours. We're very safe."

Val couldn't help doubting it with the photos of Abby fresh in her mind.

When Abby pushed open the door to the office, Val almost sighed with relief.

"Hi Mom! Why are you picking me up?"

"Come on, I'll tell you in the car."

When they stepped outside, Abby shielded her eyes against the sun, looking for the car.

"Joel's taking us home," Val said, pointing to the Charger.

He was standing next to it, talking on his phone, but he hung up as Abby ran to the car.

"Hey, kiddo," Joel said.

"Why are you here?" she asked as she climbed into the back seat.

"There's a problem with our car, so Joel is giving us a ride," Val said.

"Can we turn on the lights this time? And the siren?" she asked excitedly.

Val caught herself before she smiled at Joel, turning instead to look out the passenger window.

"Let's hope we won't need the lights and siren driving you home today," Joel said.

"Mom, guess what?"

"What, honey?" Val turned, forcing herself to turn off her racing thoughts and give Abby her full attention.

"Emily saw a real Sasquatch." Abby delivered it like a punchline. "She was at her grandma's house, and it came right into the yard."

"Really?"

"Uh huh. She drew a picture and showed us what it looked like."

As Abby described the Sasquatch, needing very little encouragement to draw out her tale with rich embellishment, Val marveled at how oblivious and content the world of a child was. A world where the threat of Bigfoot was far more real than the threat of an unknown stalker.

As they drove, her mind wandered back to the woman she'd seen Joel with. Why did she seem familiar? Val was sure she'd seen her before but couldn't think of where.

And then it came to her. She was the new secretary Kevin Donovan had hired when Val had been job-hunting over the summer.

At first, this realization cheered Val. With the strike, the secretary's visit was probably work-related. But then she tried to imagine a reason Joel would have been riding in her car, and she couldn't think of anything that wouldn't be personal in nature. Maybe they'd been thrown together because of the strike, but now it was turning into something more. After all, that's what had happened with her and Joel.

That was a depressing thought.

When they pulled up to the farmhouse, Val opened the car door, hoping to make a quick exit.

"Thanks for the ride. When do you think my car will be ready?"

"We'll get to it as soon as possible." Joel shut off the engine, and she hated how happy it made her.

Abby jumped out and ran to pet Creampuff who was lounging in the lawn. The grass was starting to green up from recent rain, losing the beleaguered look of summer.

"If it's all right, I'm going to take a look around before I go," Joel said.

Val nodded and got out of the car, not trusting herself to say anything else. Things were so awkward between them now, and she didn't know how to fix it. She felt like she needed to apologize, but for what? Trying to protect Abby?

She would never apologize for that.

Joel's only companions were the mangy stray cat and the occasional robin as he checked the exterior of the house and the rest of the yard. It was more sticker weeds than grass, and the flowerbeds were overgrown. A few weeks ago, Joel had offered to come clean up the yard, but Val had seemed embarrassed so he hadn't mentioned it again.

The old Victorian farmhouse had a decidedly more haunted look now that the hill behind the house was charred black from fire, but Joel could almost imagine hearing Jim working in the shop or smelling Mary's baking coming from the kitchen. The ever-present sights and sounds of his youth.

His work phone rang and Marnie was on the other line.

"What more have you learned about this conflict between Donovan and his brother-in-law?"

"Not much," Joel answered. "There's a chance it might have something to do with the house. Kevin's wife told me construction has stalled since their contractor quit with complaints of price-gouging. The contractor is a friend of Mason's."

"No kidding."

"Could be nothing. Could be something. In a town like this everyone's connected."

"What's the contractor's name? I'll see if I can get someone else to track him down. Sounds like you're going to have your hands full with this threat against the Fisher girl. Unless you want to hand it off to someone else?"

Joel knew that was the professional thing to do but suspected Val would never forgive him. "It's fine. It's a pretty delicate situation, you know?"

"Sure. In that case, I'll take over the financial search. Send me what you've got so far and I'll go from there."

"Thanks, Marnie. I'm almost finished here at the Rockwell place and will get it to you when I get back."

"Oh, is that where you are? By all means, take your time," Marnie said with a laugh.

"Funny," Joel said and hung up before she could

reply. He spotted Val coming back out to the porch, pulling her hair up into a messy bun as she walked.

"You're leaving?"

"Uh, yeah. Unless you need me to stay—"

"It's fine," she said. Quick, like she knew what he was going to offer. "Thanks for the ride."

"Sure. I'll call that agent as soon as I get back to the office and see if I can get some leads on who has the biggest grudge against your husband."

"That's going to be a very long list," Val said darkly. "With my name right at the top."

Yours isn't the only one.

"Let me know if you need anything else. I hate to leave you out here without a car, but I'm only a fifteen minute drive away. Ten if I use lights and siren."

He'd hoped to coax a smile, but Val looked away.

"And if your husband—"

"Don't!" She snapped the word so fast it cracked through the air.

Joel stopped.

She closed her eyes and took a breath. "Don't call him my husband. Please."

When she opened her eyes, her gaze was so fierce and furious he felt an uncharacteristic ire building in his chest and tried to smother it.

"He *is* your husband, Val."

"On paper only. You should know that better than anyone."

The way she said it, the intimacy of it and the way it wrapped around him and drew him to her, ignited the spark of indignation.

"Oh, I do. I'm reminded of it every day."

"Are the reporters bothering you too?"

"That's not what I mean." A voice in his head warned him to stop talking, but he pushed forward anyway. "I'm talking about you. It's like Jordan is only your husband when it's convenient. You toss him aside when it suits you, but then use him as an excuse to push me away whenever I get too close."

She blinked. "That's not fair. I was trying to do the right thing for Abby—"

"Were you? Or were you just thinking of yourself?"

"What's that supposed to mean? Do you think I've been playing you?" Her cheeks flushed, and she took a step closer, lowering her voice. "I didn't know any of this was going to happen. Do you think I would have allowed myself to feel what I do for you if I'd known? What kind of a person do you think I am?"

"Truthfully? I think you're the kind of person who has been hurt so deeply that you can't bring yourself to risk getting hurt again."

"Can you blame me?" Her voice rose. "What do you expect me to do? Pretend like my choices won't have any consequences? That I can just do whatever I want and no one will get hurt?"

"Of course not. And I don't blame you for being careful. But as soon as you got scared you pushed me away. You made the choice for me. And then it didn't help anyway, did it?"

"Thanks. I kind of figured that out."

"Look, my point is that you didn't trust me enough to give me a chance. You're so afraid of getting hurt that you just cut me off. And I get why that seemed the safest choice, but someday you're going to have to take risks again. You can't play it safe forever."

"Look who's talking about playing it safe! You of all people!"

"What's that supposed to mean?"

"You never did have to work at a relationship. You just went along with whichever girl was willing to do all the work to snag you. You never once took a chance on someone you might have to put in a little effort for."

The indictment hit him to the core. Val had just summed up his whole failed marriage.

"And now I see you doing it again, letting yourself get caught by the next pretty girl who won't make you work for it. So maybe you can understand if I don't want to be that girl. I don't want you to be with me just because it's the path of least resistance."

She spat the words like fire, and suddenly Joel realized that giving her space might have come so easily because that was all he knew how to do. He may have been doing the right thing, but he was doing it for the wrong reason. And while he may have fooled himself, he hadn't fooled her.

Blood pounded in his head with her accusation and he searched for something to say, but the words wouldn't come.

She took a deep breath and continued, her voice calmer.

"I know it's none of my business. You don't owe me anything, and you have a right to move on. I just didn't expect it to happen so soon, that's all. But that's what you do, hook up with whoever comes along. Whoever won't make you work for it."

Finally he realized what she was talking about and found his voice.

"Val, the woman you saw me with today, she's not my girlfriend. We're not seeing each other."

She scoffed. "You may think that, but I'm not sure she does."

Defensiveness tightened his voice. "Hannah is...I guess you could say we're friends. Barely more than acquaintances. But right now I could use a friend. You won't talk to me. Most of the guys won't talk to me after what happened at the mill. In the past two weeks I've been shot at, mocked in the press, and harassed every day just by going to work. And the thing that really gets to me is that the one guy who I could have talked to about all this and he would have understood...Carter? I shot and killed him. And I have to live with that for the rest of my life. So yeah, I could use a friend right now."

Val's lips parted in shock; the color drained from her face. "What do you mean you were shot at? Was that at the mill?"

"It doesn't matter now. I've gotta get back to work."

He couldn't get to the car fast enough, his outburst ringing in his ears. Shame gripped his chest like a vise. What had gotten into him?

"Joel, wait. Please."

He reached for the door handle, but her hand was there, pressed against the frame.

"Joel, I'm sorry. Please, don't go yet."

He stepped back, putting distance between them. Everything felt too…raw.

She leaned against the car door and folded her arms. "Look, I wouldn't even be here today if it weren't for you. You've been the best friend I could have asked for, and I've been…" The breeze blew a lock of hair forward over her eyes and she tossed it back. "Well, I guess you could say I've been a pretty sucky friend to you. I've been so caught up in my own problems that I had no idea what you've been dealing with. I *was* worried about you. I almost called so many times. But I was too worried about what you'd think of me. I'm sorry."

The tightness in his chest eased a little.

She raised a hand to shield her eyes from the sun. "I haven't been fair to you. Everything just got to be too much too soon, and I got scared because…well—" She stopped as if debating how to say it. "Full disclosure here—because I love you Joel."

The words shot through him, dissolving the ache of loneliness that had been building the past few weeks. It almost hurt how badly he needed it.

But she wasn't finished.

"I also know that love isn't enough. Maybe I never should have pushed you away, but I have to be very careful. My mother-in-law is pressuring me to stay with Jordan. If she helps him fight the divorce, any mistake could cost me. And Abby too. I want to be with you, but it's going to take time, and it's not going to be easy. I can't carry this relationship by myself. You're going to have to work at it too, and sometimes it might just plain suck. Can you accept that?"

Joel let out a breath, his head spinning. He took off his sunglasses to look her in the eyes.

"Honestly, Val, that's the best news I've heard in weeks."

He closed the distance between them in a breath. Her eyes were filled with cautious hope. He brushed his fingers against her jaw, lifting her chin, and she reached for him with a small gasp, like something between them had snapped.

He kissed her like she was the air he needed to breathe, like she was water to quench his thirst. She melted into him, her tongue seeking out his, sending a searing heat down his spine. Conscious thought fractured to sensations—the clean scent of her hair, the taste of her mouth, the rough knit of her shirt under his hands—fueling a desperate longing that was echoed by the grip of her arms around his neck like she would never let him go.

When he pulled away, she let out a deep sigh. "Man, I've missed you."

"Me too."

She slid her hands around his waist and rested her head against his chest. Holding her felt like coming home. He searched for the words to say what he was feeling.

"Since you came back to Owl Creek," he said, "I've been wrecked. Absolutely wrecked. Because I've seen the man I am without you, and I can never go back to that."

She was quiet for a moment before responding. "It won't be easy. I'm a hot mess most of the time, and I can't promise it won't get worse."

"Being with you is a privilege, Val. It always has been." He pulled away to look her in the eyes, trying to understand what she was thinking, why she couldn't see herself the way he did. The warmth of her gaze made his insides feel soft. He needed to get his head back in the game. "Are you sure you don't want me to come back tonight? I can sleep on the couch. No pressure."

Val squinted one eye as she considered. "I...no. I'll see how it goes tonight. Keep your phone close."

"Always."

She drew him close and kissed him again, a long lingering taste of late summer.

"Promise me," he murmured against her lips. "Promise me you won't push me away again."

He felt her lips pull into a smile.

"Promise me you'll push back if I do."

He kissed her one more time and reached around her to open the door. If he wanted to make this work, he would have to get better at goodbyes.

21

Val couldn't keep a grin from her face as she climbed the porch steps. The smell of Joel's aftershave clung to her skin, making her feel heady and off balance.

Just inside the door, Abby stood at the base of the stairs. Her pigtails had the limp look that came at the end of the school day, and her eyes were wide and somber. She leaned against the newel post, embracing it like it was the only thing propping her up.

"Mom, why were you kissing Joel?"

Val stopped, her grin shriveling as embarrassment sent blood rushing to her face.

"You saw that?"

Abby nodded.

"Well, Joel and I...we like each other a lot. Not just as friends."

"What about Daddy? Does that mean you're getting a divorce?"

"Come here." Val tried to take her hands, but Abby

clung tighter to the newel post. Val passed through the entry to the living room and sat on the couch in view of the stairs. She patted the seat next to her, but Abby stayed put.

All her mom instincts cried out to reassure Abby with touch. Soothe the pain of what she was going to say and make it easier to hear. But Abby wouldn't relent.

"I know this is really confusing, and it's okay for you to feel sad or even mad about it," Val began. "Yes, your dad and I are getting a divorce. But it's not because of Joel. It's because Daddy left us. And it's because of all those bad things he did to hurt those other people."

Abby's question was so soft Val almost didn't hear it. "Did he ever hurt you?"

"No. I mean, he did, but not like that." Val wracked her brain for a way to explain. "Do you remember that movie we watched a while back where it was the princess's birthday and the other girl was jealous and tricked the princess into hiding for a pretend surprise party while she stole all her presents?"

Abby nodded.

"Do you think in real life they would ever be good friends after a mean trick like that?"

Abby shrugged.

"I think it would be hard to be friends with someone who did such a selfish trick. It would be hard to know if you could trust them, and I'm pretty sure I would never invite them to a birthday party again. Well, when your dad ran away and pretended like he'd died in that car accident, that was like playing a really mean trick on us. And it hurt my feelings a lot."

Just saying the words made some of the old grief well up, and Val's voice caught. She swallowed.

"It hurt my feelings so bad that it even made me not love him the same way I used to. I know that's hard to hear, and I wish so much that none of it had happened. But I can't change what your dad did. All I can do is try to take care of you and me the best I know how."

Val's arms felt empty without Abby. She needed to draw comfort as much as she needed to give it. If only she could see what was going on in Abby's head. If only she knew the right words to say.

At last Abby released the newel post and came to Val, deliberately looking at the floor. But even with her head bowed, Val saw the glistening eyes and heard her voice quaver.

"I feel that way too sometimes."

Her face pinched like she was about to cry, and she leaned against Val. Val wrapped her arms around her tiny body and lifted her up to sit on her lap. Usually Abby kept her tears to herself, preferring not to have an audience when her feelings were intense.

Val held and rocked her, resting her chin on Abby's head and marveling to herself at how big Abby had gotten. She rubbed her back, tracing the bony ridge of her spine.

"It's okay if you feel confused about your dad. I feel confused sometimes too. That doesn't make you a bad person."

Abby shuddered and rubbed her wet face against Val's shirt.

How could she fix this?

"You haven't done anything wrong; remember that. I love you, and your dad loves you too. Just because we don't love each other in the same way doesn't mean we feel any differently about you. We both still love you just as much as we always have. And Daddy will always be your dad even when he isn't my husband anymore."

Abby's sobs dwindled to gasping sniffs.

"Is Joel gonna be your new husband?"

"No!" It came before she could stop it, and she knew immediately it was the wrong thing to say. Abby was fed a regular diet of Disney movies with happily-ever-afters that came after one kiss. She wouldn't understand why Val would kiss a man if they weren't practically engaged.

"I don't know," she amended. "Right now I don't have any plans to get a new husband. I just want it to be you and me for a while. Is that okay?"

Abby nodded. Val gently eased the elastics out of her hair and stroked her curls free.

"You like Joel, though, right?"

Abby shrugged.

"Well, he likes you if that helps."

And he likes me too, right? She couldn't believe she'd said what she had, especially since he hadn't actually expressed how he felt about her. Not concretely. What she'd said was true. She did love him. And she didn't want to be the only one putting any effort into the relationship while he just went along for the ride. But maybe she'd been too open. Too quick to share her feelings.

Stop second-guessing everything.

For now, it was enough that things weren't permanently broken between them.

"I'm going to heat up some leftovers for dinner. Then what would you say to having a little slumber party?"

"With who?" Abby slid off her lap. Her cheeks were rosy from crying and her eyes were glassy bright.

"Just you and me. You can sleep in my room tonight."

"In your bed?"

"Sure, if you want."

"Like when Daddy...when we thought he died."

"Yeah, like then."

"I'm glad he's not really dead," she said.

Val knew the line that was expected of her, "me too," but she balked. The reality was that as awful as it had been—and it had been a nightmare—in some ways her life had been simpler back when she thought she was a widow. Did that make her a horrible person? She had to search to find the part of her that was glad Jordan hadn't actually driven off that cliff into the icy waters of Lake Baruch.

"I'm glad too. I'm glad you'll be able to see him someday."

And in that moment, looking at her daughter and remembering the way she'd squealed when Jordan rubbed his stubble against her smooth cheeks or sat on his lap when they went to the movies or relished the waffles he made on the first day of school, she actually meant it.

Joel came home after dark to find his new mailbox on the ground next to the post. One side had buckled like it had been hit with a baseball bat, and the bolts were sheared off. The day's mail was scattered across the lawn.

"Seriously?" Joel muttered.

He walked across the street to the home of the high school English teacher, Jemma Patterson.

She came to the door holding a small calico kitten. "Oh! I thought you were someone else. This is the last of Molly's kittens to go, and a family is supposed to pick him up tonight. What can I do for you?"

"I've been having some trouble with my mailbox. This is the second time in a week it's been vandalized. Irreparably so."

Jemma's mouth pressed into a line. "That's deplorable. Mailboxes aren't cheap to begin with. Isn't that a felony?"

"Have you seen anyone hanging around my house? Anything suspicious?"

"Ack! Can you...?" The kitten had crawled up onto her shoulder and was climbing up the back of her neck into her hair. She turned around, hunched over, and Joel reached for the ball of fur. It was tiny in his hands, and he instinctively cradled it close to his chest.

Until it sank its claws through his shirt and skin, climbing up to his shoulder.

"Sorry!" She tried to take the kitten back, but his claws were caught in Joel's shirt.

"Here, just take…" He pulled and, with a sharp pain and tearing sensation, delivered the flailing kitten safely back into her hands. "Just let me know if you notice anything suspicious?"

"Sure, sure!" she called as she closed the door.

Joel crossed the road back to his own house and propped the smashed mailbox against the empty post. Maybe he should just commit to a PO box. Most of the residents who lived inside city limits didn't have mailboxes, choosing instead to make the daily walk to the post office with keys in hand.

He turned on the news when he got in, letting it run in the background while he changed out of his work clothes into basketball shorts and a soft t-shirt. He examined the snags in his shirt left by the kitten's claws, stretching the fabric to see if he could ease the threads back into place. No luck.

That's why he'd never had any pets. His therapist had suggested getting a companion animal after the divorce, but Lacey had taken most of the furniture, so by the time he'd replaced it, he didn't feel like welcoming a hairy creature with an excitable bladder or urge to scratch.

Now, though, he wished he had a smart German shepherd who would alert him in the night if someone were on the property who shouldn't be.

He started some rice in the steam cooker and stood

at the counter with his laptop and the notes from his conversation with Agent Giles. Giles had been more than happy to give him a few names.

"It's all such a tragedy," he'd said, "seeing how these poor people gave until there was nothing left, expecting the dividends to start flowing. I really hope none of them would stoop to something like this, but good people can do crazy things when they're desperate."

"I just want to make sure Abby Fisher is safe," Joel had responded.

"Of course. I've been thinking on it all afternoon since Mrs. Fisher called, and there are a couple who might be worth looking into."

Aaron Tuttle had been one of the first and had tied his professional life so closely to Jordan's fraudulent scheme that his business had gone under and he now faced charges of his own.

Meredith Heppner had lost the ability to pay for expensive treatment for a rare autoimmune disorder. She lived in California and had a large extended family, so she was geographically closer than most of Jordan's other victims. Joel noted the name, thinking of the woman Val reported had been calling her at work.

"Val mentioned a man accosting her once at a grocery store, claiming his father took his own life. Do you know who I'm talking about?" Joel had asked Giles.

"I wish I could say there was only one who ended up taking their lives, but there wasn't. I think I know who you're talking about, though. Reggie Goldberg is the son. He's a bit of a live wire, could very well put something like this together."

By the time they'd finished, Joel had a list of two dozen names of victims who had either suffered espe-cially catastrophic losses or had seemed unstable afterward.

More in-depth research would have to be done at work, but for now he gleaned what information he could from news articles and social media. Getting a glimpse into the damage done by Jordan Fisher, Joel wondered how the man could live with himself. How could he have destroyed so many lives and then gone home to his wife and daughter as if he'd put in an honest day's work? Pretending as if the world hadn't been made a darker place because he was in it.

What was really disgusting was how light the sentences were for these kinds of crimes. In similar cases, Joel found the perpetrator walked away with sentences of only a few years, or maybe even probation. He knew of shoplifters who spent more time behind bars than some of these sleazebags.

He dialed the number for FBI Special Agent Stacy Porter from the Eugene field office. When Porter answered, Joel apologized for calling him after hours.

"Don't sweat it. Is this about that threat to the sena-tor's granddaughter?" Porter asked.

"You talked to Giles?"

"Yeah, but I want to hear your version. Go ahead and give me the rundown."

Joel explained about the pictures and the flat tire from earlier in the week.

"We're still waiting on CCTV from the bank," he said. "Deputies canvassed the area this afternoon and found one resident with one of those new Ring door-bells. You know what I'm talking about?"

"Oh yeah, those are slick. Did you get anything?"

"Possibly. There's a hooded figure seen passing the parking lot about an hour before Mrs. Fisher found the photos. Her car isn't in the camera's view, though, so we don't know if that's our perp."

"What would you like me to do, Ramirez? I'm happy to open an investigation if you'd like. With a senator in the mix...well, I'll make sure you get what-ever you need."

"It'd be great if your lab could take a closer look at these pictures. See if you come up with anything we missed."

"Sure. Do you need any extra manpower? I could come down with a couple of agents. "

"Thanks. I may take you up on it. I've got a list of some of Jordan Fisher's victims. If you could look into them on your end and see if any of them has had an opportunity to make a threat like this, that would be really helpful."

"Absolutely. I'm happy to help. Let me know if there's anything else we can do for you."

As soon as Joel hung up, his phone rang. He grabbed it, hoping it was Val, but it was Marnie Sanders.

"How are things going with the little girl?" she asked.

"She's safe. Stacy Porter with the FBI is going to give some support."

"That's great, because things have taken a turn with

this Patriot Pride situation, and I need you at a hundred percent. We've found a connection between one of the founders—a man named Tanner Fordham—and Horace Shields."

"No kidding. What kind of connection?" Joel grabbed his laptop.

"An organization in Fordham's name is one of Shields' largest private donors. We're trying to figure out how far back Shields and Fordham go and whether or not Fordham would benefit from Shields' election."

"That would explain why Patriot Pride has taken such an interest in the protests." There was a part of Joel that was relieved to think maybe some of the protestors waving signs like, RAMIREZ MUST GO and RAMIREZ SHOT FIRST weren't his neighbors and friends.

"It's a fertile field for recruiting too. We picked up a guy here who says they've been using The Trader bar to seek out like-minded individuals."

"I thought you said they claim to be peaceful? The Trader isn't where I'd go to find upstanding citizens to support my cause."

"Good to know. I'll make some calls tomorrow to see what the feds know. They might not tell me much, but it can't hurt to ask. And Joel?"

"Yeah?"

"Be careful. If these guys are opportunists looking to take advantage of the climate in Owl Creek, there's no telling how far they'll go."

22

VAL WOKE in the middle of the night, her blood pumping fast.

The clock said 4:17 a.m., and no light crept under the curtains. She strained her eyes and ears against the oppressive darkness, trying to sense what had awakened her. Her heart thumped painfully in her chest.

She reached over and laid a hand on the warm lump next to her, reassuring herself that Abby was still there. The gentle sound of Abby's breathing and the faint rise and fall of her chest told Val that she was still asleep.

So why was Val awake?

Hating the dark that amplified every fear, she slipped out of bed and felt for her phone. Turning on the flashlight, she swept the room with the cool beam. Her bedroom took on a horror-movie quality in the dark, danger lurking in every shadow. But nothing seemed out of place.

The air coming through the window was cool, and she wore only a tank top and shorts, so she reached for a sweatshirt.

Careful not to wake Abby, Val eased the doorknob slowly as she opened the door. The stairwell loomed to her right, again taking on that haunted look by the light of her phone. She paused, listening again. When she didn't hear anything, she padded down the stairs, the grain of the wood cold against her feet.

She stopped at the bottom of the stairs, arrested by the sound of a board creaking somewhere in the house. Her throat closed.

She held the light against her chest to let the darkness surround her, straining to adjust her eyes to the shadows. The noise wasn't repeated.

Old farmhouse or stealthy intruder? Val couldn't tell the difference.

She checked the front door to make sure it was locked, then peeked out the living room windows.

Her heart stopped.

A figure stood in the yard, silhouetted against the light of the shop.

Val gasped, her hand to her mouth to stifle a scream.

Heart racing, she pulled out her phone and started to dial 911 before she realized the figure wasn't a person.

It was a mannequin.

Anger flooded in with the fear, and her hands trembled as she turned on her camera.

She snapped a picture of the mannequin and texted

it to Joel. Then, feeling a twinge of guilt for disturbing him, she called.

He answered before it went to voicemail. "Val? What's wrong?"

"I texted you a picture of my view from my front window."

She waited while he checked.

"What the…is that a mannequin? What's it doing on your lawn?"

"I was thinking of starting my own collection; what do you think?"

"Do you know how long it's been there?"

"I don't know for sure. I woke up about ten minutes ago out of the blue."

"Did you see anyone? Hear any cars?"

"No. So, my big question is, when do I start freaking out?"

Joel sighed. "Larry questioned Brett Rogers yesterday about Abby. He wasn't too keen on getting a visit from a sheriff's deputy."

"So this is his revenge?"

"I don't know. Let me get my keys and—"

He broke off and cursed.

"Joel?"

"There's one here too."

"In your yard? You're kidding. What does that mean?"

"Man, that's eerie."

"You're telling me. What do we do?"

"You haven't gotten a security camera yet, have you?"

"No. Have you?"

"No."

"We're really bad at this."

Joel chuckled. "I'm getting on Amazon right now. I'll order you one too."

"No, you don't have to—"

"It's not negotiable, Val. Trust me, you'll be doing me a favor. As much as you're a lightning rod for the creeps in this town, this will make my job easier."

Val tried to push aside the wave of shame and focused on being grateful. "Thank you."

She curled up on the couch with a gray throw that wasn't as soft as it looked. But it was thick, and she needed comfort. She couldn't pull herself away from the window.

"You remember that Will Smith zombie movie with the mannequins?" she asked.

"Yeah." He grunted. "I was thinking the same thing. It's even creepier in real life. I'm on my way out. Hold tight."

"Thanks. And Joel, I'm sorry I dragged you into this mess."

"Are you confessing to putting mannequins in either of our yards?"

"No, of course not."

"Then you don't need to apologize. See you soon."

He hung up before she could argue.

———

Larry was grinning when he got out of his SUV. "I've transported some real sketchy characters, but this is a whole new level. One of them fell over when I rounded the curve, and I about crapped my pants thinking it was alive." His round face was pink from trying to hold back laughter.

Joel snorted. "Try waking up in the middle of the night to find one on your lawn."

The mannequins did look unsettlingly like people sitting in the back of Larry's Yukon. He'd come out to Val's to meet Joel and then had followed him back to his house to pick up the other one.

Now they stood outside Brett Rogers' house. There wasn't room to park in the driveway because a tarped piece of machinery, piles of lumber, and an old refrigerator took up half the space. So they'd parked both vehicles on the shoulder of the county highway and walked in.

The scene depicting Val, Joel, and Jordan hadn't changed. The mannequins in Larry's car weren't the same ones.

Blackberries crept in around the edges of the yard, and the whole area smelled of decay. Joel approached the door, stepping over a damp pile of newspapers littered with spruce needles and moss, Larry's heavy tread on the steps behind him. A plastic chair sat next to the door with a pile of cigarette butts in a ceramic bowl. The button for the doorbell was missing, exposing a thin piece of metal and a red wire, so Joel knocked hard on the door.

A camera pointing Joel's direction sat under the

cave, and he spotted a larger one higher up in the giant spruce. He wondered how many others he couldn't see.

When the door opened, Brett Rogers looked past Joel to Larry.

"Why are you on my porch, Deputy? I told you yesterday, I didn't have nothing to do with taking pictures of that kid."

"Mr. Rogers, I'm Joel Ramirez of the Wallace County Sheriff's Office and—"

"Oh I know exactly who you are. I'll tell you the same thing I told your girlfriend. I haven't committed no crime. You have no business being here."

"We're here to ask you some questions, that's all. Let's start with where you were last night between the hours of ten p.m. and four thirty a.m."

"That's none of your business. I don't have to answer any of your questions." He wiped at his nose with the sleeve of his shirt. A few days' stubble grew on his jaw, more gray than the hair on his head.

"Mr. Rogers, one of your mannequins showed up on Mrs. Fisher's lawn the day after Deputy Shelton questioned you regarding a threat made against her daughter. How do you explain that?"

"You can't prove it was mine. And you can't prove I put it there. Maybe someone stole it from me."

"Have you had any mannequins stolen?"

"It just so happens I did. But I didn't file a report because I know how you police are. You'll use any excuse to get up in my business."

"I notice you've got some cameras. If we could take a look at the video footage, that would help us identify who took your mannequins and possibly find who's threatening Mrs. Fisher's daughter."

"Nope. I do not consent to that. And I know my Fourth Amendment rights so you can't take it without my permission."

At this, Larry stepped forward. "Look, Brett. I know you like your privacy, and you're not thrilled when we come knocking at your door. But like I told you yesterday, the sooner we can eliminate you from our investigation, the closer we get to finding who's actually responsible. If you have potential evidence that could help us find the real perpetrators, it would be in your best interest to share that with us."

Brett's face was impassive.

"You say you have a couple of my mannequins? Let me take a look at 'em."

He lit a cigarette as he followed them out to the Yukon. Larry hauled out the mannequins and rested them against the fence.

"Yep. That's Dave and Phoebe. They went missing a few days ago. Thanks for returning my property, Deputies. I think this concludes our business for the day."

"Who do you think took them?" Joel asked. "If you caught them on video you must have some idea."

"It was a dark night. Couldn't see much."

"If you'd let us take a look at the recording, we might be able to—"

"Not gonna happen. Now, I'll ask you to leave my property before I call your Internal Affairs and make a complaint."

Joel exchanged a look with Larry.

"You heard the man," Larry said. "Let's go. Thanks for your time, Brett. It's been a pleasure as always."

Brett stood by his mannequins and watched them until they'd driven away.

Joel called Larry as they drove into town. "What do you think? Any chance someone else planted those mannequins?"

Larry scoffed. "Not hardly. This is exactly the kind of stunt Brett would pull. My worry is that he'll see this as an escalation. It should help that we returned them to him. But he loves a challenge, and if he thinks Val threw down a gauntlet, this won't be the last we hear from him."

"He's not a violent offender, and it's been over ten years since his conviction. It doesn't fit that he would suddenly risk everything with dramatic grandstanding."

"I agree. If he wanted to hurt Abby, he wouldn't advertise it. And this mannequin stunt guaranteed we'd shine the spotlight on him. I don't think he's that stupid."

"Me neither."

Joel checked the clock and headed to the elementary school. School would be letting out in a while, and he wanted to have eyes on the building when Eileen picked up Abby. He parked at the baseball field where he could get a good view of both entrances to the school. The normal sounds of production drifted across the road from the mill. There weren't any picketers today, and he wondered if Kevin had finally reached an agreement with the union. Two weeks without work could mean financial disaster for some of the families in this community. They had to be pretty motivated to put an end to it.

While he waited, he pulled up the digital copies of the pictures that had been left for Val. He'd taken photos with his work phone and now got out of his car, trying to figure out where the photographer had been standing when they'd taken the ones at the school.

They were more angled than he'd realized. Now that he was standing there in person, he was certain there was no way the pictures could have been taken from this side of the road.

The photographer had to have been standing across the street at the mill.

Joel made a quick call to Kevin. "Can I get your permission to look around the mill property?"

"Sure. Why do you ask?"

"It's for another case. It should only take a minute."

Joel jogged across the road and headed into the wild areas surrounding the plant.

He continued checking his phone as he walked. It wasn't perfect, but finally he thought he got to the point where the photographer would have been at the right angle to take a picture of the school. He snapped a photo with his phone and compared the two. Not quite. The photographer must have been further up the hill, which meant they probably had a powerful zoom.

Joel walked it slowly, checking the photo occasion-ally to make sure he wasn't getting off track. As he moved further up the hill and entered the cover of trees, the long grass was replaced with native brush. Joel stopped near a tall stump and turned. The school was still visible, and now Kevin's office window was in view.

Had both the shooter and the photographer stood in this same spot? The stump could have even been used to steady a camera or a rifle. Joel tested it with his own phone, taking pictures of both targets.

Was it a coincidence? Or could the shooter and the photographer be working together? Or even be one and the same?

Joel took pictures of the stump and its mossy surface, then crouched to better examine the surrounding area. That's when he saw it. A hint of bright emerald against the dark shades of green and brown on the forest floor.

A can of Skoal tobacco.

It was a common enough brand, but he had recently seen one like this in the hands of Mason Pearson. And since the area had been thoroughly searched after the shooting, it could have only been left there recently.

As he walked back to his car for an evidence kit, he called Marnie and told her what he'd found.

"Please tell me you have a warrant," she said.

"Kevin gave me permission, but I'll call the DA's office as soon as I get off the phone."

"Good. I'm coming down there and will bring some help. I've been meaning to call you anyway because we found the contractor, and boy did he have a truckload of dirt to share."

"Like what?"

"According to him, Kevin kept racking up the

invoices, putting off making payments for months. It was making him nervous because he had to pay his subcontractors, right? Then—in early July, mind you—his good buddy Mason tells him he just found out from his sister that Kevin has a big gambling problem and has been siphoning off the construction loan to pay his gambling debts."

Joel looked back toward the mill. "So Mason's riled up and picks a fight with him over the fourth? That explains why Kevin wanted to keep it quiet."

"Actually, he said Kevin started it because he was mad at Mason for telling his contractor. Jason quit after Mason warned him about it, and things came to a head at the softball game. Of course, this is all Jason's version. We won't be able to verify it until we get those records."

"Surely he realizes the construction loan will need to be repaid. What's he going to do then?"

"You looked into the mill's books already, right? Anything look out of place?"

"No, but it was pretty cursory. I can take a closer look, but it'll take time. The thing I don't understand is, how does Abby fit into this? If Mason was on that hill—if he's the one who took those pictures—what does it mean?"

"Hmm...that's a whole other puzzle, isn't it? But if there's a connection, we'll find it."

Joel wanted to be confident, but he felt like he was missing something. What possible connection could there be between Val and Kevin Donovan's gambling addiction? On the other hand, it seemed an unlikely

CAREN HAHN

coincidence that whoever took those pictures of Abby just happened to choose the same location as the mill shooter. And if it wasn't a coincidence, that meant the pictures of Abby weren't a simple prank. They were sent by someone with an intent to kill.

23

LOADING the last of the groceries into the back of her Prius, Val sent a quick text to Eileen.

Finished up and heading back.

Eileen replied with a thumbs up.

When Val had picked up her car the day before, she'd been surprised to discover that Joel had arranged with Mike at the garage to install her new tire before she got it back. He'd acted like it was a small thing, but she'd been so relieved that a simple "thank you" had felt inadequate. Now she found herself doing a circuit of the car to check all four tires before driving anywhere.

Val's mom called just as she was getting ready to start the ignition. She tossed her purse and a file folder stuffed with paperwork on the passenger seat and answered.

"Hi Mom."

"How's my birthday girl?"

Oh, right.

With everything else going on, Val had pushed it to the back of her mind.

"Uh, I'm good. Just finished running some errands and am on my way to pick up Abby."

The setting sun was brushing the top of the fir trees crowning the hill behind Walmart. Val glanced at the clock.

"Did you do anything fun?"

"Well, I did take the afternoon off so I could come up to Pineview and get a whole boatload of paperwork notarized, copied, and overnighted to my divorce lawyer. Yay adulting!" she said in mock celebration.

"Oh Val. I wish I were there to take you out to dinner. You need someone to spoil you on your birthday; I don't care how old you are."

Val thought back to her birthday last year. Jordan had surprised her with diamond earrings and a weekend trip to New York City.

"I've had enough spoiling to last a lifetime. Thanks, though. I wish you were here too."

"So, you found a lawyer then?"

"Yeah, it's that one I was telling you about. She was able to make room for me after all, so that's good."

"The one in Medford?"

"Her main office is in Medford, but she comes to Pineview once a month, and we can do a lot over the phone. I think it'll work."

Marcene hadn't balked when Val told her who her husband was. She'd immediately launched into a list of do's and don'ts as if she'd worked with cases like this her whole career.

"Are you holding up all right?" Her mom's voice sounded weaker than Val liked, but maybe that was just the connection. "How is Abby doing?"

Val reached in her purse for a granola bar. It was late, and she'd skipped dinner. She didn't want to get in the habit of skipping meals, even though she'd had little appetite lately.

"You know, it's hard, but we're managing. I actually need to go so I can pick her up from Eileen's."

"Okay, I don't want to keep you. Just wanted to remind you how special you are and how glad I am that you're mine."

"Thanks, Mom."

Somehow Val felt sadder when she hung up. It would have been better if she hadn't remembered it was her birthday. She'd severed so many friendships over the past eight months that she had no group of girlfriends to go to lunch and commiserate about turning the big three-oh. She wasn't on social media anymore, so there would be no public outpouring of memes and emojis. Her relationship with Maddie wasn't what it used to be, and the vibe she got from Maddie's husband made her want to keep them both at a distance.

She needed friends.

Then, of course, there was Joel. They'd both been so busy that she hadn't thought to mention it. Would his feelings be hurt when he found out? Probably best not to say anything.

Dusk settled over the fields and forests as she exited

the freeway and took the highway to Owl Creek. It ran along the river, and the tight curves were as familiar to her as her address. She'd learned to drive on this road and knew exactly how much to brake and when to accelerate out of the curve.

The river ran below her on the right, black in the night except for the occasional gray boulders breaking through the surface. It was still running low and wouldn't be full again until after weeks of steady autumn rain.

A big pickup truck filled her rearview mirror, its headlights illuminating the interior of her car. She tapped her brakes lightly, warning him to back off.

At the next straight section of road, the driver swerved into the other lane and accelerated in a loud roar to pass her. As if to solidify the display of testosterone, a pair of fake testicles swung from the trailer hitch.

Val shook her head as the truck pulled in front of her, coughing a thick cloud of diesel exhaust. She might have grown up here, but there were some things she still didn't understand.

Just before it reached the next curve, the truck braked hard, the back end fishtailing and leaving a trail of rubber.

Val had only a split second to react.

She slammed on her brakes, but the tailgate was coming at her fast.

She swerved to the narrow shoulder and clipped the truck's rear wheel, which sent her spinning off the road. Bushes and trees whipped past and she scarcely registered the drop-off before the car lurched beneath her and fell into open space.

"Don't stay too late," Kim warned as she poked her head into Joel's office.

Joel looked away from his computer screen and blinked to clear his vision. "I've gotta finish this affidavit for the judge."

"Is that for a search warrant for Mason Pearson? You think you'll execute it tonight?"

"If I can. I'll let you know."

"I don't think it's a great idea to be here by yourself."

She had a point. Lately more and more protestors hadn't been going home in the evening—and the ones who stayed were fueled by alcohol and a desire for trouble.

"I won't be too much longer," he promised.

"Good. I don't want to get a call from you that you're trying to stop a brawl or something like that."

She disappeared, then reappeared a moment later.

"But actually, do call if you need to."

Joel smiled. "Will do."

When Kim shut the door, the building settled into a heavy, empty silence broken only by the radio crackling periodically in the corner. If Mason had something to do with the threat against Abby, that completely changed the direction of the investigation. The notes on Jordan's victims sat untouched on his desk while he pursued this new lead.

He texted Val a recent picture of Mason.

Have you had any interactions with Mason Pearson recently?

Over the radio he heard a call for a response to an auto accident and Kim's reply. The fire department alarm wailed down the block, sounding mournful as it echoed through the dark streets. It was a carryover from an earlier age, before pagers and cell phones, when the volunteer firefighters needed to be summoned from all over the town.

There was no response from Val, so he went back to the affidavit.

The fire alarm droned to a stop, and in the silence that followed Joel heard the distinctive sound of breaking glass followed by a cackle of laughter.

Joel's pulse accelerated, and he quickly closed his laptop to help his eyes adjust to the darkness.

He moved almost silently to the door of his office, listening for any movement in the other room. There was nothing.

His heart raced, and a detached part of him recognized it was probably in response to that day in Kevin's office. But knowing it didn't change a thing.

He peered into the other room and in the dim security light saw a large rock on the floor surrounded by broken glass. It was smooth and the size of a loaf of bread and looked like it belonged with the landscaping used at City Hall.

A siren accompanied red and white lights strobing through the window as the fire engine passed outside.

Shapes moved in the parking lot outside, letting out a peal of laughter as they ran away.

Joel swore and returned to his office for his radio. Before he could make the call, his phone rang.

"Joel!" Kim sounded breathless, like she'd run up a flight of stairs. "You'd better get out here."

"What's up? We just got a rock through the front door."

"We can deal with that later. Get your butt over here now."

"What's going on?"

"Sir, get out of the road!" Kim yelled to someone on her end. "I'm getting flares now. We'll wait for the fire department."

"What've you got, Kim?" Joel asked.

"Brian's on his way," she said, panting again like she was exerting herself. "Boone Road. Mile marker two."

She hung up without another word.

Joel grabbed his keys and left the building to find two men eyeing his Charger, faces hidden behind thick beards. One of them was urinating on the driver side door.

Joel paused.

"That's enough. Step away from the car," he warned.

Their faces were haggard under the streetlight. He didn't recognize them, but Joel had seen that look before, the thin haunted face of a user.

One of them raised his hands. "You're that trigger-happy cop, ain't you? Watch out," he said to his friend in a mocking tone, "this guy'll put a bullet in your head faster'n you can spit."

"You need to move away from the car. Now."

"Or what?" The other man wore a hoodie that cast his face in shadow, making his eyes deep holes of black. "Whachu gonna do if we don't?"

"I'll have to walk home."

"That it?" The first one laughed.

"Walking's good exercise," the second one said, his eyes on Joel.

"I agree. But a few minutes ago there was a car accident outside of town, and the responding deputy needs some help. It might be one of your friends. It might even be your grandma. The longer you mess around, the longer it'll be before the deputy out there gets the help she needs. And if she can't do her job, guess what happens to your grandma?"

The two men looked at each other.

"Whatever," the second one said as he moved away from the Charger. After a long pause to size up Joel, his friend followed.

Joel waited until they'd rounded the corner before he went to the car, grimacing when he touched the door handle.

He flipped on his lights and siren and headed out of town toward the river road.

24

JOEL SLOWED as he approached the scene of the accident. Brian was directing traffic in the glow of flares, but there was no vehicle. Brian saw him and stood aside so he could pull over behind the fire engine.

And then he saw it.

Down in the river, a little Prius lay on its side in the shallow water.

Horror crawled like insects up Joel's neck.

He grabbed his flashlight and picked his way down the hillside, stumbling on the uneven ground. The interior of the car was in shadow, and a small crowd had gathered around, obscuring his view.

Lines had been run from the axles of the car to a gnarled ash tree on the bank, and firefighters were working to set up stabilization equipment, bracing metal arms to the undercarriage of the car.

Kim stood nearby, gesturing to a man and woman standing near the rear. The river had carved away the bank, and Joel had to jump the last few feet into cold water.

"She's okay," Kim said as he approached, but her expression was grim. "That couple saw her go off the road and called it in right away."

Joel thought of the precious minutes he'd wasted at the station. "What happened?"

"They said she swerved to avoid a truck. Whoever the driver of the truck was, they didn't stop."

Joel waded toward the windshield, trying to see into the car. Val was slumped against the side.

"She's in water. That's gonna be bad for shock."

"They're working on it. They might need another pair of hands."

Joel went around the car and recognized the firefighter breaking the back window with quick, practiced motions.

"Ricky, put me to work. How can I help?"

"Now that the vehicle's stabilized and we know it's not going to float downriver, we're getting ready to begin extrication. Can you climb in through the back? It'll be a tight fit. Use this tarp to cover her and protect her from the glass while I break these other windows. Don't unbuckle her or let her move. Hold on, I forgot the C-collar."

Joel fidgeted while Ricky jogged back up the hill and returned holding a neck brace.

"Pulse and breathing are strong, and she's alert. Put this on her, and make sure she holds still. Keep her calm; can you do that?"

Joel grabbed the tarp and C-collar, relieved to have

something to do. He crawled in through the tiny hatchback window. The Prius was cramped in the best conditions, but tipped on its side was especially awkward. Groceries littered the cargo area and back seat, limp boxes of wet cardboard and a heavy jug of laundry detergent. He splashed through cold river water, murky black in the darkness.

"Val, it's me."

"Joel?" She shifted in the driver's seat. Her voice sounded distant and confused.

"Don't move. They're going to get you out but you have to stay still."

There was a pause, and then, "What are you doing here?"

It was closer to her normal voice, and Joel coughed out a relieved chuckle.

"Perks of being law enforcement."

"How embarrassing," she moaned. "This water is so cold."

He squeezed between the front seats and crouched next to her, his left leg braced against the back seat so he didn't put any weight on her chair. He swept the flashlight beam over her, and she winced. He was relieved to see no serious injuries. Blood on her shirt seemed to come from a bloody nose.

"Are you done ogling me?" she complained. "That's so bright."

"Sorry." He leveraged the flashlight in the steering wheel so it pointed straight up, giving them light without blinding either one of them.

"I'm going to put this neck brace on you."

She tried to push his hand away. "I don't need it. I'm fine."

"You can't know that for sure. Humor me."

"This is ridiculous," she said, but her speech was slurring.

"All set?" Ricky called from outside the car.

"Not yet!" Joel called back. To Val he said, "I'm going to cover us both with this tarp. They have to break the windows above us, so this will protect us from the glass."

The tarp was little more than a stiff sheet of plastic, and he leaned closer, draping it over them both.

She peered up at him, and a spark lit her eyes. "How romantic. You really know how to treat a girl for her birthday."

Joel frowned. "It's not your birthday, is it?"

"Thirty years today." She closed her eyes.

"Sorry, Val. I didn't know." Guilt washed over him as he realized how different the evening would have gone if he'd planned for it.

"It's okay. I forgot too."

She lay still against the side of the car while the windows overhead shattered and rained down on the tarp.

"We're gonna work on the windshield now," Ricky called. "How's she doing?"

"Good," Joel said. But she seemed so pale, and she was starting to tremble.

A grinding noise reverberated through the tiny car. Val stirred.

"Try and stay awake, Val. Come on, wake up."

Joel's shoulders were aching from sheltering her with the tarp. "Just a few more minutes. Come on, baby. Please, open your eyes."

Her eyelids fluttered open, and her gaze settled on him.

"You're still here." She shivered.

"I'm not going anywhere. But Val?"

"What?"

"You really need a bigger car."

Her smile was followed by a coughing laugh. She winced.

"My chest hurts."

"Hang on. We'll get you to the hospital soon."

The minutes stretched on for what seemed like hours. The firefighters giving instructions to each other. A new noise like a drill out of hell. Val's shivering increased, and Joel fought the urge to drop the tarp and wrap his arms around her to share his own body heat. Finally, the roof fell away, and Ricky shone a light on them from overhead.

Joel tossed the tarp into the back. Exposed to the open air, he felt chilled. He was wet from the knees down. Val's thin blouse and pencil skirt wouldn't be giving her any protection. More disconcerting, her shivering had stopped, and she couldn't keep her eyes open.

From the road above, Joel heard an ambulance siren.

It was another few minutes before Ricky and his crew had cut Val's seatbelt and safely loaded her onto a backboard.

"Let's get her strapped down. How are you doing,

Valerie?" Ricky asked. "We'll get you warmed up in a jiffy. Eddie, have you got those heat packs?"

The rescue team worked with calm efficiency, and soon they were starting the ascent up the steep slope to the waiting ambulance.

"You wanna talk to the witnesses?" Kim asked Joel in a low murmur. "I took preliminary statements but asked them to wait in case you wanted to talk to them yourself."

"Thanks."

Joel followed Kim to the middle-aged couple he'd seen earlier.

"Is she going to be okay?" the woman asked.

"She'll be fine, thanks to you both. Can you tell me what you saw?"

"Sure. Uh, we were driving home from our Bible study group and came around the corner and saw a big black truck stopped in the road and the little car swerving to miss it. She...uh...disappeared over the edge, and we pulled over and called 911."

"What did the truck do?"

"Just sped away."

"Did you see why it stopped in the first place?"

The man shook his head. "Probably a deer. That would be my guess."

"Could you tell if the Prius was speeding or driving recklessly?"

"No, we'd only just come 'round the corner, and it was literally a split second."

The county had a detective specifically trained in reconstructing automotive accidents, but he was usually only called out for fatalities. Thank God this wasn't one of those. Just the thought made Joel feel weak.

Kim excused the witnesses and added a few details as she and Joel climbed the embankment. "There are tire tracks on the road, two sets. One belonging to the Prius and one to a much larger vehicle. The truck stopped real sudden to leave that much rubber. She didn't have much time."

Val had already been loaded onto a gurney and moved to the ambulance. Joel climbed inside the back of the van where a paramedic was taking her blood pressure and asking questions.

"Can you tell me your name?"

"Valerie Fish—Rockwell," she said.

"Are you on any medications, Miss Rockwell? Any medical conditions we need to be aware of?"

"No."

"Blood pressure is ninety-five over sixty," he said to his partner. "Temp is rising to ninety-seven point eight. That's good."

Heat packs were propped in each of Val's armpits, and Joel knew more would be tucked in under the blanket to warm her core.

"Are you coming with us, Deputy?" The other paramedic asked, gaze flitting to the shield at Joel's belt.

"No. I'll follow in my car. But, can I have a minute?"

"Make it quick."

Joel nodded. He sat on the built-in bench and smoothed Val's hair away from her face. In the light of the ambulance her nose looked bruised and swollen, dried blood smeared on her cheek. Her eyes were pinched tight.

"Val?"

"Mmm?"

"Do you remember what happened?"

"Where's Abby?"

"You said she was with Eileen. Do you want me to pick her up and bring her to the hospital?"

"No. She'll be too scared."

"Can you tell me why you went off the road?"

Her eyes flickered open and then closed again. "It's so bright."

"Can you dim the lights?" Joel asked the paramedic.

He looked up from a small keyboard. "Sure thing."

When the lights were dimmed, Val's eyes fluttered open. Her pupils were huge.

"There was a truck. He was tailgating me at first, then passed me. Cut me off and slammed on his brakes. Really aggressive."

"Did you see what kind of a truck it was?"

"Black. GMC."

"You're sure it was a GMC?"

"I mean, I saw the letters G-M-C, so yeah, I'd say I'm sure. He had a set of those tacky fake balls on the back."

"What?"

Her hand fluttered in the air. "You know, one of those dumb things that hangs down from the hitch and looks like a scrotum?"

"That's...that's good, Val. Can you remember anything else?"

"It happened too fast." She shivered.

"Are you warm enough, Miss Rockwell?" the paramedic asked. "I can get you another blanket."

Joel leaned forward and kissed her forehead.

"Are you leaving?" she asked.

"I'll be right behind you."

He clambered out of the back and watched the first paramedic's ministrations until the other one closed the doors.

Brian stopped the few waiting cars so the ambulance could leave. No lights and siren. Joel breathed a heavy sigh.

Kim approached with Val's purse, water-stained and speckled with mud.

"Can't do anything about the groceries, and it looks like a ream of paper is floating downriver, but I thought I'd grab this before the tow truck gets here."

"Thank you."

"You look like crap."

Joel forced a smile. "Does crap feel like murder? Because that's how I feel right now."

"I know. But it was an accident, and she's just lucky it wasn't worse."

"I don't know, Kim. The way she described the truck, I think it might be the same one that almost hit me outside McGowan's."

Kim's eyes narrowed. "You've got to be kidding. You think she was targeted?"

"Maybe. I don't know. But we've got to find that truck."

"I'll put out an APB. You going to the hospital?"

"After I stop at the babysitter's to check on Abby."

"Be careful. I don't like the idea that someone might have it out for either one of you."

The Wallace County Medical Center looked like a parking garage from a distance, the way its Sixties-era architecture emphasized relentless horizontal lines striped with black glass. But inside, it had been remodeled, and the Emergency department featured new carpeting in the waiting area. Recessed lighting had replaced the long banks of fluorescents.

Joel hadn't been to the ER since his days on patrol, and he didn't recognize the two women working at the desk. They didn't question his shield, though, and he walked straight past.

The curtained bays he remembered had been replaced with walls and sliding glass doors, a detail he appreciated as he passed a room where an unseen patient was vomiting noisily.

A nurse showed him to Val's room, and he entered to find another nurse drawing blood.

Val was sitting up in the hospital bed when he walked in, a thin blanket draped over her lap like an afterthought.

"Hey," he said, encouraged at the sight of her alert and talking to the nurse who was drawing blood.

"Do you know him?" the nurse asked her casually.

"Of course," Val answered.

"Can you tell me his name?"

"Kenny de Santos," Val answered promptly. "Ran over my cat with his bike in the fourth grade."

Joel froze.

Val grinned. "Kidding. Joel Ramirez, best friend since seventh grade. Keeper of law and order and rescuer of the occasional damsel in distress."

"Sixth," he corrected.

"Seventh. You moved in during sixth grade, but we didn't become friends until that field trip to the salmon hatchery when Scottie Jefferson got sick and you had to join my group."

"That's true," Joel said to the nurse, remembering.

"Good. Are you her ride home?"

"Can she go home?" This was more than Joel had hoped for.

The nurse stuck labels on the vials of blood. "Just running a few more tests, but the x-rays were clear, and aside from some bumps and bruises and a pretty good concussion, she's doing all right."

Joel grabbed the only chair in the room and pulled it closer to the bed.

"Where's Abby?" Val asked. "You didn't leave her at home, did you?"

The nurse glanced up. "She's been asking that one a lot. She might repeat some things like she's on a loop. Just reassure her, and don't be surprised if she asks again. Will she have help at home tonight?"

Val opened her mouth to respond, but Joel beat her to it.

"Yes."

"Good. She needs lots of rest. I'll let the doctor

know you're here, and she'll see about a discharge," the nurse said on his way out.

"I lost my shoes," Val said, wiggling her bare feet at the end of the bed. "No one knows where they are."

Joel tried to remember if she'd been wearing shoes when the firefighters had extracted her from the Prius. It had been too dark, and he hadn't paid any attention to her feet.

"They must still be in the car. Or swept downriver."

"I liked those shoes." She leaned her head back and closed her eyes.

"How are you feeling?"

"Mmm. Like I drove into a river. Headache. Chest hurts to cough. And look." She pulled aside the blanket and lifted the hem of her stained pale pink skirt. Her left knee was deep purple and swollen to the size of a softball.

"Whoa! Did they x-ray it?"

"Yeah. It looks fine on the inside. Just not so fine on the outside."

"I can't believe you're not more beat up. You must have had some guardian angel looking out for you."

He reached for her hand and felt suddenly drained, like the scaffolding that had been supporting him all night had collapsed.

"Do you know where Abby is?" Val asked.

"Yeah. I went to see her at Eileen's. Eileen is going to take her home and put her to bed. She'll stay with her until we get there."

Joel checked the clock. It was already after midnight.

"I'm so glad she wasn't in the car with me. Can you imagine?"

Joel could. He'd imagined it very graphically in the horrifying moments as he ran down the embankment.

"You scared me so bad, Val." He lifted a tendril of hair from her shoulder. "I know this probably isn't a great time, but I just wanted to say—"

"Stop," she said. "Don't say it."

Joel straightened. "You don't even know what I'm going to say."

"Yes, I do. And you're only saying it now because you were scared I wouldn't come out of that accident alive. I was scared too, but that's no excuse to say something you don't mean."

"Who says I don't mean it?"

"I say. Because when you really mean it, it'll be the most natural thing in the world, and you won't feel all pressured about saying it."

"Since when were you the love police telling me when I can and can't say it?"

"You said 'love'!" Val smirked. "Get the news cameras in here!"

Joel sighed with exasperation. "You know, you might not even remember this conversation tomorrow anyway."

"That's true. It's another reason why you can't say it now. It should be over a romantic dinner with roses and candlelight."

"Stop making up stupid rules about when I can and can't tell you that I love you. Of all the scary moments in my life, never have I been so terrified as when I saw your car in the river tonight. I don't ever want to experience that again."

Val looked down at his hands holding hers. The silence grew long as he waited for her response.

"So…was that it, then? I wasn't sure if you were saying it for real or if you were just practicing. You kind of slipped it in the back door."

Joel sighed and stood. He bent over her, cradling her face in his hands.

"I love you, Valerie Rockwell." He leaned forward and kissed her softly on the lips. She smelled like hospital linens.

"Mmm. I like that. Come here." She slowly scooted over on the bed. "That chair can't be comfortable."

He hesitated, but there was nothing he wanted more than to be close to her, so he lay down next to her on the bed, his back pressed uncomfortably against the safety rails. She leaned her head on his chest, and he carefully wrapped his arms around her, marveling that she was alive and warm and his.

25

Val woke to gray daylight flickering through a box fan in the open bedroom window and a heavy wrongness. It was as if the invisible tether keeping her firmly anchored to time and space had been severed, leaving her adrift.

She eased herself to a seated position, wincing when her chest and hip ached. Why was she home in bed? Last she knew she'd been talking to her mom. It was her birthday.

She looked for her phone on the nightstand and instead found a sheet of paper with writing she didn't immediately recognize. It was wrinkled as if it had been picked up multiple times.

Today is Saturday, September 17.
You were in a car accident last night on your way home and suffered a pretty good concussion. I'm writing down the

answers to the following questions since you can't remember them no matter how many times I tell you.

Abby: She's fine. She wasn't with you in the car. Eileen brought her home, and she's asleep right now in her bed.

Shoes: They were lost in the accident.

Birthday: We'll have a do-over as soon as you feel up to it.

Marcene: I have no idea who this is, but when I figure it out I'll call her if you still want me to.

It's late (3 a.m.) so I can barely think straight. Sorry if I missed any others. I'll be sleeping on the couch so I'll be close if you need anything. -J

That explained the headache. Val threw back the light quilt and took stock of her body. Her chest ached deeply, all along the sternum, and her hip protested when she moved. Her knee was a kaleidoscope of red and purple, but it didn't hurt to bend, only to the touch.

More concerning was the fact that she wore an old tank top and no pants. That wasn't uncommon for hot summer nights, but not if she were having company. Especially *that* company.

The house was still. She felt a little wobbly as she slid out of bed and made her way down the hallway to the bathroom she shared with Abby. Seeing her reflection in the mirror made her cringe. A scab was forming on the bridge of her nose, and bruising caused dark circles under her eyes.

"You are a warrior. You are enough. You deserve to be loved," she whispered to her reflection. She repeated it until she could look herself full in the eyes as she said it without grimacing.

Back in her room, she found a baggy t-shirt to change into and a pair of long basketball shorts she hadn't worn in years.

Why are you hiding your body? He doesn't care.

I'm disgusting. He'll see how gross I am.

Let him decide. You're trying to reject yourself because you don't want him to reject you. But he might not. You don't know what he thinks. This is something you can't control, and it's okay.

I'll skip breakfast. I'm not hungry anyway, and a little restriction won't hurt.

You're going to get down there and fix a nice healthy breakfast because you've come too far to throw it away. Abby's counting on you.

The argument continued in her head as she went downstairs. At the bottom step, she checked the living room. Joel was there, asleep on the couch in a white t-shirt, one arm thrown up across his face and the other dangling to the floor. It didn't look comfortable, and the only blanket he had was the scratchy gray throw that wasn't as soft as it looked.

She paused to admire him. How did he look so good even when he was asleep? Then she noticed his discarded shirt and dress pants on the floor, and the blood rushed to her face. She turned away, feeling like a voyeur.

Her flip-flops were whisper soft on the old linoleum as she crossed the hallway to the kitchen. She started a pot of coffee, wishing for the Bonavita she'd had in her old life. But the simple Mr. Coffee was still going strong, and she wasn't in any position to upgrade.

While the coffee percolated, she looked for something to make for breakfast. There were two peaches left on the counter and half a bag of English muffins in the refrigerator. Feelings of shame stirred discontent in her stomach. This was why she didn't like feeding people. It was one thing when it was just her and Abby, but as soon as she had someone else to worry about she went into hostess mode. And it was hard to be the kind of hostess she wanted to be when she had to stretch every cent.

She thought she at least had some strawberries, but she checked the fridge twice and couldn't find them. She'd bought them thinking it would be a fun treat with waffles. Blueberries were too expensive, but the strawberries had been on sale. What had she done with them?

Then she remembered. Yes, she'd been grocery shopping yesterday, but she hadn't made it home with the food.

Mentally she calculated how much money had gone to waste. She looked for her phone to check her bank account, but her phone wasn't in the kitchen either. Neither was her purse. Anxiety surged, making her desperate. Had she lost it all in the accident? What about the car? How bad was the damage? What would that cost to repair?

She squeezed a pressure point on her wrist and breathed deeply, counting to ten.

"Hey."

Val stifled a yip as Joel walked into the room. In her stress over money she'd almost forgotten he was there.

"Sorry, did I wake you? I was trying to be quiet." Or

at least, she had been until she'd gotten frantic looking for groceries that weren't there.

"It was the coffee. Do you mind?"

"No, of course not."

She grabbed two mugs from the cupboard and handed one to Joel, a cheetah-themed one from Wildlife Safari.

"How are you feeling?" he asked as he poured a cup. He was looking a bit rumpled dressed in the same clothes she'd seen on the living room floor.

"Okay. Stiff and sore, but okay."

"What do you remember from last night?"

Val tried to think. "I remember going to the FedEx store to send a whole stack of documents to my new lawyer. Were the copies lost too?"

"Most likely."

Val sighed. They hadn't been cheap.

"After that I went grocery shopping, then my mom called while I was in the parking lot, and I chatted with her before coming home. That's it."

"You don't remember the accident at all?" He asked, leaning against the counter while he sipped from the mug. He needed a shave, but Val didn't mind the stubble.

"I don't even remember driving home. What happened?"

"You went off the road just outside of town. Ended up in the river."

"What?" Val was shocked. How could she not remember that?

"You were pretty coherent, all things considered.

You said a truck cut you off, and you lost control trying to avoid hitting him."

Val frowned. She almost thought she could remember taillights and the smell of diesel and headlights, but she didn't know if it was a real memory or imagined.

"What a disaster. As if I needed one more thing to complicate my life right now."

"So I guess you don't remember if the truck had any other distinguishing characteristics?"

"I'm sorry, no."

Joel went silent, lost in thought.

Val pulled out the package of English muffins. "I'm sorry, I don't have much to eat. I went grocery shopping yesterday, but…"

Joel nodded. "It's fine. I was thinking I'd go to the bakery and pick up breakfast after they open. I didn't think you'd be up this early."

"Sorry. That couch can't have been very comfortable."

Joel set the mug on the counter. "You keep apologizing. You haven't done anything to apologize for."

Val's cheeks warmed. "I'm so—I feel bad putting you out. What a stupid thing to do."

Joel stepped toward her and slipped his hands around her waist. "I wouldn't be here if I didn't want to be."

She let the words settle over her. *You see?*

He kissed her gently, and she wanted to enjoy it, but the pressure of his arms at her sides reminded her of how repulsive she felt. She pulled away.

"I'm sorry."

"Don't apologize. You don't owe me anything."

"It's not that. It's...someday I'll have to tell you about my abusive ex-boyfriend named Ed. E-D for Eating Disorder. He's a real prick sometimes and likes to ruin the best parts of my life. He's been really loud lately." She reached for a peach and a cutting board.

"Ah. Well, when you feel like sharing, I'd like to try to understand. For the record, you're gorgeous, Val."

Val snorted. With a knife, she gestured to her limp hair and baggy clothes. "Have you looked at me this morning?"

"Yeah. I don't know any woman who could rock the vagrant look the way you do." He grinned.

Val laughed in spite of herself, then winced at the pain in her chest. "You need to work on your compliments. Go back to gorgeous."

"It's true. I would love you even if you weren't half as beautiful, but it's a bonus that I'll cheerfully accept."

Val's hands stilled. Heat rushed to her cheeks and she struggled to see the peach clearly. Had he really just said what she thought he'd said?

"Oh, I forgot. You don't remember last night at all, do you?"

"What happened last night?" she asked nervously.

"Here's what you missed."

He stepped behind her and slipped his arms around her waist. This time she tried to ground herself in the moment instead of worrying if she were desirable enough. She focused on her own physical sensations, the warm bulk of him behind her, the strength of his hands.

His voice was low by her ear, and his breath sent a shiver of goose bumps down her spine.

"I love you, Val. It might not be roses and candle-light, but I don't want another minute to pass without you knowing the truth of it deep in your bones."

She laid down the knife and swiveled to meet him. For this moment she tried to set everything else aside and kiss him like they were the only two people in the world. Grounding herself in the taste of coffee, the scrape of stubble against her lips, and his hands pressing into her sides.

A thump upstairs was followed by footsteps running down the hall.

Joel released her and stepped away, and by the time Abby ran into the kitchen, Val was busy laying peach slices on three plates, and Joel was slicing English muffins to lay on a baking tray.

"Mom! I looked in your room, but you weren't there. Are you okay?" Abby gave her a tight hug, and Val winced at the pain in her hip when she tried to support her daughter's weight.

"I'm fine."

Abby looked her over critically. "Your nose looks all…" She made a wobbly gesture with her fingers.

"It'll heal. Are you ready for some breakfast?"

"Yes! Eileen said she was going to spend the night and make blueberry muffins."

"You got stuck with me instead," Joel said. "I'm afraid I don't know how to make blueberry muffins."

290

He placed the tray in the oven and turned on the broiler.

"We didn't even celebrate your birthday!" Abby complained. "And I made you something during free time at school. Let me go get it."

When Abby had gone, Joel pulled out his phone. "I'm going to need to go into work for a while if you're doing okay."

"On Saturday?"

"Yeah. I've got some paperwork I need to finish. Plus there are some things about last night that concern me."

"What's that?"

"The way you described the truck last night…it was similar to one that almost hit me a couple weeks ago outside of McGowan's."

"What?"

"It could be a coincidence. But if it's the same guy, that means he may have been intentionally trying to run you off the road. Either that or the two of us have the worst luck I've ever heard."

Val stared. "Why would someone do that?"

"I don't know. There's so much going on in this town right now, it's hard to say. But we need to look at the possibility that those pictures of Abby didn't come from someone looking for revenge against Jordan. They might have come from someone looking for revenge against me."

Panic shot like icewater through Val's veins. She ran her hands through her hair in frustration. "Then I have to send Abby away. If she'd been with me last night, what could have happened to her?"

"This is just a theory I want to explore. You don't have to do anything."

"I can't take that chance. If someone is trying to hurt me to get to you, I can't risk Abby getting caught in the middle. But that means..." She took a deep breath. "That means he wins. If I send her to the Fishers, Jordan will get what he wants." She shook her head, then stopped when her headache throbbed. "It doesn't matter. None of that matters now. I'll call Agent Giles—"

She stopped, then turned to Joel.

"My phone?"

"Oh, I forgot. Kim rescued your purse. It's in my car; hold on."

But Val's phone wasn't in her purse.

Joel frowned. "I'll find out where your car was towed, and we can go search it. You might get lucky."

Val shrank. "How can I function without a phone?"

"I know it's not a permanent answer, but you can use mine to make calls before I leave today. I've got Giles' number in there. But try not to overdo it. You're supposed to be resting, remember? Giving your brain a break."

But the way Val's mind was churning through worst case scenarios, she knew her brain wasn't going to rest until Abby was far away from there.

After Val used Joel's phone to make calls to family and work, Joel turned on a DVD for Abby and sent Val to bed. She looked frail in an oversized t-shirt and shorts, and the way she winced when Abby bounced around the room in a green tutu told him she was feeling more pain than she let on.

There had been something so intimate about taking care of her the night before. She'd become increasingly agitated about not being able to remember the events of the evening and less satisfied with his answers to her endless loop of questions—a loop that would sometimes restart before he'd even finished answering the last one. With her defenses down like that, he felt like he was being offered a glimpse behind the wall she'd crafted since returning to Owl Creek.

He didn't like leaving Val with no car or phone, but he promised to check in with her later. As he drove home to get a quick shower, the hum of the tires on the highway reminded him how tired he was. He'd only slept for a couple of hours, and the effects of the coffee were wearing off.

He drove into town, passing the old wooden sign that featured a log truck carved in relief and the slogan, "Welcome to Owl Creek: A Proud Timber Community." Over time the stain had faded, and the wood was weathered and water damaged. A few years earlier, someone had painted the letters for Proud in the colors of the rainbow, angering residents who worried that members of the LGBTQ community were planning a hostile takeover.

Though the city had removed the paint, the irony of

it made Joel shake his head. The town was reeking of drug abuse and domestic violence, but they thought queer people were a threat to their way of life.

As he turned onto his own street, he braked for a dog crossing the road. The skinny mutt made a beeline for a pile of garbage spilling over onto the curb. His neighbor's trash can must have been knocked over. But as Joel got closer, he realized the garbage was in front of his own home and wasn't isolated to the curb. It was spread all over his lawn and driveway and smeared across his front door. Old food, mounds of wet toilet paper, diapers split and regurgitating their contents everywhere.

And then he saw his truck.

Someone had spray-painted PUSS IS A CHILD KILLER along the side in bright red paint. Blood rushed to his head. He parked, and as he got out of the car, flies flew languidly away from the truck hood where a brown pile sat looking suspiciously like human feces.

"I'm so sorry!"

Jemma Patterson slammed her door across the street and ran over.

"I saw it this morning, and I was going to call you because I didn't see your police car and didn't know if you knew. But I didn't have your number. I guess I could have called the police station, but I didn't think of that. My husband wanted to clean it up, but I thought maybe you'd need it for evidence to try and catch who did it."

"Thanks." Joel surveyed the mess and shook his head. "Do your boys want to earn a little money today?

I've got to go to work, and I'll pay them fifty bucks if this trash is cleaned up before I get back."

"You don't have to pay them. We're happy to help out."

"Trust me, they'd be doing me a favor. Tell them to wear gloves. This is a biohazard nightmare."

"Detective," she said as he turned to leave. "They don't speak for all of us, you know. Most of us in this town appreciate your service and know that you don't deserve to be villainized like this."

Doesn't do a lot of good if you don't speak up, he thought. But he just thanked her and went inside. He headed straight to the bathroom, scrubbing off in the shower as if the smell of feces and rotting food clung to his skin. He closed his eyes and let the water run over him.

The harassment was frustrating, but not as concerning as Val and Abby being targeted. He would run the list of every single DLC union member in the DMV's database if that's what it took to find that truck. Maybe it wasn't related to the labor dispute. Maybe it was someone who had a separate grievance. But the incidents against Val had only started after news had leaked about their relationship. He had a hard time thinking that was a coincidence.

He felt marginally better after changing into clean clothes. When he left the house, the neighbor boys were already gathering trash into big black bags.

"Thank you, boys," he said on his way to his car. "If you find any mail or something with a name or address on it, set it on my porch."

He knew it was more likely the perpetrator had

raided the municipal dump rather than their own trash, but it was worth a shot.

He stopped with the door open and looked back at the boys. "Be careful, okay? Do you know what syringes look like?"

They stared at him.

"Do you ever get shots at the doctor?" That was a thing kids did, right? Vaccines and stuff?

"Sure."

"Okay, so if you see anything that looks like that, don't touch it. I'll take care of it when I get home."

"Yes, sir."

His faith marginally restored in humanity, Joel drove to the station. Immediately his cynicism returned. The protestors had given up gathering on the comfortable front lawn of City Hall and now crowded the tight parking lot of the police station. As he pulled in, he understood why.

A local news van was parked across the street, and Wesley Peters was out front, interviewing a man in front of the camera.

A sheet of plywood now covered the broken glass of the station door, and Brian stood calmly in front of it.

Joel swore when he saw the man in the stetson talking to Peters, recognizing him from his days on patrol. Able Pratt was an angry drunk, and one night it had taken a taser to get him to release the chokehold he'd had on his wife. But when they'd both sobered up, she'd switched her story to say that Able was cooperative and Joel had used excessive force.

He thought about driving around the block and

parking at the fire station, but the crowd had already seen him. They knew him now and had their own special chant. It started up before he left the car.

"Cop shot first!"

"Look twice! Don't shoot!"

They swarmed around his car, shouting in his face as he got out. A woman whose son he'd arrested in a drug sting last spring shouted, "Child killer!" A man he didn't recognize held a sign that said RAMIREZ MUST GO.

He tried to ignore them all as he made his way to the building, but Wesley Peters had other ideas.

"Detective Ramirez, what do you have to say to these people from your community looking for answers? Why did you shoot Austin Wilson, an unarmed teenager? Do you still maintain the shooting was justified? What about Carter Millston? Is it true he wasn't armed? Why did you shoot instead of taking him into custody? Is there something you were trying to hide?"

What did he expect Joel to say? He ignored Peters and tried to walk to the door, but Able Pratt blocked his path.

"Go ahead, Detective. Go hide behind your badge. We all know if you had real balls you wouldn't be shooting innocent kids who didn't do nothin' to nobody."

He stood close enough that Joel could smell the tobacco on him and see the black grit in his teeth.

Joel stepped back, trying to keep calm, but his heart pounded and his blood raged.

De-escalate.

He tried to move through the crowd away from

Able, but Wesley was there again.

"What do you want to tell these parents who worry that Owl Creek isn't safe from the police?"

Over Wesley's shoulder, someone waved a poster of Puss in Boots superimposed with Joel's face. The sight cracked his reserve, and he shot back, "If they want a safer Owl Creek, they should focus on doing their job as parents instead of worrying about how I do mine."

It was the wrong thing to say.

The crowd roared, and Wesley paused. His eyes gleamed.

"Are you blaming Austin Wilson's death on his parents?

Cursing himself for his stupidity, Joel clamped his mouth shut and pushed through the crowd. Finally, he made it to the front steps.

"That didn't look too good," Brian said as he passed. "I thought I was gonna have to wade in there and pull you out."

"Maybe you should have," Joel muttered.

He moved through the darkened reception area and didn't stop until he reached his own office. He closed the door and let out a deep, shuddering breath. What really burned him was that these people weren't saying anything about him that he hadn't already thought in his darkest hours.

He was going to need to look back on his previous cases. With the amount of hostility he felt in that crowd, and the Facebook page spreading it like wildfire, the pool of people who hated him was a lot bigger than he thought.

26

A BLACK SUV arrived at the farmhouse Sunday morning carrying two men in suits and United States Senator Jeanette Fisher. Abby ran to greet her grandma before the door of the Cadillac had even closed.

Jeanette broke into a wide grin and crouched down to catch the seven-year-old flying into her arms.

For the first time in the twenty-four hours since Val had called Jeanette, she relaxed.

Val followed Abby out as far as the porch, watching the pair as they were joined by her father-in-law. Charles kept a low profile compared to his wife, and Val hadn't realized he was coming. It moved her to see how their formal masks dissolved so quickly around Abby.

When Jeanette looked up and met her eyes, however, the mask returned.

"Val, it's so good to see you," Jeanette said, coming to meet Val with arms outstretched. "What a lovely property this is. You two look quite comfortable here."

Jeanette's hug felt stiff, or maybe that was Val. She was suddenly conscious of the unkempt grass and over-grown flower beds. The Fisher estate was an immaculate Garden of Eden by comparison.

"Thank you for coming to get Abby," Val said. "I didn't want her to travel alone, and I don't think I'm up for it yet." She was still moving stiffly from the accident, and the thought of hauling luggage down long airport terminals was more than she could bear.

"Hopefully this will be a good time for you to rest without Abby to worry about," Jeanette said, taking in Val's scabbed nose and black eyes. "You know we'll take very good care of her."

Val's heart nearly broke at the sight of Abby's smile. She was sending her vulnerable little girl back to the maelstrom they'd fled only eight months earlier. She would be physically safe, Val knew. Jeanette and Charles had the resources to protect Abby better than anyone in Val's family. But while she was there she would most likely see Jordan and endure who knows what sort of emotional campaign to undermine Val.

Maybe she was just being paranoid, but she really wished she hadn't divulged so much to Abby about Joel and her plans to divorce Jordan.

"Are you ready then, my Gabby-girl?" Val asked Abby.

Abby's grin faltered. "I wish you could come too."

"You could, you know," Charles offered. "We could set you up in the guest house, and you could recuperate there."

But Val couldn't breathe just thinking about being

back in that house. It was better to stay here and muddle along alone than to put herself in their debt any more than she already was.

"Thank you, but I've got work here. Plus we're trying to get the house up on the market, and there's still a lot to be done."

"Oh, you're selling it? That's a shame. Where will you go?"

"We'll probably stay in the area for the time being. My job is here, and Abby is making friends at school, so I don't want to disrupt her settling in."

Jeanette smiled, but it was her *I don't like it but I'm saving my opposition for the right time* smile. She ran a hand through Abby's curls.

"All right, Miss Abigail. Where are your bags?"

Abby ran inside, and Charles and a man who was built like a tank followed. They returned a moment later carrying the two bags.

Abby hugged Val and patted her shoulder. "Promise me you won't let Creampuff eat any more bunnies. And if you see Bigfoot, don't forget to take a picture. Oh, I forgot! You lost your phone."

"I guess I'll just have to draw a picture, then. Good thing you showed me what he looks like so I can spot him." She squeezed Abby tightly and kissed her on the cheek. "As soon as I get a phone I'll tell Grandma and Grandpa so you can call me every day, okay?"

"Okay."

While Charles ushered Abby to the waiting vehicle, Val pulled Jeanette aside.

"Thank you. I'm hoping it won't be more than a

week or so. When the police let me know there's no danger, I'll let you know."

"There's no rush. She'll be very safe. And it will mean the world to Jordan."

Val felt a pit in her stomach at the words. "Please be careful. She's really confused right now. Don't push her, okay?"

Jeanette's smile didn't change, but her eyes hardened. "Of course. I think I know how to differentiate between the needs of my son and my granddaughter."

"Do you?" Val said. "Because if you do, then you won't help him fight this divorce. Help him see that it's in Abby's best interest to resolve things quickly. I don't want alimony. I don't want anything from him for my sake, just hers."

But Jeanette had already closed off. "This is between you and Jordan. I'm not going to get in the middle of it."

Riiight. But Val only nodded. Abby was rolling down her window, and Val walked to the side of the car and ducked her head inside to give Abby one more kiss.

"I love you. I'll miss you. I'll see you soon."

When she straightened, Jeanette was waiting.

"Val, I know it's not any of my business, but you might tell that boyfriend of yours to keep his mouth shut. He's not doing himself any favors, and the press is eating him alive."

She delivered her parting shot with a smile and left Val standing speechless, watching as the SUV reversed out of her driveway and headed down the mountain.

Joel strapped on his vest just as Marnie pulled up. They were meeting in the library parking lot, out of sight of the Moon Apartments. It was Sunday, so the library parking lot was empty except for a minivan sitting in a space near the park.

"At least it's not raining," Marnie said as she got out of the car and reached for her own vest.

"I think it's supposed to start tonight." Joel looked up at the gray clouds.

"Suspect is inside?"

"Presumably. Vaughn and Farmer have been surveilling the apartment all morning. Truck is there and the blinds are closed."

She strapped on her ballistics helmet and handed Joel a sheet of paper. "Here's a copy of the warrant."

Joel skimmed the warrant. A fingerprint on the Skoal can he'd found had been a match for Mason, giving them probable cause for the search.

Brian met them near the ancient cedar.

"Kim's around back. You want me here or with her?"

"Ramirez says you're good with locks," Marnie said. "Stay with us."

In the apartment next door, fingers pulled down a gap in the blinds, then snatched back as if burned.

Joel climbed the steps and knocked on the door, sidearm drawn. "Mason Pearson, this is the Wallace County Sheriff's Office. We have a warrant to search this residence."

No answer.

"Mr. Pearson, if you don't open this door, we have the authority to forcibly enter."

Joel nodded at Brian. The lock was cheap and yielded in seconds.

"Wallace County Sheriff!" Brian called as he stepped inside.

The front room barely had space for a two-seater sofa and a TV perched on a low bookcase crammed with DVDs and boxes labeled by year. A plate with a half-eaten burrito rested on the couch. The burrito looked old, with dried edges hardened like it had been sitting there for at least a day. The shag carpet was stained and littered with beer bottles and dirty laundry, and the air smelled stale.

Marnie started down the hall, stopping to check the bathroom and a coat closet while Joel moved through the tiny kitchen and unlocked the back door for Kim. She wrinkled her nose as she stepped inside, looking at the garbage cascading out of the trash can onto the floor.

"Smells like he hasn't emptied his garbage in weeks."

"That's good for us. Less dumpster diving."

Kim opened her mouth to reply, but a thump sounded down the hall, followed by shouting.

Joel ran down the short hallway. Marnie stood in the doorway to the bedroom, her weapon raised.

"Drop it, Mason. Set it down slowly. Keep your hands where I can see them."

Mason's voice was high and strained. "I didn't do

anything. You've got it all wrong. I would never hurt Kevin. You've got to believe me."

Joel's pulse pounded in his ears. He edged closer to Marnie, keeping his back to the opposite wall.

"We do believe you, Mason," Marnie said. Her hand was steady, but this close Joel could see the bead of sweat on her temple. "Put the rifle down, and we'll talk about it. You can tell us everything."

"It's Puss, isn't it. He set me up. I've heard what they're saying about him. He's a crooked cop."

"That's fine. You can tell me all about it. Just put the rifle down."

"He's lying about me. Bonnie told me what he said. You've got to believe me."

"As long as you're pointing that rifle this direction, it doesn't look too good for you. I need you to set it down on the floor and step away. Good. Yes, just like that. I'm going to come in now. Put your hands up high where I can see them. High, on your head. Yeah, that's good."

Joel followed Marnie into the bedroom. It stank of unwashed bodies and pot. A rifle lay on the carpet near the stained mattress, and Mason stood in the center of the room, his hands on his head.

He swore when he saw Joel. "I told you! He's got a vendetta, man. He's setting me up."

"Sure, sure." Kim stepped forward with handcuffs, and Marnie stood watch, her weapon drawn until Mason was cuffed.

Joel crouched over the rifle.

"It's a .30-06."

Marnie's eyes were bright and determined.

Brian stepped into the room. "No camera yet, but I did find this." He held up a can of Skoal that matched the one Joel had found on the hillside behind the mill.

"So?" Mason said as Kim ushered him out. "What's that got to do with anything? Lots of people use it. I didn't try to kill Kevin. This is a setup, man!"

His voice rang down the hallway.

"Good work, Joel," Marnie said. "Finding that can may have just cracked open both of these cases."

Joel was focused and deliberate as they executed the search warrant, but the questions wouldn't rest in the back of his mind. Loyalty to his sister was motive enough for Mason to want to kill her gambling-addict husband. But what did any of that have to do with threatening Abby?

Val felt a little lost after Abby left without her regular needs for company, food, or entertainment. She was supposed to be resting, but the house was too quiet. And with orders to avoid reading a book or getting on her laptop in order to give her brain a chance to heal from the concussion, she settled on light chores. She'd just started a load of laundry when a knock came at the door.

For the hundredth time, she wished for a peephole on the front door. Although the living room windows gave a view of a white sedan out front, the angle didn't allow for her to see who was standing on the doorstep.

When she opened the door, however, she immediately recognized the woman standing on the porch.

Becca Sheffield was alone. She fidgeted with a pair of thick plastic sunglasses in her hand, and when the door opened, she spoke in a rush.

"Ms. Rockwell, I know you don't want to see me, and I'll leave if you want me to, but I'd ask that you hear what I have to say first."

"You have a lot of nerve showing up at my door. I know where those pictures of Joel and me came from."

"I'm sorry. If it were up to me those photos never would have seen the light of day. But when I couldn't get an interview with you, my editor insisted. And they belonged to *LensFlare*. I had no say in it."

"That doesn't make it better. What made your magazine a little money has started a chain of events that has made our lives a mess. Do you have any idea what we've been through?"

Becca dismissed that with a wave of her hand. "I get it. You can hate me all you want, but that's not why I'm here. Something's come up that you should know. I wanted to go to the police, but I don't know if they'll listen, and I thought this was important enough to tell you directly."

"All right. I'm listening." Val was irritated with herself for taking the bait. She couldn't send her away now until she heard what she had to say.

"I was contacted about a week ago by someone going by the handle reddawn76. He—I assume it was a man, but he never revealed his identity—offered to buy any as-yet unpublished photos of you and your daughter. I almost just dismissed him as a perv, but I did a little digging into the handle. Whoever reddawn76 is, he's actively involved with a paramilitary group called Patriot Pride."

Val frowned. "That's...weird. Why would someone like that care about me and Abby? I've never even heard of them."

"Look what's on their home page as of this morning."

Becca held up her phone. The website featured an interview with Horace Shields and the headline, "Shields to restore peace and justice to Wallace County."

Below it, a YouTube video was titled "Wallace County's corrupt sheriff supports child murderer."

Val's stomach tightened. "You think they're after Joel?"

"Someone is." She swiped at the scrub bar. "There's stuff from old cases, especially the Stan's Market shooting. But some of it's recent. Look at this video. This was taken during the strike. And this one...well, anyone could have gotten *this* clip because it's been all over the place."

Val hadn't seen the clip of Joel surrounded by protesters, but she recognized his look of barely controlled annoyance and thought back to what Jeanette had said that morning about him needing to keep his mouth shut.

"Do you know who he is? This reddawn76?"

Becca shook her head. "Not yet. This kind of stuff is way outside my wheelhouse, but I've got someone looking into it."

"I'm still not sure why you're telling me this instead of taking it to the police. Are you hoping this will convince me to give you an exclusive?"

Becca lowered her phone and flashed a crooked smile. "Nah. The offer still stands, of course. I'd love it if you took me up on it. But I thought you should know. I heard you had a bit of a scare with your daughter, and this seemed too important not to share."

"How did you know that?" Val's tone was sharp.

"I told you; I'm doing a huge feature on the Fishers."

"You knew about them coming to get Abby," Val realized. "How did you find out?"

"Don't worry, it's not common knowledge. My sources are very discreet."

"But if you found out she's headed to Chicago, who else knows?" A stab of panic shot through her chest.

Becca's large eyes were filled with concern. "You see why I thought you should know? Tell Detective Ramirez I'm happy to give him what I've got on reddawn76. He isn't taking my calls either. And if you change your mind about that interview, I'm only a phone call away."

Val took her card without thinking, even though she had no way of contacting her without a phone. After Becca drove away, she pulled out her laptop and went to the Patriot Pride website. It sickened her to watch the videos maligning Joel. After ten minutes she had a raging headache and closed the screen. Sitting alone at her kitchen table as daylight seeped away to dusk, she'd never felt more helpless.

27

Joel's phone rang as he locked his house and headed to his car, ducking his head against the rain.

"Ramirez."

"Joel, I've got it." Larry's voice was sharp with excitement. "The truck."

Joel stopped mid-stride. "Where?"

"I'm in Salmon Ridge. Drove past the feed store, and it was there. Black GMC with hitch nuts and a busted taillight on the right side. I ran the plates, and they were lifted from a stolen vehicle in Harney County back in May."

"No kidding. You still there?"

"Yep. I'm keeping eyes on it. I'll let you know when I've got something."

As Joel backed out of the driveway, he made another mental note to make an appointment at the auto body shop in Pineview for his truck. He'd had no time—he was averaging only a few hours of sleep as it was—and the angry red graffiti stood out like a livid welt against the gray paint.

Just as he pulled into his parking spot at work, his phone buzzed with an incoming text from Larry. It was a video of a man walking from the feed store in Salmon Ridge and climbing into a big black GMC truck.

Joel swore and dialed Larry.

"I've seen him before. With Hannah Quinton."

"Kevin Donovan's secretary?"

"Follow him. I'll see what else I can dig up."

Joel called Marnie Sanders as he drove to the DLC mill.

"If I send you a picture, can you forward it on to Harney County? Larry found a truck that matches the description of the one that ran Val off the road. Plates are stolen, and we need an ID."

"Send it over."

"There's more. I saw him about a week ago with Kevin Donovan's secretary. At her residence."

"Really. You going to talk to her, or do you want me to?"

"I'm almost to the mill now."

The DLC sign was streaked with rainwater, turning the wood a deeper shade of copper. He pulled into the gravel parking lot, his front wheel splashing in a large puddle.

"Hey, before you go, do you have a number for that reporter who gave you the tip about reddawn76?"

"I think so; give me a second."

"Thanks. And Joel, just to give you a heads up,

Larson is spitting nails over you getting caught on camera disparaging Austin Wilson's parents."

"I didn't disparage them. It was blown out of proportion."

"That may be, but I wanted you to know. It doesn't help that Austin's mom died by suicide last year."

"She did?" Joel's stomach tightened in the way it did whenever he thought of Austin.

"That's what the news is saying. It wasn't here; it was somewhere in California. But they're painting a pretty sympathetic picture. It's getting ugly up here."

"Yeah, well, it's pretty ugly down here too. Thanks for the warning."

Joel texted Marnie the number for Rebecca Sheffield as he crossed the gravel lot to the DLC office, the rain pelting the back of his neck. When he stepped inside, he was greeted by his own face. The reception desk was vacated, but the computer monitor angled toward the door showed a browser window open to a news site. It showed a photo from Joel's official swearing in more than six years earlier. The headline read, "Repeated blunders tarnish Stan's Market hostage hero."

Down the hall, a door opened, and Hannah walked out of Kevin's office.

"Hey, Joel! Is Kevin expecting you?"

"No. I'm actually here to talk to you."

She flashed him a bright smile. "Great. How can I help?"

As she rounded the desk, her eyes flickered to the computer screen, and her smile faltered. She quickly grabbed the mouse and minimized her browser window.

"That's awkward. Sorry. What can I do for you?"

Joel didn't acknowledge the story. With his phone, he pulled up a still shot of the man Larry had filmed moments earlier.

"Do you know this man?"

Her eyes flickered to his with amusement.

"Are you kidding? That's Trent. He's my...friend. We've kind of been seeing each other. Well, sort of. It's an off-again-on-again sort of thing. Just casual."

She flushed a little and looked away, and Joel was reminded of Val's comment about Hannah wanting more than friendship from him. Had he inadvertently gotten in the way of Hannah's relationship? Could that be why Trent had targeted him?

"What's his last name?"

"Shroeder."

"How long have you known him?"

"Let's see...I met him after I moved here which was mid-July. Not long."

"I assume in that time you've talked with him on the phone?"

"Uh, yeah." She laughed nervously. "Why?"

"I want you to think really carefully before you answer. Is there any chance that he could have been the caller you heard the day of the shooting?"

She blanched. "No way. Absolutely not."

"Are you sure? Take your time."

"No. I would know, wouldn't I? Huh-uh." She

shook her head decisively. "Why are you asking me these questions? Do you think Trent was involved?"

"Can you think of any reason he would be?"

"No. He's not from around here. He doesn't even work at the mill. He works grounds at Wildlife Safari. And what about Mason? I saw you arresting him yesterday."

"Has Trent ever shown unusual interest in your work here? Or in Kevin in particular?"

Hannah narrowed her eyes. "Do you mean, is my boyfriend only interested in me to get access to my boss?"

"I know it's not what you want to hear, but I have to know. How much does he know about your work?"

"I thought you were off this case, Detective." Her tone had lost its warmth.

The reception desk phone rang, and Hannah answered it quickly, as if relieved for the interruption.

Joel waited, even as she dragged out the conversation and delayed hanging up the phone. When she finally ended the call, she wasn't smiling.

"I need to get back to work."

"Just answer me honestly. Did Trent Shroeder know that you would be working on Sunday, August twenty-eighth? The day of the shooting?"

Hannah tossed her hair back and folded her arms. "Yeah, okay, he did. But only because he wanted me to collect sheds with him, and I told him I couldn't get away."

"Sheds?"

"Antlers. The deer and elk shed them in the fall, and

he likes to collect them. I like the woods, so I don't mind going along. But I couldn't that day, so he went without me."

"Alone?"

"As far as I know."

"So you can't say for sure where he was between noon and one?"

"I know what you're trying to say, but you're wrong. Trent's not perfect, but he's not like that. You're wasting your time, and I've really got to get back to work."

Her dark eyes smoldered with frustration. But at him or at Trent, Joel wasn't sure.

"Thanks for your time, Hannah. You have my number. If you think of anything else, give me a call."

It gave him no pleasure to introduce doubts in Hannah's mind about the character of someone she trusted. She had seemed so sincere when she said she didn't recognize Trent's voice on the phone. Sincere, but not defensive. The defensiveness had only started when he suggested Shroeder might be using her to get to Kevin.

Apparently the thought that her boyfriend had tried to kill her boss wasn't as upsetting as the suggestion he might have manipulated her to do it.

Val leaned against the teller counter and closed her eyes.

"Are you sure you should be here? Shouldn't you be

home resting?" Brandi asked, laying a gentle hand on her arm.

Val opened her eyes and forced a smile. "I'm fine. A little headache, that's all. It's really no big deal."

Brandi didn't look so sure. "I could take you home during lunch if you want. I don't mind."

"It's okay. I'd rather be here with people than sitting home staring at my bedroom walls and thinking of how much work it's going to be to paint them."

Brandi smiled knowingly. "You have a hard time sitting still, don't you?"

"Guilty. It's not something I'm good at."

"Well, maybe you need to learn. Tell you what, this weekend we're going out. My treat. Think of it as a late birthday present.

Val smiled and drew herself up to face the next customer. A man with a dark goatee and tattoos crawling up his neck approached the counter. He wore a denim jacket that looked aged to perfect softness and had a backpack slung over his shoulder.

"How can I help you?"

He fidgeted with the pen chained to the counter.

"I need to make a deposit." His voice was rich and warm.

"Of course. What's your account number, please?"

Val looked up the number while he handed over the paper bills. She printed the receipt and smiled blandly.

"Is there anything else I can do for you today?"

"That's it."

Brandi waited until he turned away and leaned in close to Val.

"Why do you always get the hotties?" she murmured, fanning herself as she watched him cross the lobby.

"You think?" He wasn't Val's type, but looking past the goatee, she supposed he was attractive.

"Absolutely. Did you see those eyes? I could melt in those baby blues."

The next customer was approaching Brandi's window, a middle-aged man with a pronounced beer belly.

Val smiled slyly. "Oh look, he's just your type."

Brandi rolled her eyes.

Val checked the clock and popped a couple more Excedrin. She probably should have been home resting, but she couldn't afford to miss work. She didn't have enough PTO, and without a clear party to claim responsibility for the accident, her insurance was accepting liability which meant she would have to fight them on every dime her Prius was worth before she could hope to replace it.

After Brandi's customer left, she turned to Val.

"So, speaking of hotties, you know I've been dying to ask. You can tell me to stuff it if you want, but I saw this picture of you the other day and you were wearing this white strapless dress and you looked so gorgeous I didn't recognize you at first."

"Thanks..?"

"I didn't mean it like that. You know."

"Yeah, I know. That was a lifetime ago."

"The caption said it was taken last year."

Brandi rested her elbow on the counter and looked at her steadily.

Val sighed, steeling herself for whatever Brandi was winding up for.

"Last year *was* a lifetime ago for me. So. What's your question?"

"Do you still have that dress?"

Val blinked. "That's it?"

"Yeah. Do you have a closet full of amazing dresses like that?"

Val glanced over at Maddie's office door and lowered her voice. "My husband is facing prison time for fraud, my boyfriend is being slaughtered in the press, and you want to know if I got to keep my formal gowns?"

Brandi shrugged. "Let's focus on what's really important."

Val laughed, then quickly stifled it.

"No, I don't have any of the dresses. Anything that wasn't confiscated I sold to get Abby and I through those first few months and pay off debts."

"That's too bad. I was going to invite myself over for a fashion show."

Val's heart felt unexpectedly lighter. "How long have you known?"

"A while. It's kind of hard to miss."

"You didn't say anything. I thought maybe you were the only person I knew who wasn't glued to social media."

Brandi swiveled on her stool and rested her elbow on the counter. "I figured if you didn't want to talk about it, I wasn't going to make you. But now that you mention it, please do share the scoop on the boyfriend. So that's not all made up? I wasn't sure."

"It's…complicated."

"Complicated sounds interesting."

"We're taking it slow and trying not to make a big deal about it for Abby's sake. I don't know what you've heard, but I wouldn't believe half of it."

Brandi glanced toward the windows that looked out on Main Street. "I think it's sick how the media is treating him. I mean, what he said wasn't great, but it wasn't that bad either. They're twisting it into something totally different."

"People hear what they want to hear."

"I just don't understand it, though. I remember when the Stan's hostage thing happened. He was a freaking hero and could do no wrong. And now? They want to crucify him for it."

"People love a hero, but they love it even more when they can turn him into a villain."

"So you have to tell me what—"

Maddie's office door opened and Brandi stopped mid-sentence. She glanced at Val and suppressed a smile. Val could have hugged her for her discretion.

Maddie's heels clicked on the tile floor as she crossed the lobby to the teller desk.

"We should be getting the ad materials soon for the holiday loan promo. I want you both to familiarize yourself so when customers start asking questions you already know what's going on."

"Sure."

"Christmas already?"

"It's late September. They need to get the word out early so customers can plan for it when they think about doing their Christmas shopping."

"Got it."

Val could almost feel Brandi's impatience crackling off her as she waited for Maddie to leave so she could resume questioning Val about Joel.

"Whose backpack is this?" Maddie asked. She bent and picked up a gray backpack off the floor. "Did a customer leave it here?"

Val recognized the gray backpack. "Yes, it was one of mine. He was here a little while ago. I'll hang onto it for him in case he comes back."

"Do you remember his name?"

The front door opened, and Eileen entered the bank.

"No, but there might be ID in it. I'll check in a minute. Hi Eileen!" Val called cheerily as she took the backpack from Maddie and placed it behind the counter. She rested it on the lowest rung of her stool.

"Valerie!" Eileen called, heading toward her. "I didn't expect to see you here! How are you feeling?"

"I'm doing all right. Did you get the message I left about Abby going to visit her grandparents? My phone was lost in the accident, and I haven't gotten another one yet. It's really a pain."

"I did, yes. I hope you're able to get some good rest while she's gone."

"How can I help you today?"

"Gordon and I have had some estate planning done

recently, and I wanted to add copies to our safe deposit box."

"That's an excellent idea. Give me a quick second to grab the log book."

She slipped off the stool, stepping over the backpack as she headed for the cabinet.

28

Joel flipped through the pictures on his work phone, looking for the license plates he'd photographed at the Moon Apartments. Hannah's gold sedan had been parked there that night, but he hadn't bothered to run the plates since he already knew who it belonged to. Now, however, he put it in the database.

Hannah's picture came up on the screen—a younger Hannah with lighter hair, cut short, and trendy glasses. Her most recent address was for Riverside, California. Not surprising, since she still had California plates on her car. Technically she was supposed to update her registration within thirty days of moving to Oregon, but lots of drivers didn't bother until their registrations expired.

Her last name wasn't listed as Quinton, though. It was Wilson. Maybe she'd been married briefly and gone back to her maiden name after the divorce. He did a quick search for both Hannah Quinton and Hannah

Wilson, using the date of birth listed on the California license. Teenage Hannah Wilson had once had a driver's license with an address in Salmon Ridge, but that was nearly ten years ago.

Interesting. Hannah hadn't said anything about living in Salmon Ridge. She'd mentioned that her mom had moved to Pineview a few years back, but never said where she'd moved from. In fact, she'd made it sound like this was her first time living in the area.

Wilson was a common enough name, which would make searching tedious. But if she'd lived here before, she might have connections to people in the area on social media.

Joel typed 'Hannah Quinton' into Facebook's search field just as his phone rang.

Marnie was on the other end.

"Trent Shroeder is just as bogus as his license plates. His real name is Gunther Randolph of Bend. He's got a couple of assaults on his record and was rounded up with some other demonstrators at an open-carry event last year in Salem. But he's not one of the main principals in the Patriot Pride group. His name isn't in any of the stuff we got from the Harney County Sheriff."

"Hmm. Hannah doesn't know of any connection between Kevin Donovan and Gunther Randolph, but she did admit that Randolph knew that she was working the day of the shooting. She also claimed he was in the mountains looking for antlers, but I checked with Brian. He said it's too early in the season for collecting sheds."

"Interesting. Because I just got the ballistics report

back, and Mason's aught-six matches the slug you dug out of Kevin's office wall."

Joel leaned back. "No kidding. Mason was our shooter after all? He must have had an accomplice. The voice on the phone wasn't Mason. If Randolph was working with him, that would explain how he knew Alex and Hannah would be working that day."

"And how Randolph knew to use the nickname. You got casts made of the tire prints on the scene, right?"

"Yeah."

"I'll add the truck to the affidavit when we bring him in. Are you sure you don't have a connection to Gunther Randolph from previous cases?"

"Not that I've found yet."

"Well, right now we have enough to charge Pearson, so he won't be going anywhere for a while. He's not cooperating and claims not to know Randolph, but I think we need to take a closer look at that secretary. She lives in his same complex, right? Mason said he knows her pretty well. She's been inside his house half a dozen times."

Joel wanted to protest but stopped himself. How well did he really know Hannah?

"I'm looking into Hannah now. I'll let you know what I find."

"Do. And keep a watch on Randolph. We don't want to tip him off until we know we have enough to charge him."

Joel hung up and turned back to his computer. He stared at the name Wilson after Hannah's name. Wilson *was* a common name. But it was also the last name of the first casualty of the Stan's Market shooting. The kid whose name was featured on the JUSTICE FOR AUSTIN signs just outside the station.

Joel went back to social media and searched for Hannah Wilson instead. As he scrolled through the results, Larry came into his office.

"Kim's taking over for me. I followed your guy to lunch and then a stop at the bank here in town."

"Thanks. We need to keep eyes on him until I get word from Marnie that she's got enough probable cause to bring him in."

Joel's phone rang, and he grabbed it, still scrolling. None of the search results matched the Hannah Quinton he knew.

"Ramirez," he answered.

Cooper's voice was sharp on the other end. "You don't know how to keep your head down, do you?"

Joel's stomach sank. *Now what?*

"I'm just trying to do my job, sir. It's getting increasingly hard."

As if in answer, a roar swelled from the crowd outside.

"I can see that. Look, I don't have a lot of time. I'm getting ready to head into a meeting with Sheriff Larson, and he's going to want to know that I've taken care of this. I want you to take some time off. Get out of the news for a while and give things a chance to calm down."

Joel hesitated. "It's not really a good time for that. Things are really hot with this case right now."

"Take the time, Joel. It's either that or a formal

reprimand goes in your file. Larson is pushing for suspension, but I talked him down."

"For a lousy comment to a reporter? They blew it way out of proportion."

"This is a political disaster right now, and we've got to calm it down. I want you to get out of town if you can. Take a break."

"But I may have just had a break-through on the mill shooting case—"

"Fill Sanders in; she can handle it. This is the sheriff's call. I don't want you back at your desk until Friday, got it?"

Joel felt jittery when he hung up. He closed his eyes, trying to drown out the sound of the protestors, trying to push away the shame.

This couldn't have come at a worse time.

He looked back over the calendar where he'd written down the events of the past few weeks. The Moyer lawsuit, the shooting, the start of the strike, the protests, the threatening phone calls, Val's accident.

Joel deleted Hannah's name from the search bar and entered Austin Wilson instead. The first suggestion was a memorial page dedicated to the young man he'd killed. A handful of Joel's personal network were mutual friends.

Joel scanned through the feed, then clicked on the posted photos. He found her in less than a minute. Hannah Wilson—the younger version with lighter hair —stood with her arm around an even younger Austin. Seeing them side-by-side, with Austin laughing at the camera, he could see in their eyes a little family resemblance.

He kept scrolling until the name Quinton grabbed his attention. A post filled with condolences for the Quinton and Wilson families over the loss of a Joanne Quinton Wilson—Austin's mother.

"How long will Abigail be gone?" Eileen asked as Val led her to the vault.

Val stood aside as she entered. "Probably a week or two. I know, it's a long time to be away from school. But it's still early in the year and—"

The explosion hit just as Val entered the vault behind Eileen. A wave of heat and pressure pushed her from behind, and suddenly the laminate table was coming at her fast, striking her chin and chest as she fell.

Everything went dark.

Joel picked up the phone to call Marnie just as a deep boom shook the earth. The building shuddered.

"That doesn't sound good," Larry called out from his office.

"What was that?" Brian said at the same time. "An explosion at the mill?"

Joel joined Larry in looking out the window at the rain-soaked parking lot.

The protestors were looking toward Main Street. Dread curdled in Joel's stomach as he listened, waiting for the call to come in from dispatch.

"I think it was closer than the mill," Brian said.

He was standing at the north wall, looking out the window at the back of City Hall. "Look, there's smoke. Can't tell where it's coming from."

The window exploded in his face.

29

THE AIR TASTED of plaster and smelled like sulfur. The tile floor was cool beneath Val's cheek. Dirt beneath her fingers felt gritty.

I'm okay, she thought with relief.

She tried to get to her feet, but another blast rocked the floor beneath her. This one came from a distance. Two explosions? That couldn't be a coincidence.

The keening wail of the fire alarm came to her muffled, as if from a great distance. She knew that sound, knew it deep in her bones from childhood. Help was on the way.

Was the ringing in her ears the bank's security alarm? Or was it just in her head? There was pain like her head was being squeezed from either side.

"Eileen? Are you okay?" Val's voice didn't sound right. Panic formed a knot in her middle.

She gathered her legs beneath her and reached out in the darkness, trying to find her way. Her left hand felt something smooth and hard that ended in a splintered lump.

A busted table leg.

"Eileen? Where are you?"

Fearful of what she'd find, she continued to grope and crawl an inch at a time until she felt something wet and warm.

She pulled her hand back with a hiss.

"Eileen?" She felt it like a gasp in her throat.

If Eileen needed help...

Val reached forward again and this time she felt a shoe with a soft rubber sole. She followed it up to find an ankle and a linen pant leg. There was no movement as she patted Eileen gently, trying to feel for injuries.

"Eileen, it's me, Val. Can you hear me?" Her ears rang even as she tried to listen for any sound from the older woman.

This was impossible in the dark. Why wasn't the backup generator turning on?

"I'm sorry, Eileen. I need to get help. I'll be back."

She didn't know if the woman could hear her or not.

Val felt her way to the wall of safe deposit boxes and used them to ground herself in the darkness as she pulled herself to stand.

A drop of something warm landed on her hand.

She felt her head, following the contours of her face. Everything felt normal until she reached her chin. It was numb and wet. Sticky.

Crap.

She should probably apply pressure but her hands

were gritty and she didn't know what she'd be applying pressure to.

She needed light.

Using the safe deposit boxes as a guide, she felt her way around the wall to the vault door. Once there, she fumbled until she found the emergency latch. But when she pulled it, nothing happened. She'd learned during her orientation that the door was battery-powered and should open even if they lost power. But she pushed with all her might, and it didn't budge.

"Hello? Can anyone hear me?"

There was supposed to be an intercom button on the wall. Val followed the seam of the door, trying to find it, but far overshot it and had to backtrack.

When she found the button, she pushed frantically.

"Hello? Can anyone hear me? We're trapped in the vault. Hello?"

She tried to listen over the ringing in her ears.

"Valerie?"

"Eileen, is that you?" Val's voice still sounded muffled to her own ears, but it wasn't as bad as before. "Let me find you. I don't have a light."

A moment later, the cold light of a cell phone flashlight pierced the darkness. Val squinted and shaded her eyes.

"I'm hurt, Valerie."

"Let me see."

By Eileen's cell phone, Val could see the broken table sitting in the middle of the floor. It had collapsed on the end where she'd been thrown against it and now leaned at a steep angle. Its surface, the floor, and Eileen's hair were covered in fine white dust.

Val made her way across the room to where Eileen sat against the wall of safe deposit boxes, looking at her lower leg. A long gash cut so deep through the fatty layer that Val could see the blood pumping with each beat of her heart.

She felt woozy just looking at it.

"That's good that you have your phone. Can you call 911?"

"I already tried. I can't get through."

"Okay." Val tried to keep her voice steady. "The good news is, help is on the way. Can you hear those sirens? They're coming for us. Let's get some pressure on your leg, okay?"

Eileen's scarf lay next to her and Val picked it up off the floor, shaking it free of debris.

"I'm really thirsty," Eileen said.

"This dust is horrible isn't it? I'm thirsty too."

She wrapped the scarf around Eileen's leg, forcing herself to pull it tightly even though she didn't want to hurt the older woman. By the time she was finished, her hands were sticky with blood. She stared at them, wishing for water to rinse it away.

"I have sanitizer in my purse," Eileen said, her breath coming in shallow gasps. "If you can find it."

Val looked around and found Eileen's purse under the table. She liberally poured out sanitizer, trying to rinse away the blood. She wiped the remnants on her pants.

"Are you hurt anywhere else?"

"My head hurts. And my ears are ringing."

"Mine too."

"Are we locked in here?"

"We shouldn't be. The door has an emergency release so we should be able to open it from the inside, but I can't get it to work. Maybe something's blocking it."

"What happened? Was it a gas explosion?"

"I don't know. I'm going to check the intercom again. But without power, it won't do us any good. I don't know why the generator isn't turning on."

The intercom didn't light up, but Val spoke into the speaker anyway. "If anyone's out there, we're in the vault. Please come get us!"

She leaned against the wall, her breathing quick and painful in her chest.

"Eileen, is there someone else you can call? Someone who could get the word out that we're stuck in here?"

"My son, Jared. You do it." Eileen held out her phone, but even that was too much and her hand dropped to her lap.

"Sure, that's a great idea."

Val hoped Eileen couldn't tell how worried she was. She took the phone from Eileen and searched in her contacts for Jared Marshall. When he answered, relief flooded her voice.

"Is this Jared?"

"Yes?" His tone was guarded.

"Jared! I'm so glad you answered!"

"Who is this? Why are you calling on my mom's phone? Is she okay?"

"My name is Valerie Rockwell. I'm a friend of your mother's. In fact, I'm with her right now, and she asked me to call you."

"Who? You keep cutting out. Is something wrong?"

"Yes. I'm with your mom. Can you hear me?"

"You say my mom is there?" His voice was breaking up.

Val took a deep breath to calm her racing heart and tried again, speaking slowly. "We're at the bank. She and I are trapped in the vault. There was some kind of an explosion—"

Jared cut her off with a stream of curses. "She's there at the bank? How is she? Is she okay?"

"She's okay, but she's a bit banged up. We're trapped here in the vault, and we can't get through to 911. Is there anything—"

A crackling noise broke into the call and she thought she heard "I'm coming down there," but couldn't be sure.

Then the call dropped.

Eileen watched her hopefully.

"The signal was bad, but he's going to get help," Val said, trying to keep her voice optimistic.

Desperately hoping it was true.

30

"How long has it been?" Eileen asked. She looked deathly pale in the cool blue light from the phone. Val had propped her leg on debris from the broken table, elevating it above Eileen's heart to slow the bleeding.

Val looked at the clock. It had been hours since she'd called Jared. Occasionally she could hear sirens, but they had long since ceased to bring her hope.

"It's been a little while," she said, using her best *glass half full* voice that she used for Abby when she didn't want her to know how bad things were.

She went to the vault door and tried the emergency handle again. Still it wouldn't open. Her mouth was dry, and she tried to moisten it with saliva before calling again.

"Hello? Is someone there?"

There was no response.

She slid down the wall to sit on the floor.

"I'm going to turn off the light again, okay?"

The phone was almost dead in spite of her best efforts to conserve power. She turned off the light and covered her mouth with her hand to stop herself from whimpering at the helpless frustration that over-whelmed her as completely as the darkness.

Jared had called three times since Val's phone call. The last time he'd handed his phone over to the fire chief. The connection hadn't improved, but the bits and pieces she got had been reassuring.

"We're going to get you out of there...make sure the building is structurally sound...engineers on the way. You're not in immediate danger, right?"

"Not exactly, but Eileen needs medical care soon."

"...clear some debris...hold tight and we'll...safely."

When Jared got back on the phone he'd sounded angry. "They're just standing around...They say in bombings like this sometimes there's a second explosion targeting the first responders...wait and make sure..."

"They think it's a bombing?"

"Yeah, because the police station was hit at the same time."

A chill had crawled down Val's spine. "Do you know...How bad is it?"

But Jared hadn't cared about the station. "I've got to go. The engineers are here, and I want to make sure they know you're in there."

He hadn't called since.

When the sound of drilling started on the other side of the wall, Val jumped up.

"Do you hear that, Eileen? They're coming for us."

She switched on the phone again.

Eileen's eyes were closed.

Val rushed to her side and patted her cheek until she roused.

"It's almost over. Come on, Eileen. They're coming."

The sound of drilling turned to a shriek loud enough Val had to cover her ears. A crack of gray daylight appeared in the wall next to the vault door and with it a long blade that reminded Val of a chainsaw. Only this saw was cutting through concrete.

She pulled the collar of her work shirt to cover her mouth, trying not to breathe the clouds of concrete dust forming from the blade.

The shrieking saw stopped and the blade retracted.

"Is anyone in here?" a man's voice called.

"Yes!" Val cried with relief. "There are two of us."

"We found them!" the man shouted.

It was several more minutes before the saw had cut a gap large enough for Val to crawl through.

She slipped the phone into Eileen's purse and tucked it next to her body, coughing against the irritation in her lungs.

"I'm getting help. Don't worry. They'll be here for you soon."

Arms in firefighter coats reached for her, helping her through the hole. Val stifled a sob of relief when she was free. In the gray light of early evening, everything looked wrong. Rain fell from the sky where there should have been a ceiling. Open street on the west side where there should have been walls and windows. Where the teller desk had once stood was now a depression in the earth. White and gray dust floated through air, coating everything. Dozens of emergency vehicles sent their red and blue lights strobing over the scene.

Val could barely register that a firefighter was holding her wrist and speaking to her.

"Can you tell me your name, ma'am?"

Val pulled her gaze away from the devastation. "Val. Eileen is still inside. She's injured."

"So are you, ma'am."

Val looked down at her shirt stained with blood and remembered her chin. She touched it and again had an unsettling sensation of numbness.

Another firefighter was climbing through the gap into the vault.

"Her name is Eileen Marshall," Val said.

"My name's Eddie," the firefighter holding her wrist said. "We're gonna take good care of your friend, so don't you worry about that. And I'd suggest you pick up a lottery ticket on your way home, because today is your lucky day. Being in that vault probably saved your life."

Val's gaze went back to the depression where the teller counter once stood.

"Is Brandi okay?" she asked. "What about Maddie?"

Maddie's office still stood, but the door was shredded.

Eddie didn't answer. He dropped her wrist. "You'll want to see a doctor to get that stitched up. Any Urgent Care will work. No need to go to the ER unless anything changes. They're pretty overwhelmed right now. I'm going to give you this tag to help the people outside know you're doing all right."

He slipped a green tag around her wrist then took her by the arm, steadying her as she climbed over curled steel and splintered wood. A twisted metal filing cabinet blocked their path, its side ripped open. As they moved around it, Val's eye was drawn to something flesh-colored resting against the black surface.

It was a woman's arm, severed above the elbow, the manicured nails tipped in gold. She gripped Eddie's arm, staring. Trying to make sense of it. It didn't look real, more like a theater prop than a human arm.

Eddie followed her gaze and gently prodded her forward.

"Let's get you out of here, ma'am."

Figures moved through the rubble, firefighters in full gear and uniformed officers. She recognized the brown and black of the sheriff's office deputies but didn't know their faces. Where was Joel? Larry? Kim?

Someone called for Eddie to help with a pile of bricks where the wall had blown inward.

"Can you make it the rest of the way?" Eddie asked Val. "There's first responders from all over the county out there. If you need anything, someone will help you."

Val nodded distractedly.

She picked her way to the front door, looking in vain for a familiar face. Brandi. Maddie. Joel.

A wall of emergency vehicles greeted her when she stepped outside into the cool air. Fire engines, ambulances, and county sheriff cars. There were cars from

Pineview's police department and a truck from neighboring Douglas County. Some unmarked SUVs she didn't recognize. News vans were parked in the distance.

None of the cars were Joel's. Where was he?

She heard a shout behind her and turned to see firefighters carrying Eileen out on a blue backboard. Val moved aside to make room and stumbled. An officer she didn't know steadied her.

"Come on out of the way, ma'am." He was dressed in black, not the brown of the county sheriff's office. He glanced at her wrist where the green tag rested. "If you could move to the other side of the parking—"

"Jameson," a man called, and the officer turned.

"Hold on, ma'am."

Val watched him walk away and shivered. The rain mixed with the dust on her skin, giving it a pebbly texture. Men and women rushed past without paying any attention to her. Near the collapsed wall of the bank stood a group of people wearing FBI jackets.

Officer Jameson returned with another man in tow.

"I'm Greg Cooper, ma'am. Lieutenant over special investigations with the Wallace County Sheriff's Office. Can you tell me what happened in there?"

A few other officers and deputies were drawing close to hear.

Val thought she should recognize Cooper's name but couldn't remember why. "I don't know. I uh…I was in the vault with a customer and then there was an explosion, and it must have blown the door closed. We were stuck in there for hours. Do you know what happened?"

"Did you see or hear anything unusual prior to the explosion?"

"No."

"Were there any packages delivered today that hadn't been opened? Or an unattended bag?"

The backpack.

"Yes." Val's throat was so dry, she struggled to get the words out. "There was a customer who left his backpack."

"Describe it for me please."

"Gray. Nothing special. I was going to check and see if he left his ID because I couldn't remember his name. But then Eileen came, and we went to the vault so she could access her safe deposit box."

Cooper's eyes were sharp and intent. "Can you describe this customer?"

"Late twenties or early thirties, I would guess. Hard to say. White. Dark hair, and…uh…he had a goatee. Tattoos. I'm not sure how tall he was because we sit on a raised platform. Maybe six feet?"

"Can you remember his name?"

Val shook her head. "I'm sorry."

"Does the bank have CCTV?" Cooper asked Jameson.

"You're talking about security cameras?" Val asked. "Yes. The video is uploaded off-site. I don't know how to access it, though."

"That's all right. We'll find it," Cooper said. "What time would you say this customer came in?"

Val tried to remember. "Let's see, I hadn't gone to lunch yet. Maybe noon? Twelve thirty?"

Rain ran down her forehead. She scanned the people moving through the emergency vehicles and into the building. Looking for Joel.

Jameson brought her attention back. "What's your name, ma'am?"

"Valerie Rockwell. Well, Fisher's on my license, but I go by Rockwell. Can you tell me about my coworkers? Brandi Federow or Maddie Gottschalk? Are they okay?"

Cooper's eyes narrowed, and he leaned in close to Jameson and muttered something Val couldn't listen.

Jameson shook his head. "We can't speak to that right now. But if you'll wait here, we might have some more questions for you."

"What about the sheriff's station? Someone said there was an explosion there too."

"Don't worry about that right now. We have people there working that scene."

"Stay close, Mrs. Fisher." Cooper moved away with Jameson following behind.

Val tried to look down the street, but it was clogged with emergency vehicles. Her lungs were tight like something was squeezing her chest. Someone in a high viz vest gave her a water bottle, and she drank it gratefully. Without fully deciding what she was doing, she headed toward the road. The drizzle was seeping through her clothes, making her shiver. She wove her way through fire engines and police SUVs, blocked by a wall of lights.

The noise changed the closer she got to City Hall.

There were people everywhere dotting the lawn, huddled in groups, holding each other, and crying. Others lay motionless on the earth, covered by blankets or ponchos. Clothes and bags, signs and debris were strewn about as if people had left in a hurry. She could only imagine the pandemonium that had led to this.

Val couldn't take it in. She wanted to be sick. She wanted to run. But she had to know. Was Joel among them?

She made her way around a group of people clustered near the fountain. At the center a man sat on the ground, his jeans bloody and torn. She caught a glimpse of a yellow tag and fingered her green one distractedly. How long was she supposed to wear it?

Before she rounded the corner of City Hall, she was stopped by a man in an unfamiliar uniform.

"I'm afraid you can't be in this area, ma'am."

"I need to reach my friend. Please, is there someone I can talk to?"

"Stay behind the police tape. For your own safety you need to stand back."

Val was sweating in spite of the cool rain on her skin. Her heart pounded painfully, but she ignored the signs of an impending panic attack. She needed to find him.

She turned back the way she'd come, but this time she followed the old City Hall building toward the parking lot. She passed around the back of the block, finally getting a good look at the sheriff's substation.

It had been leveled.

Val's heart leaped to her throat. Unlike the bank,

which mostly still stood, the pre-fab building had collapsed. Two dogs moved among the rubble with their handlers in orange vests, and Val whispered a prayer that there were survivors to find.

Val approached a crowd of people standing near the crime scene tape. She asked a woman wearing a blue baseball cap, "Do you know if they've found anyone?"

"In there?" the woman asked.

"Yes. My friend works there."

"Oh honey, it's not looking good."

Val's breath was coming fast and sharp, like she'd been running hard. Maybe he hadn't been at the station. But then she saw the Charger parked in the parking lot, covered with debris, and her stomach dropped to the ground.

Parked near the fire station was the Channel Six news van. Val walked that direction, unsure what she was doing, but needing to move. Needing to do something.

Wesley Peters was standing on the corner talking to a man in uniform. Val crossed the street and waited until he'd finished.

"Mr. Peters?"

Wesley turned, and she felt a sudden surge of anger. The last time she'd seen him had been at her house when he'd been trying to force an interview.

"Can I help you?" he asked.

"Do you know if...I'm trying to find out what happened here, but no one will talk to me."

Wesley narrowed his eyes. "Were you in the blast? Do you need a paramedic?"

"Yes. No, not here. I was in the bank. I'm trying to find out what happened to my friend. Do you know if there are any survivors?" Did he really not recognize her?

"You were in the bank when the bomb went off?" Wesley snapped his fingers to get the attention of someone standing behind her. "There's a rumor that two survivors were hidden in the vault. Can you confirm if that was true?"

"Yes, I was one of them."

"What's your name, ma'am?" He scribbled on a notepad.

"Valerie Fisher," she said, using the name that would get his attention. Sure enough, his eyes flickered with recognition. "And I'll bet you know who I'm looking for. Joel Ramirez? You haven't been too kind to either of us, but I'm hoping you'll help me now."

Wesley looked momentarily stricken but recovered quickly. "I'll help if I can, but we're getting ready for the evening broadcast. Would you consent to an on-camera interview?"

Val suppressed a grimace. "Okay, with one condition. I'll answer your questions if you'll answer mine. But only about the explosion. Nothing personal about my husband or that investigation."

Wesley nodded. "What questions do you have?"

"What happened here? Do you know if anyone survived?" *Where's Joel?* The longer he didn't arrive on the scene, the more she felt a numbness creeping over her.

"There are conflicting reports of how many were in the building at the time of the attack. I don't have names, I'm sorry. So far there's been four confirmed deaths, but I don't know how many were in the building and how many were protestors on site when the bomb went off. They're still looking for survivors."

Val's throat constricted. "Do you know who it was? Who died?"

"I don't, I'm sorry." But he wouldn't meet her eyes.

"What happened? Who did this?"

"It's unsure at this point. It's assumed it's related to the protests, but that doesn't explain why the bank was targeted. FBI and ATF are on scene now and treating it as an act of domestic terrorism."

He looked over her shoulder and nodded.

"Our camerawoman is here. Are you ready for me to ask you some questions?"

Val nodded, ignoring the sick feeling in her throat.

"Can you turn this way, please? That will get the emergency vehicles and search crews in the shot."

Wesley exchanged a few words with the camerawoman. Val took a deep shuddering breath, feeling a tingling in her hands like she needed to shake off something vile.

Then the reporter turned to her and held out a microphone.

31

"WHAT CAN you tell me about the explosion at the bank? Just tell me your experience." Wesley's voice was calm, even gentle. No trace of the aggression he'd shown when they first met in Val's driveway.

She hesitated, trying to look at something besides the microphone. But it loomed in her vision like a threat.

"We didn't have any warning," she began. Her voice betrayed her with a tremble. She paused and tried again. "I was in the vault with a customer, and the door closed from the blast. We were trapped for hours before they could get it open. But...um...it was probably the safest place we could be. Everything else was destroyed."

"Wow. That's incredible. It looks like you didn't walk away unscathed. How is the customer?"

"She was injured and taken to the hospital. I don't know how she's doing now."

"So that makes at least two survivors. Do you know if there were others?"

An image of Brandi came to her mind. If the bomb was in the backpack, Val had placed it right next to Brandi's stool. The thought took her breath away.

Focus.

"I don't know. I hope so."

"Can you describe the scene for us?"

Val shivered. The light drizzle was persistent and had soaked through her clothes. "It was…unrecognizable. I don't know how the building is still standing."

"Early reports suggest it was a bombing. Did you see anyone or anything suspicious leading up to the explosion?"

Val didn't want to compromise the investigation by mentioning the man with the backpack.

"It was just a regular day. There was no reason to think something like this was coming."

"No bomb threats or security concerns?"

"No. Not that I'm aware of."

"Do you think the explosion could have anything to do with the charges against your husband? A lot of people are angry about rumors that he might be working out a deal with prosecutors."

The blood drained from Val's face. "I said I wasn't answering any questions about my husband."

Wesley shrugged. "I know. I had to try. That's it. Let's get our footage cut for the broadcast."

As he conferred with the camerawoman, Val edged away, disgusted with the cheap shot. It was a terrible question to ask, making her feel responsible for the devastation.

She moved around to the side of the building where Joel's office had been, edging her way through the crowd to the police tape. Lights strobed painfully in her vision. A shallow crater had formed on this side of the building. If it marked the epicenter of the blast, that meant the bomb had been right by his office. Had he been inside when it detonated? Something squeezed her lungs, making it hard to breathe.

A woman she didn't know approached her with a blanket. "I saw you standing here and thought you might need this. Is there anything I can get you?"

Val took the blanket gratefully, trying to be mindful of the dried blood on her shirt. "Thank you. I'm okay."

The woman glanced at her chin. "Were you injured in the blast?"

"Not this one. The one at the bank. But I know someone who works here. I can't leave until I know what happened to him."

The woman wore a light rain jacket but hadn't bothered with a hood. Her red hair was damp and clung to her forehead. "Who is it? Larry Shelton is my brother-in-law. My sister knows everyone in the department."

"Joel Ramirez."

The woman's face brightened in recognition. "We know Joel. Do you want to come wait with us? My name is Nicole."

"I'm Valerie. Joel is my...we've been friends a long time."

The thought of having someone standing vigil with her made the cold and damp seem a little less grim. But as she followed Nicole through the crowd, a shout drew her attention. There was a flurry of movement on the far side of the building.

"They found someone," a voice in the crowd said, and excited murmurs rose, passing the news.

Val's stomach leaped. *Please...*

On the parking lot side, a knot of firefighters were banded together, making it impossible to see what was happening.

Nicole grabbed her arm. "Come with me," she said firmly.

Val obeyed automatically but couldn't take her eyes from the figures. Uniformed officers and firefighters parted, making way for a segmented aluminum backboard.

They reached a woman standing under a maple tree flaming brilliant red, and Nicole tried to introduce her to Val, but the woman wasn't listening.

"This is my sister, Meg," Nicole said. "Larry's her husband."

Val chewed her thumbnail distractedly, heart racing. Someone was being loaded onto the backboard, but at this distance she couldn't see anything more than a wall of firefighters. At last they parted, and the person came into view.

Val's heart sank. Whoever it was wore the distinctive brown of a deputy, their features indistinguishable under blood and dirt.

Meg stirred. "I'm going to find out who it is. Nic, stay with the kids."

Val hadn't noticed the teenagers standing on Meg's other side. She watched as Meg made her way toward an older man with gray hair who looked vaguely familiar. Was that the sheriff? She tried to remember his name.

In a few minutes, Nicole's phone buzzed.

"It's your dad," she said in muted excitement. "He's alive. Your mom is going with him to the hospital."

The teenagers looked ashen-faced.

"You'll come home with me tonight until your mom gets back."

Val tried to be happy for the little family. She liked Larry. This was good news, and they all needed good news. But she worried that there would only be so much good news to go around.

As if reading her mind, Nicole laid a hand on her arm and said, "This means there's hope."

Hope. It was such a fickle emotion. Whenever Val started to hope, life seemed intent on taking away whatever she cared about. If she lost Joel, she didn't think she'd ever feel hope again.

Firefighters were bringing in another backboard. She tensed, watching. She couldn't get closer, but she moved anyway, shifting angles, trying to see.

"Mrs. Fisher." Cooper was at her side. "Come with me, please."

"I can't. Not now."

"It's about Joel," he said.

Val looked at him fully now.

9.

"That's him they're digging out right now."

She exhaled. Waiting for the other shoe to drop.

"He's alive, thank God. But his condition is…he needs medical attention immediately."

"Can I go to him? Please?"

Cooper looked conflicted. "I probably should say no, but under the circumstances it might be easier to keep an eye on you both if you're together."

Val followed him past the police tape and over the lawn, wet grass clippings clinging to her sandaled feet.

A woman in a vest that said ATF Police moved and then Val could see him at last. He lay on his side on the backboard, his back toward her. His shirt was shredded, and beneath, shards of glass erupted from his flesh in a field of red, rivulets of blood drying to black down his skin.

Val moved toward the ambulance and was intercepted by the sheriff.

"You can't be here, ma'am."

"It's all right," Cooper said from behind her. "This is Valerie Fisher."

The sheriff frowned. "Mrs. Fisher. I'm not sure that under the circumstances it would be appropriate—"

"Sheriff, can I talk to you a minute?" Cooper asked.

While he pulled the older man aside, Val seized the opportunity and hurried to the parking lot where they were loading Joel onto a gurney. She picked her way over broken glass and twisted metal that littered the asphalt, passing Joel's Charger that was covered in vinyl siding and what looked like a crushed computer.

They were loading Joel into the back of the ambulance when she arrived. The driver held out a hand to stop her.

"Are you family?" he asked.

"Yes," she lied.

"You'll need to drive separately. We're taking him to Wallace County. You can follow us there."

"I can't follow. I was at the bank, and my car is…" Suddenly she remembered she didn't have a car anymore. No phone. No car. And where her purse had been was now a small crater. She swallowed hard. "Please. I need to be there."

The paramedic glanced at her chin. "All right, but don't get in the way."

She climbed in the back of the van. The paramedic directed her where to sit and showed her where the seatbelt was. As she strapped into the harness, she examined Joel. His eyes were closed, and ash and dust coated his hair and skin. Blood clotted in his hair and ran down his face. He didn't react as the paramedic strapped a blood pressure cuff to his arm.

"You his wife?" His shirt said his name was Randy.

"No."

She didn't explain further but the paramedic didn't seem to care.

"What's his name?"

"Joel."

"Do you know how old he is?"

"Twenty-nine."

Randy felt for a vein in Joel's arm, then swabbed it clean. The pad came away black, revealing a small patch of Joel's skin. His beautiful brown skin. The sight made her feel like choking, and she looked away.

One pant leg was torn, and the skin beneath looked black with blood and dirt.

As the ambulance shuddered to life and the siren turned on, Randy started an IV and taped the tube down with quick, practiced motions. Val wished she were close enough to touch Joel, but the seatbelt held her back.

She felt the ambulance turning out of the parking lot, bumping over the curb, and prayed that they would make it to the hospital in record time.

"This will help with the pain," Randy said, administering a syringe into the IV.

Val wondered how he could be so calm. What was his job like that he could treat this like just another day on the job?

She listened as he radioed someone at the hospital and explained Joel's injuries.

"Hispanic male, age 29. Multiple lacerations with embedded glass. Blood pressure is ninety over fifty. Possible internal injuries."

Val closed her eyes. The ambulance rattled and shook, jostling her with every bump in the road.

"Do you need some gauze for that?"

She opened her eyes and glanced down. Blood was dripping from her chin again.

"Here. You'd better get sutures when we get there." He handed her a clean package of gauze, and she tore it open, pressing the gauze against her chin.

"How'd it happen? Were you outside with the protesters?"

"No. I was in the bank." She felt suddenly weary as she gave him a brief explanation.

He whistled. "Too bad he wasn't as lucky."

Val's eyes burned suddenly. "There were lots of other people who weren't as lucky."

She closed her eyes, trying not to think about the gold-tipped nails resting lifeless on the end of a mottled hand.

When Joel groaned, her eyes flew open.

"Hey there, Joel," the paramedic said, an undercurrent of stress beneath his cheerful greeting. "How you doing?"

Joel moved to roll onto his back, and the paramedic tried to stop him.

"Joel," Val said urgently. "Joel, hold still. Can you hear me?"

Joel's eyelids fluttered open, but his eyes tracked without settling on her face.

She unbuckled the harness so she could lean closer to him.

"You have to stay buckled, ma'am."

"Joel, it's Val." She reached to touch his face, but hesitated. She didn't want to cause him more pain. So she rested her hand on the gurney. "I'm here. Can you hear me? You need to hold still. We're on our way to the hospital. They're going to take care of you. Just hold still."

His fingers brushed hers, and his eyes closed again. He stilled.

Randy breathed a sigh. "I need you to get buckled—"

"I won't let him go," she said. "Not as long as he needs me."

"This is why I should have said 'no.'" Randy shook his head but didn't say anything else.

Val sat hunched forward, her hand gently resting against Joel's until her back spasmed in pain from the awkward position. But she didn't mind. Because whatever pain she felt was nothing compared to what Joel was going to feel when he regained consciousness.

If he regained consciousness.

32

VAL MARKED the passage of time in the waiting room by the number of movies that played while she sat trying to get comfortable in one of the upright chairs with spindly, unpadded arms. No one was watching the television screen as far as she could see. Near her sat a middle-aged man with bed head and a plump woman whose fingers trembled like she needed a cigarette. The room filled as the night grew long, and many of the patients were from the bombing. Val recognized these straight off. The room stank of their blood and their fear.

Wallace County Medical Center had never seen this sort of catastrophe, and the medical personnel were overwhelmed. When it became too much for Val, she wandered the halls and came upon two nurses wiping their eyes and giving each other encouragement to wade back into it.

As the hours dragged on and the featured movie

changed yet again, people drifted away to other hospital wards or to go home, slowly emptying the waiting area and leaving only her.

A nice man in blue scrubs had taken her to a back room and cleaned and stitched her split chin.

Three different medical personnel had encouraged her to go home.

"Get some rest. It's going to be a long night."

"He won't know if you're here anyway, you might as well go home and take care of yourself."

"Wouldn't you rather go get cleaned up? There's no telling how long it'll be."

But each time Val was forced to face the reality that she had no car, no phone, and no friends to give her a ride. She was untethered, alone.

She was nobody.

After a while a receptionist offered to find her a clean shirt from the lost and found. Val wasn't sure what sort of sign the universe intended when she showed up with a Goldendale Ghost Town t-shirt. Val found a bathroom and gratefully stripped off the bloody Wallace Community Bank polo shirt and threw it in the garbage can, wondering if she should have asked for a biohazard bag.

Wetting coarse paper towels, she wiped up any remaining blood and tried to get as much of the dirt and grit off her skin as she could. A deep bruise was forming near her collarbone and her chest ached when she breathed.

The t-shirt smelled like institutional soap as she pulled it gingerly over her head. Her skin was still damp, and goose bumps pricked her arms and neck as she walked down the chilly hallway back to the waiting room. She hugged herself, seeking warmth. Wishing for comfort.

Someone brought her a blanket.

The front desk staff changed shifts.

Just as the darkened parking lot was starting to take on shape and dimension, indicating that night was coming to an end, the sliding doors opened and Nicole walked in. She spotted Val and headed straight toward her.

"Hi. How are you doing?" She sat next to Val and looked her over with concern.

"Hanging in there," Val said. It was becoming her rote response anytime someone asked.

"Meg told me you were here. She came through a few hours ago but couldn't stop to chat."

"How's Larry doing?"

Nicole blew out a long breath. Her hair was lighter now that it was dry and formed a soft halo of peachy curls around her face. "Most of his damage was internal. His bowels and intestines, I guess. It's pretty serious. They're sending him to Eugene. Meg went home to pack a bag and see her kids. I just wanted to see how you're doing. How is Joel?"

Exhaustion and fear felt like a vise gripping her heart. Val rested her head back against the wall.

"I haven't heard anything since they took him back for surgery. I don't want to leave in case they come out."

"Won't they call?"

"My phone is gone."

"Is there anything I can do? Can I get you some food or a coffee?"

Val looked at this stranger who had come looking for her, who had shown her kindness when she could have only turned inward with her own grief, and suddenly found she couldn't speak.

She shook her head and looked away to disguise the tears stinging her eyes.

The entrance doors slid open again, and two women entered together wearing matching expressions of grim uncertainty. Val immediately recognized Estella, Joel's sister, and she would have gone to her but the sight of Lacey kept Val glued to her chair.

Nicole saw her expression and dug into her purse until she retrieved a pen and an old receipt.

"Here's my number," she said, scribbling on the receipt. "I know you don't have a phone, but there's gotta be one around here they'll let you use. If you need anything, let me know. No one should have to go through this alone." She slipped her the number and laid a hand on Val's shoulder as she left.

Estella saw Val first, and her expression shifted quickly from shock to polite civility. Lacey, on the other hand, couldn't disguise her indignation. She looked Val up and down with a distinct challenge in her eyes.

"It's kind of you to be here, Valerie," Estella said smoothly as she approached. "Have you been here all night?"

Val nodded.

"Are you feeling okay? You look like you could use some rest."

"I'm fine. Did you drive down from Portland?"

"Yes. I wish I'd known sooner what happened. It's a good thing Lacey called me."

"I'm still listed as his emergency contact," Lacey said with a hint of smugness. She looked much the same as Val remembered her, though her thin hair was styled in a short bob that made her look older. The reeking self-importance hadn't changed a bit. She wore a wedding band of Black Hills gold, and Val wondered why she was feeling so territorial toward Joel since she'd clearly moved on. But that was classic Lacey. In high school the two of them had barely tolerated each other.

Val ignored Lacey and spoke to Estella. "I'm sorry I couldn't call. I don't have a phone right now, but if you give me your number, I'll make sure you stay in the loop."

Estella's half smile was so like Joel's it made Val's heart hurt.

"It's all right; Lacey's got it. She'll keep me updated."

Val nodded, trying not to grimace.

Lieutenant Cooper entered the waiting area accompanied by a white woman in slacks and a gray blouse and a black man in a suit. Cooper made a beeline for Val.

"Mrs. Fisher," Cooper said as he approached. "Can we have a word?"

Relieved at the interruption, Val stepped away from the other women.

"Is there any word about Joel?" Cooper asked.

Val shook her head. "As far as I know he's still in surgery."

The woman held out her hand. "I'm Marnie Sanders. I've been working with Joel on the mill shooting. And this is Special Agent Stacy Porter from the FBI's Eugene office. I've asked the hospital staff if we can use a conference room for some privacy, if you don't mind answering some questions."

"Of course not."

Val followed them down a corridor hung with local children's art and into a conference room with wide windows covered in mini blinds. She sat in the nearest chair and wished for a purse to clutch or a phone to fidget with.

Cooper and Sanders sat on one side of the table but looked to Porter—a balding man who held her gaze with direct confidence. Val fingered the hem of her borrowed t-shirt. There was a small run in the knit, and she worried it between her thumb and forefinger.

Sanders placed a digital recorder on the table.

"When did your husband, Jordan Fisher, return to the States?" Porter began.

Val looked up. "What does that have to do with anything?"

"Please, Mrs. Fisher. If you could just answer the questions."

"Let's see, I learned about it on August fourth when the marshal called to tell me. She said he'd passed through Seattle two weeks earlier." She tried to calculate the date in reverse but her mind was shot. "Sorry, I can't think what that would mean. Sometime in late July, I guess."

"And you were threatened by Carter Millston on August fifth, is that correct? An altercation which led to his death by Joel Ramirez and a deputy marshal."

"Yes."

"Have you received any other threats or have there been other incidents when you felt targeted?"

Haltingly, Val told Porter about the pictures of Abby that had been left on her car and her accident a few days later.

Sanders looked at Cooper meaningfully.

"Mrs. Fisher—"

"Rockwell."

"I'm sorry?"

"I'm going by Rockwell. I've filed for divorce and would appreciate it if you used my maiden name."

"When did you start that process?"

"Just last week. It took me a while to get a lawyer."

"That's understandable. I know this seems like a stupid question, but can you think of any enemies your husband has?"

"Joel was looking into it. He'd been in touch with Special Agent Giles from the IRS. And maybe someone from the FBI too. But I don't see what that has to do with this."

Cooper leaned forward and rested his elbows on the table. "Obviously we can't discuss details of the investigation. We're exploring the possibility that this wasn't a domestic terror event as much as an attempt against Jordan Fisher's wife."

Val shook her head, guilt stirring as she thought again of those gold-tipped, manicured nails. "That doesn't make sense. What about the police station?"

"It might have simply been calculated to prevent a rapid response to the bank."

"But there was a man, someone with a group called Patriot Pride. I told Joel about him; he used a handle called red—"

"Reddawn76?" Sanders interrupted. "Yes, Joel told me about him. Trust me, we're looking at everything. We've turned over CCTV from the bank to the FBI. If the footage was uploaded before the blast, they'll have law enforcement from San Francisco to Portland looking for him."

"Can you describe the man you saw with the backpack?"

"He was about my age, late twenties or early thirties. Black goatee and tattoos on the back of his neck. He was wearing a denim jacket and a baseball hat. I didn't recognize the logo, but it was red." Val shrugged, not sure what else to say.

"Can you describe the tattoos?"

"No, I wasn't really paying attention. Brandi, my... my coworker, she might have noticed. But..." Vall swallowed. "Do you think he's reddawn76?"

Sanders looked away. "This is a highly sensitive case. In order to maintain the integrity of the investigation, we really can't disclose anything to the public."

Val's thumb slipped all the way through the fabric of her t-shirt before she realized she'd turned the run into a hole.

"Until we know more," Cooper said, "I'm ordering a protective detail on Ramirez. If you'd like, I can request one for you as well. We've got a lot of agencies willing to help out. In the meantime, we're restricting information to the press, so if anyone contacts you, you'll need to refer them to us."

"Oh. It might be too late for that."

"What do you mean?" Sanders asked.

"I gave an interview to the Channel Six news last night."

Cooper swore and looked at Porter.

"What did you tell them?" Porter asked. "Did you mention anything about Ramirez?"

"No. I just told them about my experience in the bank. No one would tell me anything except Wesley Peters. Even you aren't telling me anything. I've been here all night, and I still don't know what happened. I don't know if my friends—" Her throat closed, threatening tears, and she took a deep breath. If she were going to lose it, she wouldn't do it in front of them.

Cooper looked at Sanders. She flipped through her notepad.

"Madelyn Gottschalk and Helen Richardson were both treated at the scene with minor injuries. They were in an office at the time, which offered some protection. Together with you and Eileen Marshall, that is four known survivors. It's presumed that everyone else is deceased."

She spoke calmly enough, but her eyes were full of compassion.

Brandi. Shaun. The cranky loan officer who'd never liked Val.

"What about at the station?"

Cooper stood. "I'm afraid we can't tell you any more than that. Thank you for your time, Ms. Rockwell."

Porter stood, but Sanders held back a little, waiting for Val.

"I know it's frustrating to wonder, but it really is for the best to control information in a situation like this," she said as they walked down the hall.

Val said nothing, but she was doubly grateful for Nicole. That connection might be the only way she would learn anything useful.

A man wearing scrubs and a hairnet was talking to Estella and Lacey when they returned to the waiting room. He made a beeline for Lieutenant Cooper.

"You're here for Joel Ramirez?"

"Yes."

Val didn't breathe.

"He's out of surgery. I tried to remove all the glass, but at this stage it's impossible to know how successful I was. Time will tell. He has multiple fractures, and he'll need reconstructive surgery on his left shoulder, but this is as much as we could do today. When he's more stable we'll have a better idea on further treatment."

Val could only concentrate on trigger words. Time. Fractures. Stable.

"What's the long-term outlook?" she asked.

The surgeon stifled a yawn. "I'm cautiously optimistic. One thing at a time. X-rays and CT scan don't show internal damage, so we're looking at secondary and tertiary injuries at this point. Contusions, lacerations, that sort of thing. Which, don't get me wrong, can be very serious. But a blast like that could kill a person from the pressure alone without leaving a mark on their body. He was lucky."

Lucky. The word was meaningless to Val.

"Can I see him?"

"He's in the ICU and is heavily sedated. You'll need to keep it brief."

"We want to restrict access for his own safety," Cooper added. "Only law enforcement and immediate family."

"Lieutenant, please," Val urged. "I know I'm not family, but he'd want me to be there. I'm sure of it." She felt Estella and Lacey's eyes on her and knew her face was reddening. Was she going to be the only one in the room excluded?

Cooper's mouth pressed into a hard line.

"Lieutenant," Sanders said, and a look passed between them.

"All right, Ms. Rockwell. But if I hear about you giving any more interviews, you're off the list."

Val relaxed. "Fine. When can I see him?"

33

If Val thought the hours had dragged on during Joel's surgery, it was nothing compared to the minutes waiting for Estella and Lacey to finish their visits with Joel in the Intensive Care Unit. It didn't bother her for Estella to go first. She was his sister, after all. But the fact that Joel's ex-wife took precedence made Val seethe. She refused to show it, though, not wanting to do anything that would make Cooper change his mind. She even tolerated a performative hug from Lacey as they passed each other on Lacey's way out.

When Val was finally able to see Joel, she was glad he was sedated so he wouldn't read the fear in her eyes. He was positioned on his left side with an IV taped to his arm and so many tubes and wires threading up and over and under she couldn't guess where they all led. The part of his face that was visible behind an oxygen mask was swollen and distorted, making him almost unrecognizable.

A single chair sat near the foot of the bed and Val dragged it closer. There were so many machines crowded into the small space that she could barely reach his hand. A monitor tracked his pulse with a steady beep.

She traced his fingers, trying not to think about the hand with the manicured nails that she'd seen when stepping out of the vault. His hand twitched in a claw-like motion and she looked at his eyes, wondering if he was waking up. His eyes stayed closed.

"Hey Joel," she said quietly. "I guess the roles are reversed this time. You just had to one-up me, didn't you?"

The joke sounded pitiful without his quip in return.

She didn't know how much to talk and worried about disturbing him with her touch. So she leaned over and brushed her lips against his fingertips. It wasn't much, but his skin was warm and she tried to focus on that. He was alive. For now it would have to be enough.

"Thank you," she whispered. "Thank you for not..." She couldn't say it. Unshed tears burned the back of her throat. Silence was easier.

Ten minutes passed too quickly. When the nurse came to get her, she wished she could do it over again.

Cooper was waiting for her when she exited the ICU.

"Ms. Rockwell, I'm going to have a deputy take you home. I understand you can't drive yourself."

"No, thank you. I'm fine staying here."

She felt panicked at the thought of leaving the

hospital and not knowing about any changes to Joel's condition.

"Ms. Rockwell, I insist. Go home. Take care of yourself. Get some sleep. He's in good hands, and you can come back this evening to see for yourself."

Evening was so far away. But the lights were making her headache worse, and she could barely remember the past twelve hours as it was.

As it turned out, Marnie Sanders offered to drive her home. Val was relieved. Marnie was a soft-spoken woman who seemed to truly care about Joel. That gave her bonus points in Val's book.

As they pulled away from the hospital, Marnie said, "I wanted to chat with you away from Cooper and the others, if that's okay."

"All right."

"I've known Joel for a long time. Larry too. Something like this...it's never happened in Wallace County. It's devastating. We'll be working around the clock to do whatever we can to find who's responsible."

"I thought that's why the FBI was here."

"Yes. It's a federal investigation now, but we know the area. We know the people. It'll be a coordinated effort. I don't want you to feel neglected, but we're going to have our hands full."

"I understand."

Marnie tapped the steering wheel lightly with her thumb as she drove. "I don't want to alarm you, but do you have a way of protecting yourself? You live alone, right?"

"I keep meaning to put in a security system, but I haven't gotten around to it yet."

"Do you have a firearm?"

"No. I was nervous about getting one with Abby around."

"Do you know how to shoot?"

"Yeah. It's been a while, but I know how."

"Sheriff Larson doesn't think we can spare anybody just now, but I would feel a lot better if you had someone keeping an eye on things. I'll talk to him and see what I can do. In the meantime, be extra cautious, okay?"

Val nodded. The morning sun was obscured by clouds, but the rain had stopped. The road was still wet, making the tires hum at a higher pitch. In a detached sort of way Val realized how completely spent she was. Voices came over Marnie's radio, but Marnie had turned it down so the chatter was unintelligible to Val.

"Thank you for advocating for me back there," she said after a while. "I don't think Lieutenant Cooper likes me much."

"Cooper is...he's pretty protective of Joel. We all are. I think he worries getting mixed up with you has been bad for him."

"Since when was that any of his business?"

"I'm not saying I agree." Marnie's gaze darted to Val. "But that comment Joel made to the press looked really bad, and Cooper's feeling a lot of pressure from the sheriff. I know, put it in perspective and it shouldn't be a big deal. But it's an election year. Everything is a big deal."

Val settled back against the seat and shook her head. "Who knew politics and police work were so connected?"

"Unfortunately, law enforcement is a lot more political than you'd think."

As they drove south toward Owl Creek, a black SUV passed them on the left going at high speed. A Pineview PD squad car followed with its lights on.

They exited the freeway, and Marnie slowed as they approached the town. Multiple sheriff vehicles and unmarked SUVs were parked on the side of the road. An armed policeman in full protective gear manned a barricade.

"Should we even be here? This looks dangerous."

"They're just taking precautions."

It looked like more than precautions, but Val didn't say so.

Marnie stopped the car, and a deputy Val didn't recognize walked over.

"We need to get through to Alderbrook Lane," Marnie said.

The deputy moved the barricade, and Marnie pulled forward slowly.

"Do you know who the guy with the backpack is?" Val asked. "He did this, right?"

Marnie hesitated before answering. "You're not going to talk to anyone about this?"

"How could I? I don't even have a phone." Marnie shot her a look and Val rushed to add, "No, I won't talk to anyone. I just want to get cleaned up, sleep a little, and go back to the hospital."

"All right. His name is Gunther Randolph. We think he's your reddawn76. We're unsure at this point if the group Patriot Pride funded this operation or if he was acting alone. He had to have had help to coordinate the bombs so close together. But we don't have any CCTV of the placement of the second bomb. That place was crawling with protestors—some of them Patriot Pride members—and all hell broke loose when the bomb went off. We're still trying to reconstruct what happened. I really can't say any more than that."

"Thank you."

They drove up the dirt road in silence. Was it the headache that made it so hard for Val to think clearly?

"Thanks for the ride," she said as Marnie parked.

"I'd like to do a quick sweep of the house, if you're okay with that."

"Sure. Let me find the spare key."

Val went to the shop and found the extra house key where she kept it in a stack of plant pots. The clouds were beginning to break, revealing a brilliant blue sky that made Val squint. While Marnie did a cursory search of the house, Val went to the kitchen. She hadn't eaten in over twenty-four hours, which was dangerous. But looking in her refrigerator now, everything made her stomach turn.

Marnie stopped in the doorway. "I'll be back at seven to take you to the hospital. Will that be enough time, do you think?"

Val looked at the clock. "I could be ready earlier."

Marnie smiled, making her look younger than Val had first assumed. "Good to know. Plan on seven for now, but if I can get away sooner, I will. In the meantime, lock your doors."

Val showered, washing as carefully as possible and taking stock of every bruise and sore muscle, then collapsed into bed with her hair still wet. When she woke, the late afternoon sun was coming through her bedroom window, and she was flooded with alarm. What day was it? Where was Abby? Why was she sleeping? When her thoughts ordered themselves, they coalesced to one thought.

Joel.

She huffed in frustration at not having a phone and pulled out her laptop. She pulled up article after article about the bombing. The reports were anemic and limited, and she didn't learn anything more than Marnie had told her, except that the feds had performed a search at a residence in Pineview earlier that day.

She saw her own interview—"Wife of Jordan Fisher survives bombing"—and was shocked at how wild she looked. She looked twenty years older with her hair coated in dust and dirt settled into the lines of her face. Her chin was a matted, dark mess. She couldn't believe Wesley had dared to air the interview, but it was trending, so maybe he'd known what he was doing.

There was no mention of Joel or Larry, or any named casualties from either bombing.

After a while it became clear that every article was

giving the same information with a different spin. She put the laptop away and set about picking out the tangles in her hair. It had dried into a knotted mess while she slept.

When there was a knock at the door, Val's heart leaped. She hadn't expected Marnie for another hour. Maybe she'd finished early after all. Val slipped on a zippered hoodie and canvas shoes and crept downstairs. A gold sedan was visible through the living room window.

Val opened the door to find Hannah, Joel's friend.

"Hi. You're Valerie, right? My name's Hannah and I'm a friend of Joel Ramirez." Her dark eyes were wide and intense. "I was wondering if you've heard anything about how he's doing. I tried calling, but he hasn't responded, and then I saw your interview and wondered if you knew what was going on. Do you know if he's okay?"

Val felt a pang of something she couldn't quite identify. Was it jealousy? Just because Joel didn't have feelings for this woman didn't mean that she didn't have feelings for him.

"I'm sorry," Val said. "I'm not supposed to talk to anyone. I already got in trouble for that interview. It's an ongoing investigation, and they've asked me not to say anything."

"So you *do* know how he's doing? Please, I'm not a reporter. Just a friend." Hannah looked hopeful and guarded at the same time.

Val wavered. She knew how frustrated she'd felt when Porter and Cooper wouldn't tell her anything. She knew how it felt to be an outsider when Estella and Lacey had walked into the room.

"He's in the hospital. I can't say more than that."

"So he survived?" Hannah released a loud breath. "Thank you. I...thank you."

She turned as if to leave and then turned back.

"Are you going to the hospital to see him? I'd love to tag along if you don't mind."

Val did mind. "Visitors are restricted, so I don't think you'd be able to get in. I'm waiting for a ride to go up this evening, but even I could barely get in to see him."

"I could take you. I have my car here. We could leave right now."

Val wanted to say no, but the idea was tempting. She didn't know how she would keep herself occupied until Marnie was available. And what if Marnie was delayed? Or worse, couldn't come after all? This might be her only guaranteed chance to get to the hospital.

Watching her deliberate, Hannah added, "I'll just drop you off and then wait for you in the car. I'd like to hear how he's doing, even if I can't see him myself."

"All right. Let me leave a note for my ride."

Val went back inside and found a piece of blank paper next to Abby's markers. *Caught a ride to the hospital with Joel's friend Hannah*, she wrote. *See you up there.*

She paused, thinking of Marnie's warning to be cautious. Adding another note on the inside, she pinned it in the screen door frame where Marnie shouldn't miss it. Then she followed Hannah to the car.

34

MARNIE SANDERS FOLLOWED the mountain road, looking for markers from when she'd driven Valerie Rockwell home earlier that day. Valerie had been able to guide her then, but without her in the passenger seat, all the turnoffs looked the same.

Marnie only marginally trusted her GPS. She'd once responded to a call in the mountains outside of Pineview, but the GPS had taken her on the wrong approach and she'd ended up being run down by an angry prepper who blocked her path and threatened her with a rifle. Since then, she never felt comfortable traveling roads like this alone.

That mailbox with the reflective tape looked right. The road was rutted and washboarded, but felt increasingly familiar. Eventually she rounded the last corner, and the old Victorian farmhouse came into view against the backdrop of the burned hillside.

She got out of the car and marveled at the serenity of

the location. Even with the blackened scar from a recent fire, it felt like a place someone would want to call home. Then she noticed the giant antenna mounted to a metal pole like some Cold War relic and decided she preferred her little house in Pineview where she got high speed internet to binge watch all the historical dramas she liked.

When Valerie didn't step out right away, Marnie headed to the porch and noticed a folded sheet of paper stuck in the screen door. She read through the message and felt a jolt of alarm.

The feds had arrested Gunther Randolph in Pineview that afternoon but were still looking for Hannah Quinton as a possible accomplice. If Hannah had shown up on Valerie Rockwell's doorstep, it couldn't be a coincidence. She opened the paper to make sure she hadn't missed anything and saw that Valerie had written,

Gold Impala
6GBH112

Marnie had passed a gold sedan on the county road only ten minutes earlier.

She ran to her car to call it in.

Val relaxed a little as Hannah turned onto the county road. She had a lead foot, and Val's sore muscles had felt every jarring bump on the rough Alderbrook Lane.

But the asphalt on the main road had been recently repaved, and Val eased her grip on the passenger door handle.

"How was Joel when you last saw him?" Hannah asked.

"He's in the ICU. He wasn't awake, but considering what he's been through, he's lucky."

Now she was guilty of using that trite phrase. But what else could she say? *He was barely recognizable. I wanted to yell his name and make him open his eyes so I could see the Joel I love.*

"We're going to have to go the long way," Hannah said. "They've got Main Street closed and there's a big manhunt going on that's closed the river road."

"Really?" Val looked at her with interest. "Have they found the suspect?"

"I don't know." Hannah's face was grim.

Val looked at the clock and tried not to let her annoyance show. If she'd waited for Marnie, could they have cut through the blockade?

The sun was setting behind hills fringed in douglas fir and cedar when they turned off onto the bypass road that skirted around the town and rejoined the highway on the other side. But they'd only gone a mile or so when Hannah turned onto Skyline Road, the smaller back way leading through the mountains to Salmon Ridge.

"Uh...where are we going?"

She looked over at Hannah, but the younger woman's face was fixed forward.

"Hannah, this is the way to Salmon Ridge. The hospital is in Pineview."

"We're going to make a detour."

"What kind of detour? This is the wrong way."

"There's something I have to do first."

Hannah grew silent as they drove further up the mountain, and Val's annoyance grew. If she'd known Hannah wasn't going straight to the hospital, she would have stayed and waited for Marnie. Something didn't sit right with her but her mind was still moving sluggishly and she couldn't put it into words. So she kept her mouth shut and tapped her toes impatiently in her canvas shoes.

Homes were few and far between up here, and the road snaked along the river. Night descended quickly in the forest. The world shrank to the cabin of the sedan and the headlights tunneling the darkness of the road in front of them.

"I think I'd rather you take me back," Val finally said. "I didn't realize we weren't going straight to the hospital. I'll just wait for my ride instead."

"I don't think so," Hannah said with a small smile.

"Excuse me?" Val wondered if she'd misheard. "Look, I appreciate the ride, but it's not like you can keep me here against my will." She meant it as a joke, but Hannah's response sent a jolt through her.

"Actually, I can." Hannah reached down beneath the driver's seat and pulled out a handgun.

Val swore fiercely and shrank against the seat, but there was nowhere to go. Not driving more than fifty miles per hour on a back country road.

"What are you doing?" Val's voice was strident with fear. "Is this because of Joel? Look, I know you're in love with him, but if you think—"

At this, Hannah burst out a laugh. "Sure. Yeah, that's it. If it makes you feel better to think this is some love triangle, go for it."

Val stared. "Then what is it? If you aren't in love with Joel, what's going on?"

Hannah held the gun with her left hand while she navigated a tight turn with her right. "This is no love triangle, Valerie Rockwell. It's called justice. When a police officer kills someone, does he get justice? No. He gets a promotion. So I'm here to make sure justice is served."

"Are you talking about Carter?"

"No." Hannah's gaze flickered to Val. "Carter wasn't innocent, but he still deserved a trial of his peers, not a trial by bullet. I'm talking about a poor kid who had barely turned eighteen who was scared out of his mind because some idiot made him rob a store and a trigger-happy cop decided that playing a hero meant killing a kid."

"Austin Wilson."

"Yeah. Austin." She said the name like it hurt her.

Val's mind reeled, searching for the right words to say.

"Joel wasn't trying to be a hero. He never felt like a hero, and hated all the attention. In fact, he's really sorry about it."

"He's sorry? My little brother is dead and he's *sorry?*"

Val cringed, her eyes on the barrel of the gun. "I'm just saying, he's not a monster. Surely you've seen that. You've been pretending to be his friend all this time. He trusted you. You have to know he's not a bad person."

"Austin wasn't a bad person either. He was a good kid who was in the wrong place at the wrong time. But he didn't get a second chance."

Val's heart hammered in her chest. "So, why am I here? I didn't have anything to do with it."

"You all did. As far as I'm concerned, this whole stinking town deserves to rot for how they celebrated Austin's death. You might have forgotten, but we never forgot. My mom shot herself last year, and that's when I knew that I was doing it wrong. I'd been trying to put it behind me, but I couldn't do that until Ramirez paid for what he did. And when that reporter published the pictures of you two together, I knew there was a better way. Why kill him outright when I could make him suffer like I have these past three years?"

Hannah braked hard as a deer bounded across the road. Val moved before the thought had fully formed, grabbing for her seatbelt and the door handle at the same time. She pushed the door open and braced it with her left foot, lunging out of the car as it slowed.

She hit the gravel shoulder hard, feeling a sharp pain in her elbow. She rolled with the force, bits of rock tearing at her skin. Pain didn't matter, not with the sedan braking ten yards ahead.

Val scrambled down the embankment, grabbing at plants that whipped and stung her skin. They were wet from recent rain, their cold leaves trailing and clinging as she pushed through. Her breathing became a desperate panting that drowned out the sounds from the road overhead. Blackberry thorns scraped her ankles and she veered to the right, trying to put as much distance as possible between her and Hannah.

The creek lay below her, murmuring with the sound of water rushing over rocks. Val needed to find somewhere to hide, but in the dark she couldn't orient herself. A light shone to her left, sweeping over the bank.

A ghostly shape was briefly illuminated by the beam, and suddenly Val realized where she was. That was the historical marker that marked the bank of the stream where a mining accident had taken place over a hundred years earlier. Which meant the trestle bridge wasn't far, and beyond that lay the remnants of Goldendale.

The steep terrain funneled her toward the creek in spite of her efforts to stay away from it. From above, it would be easy to see her silhouette against the river. She needed cover.

The flashlight beam was sweeping closer. Val dropped to the ground, hoping the ferns and blackberry bushes would disguise her. But her clothes were too light. There was no way Hannah wouldn't see her if her beam got close.

Hannah was still up on the road, but the flashlight was bobbing closer. Val was going to have to make a run for it.

She didn't know how good of a shot Hannah was.

If all she had was the handgun, Val might stand a chance. But if she'd brought a rifle...

She couldn't think about that now. She waited until the beam had swept away then darted out of the brush, heading down the bank toward the creek. If she could get around the bend, she could cross the creek out of sight and might be able to make it up the other side before Hannah saw her.

Suddenly the light was on her, chasing her down the slope. A gunshot cracked overhead and Val flinched but kept moving. Heart racing, blood pounding in her ears, she stumbled and her knee erupted in pain.

At last she reached the edge of the creek. With the water running low in late summer, the rocky beach was wide. Large, flat boulders jutted out into the water near the river bend. She headed for the largest boulder, scrambling across the pitted slab and feeling grateful she'd chosen to wear canvas shoes and not slippery flats.

Nearly blind with terror, Val tripped in a hole just as another shot cracked overhead and the rock splintered in front of her. She pulled herself forward until she slid down the other side of the boulder and into the water, gasping at the cold.

The light disappeared, and Val knew Hannah was on the move. Huddling close to the outcropping to stay out of sight, she moved upstream, trying to keep her splashing minimal. But the stream bed rocks were slick with algae, and the overwhelming darkness made her frantic.

Something brushed against her leg, and she covered her mouth to stifle a yelp. Heart hammering in her chest, she kept moving, hugging the rock as the water deepened. What if Hannah anticipated her direction and cut her off? She could be waiting just ahead in the dark where the trees overhung the water.

Val shivered from cold and fear. She'd have to cross the river sooner or later if she wanted to find shelter.

With blood rushing in her ears, she left the safety of the boulder and waded further into the water. She felt like a sitting duck with her pale clothing, but she forced herself to go slowly, gingerly feeling her way without making a splash. Her shoes were waterlogged and filling with grit, but she was grateful for the protection against sharp rocks.

A few feet from the rock the ground gave way and she sank to her waist, the shock making her gasp. She paddled quietly forward until she felt rocks beneath her again. In the back of her mind a warning drilled into her since her youth reminded her how dangerous the wet and the cold was in the mountains this time of year. Another thing to fear.

She risked a glance to the opposite bank as she pulled herself out of the water. From this distance, she thought she could see the glow of brake lights on the road. Was Hannah in the car? Was she still searching the riverbank? Val prayed she would give up.

She wasn't far from the swimming hole under the old trestle bridge. The shape of it loomed ahead against the night sky. A bank of clouds blocked the moon, but the air over the river was cold and Val's clothes hung wet and heavy. She picked her way to the bridge, looking for the trail she remembered from her childhood.

Sure enough, it was still there. Generations of teenagers had worn the path sandle-smooth.

Val hurried up the trail, shoes squelching with each step.

The climb warmed her body, her lungs burned from the cold and the exertion, and she reached the top out of breath. She paused, hidden from the road by shrubbery that hadn't yet lost its summer leaves.

The water beneath the bridge was still and quiet, and once her breathing calmed, Val strained to hear the sound of a motor above the night sounds of insects and frogs.

Ahead of her yawned the inky blackness of the railroad tunnel. She shied away from going in without a light. What if Hannah waited for her inside?

But the only other option was to cross the trestle bridge, and that would expose her to the road.

The tunnel it was.

Val climbed out of the brush and ran to the tunnel, limping from the pain in her knee. She stayed away from the edge where the gravel crunched noisily underfoot and echoed through the tunnel. Instead, she felt her way over the railroad ties, keeping the steel rail on her left as an anchor. The pungent smell of oil and tar bit her nose, and she put her arms out defensively. A current of air gusted from the other side, chilling her further.

Total darkness made her heart race and played tricks with her perspective, making the tunnel seem ten times longer than she knew it was. At last, the exit became visible as a lighter black than the deep dark of the tunnel. Val quickened her pace. If she could get safely to the other side, she could find shelter in the abandoned church or post office.

But then another thought crossed her mind.

If Hannah knew of the ghost town, she might look for her there. Val needed to find shelter, but not somewhere so obvious. With the tunnel behind her, she felt exposed again. Why hadn't she thought to cover her skin and clothes with mud to make her harder to see?

It was too late now to go back to the river.

Light suddenly illuminated the railroad track ahead of her, and Val caught her breath. The clouds had broken and a full moon was shining overhead. Alarmed, Val looked for cover, but the railroad line had been cut out of the mountain, leaving a steep cliff on one side with an abrupt drop on the other.

So, in spite of gravel beneath her feet and the moon betraying her from overhead, she ran.

35

Val watched the empty church from behind a large madrone tree. She was shivering with cold, and the building taunted her with the temptation of warmth. Even with gaps in the planking and open windows, it had to be less chilly than the open air where she sat hugging herself.

How long could she hide? How long before someone would come looking for her? Without a watch or a phone, she had no idea how long she'd been gone. And no one would think to look for her here.

She wondered if Marnie had found her note. She'd left Hannah's license plate just to show extra caution like Marnie advised, not because she actually thought she'd need it. But if Marnie had been delayed or the note had blown away in the wind, it would have been for nothing. And even if Marnie found the note, she'd have no reason to look for her in Goldendale.

She was on her own.

As the minutes stretched long, her muscles cramped and she slowly shifted positions. The sleepless night was catching up to her, and she desperately wanted to lay down and close her eyes. But the thought of not watching the buildings below made her panic. To keep herself occupied, she grabbed moist moss and loam from the forest floor and rubbed it on her clothes and skin. Anything to stop from shining like a beacon when she stepped out into the moonlight.

Anyone who came to the ghost town would have to come through the tunnel. She had the advantage as long as she didn't close her eyes.

And then what?

Val had avoided thinking about that. What if Hannah tracked her all the way to Goldendale? It wouldn't take her long to figure out that Val wasn't in the buildings. Would she then do as Val was doing now? Hide at the other end of the tunnel and wait for Val to emerge?

It was a game of cat and mouse where the mouse found out too late the rules of the chase.

Her stomach growled, her throat burned with thirst, and her elbow ached where she'd landed after jumping out of the car. Her chin throbbed and she hoped the glue securing her stitches had held.

The longer she sat, the angrier she got. Joel had called Hannah his friend. He'd trusted her, and she'd deliberately deceived him. Just to get close enough to kill him.

Val felt so stupid. Those weeks apart from Joel meant she didn't know anything that had been going on. Had the shooting at the mill been about Joel all along? What about the photos of Abby? The car accident? The bombings? It was staggering to consider.

None of this solved the question of what to do next. How would she get out of there alive?

Val looked up at the sky and breathed a silent prayer. Unformed, uncertain, and uncomplicated.

Please...

When she looked back toward the railroad track—the gravel pale gray in the moonlight—her stomach flipped. A figure darted forward, the flashlight in her hands sweeping the clearing.

Hannah.

As soon as she rounded the cliff, Hannah stepped off the track as Val had done, heading for the cover under the trees. Val pressed herself against the cool earth. Hannah extinguished her light, but from Val's vantage point she was silhouetted against the moonlit clearing. She moved closer to Val, but her profile suggested she was looking toward the church.

Val scarcely breathed as a plan took shape in her mind. If Hannah searched the church, that might give Val an opportunity to sneak back down to the railroad track unseen. If she could get to the bridge ahead of Hannah, she would have a head start. She could even make it to the road and maybe escape in Hannah's car, especially if Hannah took her time searching each of the structures.

Hannah approached the church from the wooded side. The windows were too high off the ground to see in properly, but she held still, appearing to listen. Then she moved around the corner and out of sight.

Go! a voice in Val's head said, but she held still. She couldn't see Hannah, but that didn't mean she was safe. She waited, and soon the figure appeared again around the other side, this time moving toward the door. Hannah climbed the steps confidently. The hunter thought her prey was trapped.

Val raised up into a crouch.

As soon as Hannah went inside, Val scurried through the dark toward the railroad track. But before she broke out into the open, Hannah appeared in the doorway.

Val stopped and dropped to her knees, heart pounding.

She'd misjudged how quickly Hannah would realize the church was deserted.

Hannah strode more confidently toward the post office. Val remembered a large wooden counter and cupboards that surely would take longer to search. But if Val were going to run, she had to do it soon.

Again, Hannah did a sweep of the exterior then mounted the steps. She pulled the door open slowly, her flashlight in one hand and gun in the other. As soon as she disappeared inside, Val bolted out of the trees. Her wet clothes dragged at her, making it hard to move, and her knee screamed in pain.

She reached the railroad track and sprinted down the gravel shoulder, choosing speed over silence.

It was a mistake.

Just as she rounded the bend, a noise echoed behind

her. The unmistakable sound of a wooden door banging against its frame. She had a head start, but Hannah had a gun, and now she was caught on the narrow ledge with nowhere to go but forward.

Val's lungs seized with pain. She couldn't hear footsteps behind her over the sound of her own panting and the scattering of gravel beneath her feet. The tunnel was just ahead. She had to reach the darkness before Hannah could get a clear target.

A shot rang out just as Val passed through the entrance. She risked a backward glance. Hannah was less than fifty yards away.

Fish in a barrel.

Her thoughts were disconnected as she tried to keep up her pace, desperate to round the tunnel curve before Hannah closed the distance.

She kept one hand on the tunnel wall as she ran, pacing the ribbed supports with her breath. Just as she felt the tunnel curving, a light swept over her from behind. Three quick gunshots and strobing light, and she rocked forward with a force like something struck her from the side. She staggered, but rounded the corner and saw the trestle bridge ahead, bathed in moonlight. She felt her hip, and her fingers came away wet.

Please, God...no...

Gasping for breath, she staggered out of the tunnel and veered to the side out of range of Hannah's light.

It was no good. She could never make it across the bridge without giving Hannah a clear shot.

A thrumming sound came to her from a distance, but it took several heartbeats to recognize it.

A helicopter.

Val scanned the night sky and saw flashing lights in the distance. Whoever it was, they weren't close enough. She had to do something, or she would be dead before they reached her.

She scanned the embankment looking for something to use as a weapon. To the side of the gravel was the pile of iron railroad spikes that had drawn Abby's attention when they'd visited. It wasn't much, but it was all she had.

Footsteps echoed from inside the tunnel, slowing as Hannah neared the entrance.

Val waited, her throat burning with exertion. Her hands trembled. She balked at the idea of driving an iron spike into another human being. But somehow she had to find a way if she ever wanted to see Abby again. If she ever wanted to see Joel again.

Thinking of Joel and Abby, she wiped her sweaty hands on her pants and steeled herself, stoking a rage to push away the fear.

Hannah stepped cautiously out into the moonlight and immediately looked to the left where Val stood.

Val brought the spike down hard, aiming for Hannah's neck, but Hannah reacted fast, bringing her arm up to block it. The spike bounced off her shoulder, and Val stumbled forward, grabbing for the handgun instead. Hannah fell back and Val fell with her, pain erupting in her head as Hannah punched her awkwardly with her left hand. The gun skittered away.

Scrabbling in the loose gravel, Val kept her weight on Hannah and strained to reach the gun. Hannah gasped and writhed beneath her. Val cried out as hot pain shot through her hip. A bright light flooded them from overhead, and the deep pulse of a chopper rotor thrummed through Val's chest.

Desperate to keep Hannah from the gun, Val leaned her forearm against Hannah's throat. Hannah thrashed and kicked, knocking Val's grip loose with a grunt and clawing her way out from under her. Val lunged for the pistol, rocks biting her hands as her fingers closed around the plastic grip. She swayed unsteadily as she came to her feet and turned to point the barrel at Hannah.

Someone was speaking over a loudspeaker, but Val couldn't make out the words over the pounding in her head. The bile in her throat. The thrumming of the helicopter blades and the wind blowing dust into her eyes.

Hannah's face was twisted with fury.

Val's hand shook and she breathed deeply to steady it. Her finger was on the trigger, and her thumb found the magazine release. If she unloaded the pistol, she would lose the upper hand. Would Hannah make a run for it?

"Drop your weapon," a man's voice said through a loudspeaker. "I order you to drop your weapon."

Val started and looked up, realizing they were talking to her. Of course. She was the one armed. She looked like the perpetrator.

Hannah took a step backward toward the tunnel.

She was going to make a break for it. Val wavered, thinking of Joel. Brandi. Larry. Eileen. So many good people who'd been hurt in Hannah's hunt for revenge. She couldn't let her get away.

The voice over the loudspeaker was urgent. "We don't want anyone to get hurt. Lay the gun down on the ground and step back. Place both hands where we can see them."

Would they shoot if she didn't comply?

What about Hannah?

But what other choice did she have?

Val dropped the gun and raised her hands above her head.

Hannah disappeared into the tunnel, and Val choked out a sob of despair. She was getting away, and Val couldn't stop her. She was trapped.

Sirens drew closer with flashing lights turning off the main road.

"On the ground. Get on your knees," the voice boomed overhead.

Val swiveled. Headlights shone across the trestle bridge, their beams illuminating the tunnel.

The tunnel was empty, but she didn't dare lay on the ground. She didn't dare turn her back to Hannah.

Boots sounded heavy on the metal grate walkway, and Val tried to point and shout, "She ran into the tunnel!" but no one was listening.

"Get down on your knees!"

Figures were silhouetted against the headlights, moving toward her with semi-automatic rifles. She dropped stiffly to the ground, crying out as she hit her knee. Why weren't they going after Hannah? Why couldn't they see what was going on?

Rough hands grabbed her arms and twisted them behind her. A half dozen figures moved past her toward the tunnel, rifles at the ready. She barely registered the cold handcuffs around her wrists.

"It wasn't me! It was Hannah! She ran into the tunnel. You have to go after her."

Val was hauled to her feet and cried out as her hip flared with pain.

"Watch it. She's injured," a man in a vest said. "What's your name?"

Finally.

"Valerie Rockwell. She was trying to kill me. That was her gun, not mine."

"Do you have ID?"

Val thought about her purse that had been mere feet from the backpack. It was likely in a million fragments now. "No, I don't have ID. Ask Detective Sanders with the sheriff's office. Or Lieutenant Cooper. They know who I am."

Two men wearing FBI jackets escorted her across the trestle bridge, but their grips weren't as rough as before.

"I need to sit down." Val was suddenly lightheaded and weak.

Shots rang out, echoing over the ravine. Val jumped and ducked, then started trembling.

"Are you all right, ma'am?" one of the agents asked.

"Please. I don't care if you arrest me or not; I have to get out of here."

"We're going to get you to a hospital. Just sit tight."

They put her in the back of a police car, and Val collapsed onto the seat. She was surrounded by law enforcement, but she didn't feel safe. She doubted she would ever feel safe again.

36

A LOCAL ANESTHETIC had eased the pain in her hip, and Val was just closing her eyes when the door to the ER bay opened. Marnie Sanders stepped in, followed by Lieutenant Cooper. They both looked haggard and worn.

Cooper spoke first. "Ms. Rockwell, I've spoken with Special Agent Porter, and you're free to go. Marnie is going to take your statement, and then she'll drive you home. I wanted to let you know that your actions tonight helped us apprehend Hannah Wilson, and we're all very grateful to you."

"I didn't do anything except try really hard not to get shot. And even that I failed."

The bullet had grazed her hip, leaving two ugly wounds with a bridge of skin between. Too wide to be sutured and too shallow to be of serious concern, the doctor had cleaned it, slapped on a bandage, and given her a lecture on preventing infection.

The whole time an FBI agent had stood outside her door, and Val hadn't known if it was for her protection or to take her into custody as soon as the doctor finished.

Cooper glanced at the clock. "In any case, I just wanted to let you know that you're no longer a person of interest in this case. Good luck to you."

He ducked out the door, and the FBI agent left with him.

Val grimaced. "I still don't think he likes me much."

Marnie sat in the chair and pulled out a notepad. "I think he's getting tired of reports coming across his desk with your name attached to them." She added a smile so Val knew it was a joke.

"In fairness, Hannah's vengeance had nothing to do with me. She's Austin Wilson's sister; did you know?"

Marnie nodded. "We took Gunther Randolph into custody yesterday, but she got away. Going after you was a last ditch effort to get revenge."

"Gunther Randolph was reddawn76?"

"Yes. We're still working out their relationship and whether or not they were connected to Patriot Pride, but it appears they were acting on their own."

"I can't believe they killed all those people. I understand bitterness, I do. I even understand being angry toward a whole community. But to go that far for revenge? To hurt innocent people like that?"

Val leaned back against the pillows and closed her eyes. Physically, she felt relaxed with minimal pain as long as she didn't move too much. But mentally, she still felt on edge, like any little thing would set her off.

"Whenever you're ready," Marnie said, pulling out her phone and setting it up to record, "I'd like to get a statement from you on what happened tonight."

Val told her about Hannah showing up at the house and explained why she thought she could trust her.

"Joel said they were friends. I saw them together once and...I actually thought she liked him. Like, romantically. So when she started acting weird I thought maybe she was just jealous."

"Did she say anything about her brother?"

Val repeated their conversation as well as she could remember. When she described jumping out of the car, Marnie stopped writing and looked up as if unsure whether or not to believe her.

"It was the deer. She had to brake suddenly and wasn't watching me. I didn't know if I'd get another chance. The car wasn't going that fast, but...holy crap, it hurt." She could barely move her elbow, and her forearms were covered in abrasions.

Marnie looked like she was fighting a smile as she continued writing.

When Val couldn't think of anything more to say, Marnie put down her notepad and stopped the recording.

"I've been thinking, Valerie. I'm ready to give you a ride home when they discharge you. But if you'd rather not be home alone, you can stay at my house. We have an extra room and I live here in town. You'd only be ten minutes from the hospital."

And Joel.

"Thank you. That's...honestly I can't bear the

thought of going home yet. I don't know how I'll ever sleep again."

Marnie's eyes softened. "It'll come. But you don't need to rush it. We'd be happy to have you."

"I'd need clothes and an overnight bag…"

"We can fix you up for tonight. The night's half over anyway. I'll take you home tomorrow to get a bag. Just think about it."

"Thank you. That's very generous."

"Well, we like to take care of our own."

Val warmed at her words. A few weeks ago the thought of people knowing about her relationship with Joel had sent her into a tailspin of anxiety. But now, she appreciated the validation. From Marnie, at least, she felt acceptance.

It was another hour before the nurse came with discharge papers and a warning that they didn't want to see her again for six months at least.

Val had one request before she left. Marnie nodded thoughtfully.

"It's after hours but I'll see what I can do."

As it turned out, when you were at the center of a federal investigation, people tended to be a bit more accommodating than with the average citizen. Val was ushered into the darkened ICU and led to Joel's bed.

"I'll be right outside," Marnie said softly, leaving her alone.

Seeing him there, even in his drugged state with tubes and wires and monitors beeping in the dimness, released something in Val she didn't realize she'd been holding in. She crumpled into the chair and laid her head on the bed near his and wept. Deep, shuddering sobs in near silence—so as to not be overheard—she let it all go.

It wasn't a specific feeling, not pain or loss or fear or relief. It was all of them and nothing, washing over her in waves.

When she had cried herself dry, she leaned close to his ear and whispered, "I'm here."

Two simple words. She was still here. In spite of all that had happened. In spite of hiding for her life in the mountains only six hours earlier, she was there. And she would be there tomorrow and the next day. However long it took until he came home.

37

JOEL FUMBLED with the buttons of his shirt, breathing through the pain.

"Do you want me to help you with that, sugar?" The nurse, Denise, had to be twice his age, but she was stronger than she looked and had helped him shower and dress with gentle efficiency.

"I got it, thanks," he said.

She'd helped him shave too, and he looked critically at his reflection in the mirror, noting an uncharacteristic puffiness from three long weeks spent bed bound with fluids pumping directly into his veins. It would be weeks, maybe months, before he could exercise normally again. The doctors had been very firm about not overdoing it, and Joel was trying to accept that his loss of muscle tone would be the new normal for a while.

He sat on the reclining chair near the window while Denise pulled on his socks and helped strap the sturdy supportive boot around his right leg. If he ever had to be in a hospital bed again, it would be too soon. It was disconcerting how weak he felt after something as simple as getting dressed. But at least he didn't need a walker to move around anymore, so that was something.

The door opened with a knock.

"Can I come in?" Val asked, poking her head around the door.

"Come on in; we're about done here," Denise called cheerily. She looked up at Joel, her cheeks pink from crouching over his shoe. "I'll be back in a jiffy with a wheelchair, and then we'll get you out of here."

Joel sighed. One more indignity. But better than risking the alternative—collapsing on his way out to the parking lot because he'd overestimated his endurance.

Denise chuckled. "Don't worry, you'll be out catching bad guys again before you know it. But for now you've gotta let us pamper you a little bit longer." She winked as she went out the door.

Val wore a light jacket against the October chill. She paused for a minute, taking him in.

"Wow. You clean up nice."

"You didn't like the beard?"

"I mean, the swarthy look was good too, but maybe ease off on the homeless vibe next time." She grinned. "Man, you look good."

She bent over to kiss him, and the smell of her was so familiar and fresh and nothing like hospital products that he had to hold back a little moan.

"Come here," he said, reaching for her hands.

HUNT AT OWL CREEK

"Are you sure? I don't want to hurt you."

"I've never felt better." He pulled her to him, and she sat on his lap, gingerly at first, then settling against his chest and resting her head against his.

"Nicole is bringing dinner tonight, so we don't need to worry about that. She's been amazing. She took me grocery shopping and helped with laundry and cleaning."

Joel cringed. "Val, I'm sorry. You shouldn't have to—"

"Stop. I wanted to. I'm just so excited that you're coming home. I hope you don't mind," here she pulled away to look him in the eye, "but I packed a bag. I thought I could sleep in the guest room, just until you're doing well enough to be left alone."

His first instinct was to say no, that he'd be fine and didn't need her help. But her eyes didn't hold pity. Instead, he saw fear.

"It's been harder than you've admitted, hasn't it?" He examined the fresh scar on her chin, still faintly purple.

She looked away, frowning. "I can't sleep at the house yet. I try, but it's too…I'm hoping it will be easier if I'm not alone."

"Stay as long as you need to. But don't do it on my account. I'll be fine."

Val scoffed. "Right. You didn't just survive a bombing and spend three weeks in the hospital. You've got this all under control."

She kissed him again, and the warmth of her was so

405

soothing that he said, "Does it have to be the guest bed?"

She laughed, her eyes lit with humor. "Yes. At least…for now. Look on the bright side. You can finally show me *Stranger Things*."

"Not just *Stranger Things*. Get ready for so much Netflix bingeing."

"Fine. But I have one condition."

"What's that?"

"Take Lacey off your emergency contacts."

Joel laughed. "That's fair."

The weight of her pressing him against the chair was starting to be too much for his back, but he didn't want to let her go. The nurse returned with the wheelchair all too soon.

Val made herself busy gathering Joel's few belongings as Denise helped him into the chair. He pushed away the sense of humiliation, reminding himself that it was temporary. Denise wheeled him out to the hallway where four other nurses in brightly colored scrubs were waiting to tell him goodbye and wish him luck.

He avoided looking at Val, knowing she wouldn't be able to hold back a smirk if he did.

"You're like a regular celebrity," Denise said as they approached the elevator. "The last of the bombing victims to leave the hospital."

Joel didn't correct her. It was true for the Pineview hospital, but Larry had been transferred to a renowned research hospital in Portland to receive more specialized care and there was no talk about him coming home. The thought sobered Joel.

As Val held the elevator doors open, he said, "I'm sorry you had to postpone your trip to get Abby."

"It's okay. Jeanette and Charles are spoiling her to death. And now that I've finally got a phone, Abby checks in with me every day. I hate that she's so far away, but I'd like things to be a little closer to normal before she comes back."

"Do you know if she's seen...?" Joel hesitated. Val didn't like to talk about Jordan around other people.

Val's expression clouded over. She nodded, but didn't say anything more.

The elevator rocked to a stop, and the doors opened onto a large lobby.

Val stepped out first. "I'm going to go get the truck and bring it around. A truck which is now free of graffiti, I might add. You're welcome."

"YouTube?"

"No way. I wouldn't dare do it myself. I took it to Mike. He did a good job. Oh, and no criticizing my driving. I'm used to my little Prius. Your truck is a beast."

She moved toward the parking lot, and Joel noticed a slight hitch in her step. She never talked about her own injuries, and Joel still wasn't sure he knew everything that she'd been through. They had a lot of catching up to do, and if she'd be staying over, they'd have ample time to do it. The thought cheered him.

"What a sweetheart," Denise said, watching her go. "You're a lucky man. You listen to her, all right? Take it easy, and I don't want to see you back here again unless you're bringing flowers and chocolates, got it?"

Joel smiled. "I'll do my best."

Val frowned at the winding road. "I'm not sure this is a good idea. We can do this another time."

"I want to see it."

Joel had grown quiet the longer they drove, and Val worried he was in pain. So when he'd asked to go to the trestle bridge, she'd been surprised.

"We can go for a drive another time. Let's get you home and put you to bed."

"Val, please." He'd shifted in the seat and winced. "Besides, it's my truck."

"Oh, well, in that case. Great Master of the Truck, I'm at your command," she'd replied sarcastically as she turned onto the mountain road.

But now, she gripped the steering wheel and found herself taking small, shallow breaths. It was mid-afternoon, and the river was flowing robustly with recent rain, pools of still water broken by white riffles over submerged rock. The maple, oak, and ash trees were in full blaze of autumn color—yellow, orange, and red—and the sun was warm through the windshield. Golden leaves dappled the road, and sunlight flickered through the trees as they passed under arching branches overhead. It was a scene of postcard beauty.

But Val was lost in a memory of darkness and fear. Every view of the river reminded her of slipping over rocks in the dark, biting back a cry of pain as she

HUNT AT OWL CREEK

grazed her shins. The overwhelming terror that had driven her blindly on, alone and hunted.

Pressure just above her knee brought her back to the present. Joel's hand rested on her leg.

"I'm here. We'll do it together."

She swallowed.

When the trestle bridge came into view, the aged steel glowed from the late afternoon sun. Val turned off the main road and parked in the pull-out. The ravine was quiet and deserted, theirs the only vehicle. Dust settled around the truck as she turned off the engine.

"Let's get out," Joel said, reaching for the door handle.

"No, you really shouldn't——"

But he had already unbuckled and was opening the door.

Val opened her own door and stepped down with a little hop. The truck was so big, she wasn't sure she would ever get used to it. But she did like the feeling of being so high. When she replaced the Prius, maybe she would get something bigger.

Val hurried around the truck to help Joel, but he was already standing on the hard-packed ground, looking toward the tunnel.

"Show me," he said and reached for her hand.

She walked with him to the trestle bridge and followed the metal walkway for pedestrian traffic, looking at the sky, the trees flaming amber and crimson, the river burbling below their feet. Anywhere but at the tunnel.

They caught her, she reminded herself. *She isn't hiding in there waiting for you.*

Still her pulse picked up.

She stopped when they got to the other side.

"Not the tunnel. I can't...not yet."

"That's all right. Do you want to tell me what happened?"

She didn't, not really. But somehow, as she started describing that night, her voice uncertain at first, something shifted. It wasn't as terrifying. She was just relating facts. Joel occasionally asked her questions, and she found she couldn't always answer them. Already, some of the details were slipping away.

In the weeks since Hannah had been apprehended, the nature of her relationship with Gunther Randolph had been revealed. After her mother's suicide, Hannah had connected with him through the newly organized group Patriot Pride. He was eager to make a more dramatic statement, and Hannah's desire for revenge had made the two natural partners. Carter's death had been the trigger to put her plan in action. And with Owl Creek embroiled in a labor dispute and a lawsuit against the sheriff's office, it had been easy enough to fit their plans into the turbulent social-political climate.

"I heard the charges were dropped against Mason," Val said. "They really don't think he was involved?"

"He made a perfect scapegoat. Hannah befriended him and had easy access to his apartment and his rifle. The dumpster is shared by the tenants, so lifting the Skoal can covered in his prints was easy. When I think of how much she influenced the investigation, and I was too trusting to realize it…"

"Well at least you weren't so worried about hurting her feelings that you didn't even realize you were being abducted."

A cool breeze blew up from the river, and Val shivered. She'd left her jacket in the truck.

Joel wrapped his arms around her from behind, cradling her against him. She let out a sigh of contentment.

"I should have been there for you," he said, murmuring into her hair. "I'm sorry I couldn't protect you."

"It's not your job," she said.

"Um…it's literally my job to protect and serve the people in this county."

"You know what I mean. I need to be able to take care of myself."

"Says the woman who wouldn't let me go home from the hospital alone."

"That's different. I'm not talking about recovering from a traumatic injury. I'm talking about rebuilding my life from the ground up."

"I know. You're the only one who doubts your own capability. Honestly, Val, I always thought you were too good for me."

"Whatever."

"No, seriously. You were so smart and funny and beautiful and you excelled at everything you did. Everyone liked you, and your family was amazing, and of course you would go to Purdue and marry the rising son of a US senator and change the world."

Val's shoulders sank a little. "Don't remind me."

"The thing is, none of that even compares with what I've seen you do these past few months. And I'm blown away by—no, sorry, wrong phrase."

Val chuckled quietly. "Too soon."

"I'm *floored* by what you did to get away from Hannah. Jumping out of a moving vehicle? That's intense. I don't know how you did it."

Val didn't respond. She didn't know either, and she didn't want to remember the desperate fear that had pushed her to such recklessness.

Joel shifted his stance and she settled against him, trying not to let him take too much of her weight.

"I can't help feeling like it was all my fault," he continued. "None of this would have happened if I hadn't killed Austin Wilson. You wouldn't have been hurt if it weren't for me. Abby never—"

"Stop. Hannah didn't have to use her grief for revenge. And taking those innocent lives…there's no excuse for that. You certainly aren't to blame." Val still struggled to comprehend it. She'd barely made it through Brandi's memorial, and even then it was only because Nicole had offered to sit with her.

They'd lost three employees that day at the bank. Brian and Kathy had been killed in the station bombing, and Larry was receiving specialized care in Portland. Five protestors had died, and many more had been injured. It was a staggering loss for the small town.

If there was a silver lining to it all, it was that the

divisiveness had apparently resolved overnight. The protests had come to a halt, and Main Street had returned to its normal languid state. Even the creepy mannequins had been draped in black as if in mourning.

"Intellectually I know it's not my fault, but I can't help how I feel," Joel said. "When I think about how much pain Austin's death caused, and how many more people are dead because of it, it's hard not to feel responsible."

"I know what you mean." Val still fought her own feelings of guilt any time she thought of the backpack that she'd placed right by Brandi's stool. "It's not fair that they're dead and their families have to spend the rest of their lives without them. But it's not your fault any more than it's my fault they targeted the bank."

"Yeah, but even you never would have been a target if we hadn't been together. So even that is my fault."

"If you recall, we weren't together when the news decided to tell the world about our relationship. That's what made me a target, and they only did that because of Jordan. So if anything, we should be blaming him," Val added with a smile.

Joel sighed, and his warm breath tickled her ear. "I hate to put you at risk. It goes against everything I stand for. And I can't help but question what I could have done differently."

Val swiveled in his arms to face him, her eyes searching his. He looked so tired, she felt guilty for bringing him there instead of taking him straight home.

But there was a poignant vulnerability to the moment that made her loath to end it.

"There's a lot that we both could have done different. But if we had, we might not be here right now. Together. Your job is never going to be easy, but I've dragged you into my own share of crazy, and you haven't run away yet. I'm not running either."

His wry smile warmed her. "That's good because I'm in no condition to chase you."

She raised her face and kissed him gently. Her hands rested on his chest and she reveled in the feeling of his heart beating. He was alive, and he was hers, and for now that's all that mattered.

"Are you ready to go home now?" she asked.

"Yes. Let's go home."

THANK YOU FOR READING!

If you enjoyed *Hunt at Owl Creek*, please consider leaving a review on Amazon or Goodreads. (Or both for you overachievers!) Thanks for helping get my work into the hands of other readers like you.

As a special thank you, I'm delighted to share with you a bonus scene that takes place during Joel's recovery. Yes, they finally watch *Stranger Things*. But more significantly, it's a time of physical and emotional healing.

This exclusive epilogue is available to download when you sign up for my newsletter. If you can't get enough of Val and Joel, you won't want to miss it. As a special perk, you'll also be the first to know when the next Owl Creek book is released.

Here's a short excerpt from the bonus scene:

Another rumble of thunder drew her gaze to the window. The open blinds offered a view of fir trees shrouded in heavy gray clouds. Rain pattered against the glass, stirring nostalgia. It was the kind of day to stay indoors with a hot drink and a favorite book. A day that hinted of falling leaves and muddy trips to a pumpkin patch.

The door to the master bathroom was closed, and the unmistakable sound of the shower turning on brought Val back to the present with a disorienting sense of both the familiar and the startlingly new. It was a sound that evoked countless mornings of waking to hear Jordan already started on his day.

But the man showering in the next room wasn't her husband.

Want more? Download the full scene at carenhahn.com/huntbonus.

ACKNOWLEDGMENTS

First, my heartfelt thanks goes to you, dear reader. It fills me with awe to see people around the world falling in love with my stories. However you happened to discover Owl Creek, thank you for lingering.

I'll be honest; this book surprised me. Initially, I didn't intend to write a sequel to *Smoke over Owl Creek*. But after a conversation with my agent at the time, April Eberhardt, I realized that not only was a sequel possible, it needed to happen. It was too limiting to expect that Val and Joel's happily ever after would come so easily, and it didn't take long to realize that the consequences of the events in *Smoke* could be disastrous.

Following those consequences down their natural paths gave me a chance to explore what became the central theme in *Hunt at Owl Creek*. Having grown up in a rural logging town, I've seen how tragedy can just as often rip a community apart as pull it together. I've experienced the benefits that come with having close connections with your community, and then the fracturing that takes place when that community turns on one of their own. Although Owl Creek and the characters who live there are fictional, that dark side of small town life is not, and I've learned for myself that those scars can last a lifetime.

This book required more research than any other to date, and while the internet is a rich source of information, nothing beats getting perspectives from experts working in the field. I'm particularly grateful to those who answered round after round of questions regarding their particular areas of expertise, from law enforcement to explosives to first responder and FBI procedures. Todd Spingath, Michael Hahn, Scotty Edwards, and Bob Schofield contributed crucial insights that shaped the novel in a more authentic way, patiently answering questions until I had more material than I could possibly use. Any and all mistakes that persisted despite their efforts are entirely my own.

Adam Richardson was an invaluable resource, giving me a better understanding of the life and work of a detective, particularly in how they relate to plot and character development. Adam was unfailingly patient with my endless questions, and I would often leave our conversations with my brain bursting with new ideas. I highly recommend his podcast, the Writer's Detective Bureau, and for the writer wanting to take a deeper dive into the police procedural side of things, his Writer's Detective course is a game changer.

My brother, Chris Schofield, deserves a shout-out for letting me tap into his mischievous past for a couple of scenes. When your natural personality is as cautious as mine, it can be useful to have a more adventurous (dare I say, reckless?) sibling whose teenage years created endless fodder for interesting fiction. I'm even more grateful that he survived them.

Being a writer means I'm always interested in life experiences that are different from my own. Thanks to Katie Keller who first told me about collecting sheds and helped me get that particular detail right. I couldn't ask for a better physical therapist, and I'm even more grateful to call her a friend.

I always appreciate those who can see past the roughness of a new manuscript to envision what it can become. Beta readers for this project included Crystal Brinkerhoff, Jenny Hahn, and Andrew Hahn. Rachel Pickett provided critical editing support in helping me polish it up into something worthy to share, and it's much stronger because of her careful attention to detail.

I'm especially grateful to my family for their love and support, especially when the mom part of me has to take a back seat to the writer. I couldn't ask for a better partner in crime than Andrew. He not only designed the stunning cover of this book, he did it with minimal complaining about how hard I am to please. Raising six children with him has been the greatest privilege of my life.

ABOUT THE AUTHOR

Caren Hahn grew up in a tiny logging community with more than its fair share of tragedy and violent crime, giving her early exposure to the dark side of small town life. She specializes in relationship dramas featuring empathetic characters who are exquisitely flawed—the stuff of great book club discussions. Her

Photo by Rachel Pickett

richly layered plots and can't-put-it-down conclusions offer readers a thrilling ride blended with deep emotional resonance. Caren is blessed to live in the Pacific Northwest with her husband and six children.

Sign up to get updates at carenhahn.com and receive a free collection of short stories. Follow her on social media to learn more about her upcoming projects.